Next TIME

Books by M. Jacqueline Murray

Maddie and Nate Series
Out of Time
Next Time

Stay up to date by signing up for my mailing list:
https://www.mjacquelinemurray.com/subscribe

Next TIME

A Novel

M. Jacqueline Murray

COLE JACOBS BOOKS LLC

Title: Next Time
Copyright © 2024 M. Jacqueline Murray
Published by Cole Jacobs Books LLC

Cover design by Cathy DardenLentz

ISBN: 978-1-963394-00-9 paperback
ISBN: 978-1-963394-01-6 hardcover
ISBN: 978-1-963394-02-3 jacketed hardcover
ISBN: 978-1-963394-03-0 ebook

DEDICATION

For believers in the magic of love and the power of destiny.
May this story whisper to your heart that love, once sparked,
will always find its perfect moment, and true love,
once kindled, will ultimately have perfect timing.

Author's Note

Love and friendships are never straightforward; they are a puzzle of emotions and intricacies. The choices made by individuals, driven by their own needs and desires, have the power to either bring two people closer or push them further apart. It's the conflicting emotions and difficult choices we make as we navigate our lives and relationships that inspires me to write stories of lives lived and loves loved.

This story begins in the 1970s when women in science and engineering professions were exceedingly rare and nearly non-existent in the senior and management ranks. Paying tribute to those trailblazing women who paved the way for me to pursue a technical career motivated me to give Maddie a non-traditional career for a woman of her generation.

In addition, I want to note that this story touches upon controversial themes and subject matter which may not appeal to all readers, such as open-door sex scenes and instances of infidelity. These elements are integral to the narrative and are presented with the intent of portraying the complexities of human relationships and emotions.

Thank you for choosing to embark on this journey with Maddie and Nate. Like "Out of Time", the first book in the series, you will find I've used both American and Canadian spelling conventions. This choice is intentional and serves to emphasize Maddie and Nate's diverse backgrounds and voices. We hope this enriches your reading experience by highlighting the individuality of their perspectives.

My hope is that you find the story both engaging and thought-provoking. If you enjoy the book, please leave a review on your preferred review site or retailer.

CHAPTER 1

In a blackout, the whirr of the world falls silent. Without the hum of lights, fans, and motors to muffle them, the voices of the other patrons were so clear they were distracting.

Harvey, the bartender, pointed to the empty glass in front of me. "Another one Mr. Jacobs?"

I put down the contract I was struggling to read by the light of the oil lamps Harvey had positioned around my usual spot at the bar. "Might as well."

He set a perfectly poured pint in front of me. "I just heard from the manager that the power is out for the entire city, not just the hotel."

"Hopefully it comes back on soon." I took a sip. At least the beer was still cold. I picked up the contract and tilted the paper towards the lamp to get as much light as possible. I wanted to review the rest of the documents before my morning meeting. It was slow going in the dim light.

Harvey slid another lamp closer to me. "Who'd a thought we'd need our lamps from 1876 in 1976."

He retreated to the far end of the bar to let me work. I'd done a lot of deals for Bond as their General Council, but this was by far the most complex. Every trip to Toronto to meet with our bankers added to the mountain of material I needed to review. I'd been working through dinner at the bar more often as the deadline to submit our acquisition agreement approached.

"Excuse me, Sir," said a voice beside me.

My irritation at the interruption evaporated when I realized the attractive woman in a business suit was leaning over the bar, trying to get Harvey's attention.

"Yes, Ma'am. What can I get you?" Harvey's deep voice embodied the refined elegance of the Royal York Hotel's Library Bar.

"I was wondering if you know if trains are arriving at Union Station tonight. I'm waiting for a friend. He's staying here, but he's not checked in yet."

"There have been many delays. If you check with our concierge, she may find out for you."

"Thank you." She turned to go, then turned back. "Sorry, but how do I find the concierge?"

"She's in the lobby, past the reception desk. Give me a moment and I'll grab a flashlight and walk you over."

"I can show you, Miss," I offered. There was something about her that inspired me to want to help.

"You needn't trouble yourself, Mr. Jacobs," said Harvey.

I extended my hand for the flashlight. "You've been run off your feet all night. It will do me good to get off this stool."

Harvey flashed his big toothy smile. "We'll have to put you on the payroll."

I escorted the woman through the lobby to the concierge desk.

"Hello, Annette." I knew her by name since she had assisted me countless times during my frequent stays over the past year.

She smiled, but she looked weary. "How can I help you, Mr. Jacobs?"

I turned to the woman I'd escorted. "Not me. Miss…"

"Tobias. Mrs. Tobias."

I stepped back a few feet from the desk to give her some privacy as she explained her situation to Annette. Annette made a few calls, and I overheard her explaining that the trains from Ottawa had been canceled due to the power outage. She also mentioned that if her friend had not arrived, it was unlikely that he would until the next day. The woman then asked about getting a taxi to take her home. Annette called the taxi company and informed her it would be at least an hour.

"I could walk home in an hour." She frowned and ran her fingers through her dark blonde shoulder-length hair and looked down at her feet while considering her situation. "Given the weather, and my shoes, I guess I'll wait."

"Perhaps you'd permit me to buy you a drink?" I asked, stepping forward with the flashlight, feeling inexplicably happy that she wasn't leaving right away.

Her gaze shifted upwards, looking directly into my eyes. "That would be nice." She continued to lock eyes with me, her face brightened, and she smiled. "No sense standing around in the lobby when there are perfectly good stools at the bar."

"One more thing, Mr. Jacobs," called Annette from behind the desk. She motioned for me to come over. "When the power went out, I asked housekeeping to put a bucket of water in your bathroom and fill your pitcher and ice bucket. When the power goes out, the hotel water system stops flowing as the pressure in the system drops. They do it automatically for the suites, but I added you to our VIP list."

"You're the best, Annette. Thank you." I turned back to Mrs. Tobias. "Shall we?" I swept the beam of the flashlight down the lobby towards the bar to suggest we head that way.

We walked back to the bar. Harvey had placed a reserved sign in front of the place where I'd been seated. I pulled out the stool beside mine and slid it under her as she sat down. I asked what she'd like as I resumed my spot with my contract and beer.

"Rye and ginger, please," she said to Harvey, who nodded, reached for a glass and bottle and filled her order promptly.

I shuffled the pages of the contract together and set them aside.

She nodded at my stack of paper. "Please don't let me interrupt your work."

"It can wait. Besides, I can't read well in this light."

She lifted the glass towards me in a gesture of gratitude. "Cheers and thank you."

"My pleasure." I lifted my beer in return before taking a sip myself.

"So… Mr. … Jacobs? Was it?"

"Yes, Nate Jacobs. Please, call me Nate."

She extended her hand. "Maddie. Pleased to meet you."

"I couldn't help but overhear you were waiting for a friend?"

"Yes. We were supposed to meet for dinner hours ago."

"Are you hungry? I bet Harvey's got some snacks hidden back there…"

"I'm fine. Thank you."

"Would you two like some ice cream?" asked Harvey, "It's thawing in the kitchen, and they don't want it to go to waste."

"I've always got room for ice cream," said Maddie, looking considerably happier, so I suspected she was hungry and had not wanted to admit it.

"Mr. Jacobs?"

"OK. Just to help out the kitchen…"

We chatted over our drinks and ice cream. Maddie asked what brought me to Toronto. Although I didn't mention the specifics, I told her I was working on an acquisition that required me to be in town regularly. She offered suggestions for things to do and see in the city during the summer. I was happy to have them, as I was planning for Betsy, my wife, to accompany me on my next trip. I didn't get a chance to ask her about herself before Annette came to let her know her taxi had arrived.

"Thank you, Nate, for the drink and the good company. Sorry to drink and run," she said with the loveliest smile.

"You're welcome." The time had passed quickly and I was disappointed she was leaving so soon.

Maddie reached into the leather briefcase she had over her shoulder. "If you're in need of engineering support… we do a lot of assessment work. Feel free to give us a call." She handed me a business card.

I took the card and reached out to shake her hand. "Thank you. I will." I looked at the business card she'd handed me as she walked away. I was sure she'd said her name was Tobias, but the card said Madeleine Cole, P. Eng., Sr. Project Engineer.

I was impressed by her title. I guessed she was a few years younger than me, mid-thirties perhaps. She seemed young to be a senior anything. I'd worked closely with engineers at Bond preparing their patent applications, but none of them were female and definitely not as attractive as Ms. Cole.

I tried to resume reviewing the documents, but my eyes were tired. The light was too dim, and I couldn't focus. It was late. Normally I'd be back in my room by now. I shuffled my papers back into their file folders and nodded to Harvey, who came over immediately.

"Could you close out my tab for tonight?"

"Already done Mr. Jacobs. Tonight's rounds are on the house, on account of the conditions. I can call someone to show you to your room if you're ready to head up."

"I'm sure I can find my way."

"It's darker than you think. Take the flashlight. You can drop it at the front desk in the morning."

I thanked him, wished him goodnight, and headed for the stairs.

Luckily, this week, my room was on a lower floor. My footsteps echoed and sounded unusually loud in the eerie silence. There was no hum of ventilation or sounds coming from the hallways as I passed the door to each floor, propped open with washcloths stuffed under them as makeshift doorstops. The only light in the stairwell came from the red glow of the exit signs above the doors.

I was grateful for the flashlight as I made my way down the inky hallway and, even more so, when I tried to get my key into the lock. Inside my pitch-black room I instinctively opened the window curtains to get some light. But the only light outside was from the sliver of moon that occasionally broke through the clouds. I undressed but decided against putting my pants into the press of the valet stand in my room for fear of mis-aligning the creases.

As Annette had arranged, there was a large bucket filled with water sitting in the tub and a pitcher of water and full ice-bucket on the credenza. I brushed my teeth using a glass of water from the pitcher before getting into bed.

The power had been restored by the time my phone rang with my wake-up call. While walking up Bay Street to the Dominion Bank offices, where our M&A team for the Oakland Chemical acquisition conducted their meetings, I couldn't help but be surprised by how little the city seemed to be affected by the widespread outage. Throngs of people streamed from Union Station, and I wondered if Maddie's friend had made it to town and if she'd be back at the hotel to meet them that evening. I felt a pang of disappointment that I wouldn't be there to find out.

I was the first to arrive at the office. Because the receptionist wasn't in yet, I had to be let in by the security guard. I settled into my usual seat at the table and pulled out my files from my briefcase. I needed to get through the documents I'd given up reviewing in the bar.

I'd just finished the last one when Franklin Ball, the guy heading up the Dominion Bank team, came in and sat at the head of the table. "We really need to teach you how to work bankers' hours."

Franklin's assistant Joyce followed him, carrying his coffee and a box of donuts. She set them in the center of the table before taking her seat at a small desk near the door with her steno pad.

"I do work bankers' hours," I countered, "but that only takes half my day."

Despite Franklin's disapproving grumble, his face betrayed his enjoyment of the banter. "Then we better dive right in so we can get to lunch on time."

The remainder of the team had trickled in, and we spent the rest of the morning going through my comments on the supplier and quality agreements I'd reviewed. I'd identified some concerns with regards to the lack of specifications for minimum safety stock quantities and delivery time commitments but, overall, I was pleased with their raw material supply and that their procurement and distribution systems were consistent with our processes or could be harmonized without significant effort.

"When you get back, we'll start on the facilities and real estate holdings," said John Ellis, Dominion's real estate expert. He slid a stack of reports my way. "A little light reading for your flight to Boston."

I jammed the reports into my briefcase. "I'd better be off. I need to get to the airport."

Franklin pushed his chair back from the table, signaling the meeting was adjourned. "You're joining us for lunch. Right?"

"Not this time. My flight's at two."

John stood up and stretched as if he'd just finished working out. "You should change your flight. Reservations at Napoleon are impossible to get... without connections."

I made a mental note of the restaurant's name. It sounded like the sort of exclusive place Betsy would like. I elbowed John on my way out of the room. "I'll be counting on using your connections for my rain check."

CHAPTER 2

The night had not gone as planned. I'd been looking forward to seeing my friend Robbie. Instead, I'd wasted the entire evening waiting in the hotel bar for him and then for a taxi. Riding home through the dark streets, I consoled myself that at least I'd had the chance to pass out one of my brand-new business cards. Dave, my boss and mentor, had been encouraging me to get my name out there whenever I could. It would be great if something came of meeting Mr. Jacobs. He'd not said where he was from, but his accent sounded American. It was a long shot, but if I was going to make partner, the first female partner no less, I had to bring in new business and that started with getting better at handing out my card.

I rubbed my throbbing elbow as I got dressed to go to the office. I'd tripped and banged it on the hallway door the previous night as I hurried through the pitch-dark house to the kitchen to answer the phone. I was wincing and breathless by the time I got there. It was my husband, Will.

"Are you OK?"

"Yes… No. Just cracked my elbow on the door. The lights are out."

"I heard. That's why I called. Bill called Jeannie and she told him the whole city was out. She was hysterical. So… Bill thought I should check on you."

"I'm not hysterical."

"So… you're fine?"

I could tell he was anxious to get off the phone. "You can get back to the beer cooler. I'm fine. Going to bed. I've a meeting first thing."

"Great. Night Mads. See you Sunday."

The blackout was over, but the grief it caused continued when I arrived at the office. The reports I needed for my meeting were still in pieces on the big tables in our drafting office. Mark, our head draftsman, was standing over the map printer with a large mylar I recognized as one of my maps.

I started looking through the stacks on the table. "How many copies have we got?"

Mark sighed like my question was irritating. "Five. I couldn't finish running the maps yesterday on account of the power out."

I could make do with five but I needed them assembled. I walked to my intern Steve's office, but he wasn't at his desk. I looked at my watch. Eight-thirty. The meeting was at nine. I didn't have time to go running around looking for him, so I headed back to the drafting office.

"Is there someone to help put these together?" I asked Mark.

He shrugged and took a drag on the cigarette that hung from his bottom lip. "Do ya see anyone?"

Fortunately, during the years I worked my way up through the ranks to my current position, I'd assembled a lot of reports. I punched and bound the five copies and asked Mark to bring me the rest as soon as they were done. After making a quick stop in my office to gather my things, I headed to the conference room.

As I passed Peggy, our receptionist, she nodded at the conference room door. "Mr. Smith has arrived. He's in there."

The mystery of Steve's whereabouts was solved when I entered the room. He and Mr. Smith were both seated at the conference table, leaning back in the large leather chairs. Steve jumped up when he saw me and took the stack of reports from me.

"Can you bring me a coffee, Doll," said Mr. Smith.

My shoulders and jaw tensed up. I took a breath before answering. "How do you take your coffee?"

"Just cream. Thanks."

I looked at Steve. "Can you please get Mr. Smith his coffee and bring one for me as well."

He set the reports down and headed for the door. "Yes, Ma'am."

"And please check with Mr. Bennet to see if he'll be joining us this morning."

Our guest looked at me with a puzzled expression, seemingly bewildered by my behaviour. "Dave assured me he put his best engineer on it, Cole I think his name was. Will he be joining?"

I took out my business card and handed it to him along with one copy of the report. "Let me introduce myself. I'm Madeleine Cole, project manager and senior engineer assigned to your project."

He looked stunned and studied the card I'd handed him. I focused on opening a copy of the report, unfolding the maps and laying them out on the table. I'd rehearsed in my head how I would present my findings. Dave had warned me that, although Dan Smith was a savvy developer, making millions buying property and building on it, he hadn't much technical knowledge. He'd confided that, if not for the generous donations his family made to his college, he wouldn't have a degree at all.

Steve returned with three cups of coffee on a small tray. "Mr. Bennet said to go ahead with the presentation. He'll join us later."

Mr. Smith's mouth was pressed into a thin line and his eyebrows were furrowed, he made a little grunt sound but said nothing.

"Thank you, Steve. Now if you'll open up your report to page two, I'll start by reviewing the executive summary." I'd decided that giving him the overview and conclusions first would be best because the site investigation had been quite complex.

The site was located on the shore of Lake Ontario and had a long history. The property records for the site dated back to the late 1800s. Of particular interest regarding the suitability of the site for redevelopment was the previous land use. There had once been a secondary railway yard on one part of the property and the other portion of it had been created, pre-1930, by infilling a small cove of the lakeshore with coal ash and domestic waste.

We had drilled four investigational holes through the overburden and into the underlying bedrock. As we suspected, the subsurface environment reflected more than a century of impacts. The good news was that, despite finding fragments of glass bottles and ceramics in our core samples, the structure of the soils did not raise any concerns regarding soil stability. However, the investigation also determined that the site had a high watertable and bedrock of a highly weathered shale with clay seams. As a result, we recommended conducting field plate-loading tests in order to determine the foundation requirements for building design.

"I'd like to hear what Dave has to say about this."

"I've reviewed the findings with him. He concurs with my assessment."

I had my back to the door, so I didn't see that Dave had entered until he spoke. "Indeed, I did, Dan. Although Ms. Cole doesn't need my approval. She's our expert on subsurface structural stability. She has more than a decade of international experience in this type of investigation."

Mr. Smith straightened up in his chair, looked at Dave, and then back at me. "I didn't mean to imply...to question..."

As much as I hated that Dave should have to back me up, I was grateful that he'd always treated me with the utmost respect. He'd supported my professional development. He never refused my requests to attend conferences and take courses so I could stay current and keep our firm at the forefront. He also encouraged me to work with my colleagues in academia and government to co-author research papers to build my professional reputation.

"Ms. Cole has signed off on these reports. I have full confidence in her conclusions."

"Thank you, Dave." I intentionally used his first name. It was something Dave had suggested I do to emphasize my status as an equal.

Dave gave me a nod, indicating I should continue with my presentation.

"There's just one additional point I'd like to make. If you'll turn to the final page."

I explained the disclaimers because I wanted to make sure Mr. Smith understood that our conclusions and recommendations were based on the conditions observed in the four investigational boreholes and the information available at the time of preparation of this report. Due to the variable nature of the man-made infilled lands, further investigation would be required to fully characterize the site.

"So… what you're really saying is I need to give you more work?"

Dave patted Mr. Smith on the back. "How about we take you to lunch after we discuss the details."

"I'll be ordering something expensive because I suspect this is going to cost me."

"I'm sure Ms. Cole's recommendations are a small price to pay to make sure those lakefront towers you're dreaming of are as stable as they are beautiful."

I really didn't have time for a long business lunch, but I knew that Dave was including me because it was important. He wanted me to manage more of our large clients and the Smith account could be a very lucrative one. The family real estate holdings were extensive, and they had numerous large-scale developments in progress.

I gathered up the copies of the report and handed them to Mr. Smith and turned to Dave, "Should I ask Peggy to …"

Dave stopped me with a disapproving shake of his head and looked at Steve. "Please work with Peggy on reservations for three at Barbarians or Tom Jones? In the meantime, we'll go through our proposal for the next phase. Ms. Cole, please continue."

I smiled at Dave. We'd worked together closely for more than a decade and I knew he was once again setting me up to take on a more significant role. I wasn't going to let the opportunity pass. I pulled the proposal from under my notebook. "All right then. Let's start with the recommendations for plate testing."

CHAPTER 3

I held the locker room door open for Bob, my golf buddy. "You have the honors, just like all day."

"You know I like it when you're off your game, Nate, but today you really stunk."

I sat down on the bench and started taking off my shoes. "This deal I'm working on… not enough hours in the day with me away two weeks of the month."

"Are you going to let me in on it?"

"You know I can't. But at least you're up $50 today."

Bob nodded towards the men-only bar area across the hall from the lockers. "Then I guess I'm buying the first round."

"The girls are meeting me for lunch." I pulled out my wallet to pay up, but Bob waved the money away.

"You'll get a chance to even things up. Next Saturday?"

Closing my locker, I extended the money again. "I'll be back in Toronto. I'll pay up now. Gotta go, don't want to keep the ladies waiting."

My wife Betsy and my daughter Ann were dressed in their tennis whites and sipping lemonade on the patio when I came out of the locker room.

"Hello, my lovelies." I put my hand on Ann's shoulder. "How was your lesson?"

"Nothing but backhand drills. Lessons are boring."

Betsy shook her head. "Mr. Martin said she's really improving. A contender for Junior Club Champion this year. If she keeps it up."

Ann looked up at me. "He's just saying that so you'll keep paying for lessons."

I gave her shoulder a gentle shake. "When did my little girl get so cynical?"

Ann's face crumpled and she crossed her arms. "Since she's not a little girl."

Ann was growing up. Much too fast. The nine years since we'd adopted her had flown by and it was hard for me to imagine she was going to be a senior in high school in the fall. She'd gone from playing with dolls to driving lessons in the blink of an eye.

Despite being adopted, she and Betsy were remarkably alike, sometimes much to my dismay. I'd fought sending her to an exclusive private school, not because of the cost, but because I wasn't a fan of the prep-school crowd. I was irritated by their entitled attitudes. They'd had everything given to them. They didn't have to work to pay for college, as I had, and their first jobs were arranged for them in the locker rooms of country clubs such as this one. I resented how quickly they rose through the ranks. I thought going to a good public school would be beneficial for Ann.

Betsy insisted it would be beneficial for her to be associated with the right people from an early age, and she had convinced Ann of its importance. Betsy chose Notre Dame, a prestigious all-girls school near us in Boston, so Ann wouldn't have to go away. But after her first year, Ann pleaded to be allowed to board with her friends. She argued that being a day student meant she didn't get to take part in important extracurricular activities. I suspected the ones she didn't want to miss were not those organized by the nuns running the school. Despite wanting Ann to be at home with her, Betsy was proud that Ann was friends with the daughters of several influential people, and she agreed that boarding was the best solution.

"Should we have lunch in the dining room? No one is eating on the patio today." Betsy stood, making it clear she wasn't asking.

I followed Betsy and Ann into the clubhouse and the hostess instinctively led Betsy to her preferred table. Once we were settled, I broached the subject of the trip I was planning. "I've been looking at activities for our trip to Toronto."

Betsy stiffened. "I don't think we should leave Ann while she's off on summer break."

I'd anticipated her objection. "I was thinking we could all go together. We'll head out Friday and come back the next weekend."

"That's when I'm going to Nantucket with the Kellys. You already said yes," hissed Ann.

"Maybe you could go a different week?" I knew it would be harder to get Betsy on board if Ann didn't come along.

"No. It's Mel's birthday and everyone will be there." Ann's voice sounded desperate. She looked to her mother for support. "I can't be the only one to miss it."

Betsy picked up the menu. "Ann already accepted. It would be rude to back out at this late date."

"Since Ann is away… we could still go… just the two of us?"

Ann's face changed from pouting to hopeful. "Mel said I can stay longer. Even all summer."

I shook my head at Ann. "That won't be necessary."

"If we go at all," said Betsy.

"I have to go. I've got meetings that week."

"But I don't."

"We've been invited to dinner. Franklin said his wife is looking forward to meeting you."

"She'll understand. She wouldn't expect me to come from out of town to attend."

"I thought it would be a good reason to spend the week there. Get to see more of Toronto."

"I've no desire to see more." Betsy picked at the salad our waitress had placed in front of each of us.

Despite her objections, I wanted this trip to happen. If the acquisition went forward, I'd already been approached about taking the job of President of the new Bond Canada division. It would be a significant promotion and the opportunity I'd been working towards for the past several years. Along with the increased responsibility of running an entire division, it came with a commensurate increase in both salary and benefits. But for me to take the job, we'd have to relocate to Canada. I hadn't told Betsy that the promotion was increasingly likely. I hoped that by introducing her to the area and helping her make connections, she would be more open to the idea of moving if I got the job offer.

It would be a big change for her, and I understood her resistance. We'd been living in Boston for almost twenty years. We'd moved from St. Petersburg, Florida shortly after we were married. Betsy had lobbied for me to take a job at her family's law firm rather than the job with Bond. But a career doing wills and trusts for rich people was not what I wanted. I wanted more career opportunities that weren't possible at my in-law's small local firm.

After we'd adopted Ann, we moved to a larger house in a more affluent neighborhood. Betsy had insisted we needed to live in a better school district. I suspect the address, not the school system, was Betsy's primary motivation because, only a couple of years after that, Ann was off to Notre Dame High School.

Betsy had a talent for navigating 'high-society'. I focused on work and advancing my career and I entrusted orchestrating our social connections to her. She decided which country club I should join, where we should rent a house for our summer holiday, and what charity events we should attend. I knew she would thrive in the role of "First Lady" of Bond Canada, and I was doing everything I could to earn the promotion.

I tried again. "There's a lot of outdoor events now that it's summer and if it's hot, there are museums, restaurants, art galleries, theaters..."

Betsy put her fork down and glared across the table. "You aren't going to let this go."

"You liked staying at the Royal York. No cooking or cleaning for a whole week."

"Why would I look forward to being left alone in a hotel, all day, while you go off to work?"

"I'll take some afternoons off. I'm looking forward to being a tourist for a change."

"That's hardly consolation. I'll be alone, in a foreign country, where I know no one. It'll be like Paris all over again."

"They speak English in Toronto. It's not that foreign, and there are lovely shops for you to explore."

Ann perked up at the mention of shopping. "You'll bring me back something right?"

Betsy sighed. "Fine. I'll go."

"Wonderful. I'll call the travel agent this afternoon when I go back to the office."

Betsy looked down at her plate. "The office?" Her tone made it clear she disapproved.

"I need to get caught up."

Betsy looked at Ann. Ann rolled her eyes.

"You two just don't understand. I have a lot of responsibility. People are counting on me."

Betsy raised one finger to signal our waitress as she passed our table.

"What can I get you, Mrs. Jacobs."

"Mr. Jacobs will be leaving. Please ask the valet to bring up his car."

I bristled at Betsy dismissing me publicly, but I swallowed and said nothing until our waitress had walked away.

I leaned toward Betsy and whispered, "That was unnecessary."

"As are you at this table."

My fists clenched under the table.

Betsy didn't look at me but at Ann. "We'll need to go shopping for Mel's birthday gift and a hostess gift for Mrs. Kelly. We can't have you going empty-handed."

I was still seething, but I took a breath and got up slowly so as to not draw attention to us. "I hope you ladies have a nice afternoon. I'll be home before dinner."

My car was one of only a handful in the company parking lot, but I still took my usual spot three spaces from the front entrance. I had to knock on the door to get our security guard to let me in.

"Good afternoon, Mr. Jacobs. What brings you in on a Saturday?" he said as he relocked the door behind me.

"Just catching up on a few things. I shouldn't be long." I crossed the lobby and up the spiral staircase to the executive floor where my office was located. I stopped at my secretary Mary's desk, retrieved my office door key from her top drawer, and let myself in.

Fanned out in the center of my desk were several letters awaiting my signature. Placing my briefcase on the credenza behind the desk, I sat down to review them and get them out of the way. I put the signed letters in my outgoing mail tray and started unpacking my briefcase.

I pulled out the reports John had handed me on my way out of the office the day before. As I did, a business card fluttered to the floor. It was the card that Maddie, the woman I'd met in the hotel bar, had given me. I set it aside with the intention of filing it later and started making a list of the documents and who on my team would need to review each of them. In the stack were several site evaluations for both developed and undeveloped land owned by the company. It occurred to me that we might want to have a third party review the evaluations since the company's consultants had conducted them.

I picked up the card and read her title again, Sr Project Engineer, DB Engineering. I thought of Maddie's comment that if I needed engineering support, I should give her a call. The idea of having a reason to talk with her again was enticing. As I thought about our conversation in Toronto, I realized I was smiling. There was something fascinating about her. I set the card on the stack of site evaluations and made a note to ask John if he was familiar with DB Engineering and get his thoughts on reaching out to them for consultation.

I read through several more of the reports, making notes. When I was finished, I put them in large brown envelopes marked confidential for distribution to the appropriate team members. There were only a few people who had signed non-disclosure agreements and had been cleared to work on this acquisition, and these reports were for their eyes only.

I looked at my watch. It was approaching five. I put all the documents into my credenza, locked it, and then locked up my office and headed home. I hoped the afternoon of shopping had gone well.

CHAPTER 4

The Friday traffic on the 401 was heavy and the drive to Will's parents' house was taking longer than usual. Our six-year-old daughter, Anne, was climbing back and forth between the front and back seats of our station wagon. It wasn't just the drive making her restless; she was anxious about her first time at Camp Nibi Nagamo.

We weren't forcing her to go. I'd told her stories about my experiences spending the summer at the same all-girls camp. I'd gone every year for 8 years and I loved it. I'd learned to swim, dive and paddle and many other outdoor skills like fire-making and shelter building. She'd begged me to let her go. I'd promised, when she was old enough, she could. But now she was re-asking every question she'd asked since we'd made the final arrangements and paid the non-refundable deposit. I wasn't going to let her back out because she was afraid of trying something new. I never wanted her to be limited by fear when it came to trying new things.

Anne popped into the front seat for the umpteenth time. "What if I don't like camping?"

"Then you don't have to go next year."

"Why can't I just leave?"

"It's only two weeks."

"Are you sure there's washrooms in the cabins?"

"I'm sure. Remember we saw them when we went for a tour back in June."

The barrage of questions continued. I was relieved when I spotted the red barn mailbox that marked the laneway to Verna and George Tobias' farm.

George waved to us from where he was sitting on the front porch steps as we pulled up beside the white and green farmhouse.

Anne hopped out of the car and ran up to the porch. "Hiya, Gramps!"

"Hello, Pumpkin. How was the trip?"

Anne let out a theatrical sigh. "It took forever."

Verna came out the screen door onto the porch. "Well, you're here now. Come inside and get washed up. I've got supper ready."

Will and I took our two small bags out of the car, leaving Anne's bulky camp duffle in the back. We'd be dropping her off at camp first thing in the morning, so she didn't need more than the change of clothes, her PJs and toothbrush I'd packed in my bag for her tonight.

George nodded towards the kitchen. "Will can take those up. Verna's through there."

I found Verna coaxing butter tarts from their baking tin onto a plate, and Anne hovering at her elbow.

I smiled seeing Anne's glee at the sight of one of her favourite desserts. "Your Nana spoils you."

"Special occasion. Our first grandbaby going off to camp all by herself. What a thing!"

George came into the kitchen with two beers, followed by Will. George handed one to Will. "We never had to send our kids away in the summer. Your mamma was home to mind 'em."

"Never you mind him," said Verna to me. "Had nothin' to do with it. Wanted the free farm labour, he did."

Even before Will and I were married, I was aware of George's disapproval of my choice to work outside the home. Will's two sisters, Valerie and Laura, were married with children. Both stayed at home as did Pam, his brother George Jr's wife. G.J., as he was called, was the oldest and Will the youngest of the Tobias children. Will was the only one who had left the small town of Verona. All his siblings still lived within fifteen minutes of the family farm. Although Will had moved away before I'd met him, I think his father still holds me responsible for him not returning to raise his family nearby.

The farm hadn't changed much in all the years we'd been coming to see Will's parents. The main floor of the house had high ceilings and included a kitchen, sitting room and bathroom. The largest room was the kitchen. It had a substantial oak table with at least a dozen pressed-back chairs around it and two walls of cupboards that extended up to the ceiling. Verna kept a little ladder behind the door so she could climb up to access her vast collection of tools and containers she used for her constant cooking, canning, freezing, and baking.

The house had three bedrooms upstairs. When we first started coming, we weren't married, so we had to sleep in separate bedrooms. Will slept in the room he had shared with GJ. GJ and Valerie were already married so I bunked with Laura. I thought back to the time when I slept in the room where I had just tucked Anne in after her Nana had stuffed her with fried chicken and butter tarts.

I remember one Canada Day weekend, not long after Will and I had announced our engagement, we went up to stay at the farm. The main event was an all-day family picnic that his sisters had planned. GJ, a member of the volunteer fire department, was responsible for putting on the town's fireworks display. He was excited about it and had told his sisters which spots would have the ideal view. His sisters planned to spend the day holding the best spot by having a picnic.

We carried several lawn chairs, blankets and old quilts from the cars and staked out our territory with them. Verna, her daughters, and daughter-in-law had prepared lots of food that was packed in large hampers and coolers. There were two big thermoses filled with tea and one cooler was filled with cokes and beer packed in ice. They'd also brought a little orange portable grill and when it got close to supper time, Hank, Valerie's husband lit the charcoal so he could grill the hot dogs and hamburgers.

Both GJ and Valerie had small children who were delighted to have a whole day at the park on the shore of a small lake. The kids played on the swings, climbed the jungle gym, made sandcastles, and went swimming. Their mothers took turns minding them and I helped by taking over when I went for a swim. For the most part, the men drank beer and pitched horseshoes and the women sat on the picnic blankets talking and doling out food.

Much of the conversation revolved around the antics of the children, including our grown-up boys drinking beer, and about plans for the summer. Laura was the one to bring up Will and my upcoming wedding.

She gave me a sidelong hug. "Not long now and we'll have another sister."

The whole idea seemed strange. Being an only child, I wasn't sure I wanted any sisters. "It's still nine months away."

"Only nine months until you can quit working and stay home," said Valerie.

"Oh… I'm not going to quit working." I didn't anticipate the condemnation I saw on their faces.

"Is Will OK with that?" asked Valerie.

"Why wouldn't he be?" I was genuinely perplexed at her surprise. She worked. It was at the local grocery store but she wasn't at home all the time.

Valerie shrugged. "He wasn't happy about you going to Japan."

"That was a unique opportunity I couldn't turn down. I doubt I'll be spending months away again, a week or so at most."

Pam had come back to the blanket to help herself to more tea. "You'll be away? After you're married?"

"Most of my work doesn't require me to go away."

"But you don't have to work. Will makes a good living."

I was starting to get defensive. I made good money too. "I didn't work this hard to stop just because I get married."

"I'm sure you think your job is important, but so is being able to support your husband by taking care of things at home," said Valerie.

I reminded myself that they had no idea what it was like for me and what I'd had to do to get to where I was. I needed to lighten things up, so I laughed off Valeries's comment. "Now you're starting to sound like my mother. I thought we were going to be sisters."

Laura snorted and poked at Valerie. "Just because you want to quit your job, like I did, doesn't mean everyone should."

Just then, a beach ball landed in the centre of the blanket and our conversation was interrupted by the chaos of potato chips and cookies flying through the air.

"That was thanks to one of yours," said Pam who liked to needle Valerie and couldn't resist adding, "Maybe if you were home more, Hank Jr wouldn't be such a monster."

Will never came right out and asked me to give up my career, but he didn't fully support it either. His father had much less restraint on the subject. Even after we'd been married for years, he continued to criticize me for not staying home. If anything, the older he got, the less he filtered his comments.

What upset me most was when he said things in front of Anne. I worried she'd get mixed messages, especially when she was staying with Verna and George on her own. She had her first solo week with them during spring break. I was happy she was experiencing the countryside and life on the farm. She'd enjoyed playing with her cousins and having them sleep over at Nana's house with her. But she came home asking questions like why did I have to go to work and was angry she had to go to my parents' house after school instead of coming home.

I hoped that the experience at Camp Nibi Nagano would be positive. I knew from my time there that they believed that girls could do everything. She would learn new sports, get stronger physically, build with her hands and create with her imagination. I wanted her to be fearless and feel empowered to do or be whatever she wants in life, and I hoped the camp experience nurtured her confidence to do it.

Dropping her off at camp had been a rollercoaster of emotions. More so for me than for Anne.

Will thought going to a camp like Nibi Nagano was elitist and he had objected to her going. "I don't want my Annie turning into a snob."

I was offended. "So, you're saying I'm a snob?"

"I didn't say that."

"There's nothing snobby about it. If anything, it turns prissy princesses into strong independent women."

"My Annie is already strong, and she's going to miss two weeks of softball."

I was relieved when Anne had chosen to go and I thought the subject was closed. But Will still gave her the option to back out as we pulled into the camp to drop her off. I was furious, but Anne thought he was kidding and had happily trotted off with her duffel bag, turning only once to wave goodbye before being swept up with introductions and instructions from the camp leaders.

19

CHAPTER 5

I was uneasy flying to Toronto with Betsy. I'd made the same trip a dozen times or more for work. This time was different. I needed it to go flawlessly. I'd met with our company president, and he'd informed me that if the deal went through, the job of leading the new division was mine. Considering the increasing possibility of us relocating, I'd meticulously planned this trip to introduce Betsy to the area in a way that would appeal to her.

Even if she was less than enthusiastic about the trip, I was looking forward to the events I'd arranged; tickets for an outdoor concert, theater tickets, a private tour of the city and an excursion to the Shaw Festival and Niagara Falls on the weekend. I'd compiled a list of restaurants that I thought she'd like, and I'd assembled information on the special events at several museums and galleries, so she had some options for things to do while I was at work.

By Monday morning, I felt relieved leaving for the office. Our hotel room at the Royal York, although elegant, had started to feel very small and I think both Betsy and I needed a little space.

John was in the conference room when I arrived. He made a show of looking at his watch. "You get lost? You're never this late."

"My wife is with me this week."

He gave an approving nod and a wink. "I see. A little romantic getaway on the company dime. Good for you."

I pulled a stack of reports out of my briefcase. "I have some concerns about these properties. I think we should get an independent assessment."

"What sort of assessment?"

"At least an expert review of these reports to validate the conclusions."

"It could take some time to get someone on board."

"I have a contact at DB Engineering…"

"Good choice. See if they have someone who can turn this PDQ."

When we had a break later in the day, I went into one of the open offices. I pulled out the business card I'd filed in the back of my day-planner, dialed the number, and asked to be connected to Ms. Cole.

"Hello. This is Nate Jacobs. I don't know if you recall, but we met at the Royal York, during the blackout."

"Of course, Mr. Jacobs. How are you?" Her voice was modulated and professional.

"Very well. Thank you. And yourself?"

"Busy. But that's a good thing."

"Is this a bad time?"

"No. Not at all. How can I help you?"

I gave her a brief overview, and we agreed to meet over lunch to discuss the project in more detail. She suggested a restaurant, the Silver Rail on Yonge Street, and we met there the next day.

I arrived early and was already seated when Maddie walked down the staircase into the dining room. I watched as she weaved her way through the restaurant to join me at our table. I remember being surprised by the pantsuit she wore. Although it was made of traditional pinstriped wool, there was nothing masculine about her in it. She had a determined stride and appeared oblivious to the businessmen who looked up from their meals, some unabashedly ogling her. I felt a little rush of pride that this gorgeous woman was my lunch companion.

I stood as she approached the table.

She extended her hand. "Hello, Mr. Jacobs. Nice to see you again."

I extended my hand in return. "Nice to see you again, too, Ms. Cole. Please, call me Nate."

A waiter swiftly approached our table, sliding her chair in before I had a chance to offer my help.

"Good afternoon. I'm Paul. I'll be your waiter today." Paul placed her napkin on her lap.

She sat up straight, her posture exuding confidence. "I hope you don't mind if we get right to the reason for our meeting. I've a full schedule today."

I suspected setting a time limit was her way of asserting control and a clever way of avoiding consuming an excess of alcohol with a stranger. I'd made a lot of deals during business lunches. However, that rarely happened until after the social meal was completed and after consuming several cocktails.

Paul may have picked up her cue to hurry things along and was hovering nearby. "Can I start you off with a cocktail?"

We ordered drinks from the extensive bar menu he'd handed each of us.

I wanted to assure her I wasn't going to drag things out. "I completely understand. I appreciate you meeting with me, on such short notice."

"A girl's got to eat, and drink." Her eyes flashed mischievously but quickly dissolved to a more serious gaze and she looked down to study the menu.

I set my menu aside having decided on the steak for lunch. "This seems like a popular spot. Come here often?"

She tilted her head and her eyes narrowed and, seeing her look, I realized my words sounded like a bad pickup line.

"It's a Yonge Street fixture. Good for lunch, dinner, and drinks." Her voice was cool and matter of fact.

We ordered our lunch, and she pivoted the conversation back to business. "I'm pleased you're considering DB for the engineering reviews you mentioned on the phone."

"Maybe you could start by telling me a little more about you… I mean… your firm." I was uncharacteristically stumbling over my words; caught off guard looking into her bright and expressive eyes. They seemed to change color from green to brown to gray as she went from charming to all business.

She pulled a folder from the briefcase she'd set on the floor beside her chair. "I prepared some information about our capabilities. I've included a summary of our areas of expertise and the CVs for our leading expert in each area. We'll select your project team based on the expertise you need."

She handed me the folder. I opened it and looked through the sheaf of printed pages while she pitched her firm's capabilities. From the questions she asked, it was obvious she knew a lot more about the subject than I did, and it was humbling. I prided myself on being up to speed with technology. Chemistry and engineering were, after all, at the core of our business at Bond Technologies.

Our lunch arrived, and I set the folder aside. "If you don't mind me asking… I noticed the name on your business card is Cole, but you introduced yourself by another name at the hotel."

"Cole is my maiden name. Tobias is my married name. You can call me Maddie. That's always correct."

"Alright then. Maddie it is. So, how did you come to be in this line of work?"

She rattled off her credentials, her background in mining engineering, her experience with soil and rock investigations, and that she was the head of their geotechnical group. I'm ashamed remembering my disbelief that this attractive woman could be an expert in that sort of thing. The surprise made her even more fascinating.

I wanted to hire her on the spot. "I'm confident your firm can help us."

"I presume you'll want a proposal?" She slid her plate off to the side and pulled out a leather notebook and pen. "If we could go over the scope of work, I'll prepare something."

"We need this assessment done as soon as possible. I'd like to get started immediately."

"That's not a problem. If I understand correctly…you're looking for a review of previous investigations and a report with our professional opinion."

"That's correct. We would need to have your experts come to our offices to review the reports and, of course, sign confidentiality agreements."

"Where are your offices?"

"On Bay Street, the Dominion Bank Building." I took out one of my business cards from the leather portfolio I'd brought with me to take notes. "I've written the phone number and address of our temporary location on the back of my card."

"That'll be no problem. It's not far from our offices. If you could tell me how many reports and what the subjects are, I can determine who would be the appropriate experts."

"Would one of the experts be you?"

"Would that be a problem?"

"Of course not. I was just curious." I took out a typed sheet from my portfolio. "Here's a list of the subjects. There are 20 reports in all. Some are quite short, but there are several that are quite thick."

"This will be enough for me to put together an estimate."

"Perhaps we can begin on a retainer basis…"

Maddie tapped her pen on her notebook. "That would be unusual. Normally we scope a project, or if the scope is to be determined, on an hourly basis. I'd need to discuss it with our senior partner. Can I get back to you on that later today?"

"Tomorrow is fine. I don't expect you to rush back to the office today."

"I was planning on going back. It's no problem."

"Then it's a done deal. Shall we have dessert?"

"Nothing for me. But please go ahead."

Although her words were gracious, she started putting away her notebook, and I sensed she wanted to leave.

"I don't need it."

She signaled Paul. "I'll take the bill when you have a moment."

Paul nodded. "Yes Madam. I'll be right back."

I was taken aback by her speed at requesting the check. "You needn't pick up the tab."

She narrowed her eyes and looked at me sternly. "It's customary for the consultant to treat the client. And I'm looking forward to being your consultant." Then she smiled, and I realized she was toying with me.

"Well, next time it's on me." I watched her review the bill and then place her credit card on the tray.

While we waited for Paul to return, she asked, "Should I use the information on your business card as the primary contact for the proposal or your temporary address?"

"The primary address. But I'll be at the temporary address for the next two weeks, so you can reach me there."

Once she had signed the slip, she stood up and extended her hand. "I'll be in touch."

CHAPTER 6

I had a feeling this review job could turn into something bigger. I wanted to make good on my promise to get an answer to Nate by the end of the day. So, after lunch, I went straight to Dave's office. I poked my head into his open door. He was on the phone but waved me in. I took a seat in one of the chairs across the desk from him, took out my notes from lunch, and waited until he hung up.

"How'd it go?"

"Good. Mr. Jacobs would like to get started as soon as possible."

"Did you get a good sense of what they need reviewed?"

"From the list he provided, most of the reports are site audits and soil investigations."

"Nothing we can't handle."

"Have you got a feel for how much work it'll be?"

"There are 20 reports in all. He indicated some were short."

"How long do you think it will take you?"

"I'd say at least a week. Maybe two."

"Are you sure you can handle it on your own?"

I was taken aback. I'd been irritated by Nate's surprise at my credentials, but Dave was not one to question them. I didn't hide my displeasure at the suggestion I needed help with such a straightforward assignment.

Dave leaned forward and smiled. "Don't get mad. I only meant do you have time? You're already putting in long hours."

"Anne is at camp for another week. So, if they want to start right away, the timing couldn't be better for me."

"Anything else?"

"He suggested a retainer…"

"We can get around that. On our end, we'll set it up like a regular project, but in the proposal, we'll describe it as a retainer. That way, they'll feel like we're working on their terms. Commit to up to 80 hours of professional review and consultation services to be completed by the end of August. Include an option for them to renew it at the end of the month."

"Ok. I'll give him a call, agree to a retainer, and let him know a preliminary cost based on my rate."

"Calculate the hourly rate at a premium. We'll want some wiggle room."

I got up and gathered my briefcase to go back to my office. "Will do. Thanks."

"Good job hunting this one down."

I went to my office and got out my calculator and a pad of paper. I did a few calculations and then got out Nate's business card to give him a call. Before I could, my phone rang. It was Will.

"Hi Mads. Did you get my message?"

As he said it I noticed the pink slip of paper in my inbox. I picked it up. Call Will was all it said.

"I just saw it. What's up?"

"I have a game tonight and I can't find my baseball shirt."

"It's hanging by the washer downstairs."

"Ok. Thanks. When are you going to be home?"

"Probably a little late. I've got a proposal to write that I want to finish tonight."

"So you're not making dinner?"

"There's leftover chicken casserole in the fridge."

"It'll be cold."

"You can reheat it. Just put it in the oven for a bit."

"I'll get something after the game."

"Make sure that something is more than just beer."

"If you weren't sending me out on an empty stomach, it wouldn't be a problem."

"Heat up the casserole."

"Uh, no. Ok. See you later."

"See you later."

I looked at my watch. It was just after five and I wondered if Nate was still in the office or if I'd missed him for the day. I dialed the number he'd written on the back of his business card.

I let it ring seven times, and I was just about to hang up when someone answered.

"I'm calling for Mr. Jacobs."

"Speaking. Maddie? Is that you?"

"Yes. I'm calling about the project we discussed." I outlined the retainer parameters and gave him the rough estimate I'd calculated. I could hear him writing things down as I spoke.

"That sounds reasonable. Can we get started tomorrow?"

"I'll have the proposal to you tomorrow…"

"I mean start the review. We're on a tight timeline."

"That quickly? I could start Thursday. I'll need tomorrow to clear my desk of some other projects."

"You'll be doing the work yourself?"

"Based on the titles of the reports you provided, yes. If other expertise besides mine is needed, I'll arrange to have them brought in."

"I presume you'll need a payment to get started…"

"I can courier the proposal with all the details and terms tomorrow morning. I should point out we're only estimating a desk review. If we see the need for any field investigations, that would be a significant change in scope."

"Understood. See you Thursday. Nine o'clock?"

"I'll be there."

I hung up and went back to Dave's office to let him know.

He sat back in his chair and smiled. "You and Will should go out and celebrate tonight."

"I need to get this proposal done so it can go out in the morning."

"Then bang it out and leave it for Peggy to type in the morning and go toast your new client."

"Will's got a baseball game."

"Then we'll have that drink now."

If it was anyone else but Dave, I would have said no. But we had a special relationship. He was my boss and my friend, which was a tough tightrope to walk sometimes. He believed in me and had created opportunities for me to grow professionally, like working on a project in Japan very early in my career. But he also knew me better than anyone else in the office and we kept each other's secrets.

Dave opened the cabinet above his credenza and took out two glasses and a bottle of scotch. He poured us each a drink. I took mine and settled onto the sofa by the window of his large corner office. Dave sat at the other end and raised his glass in the air. "To Maddie. Who'll be running this company one day."

I laughed. "Maybe then guys will stop asking me to type up their reports."

"When was the last time you typed someone else's report?"

He had a point. I'd gotten quite adept at deflecting, although I usually typed my own letters and reports because the girls in the typing pool often left mine to the end. Especially the single gals who prioritized the eligible bachelors' work, hoping to snag a husband.

There once was a time when I too thought having a husband would be to my advantage. Turns out most of the advantages of marriage are reserved for men who have wives at home to take care of things while they're getting ahead in their careers.

I'm sure the single girls in the typing pool would jump at the chance to marry a guy like Will. He was a very acceptable catch; handsome, funny, owns his own business and an all around good guy. Marrying Will had been a sensible choice since the alternative of being single into my thirties would have made me a true old maid and social pariah. I'd barely made it under the wire, marrying Will shortly before my 30th birthday.

Both of our careers had evolved in the eight years since we got married. Will's electrician business had grown. He'd gone from doing the work to overseeing the work of his staff of electricians and apprentices. In many regards, his job had gotten easier, while mine had gotten more demanding. Yet, he still resisted doing anything around the house that he considered women's work, so the burden of the cooking, cleaning and laundry was all mine.

He did, however, help with Anne, especially when it came to her sports interests. Anne loved all sorts of sports. She took swimming lessons, played softball and this fall she'd be starting ringette. Will never complained about taking her to lessons or games and he was happy to practice with her whenever she wanted. He loved that she wasn't too girly, and he was happy to go to the park and play with her. I can't count how many times they came home all muddy and laughing about tree climbing or frog catching or some other misadventure.

He didn't initially think he'd be the one looking after Anne. When I told him we were expecting, his initial reaction was to hug me. "This is great!"

"I'm glad it's a good surprise."

"I was starting to think we couldn't, since it hasn't happened."

"The doctor says we have about seven and a half months to get ready."

"Time for you to sort things out at work."

"I get fifteen weeks of paid maternity leave. It's only two-thirds pay, but we'll be ok until I go back."

"What do you mean go back?"

"Back to work."

"You don't have to go back. You can stay home."

"I don't want to stay home."

"But you need to… you're… the mother…"

"I can be a mother and work."

It had taken several discussions, a few arguments, and the hiring of a nanny in order for me to return after my maternity leave. We had our nanny, an Italian woman named Maria, until Anne started kindergarten. From age 5, Anne started spending after-school time with my parents, or Rosa our neighbour until Will or I got home from work.

It was good that Anne was at camp with this new project starting. It would be ideal to get the bulk of the work done before she got home. Nate seemed anxious to get started, and I had a feeling that I'd be working long hours trying to turn it around quickly for him.

CHAPTER 7

There were several surprised faces when Maddie walked into the conference room Thursday morning. She wore a light blue pantsuit, the short-sleeved jacket buttoned over a bold dark blue and white striped collared shirt. She towered over us on account of the platform wedge shoes she was wearing.

I got up to greet her and made introductions. "This is Ms. Madeleine Cole from DB Engineering."

John pointed to a chair beside Franklin's assistant Joan. "You can set up there."

Maddie didn't move towards the chair. "I'll need a much larger area to work… to spread out the site plans. If you have an empty office or conference room, that would be preferable."

John looked at me and raised his eyebrows.

I pulled out the chair closest to her, which happened to be beside Franklin, near the head of the table. "I'm sorry Ms. Cole. Please take a seat. I've arranged for an office. You can begin as soon as we get these documents signed."

She set her briefcase on the floor and sat on the front edge of her seat with her back very straight. "We can proceed as long as you've signed our proposal indicating you agree with the terms…"

I went back to my seat. "Of course. I have your copy right here." I passed her the proposal, she checked the signature page, and placed it into her briefcase.

I explained that due to the confidential nature of the acquisition, we would require her to sign a non-disclosure agreement. I handed her the documents.

She took them and flipped through the pages. "I'll need a few minutes to review them before signing." She leaned forward and started reading.

"Do you need me to explain it to you?" said John.

Maddie didn't look up from the papers. "Should I need clarification on anything, I'll ask."

John sat back in his chair and scowled. Although I didn't let on, I enjoyed watching her put him in his place. John thought himself quite the ladies' man, but in the tales he told of his conquests, he invariably portrayed himself outsmarting gullible women, which I found appalling.

She quickly read the agreement but didn't pick up the pen to sign. "I can't agree to section seven. Exclusivity isn't possible since I have other clients. This appears to be a non-disclosure agreement for an employee."

I reached over and pulled the agreement towards me. "So it is."

She sat back a bit in her chair and looked at each of us in turn as she spoke. "As a professional engineer, it is my duty to respect the confidentiality requirements of my clients… so if you indicate which information you share is confidential, a separate non-disclosure agreement is redundant."

John sat up. "You're the engineer Dave assigned to this project?"

Maddie ignored his comment and continued, "However, if you remove section seven, or provide a different agreement that is specific to contractors, I'm authorized to sign it."

I was embarrassed that we'd given her the wrong agreement. Despite her controlled answer, I sensed we were getting off to a rocky start and I wanted to demonstrate my good faith and trust in her.

"I'll get another agreement drawn up this morning, but there's no reason you can't get started with the understanding that everything you hear, read, or discuss in this office is confidential. I'll show you to your office now, so you can begin your review."

I gave Maddie a brief orientation to the office, the location of the break room where there was always coffee and tea and the restrooms before showing her to the office I'd arranged.

Maddie set her briefcase on the desk and took out a notepad, pens, and a roll of masking tape. She pointed to the stack of reports on the desk. "Are these all of them?"

"Yes. Do you have everything you need?"

She reached for the stack and shuffled through them. "I'll get started right away."

"Then I'll leave you to it." I nodded towards the phone on the desk. "I'll be at extension 333 should you need anything."

She sat down at the desk, looked up at me, smiled and said, "Thank you."

I took that as my cue to go. I went back to the conference room where Joan was moving around the table, serving fresh cups of coffee to each of us.

I returned to my seat and opened the file of financial statements we'd been reviewing. "Shall we start to sketch out our offer?"

John leaned back in his chair. "Before we start, you should know I just got off the phone with Dave Bennet. He's the DB of DB Engineering and we go way back."

"And?"

"He only had good things to say about this girl."

I was irritated he'd felt the need to call her boss. "Then we should just let her do her job and we'll do ours."

It wasn't just that he was second-guessing my decision to hire Maddie, but something about the way he referred to her as a girl bothered me. From our few encounters, I was certain that Maddie wouldn't have taken kindly to the remark. Fortunately, John didn't make any further comments, and we dug in to work through our valuation.

After a couple of hours, we'd hashed out the equipment and other assets and I needed a break. I stood up and stretched. "Shall we stop for lunch and pick up on the employee retention portion this afternoon?"

Franklin pushed back from the table and nodded. "Joan, please call and get us a table at the club."

Joan put down her steno pad. "If Ms. Cole is joining you, perhaps you should consider somewhere else?"

John grumbled.

I wanted to check on Maddie's progress anyway, so I offered to go ask her if she was joining us for lunch. Her office door was open, and I paused outside, watching her. She'd taken off her suit jacket and was reading one of the three reports she had open in front of her. There was also a large map, unfolded, covering the remainder of the desk surface.

Reluctant to interrupt her, I stood just outside the office door and leaned in. "Care to join us for lunch?"

Maddie marked the spot where she was reading with her finger and glanced up at me. "No, thank you. I brought lunch."

"Do you need anything?"

"No. I'd just like to get as much done today as I can." Maddie tore off a piece of tape and made a tab on the edge of the page she was reading.

"What do you do with the tape?"

"I use it to make numbered notes. It makes it easier to refer back to the original data later."

"How clever."

Maddie stopped what she was doing and looked over her shoulder at me. "These reports can be quite confusing for non-technical people. This will help you follow the logic of my analysis and conclusions."

"I'm used to reviewing highly technical information, but I appreciate your thoroughness in documenting your findings."

"I didn't mean to imply you wouldn't understand." Maddie's tone suggested that was precisely what she meant.

I had considered asking her to plan on going out for lunch with me on Monday, but our awkward conversation made me doubt she'd be interested. So I left her to her work.

I told John she wasn't coming, and he was relieved. He made a point of telling us, as we made the short walk to the Albany Club, how much simpler it was to just go to the club instead of trying to find a table for mixed company. Rarely did I agree with John when it came to his attitudes towards women, but I don't think we would have enjoyed our lunch as much if I'd pried Maddie away from her desk to join us. I found it surprising she had an all work and no play attitude, given how warm and fun she'd seemed when we first met.

The new non-disclosure agreement for Maddie was ready when we returned from lunch. I had Joan take it to her for her signature because I wanted to hammer out the details for the employee retention packages we discussed over lunch. But before I left for the day, I felt a sense of obligation to check in on Maddie again.

Once again, I poked my head into her office. "I'll be out of the office tomorrow, so if you need anything, just ask Joan. She generally gets in about 8:00, so you can start any time after that."

Maddie continued to write in her notebook, but turned her head slightly towards me and nodded. "Ok. Thank you."

"You can stay as late as you like. The security guard will let you out and lock up behind you."

She closed the report in front of her, set it aside and picked up another. "I shouldn't be much longer today."

"I'll see you Monday then?"

Maddie set her pen down and swiveled her chair to face me in the doorway. "You're not heading home to…"

"Boston. No. I'll be here through the end of next week."

"I see." She pressed her lips together, looked up and away as if calculating, and then looked back at me. "I'll aim to have something for you by then."

"Are you sure that's enough time? You said two weeks…"

"I've gone over everything at a high level today. I don't think it will take all next week."

"You've read all the reports?"

"I've read the executive summaries and have identified the conclusions that I want to evaluate further. There are a few areas I want to investigate. I've made a list of air photos and maps I'd like to consult."

"Air photos?"

"Photographs taken from the air. We have a library covering most of Ontario in our offices. I'll call our librarian tomorrow morning and have her assemble them for me. I'll pick them up at our offices over the weekend, so I'll have them for reference next week."

"And you'll wrap up next week?"

"I'll still need a couple of days for one of my colleagues to review it. It's standard practice for all reports to be reviewed internally before presenting to the client. But I can give you a preview of key findings even if the report isn't finalized."

"I'll look forward to it, then. Ok. I'm off."

She turned back to writing in her notebook, calling over her shoulder, "Bye. Have a nice weekend."

I stood in the doorway for a few seconds, a little stunned. Although her words were pleasant and polite, I felt as if I was being dismissed. In the hotel bar she'd been chatty and engaging to talk to, but now she seemed distant and disinterested in conversation. I wondered if I'd done something to make her dislike me, but I had no idea what it might be.

CHAPTER 8

The bank security guard held the door open for me. "Good morning, Ms. Cole."

I could barely slip past him with my arms full and my loaded briefcase over my shoulder. "Thank you. Good morning… I'm sorry, I don't know your name."

"Dominic. Not to worry." He tilted his head and raised an eyebrow. "It's my job to know who everyone is," he said in a serious tone

I stopped and turned to face him as he relocked the lobby door. "Good morning, Dominic. Sorry it took me all week to ask."

He grinned and nodded towards the elevator. "You have a good day, now."

I hoped it was my last day of having to work at the bank offices. As luxurious as they were in the towering building over Bay Street, I felt more comfortable and productive in my own space. On several occasions, I had to go, after hours, to my office to pick up supplies, like tracing paper and my drawing tools, in order to do my analysis of the reports prepared by other consultants. And yesterday evening I'd gone to my office with my draft report for Dave to review and then I'd stayed until well past midnight typing up the final version, in triplicate, to submit to our client today.

It had been a whirlwind eight days since I'd started this assignment. I'd worked hard to get this job done as quickly as possible, both for my sake, as I felt out of the loop being away from my office so much and for Nate, as he seemed very anxious to get the results. I'd gleaned as much information as I could from the materials they'd provided, and I'd identified several areas where I had concerns that the consultants had missed or under-reported potential liabilities.

I dropped my briefcase and the reports I was carrying on my desk and went in search of coffee. Nate had arranged for me to be allowed into the building early, before the office staff arrived, and I'd made coffee the last couple of days. But today the large coffee urn that was normally in the breakroom wasn't there. I opened all the cupboards finding extra ground coffee, sugar, and cups but no urn.

Nate came in as I was closing the cupboards. "No coffee yet?" He frowned and looked annoyed.

I was irritated he thought it was my job to make the coffee. "No urn even," I said, leaving him standing in the breakroom.

I didn't have time to fiddle with making coffee. Although I'd already prepared the acetates with the maps and diagrams, I'd waited to finalize my report before preparing the summary acetates. I wanted to get those done early in the day, so I'd have time to rehearse my presentation before this afternoon's meeting.

"You've got this," Dave assured me after I'd run through the presentation with him before we were summoned to the boardroom. We'd debated whether or not Dave should come to the presentation meeting. I didn't want his presence to imply that I needed him there, but in the end I agreed that having the company president attend would demonstrate that we valued them as a client and it could help solidify the relationship. Landing Bond as a client would be a major win for me and a step closer to demonstrating I was partner material.

My presentation went smoothly despite having to deliver bad news about three of the properties under consideration. On the site plan for one of the company's manufacturing facilities, I'd found an area referred to as a 'used barrel area'. There was no information in the reports as to what had been stored there, so it warranted a follow-up question to confirm whether the barrels had contained hazardous compounds.

I'd also found an area labelled 'waste dump' on the site of a paint manufacturing plant that the previous consultant had not identified or investigated. Given the nature of the types of chemicals that could have been dumped and the sandy soils of the site, I concluded that it was likely that there was contamination beyond the small bermed pit at the edge of the property.

The site that gave me the most concern was a vacant lot adjacent to the company headquarters, which was formerly a chemical storage facility, but the building had burned down. The consultants had categorized the property as ready to be redeveloped for the expansion of the corporate offices as the site had been cleared of what had remained of the burned structure and graded. I'd pulled airphotos of the site from a year before the fire and there was evidence of several underground storage tanks but I found no record of them being decommissioned in the reports.

"What's the worst-case scenario?" asked Nate after I'd finished describing all three areas.

"That the storage tanks were never properly emptied and decommissioned, are now damaged and leaking, and the entire site will need to be excavated and all the soil removed before any construction can be done."

John looked at Dave. "That seems like a hysterical assessment."

Dave didn't answer John but looked at me, signalling I should answer.

I'd anticipated the question and I pulled out an acetate I'd prepared that listed the areas of concern and the possible costs associated with each one. "Here are some ballpark numbers for investigating each of these sites. Without the results of the investigations, I can't accurately predict the cost of rehabilitation. However, I have provided a range of remediation costs based on other projects we've completed on similar sites."

Dave gave me a subtle nod to let me know he approved.

"This is extremely helpful," said Nate. "Have you included these estimates in your report?"

"They are included in the discussion section of the report, but they are not a formal estimate or prediction of future costs. They are for information purposes only." I picked up the copies of the report and made my way around the table to distribute them.

Nate smiled up at me as I handed him a copy. "Understood. Really excellent work Ms. Cole. Thank you."

Franklin opened his copy. "We appreciate how quickly you've been able to get us this information."

Nate turned towards the far end of the table where Franklin was sitting. "I think we'll need to account for these potential liabilities and reconsider some of the contingencies based on these estimates."

John stood up and patted Dave on the back. "You've really delivered for us."

Dave gestured towards me. "Ms. Cole is the one you should be congratulating. She's got a gift for seeing what others overlook. It's why I told you she was the best person for this job."

"I hope this is the beginning of a great partnership," said Nate getting up from the table. "We should go for a drink to celebrate."

I started to decline, saying, "I have a box of my things I'd like to take back to my office now that we've wrapped up."

Dave gave a subtle head shake. "I've got to go back to the office anyway. I'll drop your box in your office. Please take our new favourite clients for a drink."

"I'd be delighted to," I said picking up on Dave's cue even though I wasn't thrilled about having to take the three of them for drinks without him. It's not that I was uncomfortable in the company of men, but I was outnumbered by the client and it would be more relaxing if Dave were there to do some of the entertaining.

Dave followed me back to my temporary office. He picked up my box and we walked together to the lobby.

"See you back at the ranch on Monday." He left me to wait for the others.

Nate arrived first with his briefcase in hand. "It looks like it's just us. John and Franklin have personal obligations."

"We can do this another time."

"No time like now. Besides, I'd like to run some things by you. Just one drink?"

I was relieved that I wouldn't have to entertain all three of them solo and given that Nate had been very easy to talk to and had bought me a drink on the night of the blackout, I liked the thought of having a chance to return the favour.

We slid into a booth in a quiet corner of Bardi's Steak House.

We ordered drinks and once the waiter had moved off, Nate leaned a little closer across the table. "I hope you'll keep this in the strictest confidence." He spoke in a low voice so no one would overhear our conversation, but I could sense his excitement. "The reason these properties are such a concern for me is, if this deal goes through, I'll be named President of the new division. They'll be my problem if I take over."

"What an extraordinary opportunity."

"It's not a sure thing the deal will close, nor a sure thing I can take the job."

"Why wouldn't you take it?"

"My wife's not happy about it."

"I would think she'd be very proud of you."

"Pretty big deal for the son of a bus driver."

"I sincerely hope you get the job. I can see it means a lot to you."

Nate sat back and smirked. "You're just saying that because you want to secure Bond as a client."

I batted my eyes and feigned innocence. "It never even crossed my mind."

"Don't get me wrong. I admire your tenacity. Hunting me down. Getting me to hire you."

"I don't remember doing much hunting given you called me. But the client is always right." I picked up my rye and ginger that the waiter had delivered. "To a long and mutually beneficial relationship."

"I'll drink to that," said Nate, picking up his beer and tapping my glass with his.

"You caught on to why I wanted to go for a drink, eh?" I gave him a sidelong look and a wink to make sure he knew I was teasing.

"I hope that's not the only motive." His tone was friendly without being overtly flirtatious.

"No, I also had to reciprocate for the night of the blackout."

"May I say, you're an intriguing lady, Ms. Cole. I hope we can be friends, not just client and consultant."

I smiled and raised my eyebrows. "Let's just be clear. I am angling to be your consultant."

"Alright then. Our first project is getting my wife to agree to move to Canada. Got any ideas?"

"Not sure I'm qualified to help with that one."

"What would convince you?"

"Probably nothing." I held up my hand with my thumb and forefinger about an inch apart. "I'm this close to becoming the firm's first female partner. I wouldn't want to give that up."

"That's understandable, but my wife doesn't work."

"What does she say about it?"

"Besides, no?"

"What reasons?"

"Our daughter is in her senior year."

"That's a legitimate concern, I suppose."

"But she'll be leaving for university soon."

"Do you have other children?"

"No, just the one."

"Perhaps you can delay relocating?"

"I have to be here to take the job."

"Get a small apartment for a year, then make the move once she's done her senior year."

Nate made a humming sound and tapped his fingers on the side of his glass. "That might be an option. I knew you were going to be an invaluable consultant."

"Consultation services beyond engineering are not guaranteed for quality or accuracy. Too many unknown variables."

"You've given me lots to think about today. Both in and out of the office."

"I'm happy to help."

"I'm getting hungry. Would you like to join me for dinner?"

"I can't this evening. My husband is expecting me."

"He should take you out to celebrate your success..."

I didn't think it was appropriate to tell Nate that Will wasn't overly supportive of my career. I scrambled for a natural way to change the subject.

I noticed Nate's beer was empty. "Would you like another beer? I can order you one before I ask for the check."

"No, no, no. You've been providing plenty of free advice this afternoon. I'll get it. I'll wait for you to buy me dinner."

I slid out of the booth. "All right then, I owe you dinner. In the meantime, give me a call if you need anything. DB is at your service."

I would have liked to stay for dinner with Nate. Talking with him was easy and fun. It felt empowering to have a smart, accomplished, and attractive man genuinely seek my advice and value my thoughts and opinions. If we'd crossed paths at a social gathering, I have no doubt we would have hit it off and become friends.

But I didn't want things to get too personal. If the acquisition went through, there's a good chance for a large project related to the properties we'd discussed in the meeting. Cultivating Nate as a client was just the sort of business building Dave had been telling me I needed to demonstrate. I wasn't going to let anything, or anyone, get in the way of landing the business.

CHAPTER 9

Randal, the retiring president of Oakland Chemical, led me through the executive floor to the corner office. The brass plate with Nate Jacobs, President, was already in place on the door.

Randal opened the door and stepped aside for me to enter. "We had it cleaned and painted, but we left my furniture for now. We thought you, or your wife, might prefer to do the redecorating."

The office was enormous. Although the walls were painted a neutral white, the décor was much too bright for my taste. The sofa and two wing chairs were upholstered in orange, and the side tables featured lamps in shades of orange and yellow. The desk, at least what I could see of it under the assortment of bottles and gift baskets covering it, was dark wood and much larger and nicer than the one I'd left behind in Boston.

I walked behind the desk and pulled out the large leather chair. "It's all very nice. It'll work just fine as is."

Randal looked over the gifts on the desk. "Good thing some of our suppliers have taste, they've stocked your bar for you." He picked up a bottle of champagne. "This one is from all of us. A welcome gift for you and your wife."

"Thank you. I look forward to working with you."

"I hope it'll be as rewarding a job for you as it has been for me. I'll leave you to settle in."

Although Randal would be staying on for a few months to help with the transition, I got the feeling he was at peace with handing over the reins to someone else. I was grateful he was as excited about retiring as I was about taking this job.

After he left, I took a better look at the bottle of champagne. Dom Perignon. Betsy would have been impressed, if she'd been here. But she was back in Boston. She wasn't at all happy I'd accepted this job.

"Why can't you be promoted here?" she asked.

I tried to explain how important the promotion was. "If I don't take this job, there's no way that I'll get promoted again. I'll be stepping off the track. This is the opportunity to prove I can lead a division and, maybe down the line, the whole company."

"It doesn't sound like a big deal to me."

"Being named President isn't a big deal?"

"It's progress. You've come up in the world since we first met." Her words evoked the familiar anger I had experienced throughout our relationship whenever she used our differing social statuses as a tool to assert dominance and manipulate me into doing her bidding. I'd not been as bothered by it early on because, the reality was, I didn't have family money or status to bring to the relationship.

I learned early on how important both those were to Betsy. I have never forgotten how annoyed she was with me after the first big dinner party with her parents and their friends following our engagement.

"You've got to stop saying your father is a bus driver." She'd scolded me in the car on the way home.

"But it's the truth." I'd been asked what my father did for a living and I didn't see any problem.

"Say something true but less… embarrassing. How about saying your father is a civil servant in the Baltimore area?"

So that became our story.

I remember the disappointment on my dad's face when he overheard Betsy say it to one of our wedding guests. His face deflated and his shoulders slumped from the happy-proud stance he'd held all day. I felt like a terrible son.

Looking back, I wished I'd not given in to Betsy and stood up for my dad. I wasn't ashamed of him; I looked up to him. He was loyal, hardworking and a gentleman. But Betsy made me feel like that wasn't good enough. She needed to remake him and me to be more acceptable in order to fit into her world.

Dad had long ago forgotten or pretended to forget about that incident. I'd apologized on behalf of Betsy and had told him she was prone to exaggeration when it came to talking about me.

I'd called my parents the day I'd accepted to tell them about my promotion.

Dad had congratulated me. "My son, the President," he'd said with pride. "You earned this."

I treasured those words more than all the other congratulations I'd received.

A timid knock on my door snapped me back from my memories. "Come in."

The door opened just enough for a blonde head to poke through. "Mr. Jacobs?"

"Yes. Please come in."

The head was attached to a slender woman, very pretty, wearing a pale blue dress with a matching scarf tied around her neck.

"I'm Jenni from the secretarial pool. Jenni with an i, short for Jennifer." Her voice was high pitched and she giggled as she extended her hand.

"You're here to interview to be my assistant?"

"That would be cool," she said, perching on the edge of my desk and tilting her head to one side.

I tried to not look annoyed. I pointed to the chair on the other side of my desk. "Please take a seat."

She hopped off the desk and sat on the edge of the chair, looking at me with a bright smile. It made me think of the look someone might give if they were hoping to be asked to dance.

"So Jenni, please tell me a about yourself."

"Well…" She paused, looking up and biting her lower lip. "I'm 5' 5", I like dogs. I'm great with kids and I love to cook…" Her list was more like a personal ad than a resume.

I tried to steer her in the right direction. "How about your office skills?"

"I type 82 words a minute and I'm very punctual. I haven't been late once in the whole time I've been here."

"That's good. How long have you been here?"

"Ages. Three months. It's the longest I've been at one job." She smiled proudly, oblivious to the red flags she was throwing up.

I felt I needed to give her at least a little more time. "Do you have any questions for me?"

"Oh yes," she said, with such enthusiasm I thought maybe I'd misjudged her. "How do you take your coffee?"

"Black. Any other questions?"

She twisted her finger in her hair and scrunched up her face and looked up and down and sideways. "I don't think so…"

"All right then. I have a few other ladies to talk to, but HR will let you know if you get the job."

"Right on. I'm stoked about this, Mr. J."

I stood up to signal it was time for her to leave, thinking to myself that Jenni with an 'i' was pretty and bubbly, but her voice jangled my nerves. I would go without a secretary before hiring her. I opened my office door and followed her out into the hallway.

I looked around to see if my next appointment had arrived. There was a woman, about my age, sitting at the desk just outside my office. She wore a lavender sweater set and matching lavender skirt and she had a small string of pearls around her neck.

She stood up. "I'm your next appointment." She handed me a piece of paper with three names on it with meeting times.

"Then please come in…" I looked at the list for her name. "Miss Spring."

"It's Mrs. Spring, but please call me Delores."

She surveyed my office as she entered, taking a long look, frowning, at the gifts on my desk before settling into the chair across from mine. I decided to take a different approach with Delores than I had with Jenni.

"Thank you for your interest in the position as my assistant. It will entail taking dictation, typing as well as note-taking for meetings. Do you have experience with these?"

"I use shorthand to capture both dictation and meeting notes. I type at least 90 words a minute and I've been an executive assistant for 12 years. Before that, I worked my way up from the typing pool through various secretarial positions." She spoke in a moderate voice, that was clear and didn't grate on my ears as Jenni's had.

"That's great. So, if you were to begin this job today, what would you do first?"

"I'd clear all this off your desk and box it up. I'd prepare a list of all the gifts and givers and recommend which will require thank you notes or phone calls and I'd make sure we had note cards on hand so I'd be ready to prepare the notes per your instructions."

I was impressed. "That would be very helpful."

The phone on my desk rang. I reached for it but Delores waved me off. She stood up, reached across my desk, picked up the receiver and pushed the lighted button.

"Mr. Jacobs's office." Her voice was calm and even and after a pause listening to the caller, she looked directly at me while speaking. "Good morning Ms. Cole, please hold and I'll see if he's available." She then pressed a button putting the caller on hold and announced, "It's Maddie Cole from DB Engineering. Would you like to take her call?"

"I don't want to interrupt our interview…"

"That's all right. We can pick it up later. I'll be at my desk."

"Where's your desk?"

"Right outside your door?" She smiled and raised her eyebrows.

"But there's another candidate after you."

"I'll send her in when she arrives if you're finished your call with Ms. Cole."

"You seem confident."

"Isn't that a good thing? You wouldn't want a pushover for your assistant would you?"

I chuckled. "Can you sit in for me as my assistant for today?"

"Absolutely, Mr. Jacobs." She pressed the blinking button on the phone. "Hello, Ms. Cole. Yes, he is available. I'll put you through now." She put the call on hold and handed me the receiver. "Push the blinking one to take the call."

Delores slipped out and closed the door silently as I answered.

"Congratulations, Mr. President." Maddie's voice sparkled with enthusiasm.

"Thank you. You were on my list of people to call once I got settled."

"I saw your appointment announcement in the Globe and Mail this morning."

"We announced it internally last week but it's my official first day today."

"You must be very busy then. I won't keep you. Once you're settled, I'd like to invite you to lunch to celebrate your new position."

"I've not forgotten that you owe me dinner."

Maddie chuckled. "Well then, I'll invite you to dinner. I always pay my debts."

"I also need to introduce you to our director of facilities to address the issues you identified in your investigation."

"I really was just calling to congratulate you. But now that you've brought it up… I'd be delighted to meet with you about providing our services as well." Her cheerful tone made me smile. I knew she had professional motivations behind her call, yet I felt she was being sincere in her congratulations.

"I'll get my assistant Delores to schedule a meeting. Would you be available later this week?"

"Yes, of course. But if you're too busy we can do it at a later date."

"I want to get started right away. Based on your recommendations, we included several contingencies, so it's imperative we get these works underway as soon as possible."

"I look forward to working with you again."

I was looking forward to seeing her again too. I was convinced by our earlier interaction that Maddie was not just a good engineer, she was a brilliant one. I hoped she knew I trusted her, and she could stop trying to prove herself to me. It would be more comfortable working together and I had a feeling she'd be an interesting person to be around if only she'd let her guard down. We were just starting to get to know one another after our week working together a couple months back. I hoped we could become friends.

My thoughts of Maddie were interrupted by the buzz of my phone. I answered it.

"Your next interview is here," said Delores.

I sighed. "Ok. Send her in. And could you please arrange a meeting with Ms. Cole for later this week and invite our Director of Facilities?"

"That would be Kurt Klein. Consider it done, Mr. Jacobs."

CHAPTER 10

I was glad to see that Will had shovelled the driveway. Our house matched my festive mood. The red and green Christmas lights we'd wrapped around the small evergreens in our front yard glittered under the fresh snowfall. With only a week to go, there was a good chance we'd have a white Christmas.

I slung the straps of my briefcase and purse over my shoulder and grabbed the bottle of champagne with the big red ribbon by the neck and hurried into the house. I couldn't wait to share my news.

"I'm home," I called out as I pried off my boots in the front hall. "Will? Anne?"

I got no answer. Still with my coat on and carrying everything, I went down the hall to the kitchen at the back of the house. I put the champagne bottle on the lowest shelf in the fridge to chill.

There was a note from Will on the kitchen table.

Gone skating.

I'd have cold and hungry skaters home soon. I put a pot of milk on the stove to make hot chocolate for Anne.

Will had been helping Anne improve her skating since she'd started playing ringette in the fall. Will was one of her team's coaches. Anne was the youngest on the team, but she was determined to keep up with the more experienced players. She wasn't going to be satisfied until it was her turn to take home Mr. Stickles, the team's stuffed bear and mascot, for being the game MVP.

Anne loved winter and summer sports and I was happy that she and Will had that in common. I think they enjoyed their father–daughter time travelling to tournaments. She got her love of playing sports from him, but her competitive streak came from me.

Other than curling on Wednesday nights with the business girls' league and the occasional bonspiel, managing my career and home responsibilities didn't leave much time for other activities. I got my fair share of physical activity working. Overseeing site investigations and lugging samples and survey equipment around helped keep me in shape.

During the past two months, I'd done little else but work on the Bond

Canada project. I'd been at meetings at their Oakville offices or on-site at the three manufacturing facilities we were investigating. It had been challenging to get the assessments done before the end of the year as Nate had required, but we'd delivered. I'd kept three teams working continuously through the project and I'd proven to Dave and the other partners that I was capable of bringing in major work. Dave told me in private that this latest project made it impossible for the other partners to veto my promotion.

A commotion in the front hall alerted me that Will and Anne were back. I looked towards the front door in time to see Anne bouncing down the hall towards me followed by Will.

"Hot chocolate for our super skater." Will ruffled Anne's hair that was plastered to her head from being stuffed into her wool hat.

Anne brushed away Will's hand, puffed up her chest and stuck her nose in the air triumphantly. "I skated backwards the whole way around. Without one stumble."

"That's great, Monkey! I have the milk warming for a backward skating celebration and something chilling for us grown-ups. I've got some news too."

Will looked around the kitchen and over my shoulder at the stove. "What's for dinner?"

"I just got home. I haven't started anything but the hot chocolate. I thought we'd order pizza to celebrate."

"Celebrate Anne's skating?"

"That too but you're looking at DB Engineering's newest partner." I couldn't help but do a little shuffle step. I was still floating high from the meeting with Dave and the partners earlier in the day.

"Hmm," said Will, pressing his lips together. "So you worked a zillion hours and now they want you to put money in?"

"It's not like that. It's… recognition."

"Don't you see? They are just getting their hooks in deeper, so you'll never leave."

"Why would I want to leave?"

"Because you don't have to work now. I'm making more now and working less. You just work more and more and more."

I was too happy to let the same old argument bring me down. "How about we order our celebration pizza?"

Anne raised her arms in the air and shouted, "All right!" and then rummaged for the pizza menus in the cupboard by the kitchen phone. "Can we get Marios? Extra extra cheese and bacon?"

I grumbled. "Can we at least get one vegetable to make it a complete meal?"

"Doesn't tomato count?"

"Tomatoes are fruit."

Anne scrunched up her face. "So we can put fruit on pizza. Can we get pineapple?"

"Pineapple doesn't belong on pizza. It's the wrong fruit," said Will.

"How about mushrooms?" I suggested.

"Mushrooms are ok," said Anne handing me the pizza menu for Mario's, looking crestfallen at her failed attempt to get pineapple. "But no peppers. They're yucky."

I started dialing the number on the menu. While I waited for them to answer, I looked over at Will. "I'll order. You go pick it up. Ok?"

"I'll need my assistant to hold the box level. Get your coat Annie-Bananie."

Anne zoomed down the hall and practically leapt into her boots.

While they were gone, I set the table and pulled out two champagne glasses from the china cabinet in the dining room. I had to wash them. They hadn't been used in ages.

My efforts were in vain. When Will got back with the pizza he said he'd rather have a beer with his pizza and it seemed a waste to open the bottle just for me. I supposed we could save it for Christmas, or New Year. It would keep. I got out mugs and sent Anne to the basement to get a root beer, so we'd all have beers to drink with our pizza.

"Do you think Santa got my letter yet?" asked Anne through a mouthful of pizza.

"I should think so. But I hope talking with your mouth full doesn't get you on the naughty list." I was determined to get as much good behaviour out of her belief in Santa.

Anne swallowed and took a gulp of root beer. "It's really important. I need new skates. All the girls have CCM Super Tacks."

Will shook his head. "I really hope you get them. We have a lot of big tournaments coming up in January and February. Maybe I should write Santa and ask him for your skates. Just in case you're too naughty."

Anne snorted. "You're too old to get presents from Santa."

"I am not. I'll write him today, ask for your skates and … a new station wagon for me."

Will knew full well we'd already bought the skates for Anne, but now he was angling to get a new car by using my desire to solidify Anne's belief in Santa. I shook my head at him and sighed as I started to clear the table.

"Santa brings toys," said Anne. "He can't put a real car in his sleigh."

Will wasn't going to give in. "If he's so magical he can bring toys to all the good girls and boys in one night, he should be able to get a car to me."

Anne scrunched up her nose, tilted her head and looked at me for an answer.

I shrugged. "I don't know. I guess we'll just have to wait and see on Christmas morning. In the meantime, we should do your reading before it's bedtime. Go get your book.

Anne's reading had vastly improved since we started our nightly half hour of reading. The Bobbsey Twins at London Tower was our latest book. Anne liked that the younger twins were her age, and they were constantly running off.

"Can we go to London on a ship too?" asked Anne.

"We can someday, but we'd take a plane. It's much faster."

"Why did they take a ship?"

"That would have been how they went in the time when this book was written." I turned the copyright page of the book and showed her where the date was. "See 1959. Flying across the ocean was not that common and would have been much too expensive for a family of six."

"Have you been to London?"

"No."

"Then how do you know a plane can make it."

"I've been in a plane that crossed an ocean."

"Really? When?"

"Before you were born. I went to Japan."

"How come?"

"For work. We had a project in Tokyo."

"Did Daddy go?"

"No. It was before we were married. Come now. Let's finish this chapter."

She cocked her head to the side as if she was working out a problem in her head. "No Daddy… so you didn't have to be home to make dinner."

I didn't like Anne believing that the wife had to be home to make dinner. It annoyed me that I had to counter the attitudes of my mother and Will and his family. I sympathized with my father's exasperation when he tried to counter my mother urging me to quit working.

"There's nothing wrong with daddy making dinner when mommy is working."

"But Mrs. Bobbsey makes dinner."

"That was normal back then. Just like we travel across the ocean with airplanes and not ships. Things change. If you want to work, you can. You can be anything you want to be."

Anne looked skeptical but didn't ask any more questions and we went back to reading about the twins helping the police catch a slippery thief called Smitty.

CHAPTER 11

My last weekly one-on-one meeting ended, and I stood up, stretched, and then walked out of my office to check with Delores for messages.

"Ms. Cole called. She asked if you wanted to reschedule dinner on account of the snow?"

I'd planned a special dinner for her and I didn't want a little weather to get in the way of it. "I'll call her. Any other messages?"

"No, but this package came for you." She handed me a large envelope.

"Yes. The mortgage paperwork. Thank you."

I took the package and went back to my desk to call Maddie. I let her know dinner was still on if she was up for it and she agreed. I was delighted she didn't cancel, as I'd been looking forward to tonight all week.

The first five months of my new job had been the most challenging and rewarding of my career. Maddie had been a constant support throughout. Working with her gave us a chance to get to know each other, and we'd become good friends.

The day of our first project meeting, when I'd introduced her to my Director of Facilities, I'd asked her if she could stay after the meeting had ended. I didn't want her to leave without having a chance to talk with her privately.

"I want you to know that I took your advice," I said once we were alone.

Maddie crunched her eyebrows together. "I know. The project scope is essentially what I recommended last summer."

"No. I meant your advice about putting off moving my daughter until she finishes her senior year."

"I'm sure you could have come up with that on your own."

"I might have. But I was under a lot of pressure not to take the job."

"But you did."

"I don't think my wife would have agreed if I hadn't proposed this arrangement."

"I'm glad it worked out." Maddie looked at her watch.

I glanced up at the clock across from my desk. "It's almost noon."

"My cue to leave. Don't want to keep you."

"You're not. I was hoping you'd have lunch with me."

Maddie let out an exaggerated sigh. "I suppose that's part of the consultant's responsibility, buying lunch for their clients. Especially at the start of a new project."

"No. No. My invitation. My tab. But I can't guarantee I won't ask for free advice."

"I do have to be back at the office this afternoon. But I have time for lunch." She looked me in the eye and smiled and I instantly had that swirling feeling in the pit of my stomach when something feels familiar; like you've lived that moment before. I couldn't help but smile back.

I was thrilled she agreed to have lunch. "That's great. I'll just check in with Delores, and then we can head out."

I escorted Maddie down and out of the building. "I'll drive. If it's ok with you?" I pointed to my car in the first spot outside the main office door and I hurried over to open her door for her.

"My car is… older… so I think you'll prefer yours." Maddie looked over the car as she slid into the passenger seat and took in a long breath. "Very nice. New?"

"Just delivered yesterday."

"It has that new car smell."

"It's my company car. I turned in my previous company car in Boston and I've had a rental for the past few weeks here. I have my wife's car to drive when I'm there."

"How often do you get back?"

"Every couple of weeks or so."

"And you've found a house here?"

"Temporary accommodations."

"You're not still living in a hotel." Her voice was disapproving.

"I've got a small apartment here in Oakville."

"At least you don't have a long drive to the office."

"I need to start looking for a house."

"I presume your wife…Betsy right?" Maddie paused and I nodded. "She's coming to look too?"

"Let's just say she's delegated the search to me."

"I find that hard to believe. I'd want a say."

"I'm happy for you to have a say."

"Funny."

"Seriously. Maybe you could look at some of the listings."

"Is that the free advice you were talking about?"

"I hadn't thought of it until just now. But who better to consult than someone born and raised here?"

"How do you know I'm not some transplant who moved to the city for work?"

"Because you told me so, the first night we met. You said you'd lived in the area your whole life."

"I did?"

"Yes. And you told me blackouts like that were very unusual."

"You remember that?"

"You might have made an impression on me."

"A good one?"

"Very good. And it's turning out to be very accurate."

Maddie blushed but didn't look away. She looked me in the eyes, her lips slightly curled up into a mischievous grin. "Are you perhaps flirting with me now?"

"Not intentionally."

"Good, because that could get messy…"

"And I'm hiring you to take care of messes. Would be counterproductive to make more."

"I'm happy to give you my non-professional opinion on your house options. But my free advice is worth what you pay for it."

Our banter was playful as we ate our plates of schnitzel, spaetzle and boiled carrots that were the lunch special at the family-run german restaurant that Delores had suggested. We chatted about what we'd both been doing since last summer when we'd last seen each other.

Maddie's daughter had started second grade and had just started playing a sport I'd never heard of; a sort of hockey for girls played with a ring instead of a puck. I learned that Maddie liked winter sports. She skied, skated and curled, another sport I'd no clue about.

"At least I like hockey," I'd said in my defense when she'd teased me about my deficient understanding of winter activities.

"You're gonna need to do better than that if you're gonna blend in here."

"I thought Canada was a mosaic? So not blending in should be Canadian."

"Where'd you hear that?"

"In the 'Things to Know Moving to Canada' pamphlet our HR guy gave me."

"If you're counting on pamphlets for your information… I've definitely got my work cut out for me educating you on all things Canadian."

"That sounds like an offer…"

"Might be fun."

"House hunting and Canadiana training… we might be spending a lot of time together." The idea made me feel a flutter of excitement.

"That might not be a bad thing." Maddie's voice was low and sultry.

"Are you flirting with me now?"

She launched into a lengthy rant. "Absolutely not. I don't want you to misconstrue my comfort spending time with you as anything more than friendship. Since my university days, I've had more friends that are men than women, because, frankly, there just weren't a lot of women to be friends with in my line of work."

I assured her I understood where she was coming from. But there was a pang of disappointment in the pit of my stomach. It wasn't just that I found her very attractive, our conversation was engaging, and I wanted more time with this smart, funny lady. If we'd met under different circumstances, at a different time, I would have definitely wanted more than friendship.

In the weeks that followed, Maddie was instrumental in helping me find a house. The package of mortgage documents in front of me waiting to be signed was the last step in finalizing the purchase.

It was up to me to find a suitable house for us, as Betsy had made abundantly clear. I'd shown her listings every other week on my trips home to Boston. She'd eliminated most of them with reasons that were often contradictory: too big, too small, too old-fashioned, too new.

"At least you can see what we need to do to get this house ready to sell," I'd said when Betsy pointed out the flaws of the houses I proposed.

"I don't want to sell this house."

"We have to move."

"But it's temporary. We're going to come back."

"But it won't be for some time."

I'd planned to sell our house in Boston and use the proceeds to fund our new home, but Betsy was obstinate. She wasn't going to sell the home that Ann had lived in for most of her life. I lay awake many nights trying to figure out how I was going to make it work. I worried about the burden of a bigger mortgage and we'd have to rent the Boston house.

In the past five months, Betsy had come for just one visit, just after New Year. She'd been unimpressed with the neighborhoods we toured and bemoaned having to move the whole time.

It was Maddie who helped me narrow my search to a couple of areas and had given me her thoughts on the listings my agent had sent me. Once I'd decided on houses to visit, Maddie accompanied me to see six of them. The first five were not what I was looking for, and I was getting discouraged and frustrated. Maddie had agreed with me about the deficiencies of the houses, but had remained positive and enthusiastic that we would find the perfect house if we just kept looking.

When we toured the last house, the one at the base of Chartwell Road in

Oakville, we both knew we'd found the right one.

"You two are just so copasetic," said the real estate lady. "I bet you'll have some really great parties once you get settled."

When we'd gotten back to my car after leaving the house, Maddie turned to me and said in a voice mimicking the real estate lady, "We're copasetic."

 "Did you see the look of panic when you said 'I'm sure your wife will like it'. She almost threw up."

We'd laughed so hard I could barely breathe.

When Maddie caught her breath she said, "She was terrified she'd lost the sale. I'm sure she'll recover when you make an offer."

Maddie had turned a chore I'd been dreading into one of the most fun days I'd had in a long time. That day had led to signing the papers I pulled out of the package Delores had handed me. In sixty days, I'd have the keys to our new home.

I checked that I'd signed and initialed where required, and I reorganized the papers and put them back in the envelope. Then I phoned the relocation coordinator Bond had provided to let him know I'd be sending the closing documents by the end of the day.

"Do you have a target moving date?" he'd asked.

"It will be some time after the first week of June."

"We can move ahead with having the moving company estimate your packing and transport needs."

"I'll be back in Boston in a couple of weeks. Can we do it on a Saturday?"

"You don't need to be there. We just need someone home who can indicate to the estimator what stays and what goes. I'm sure your wife can do that without you."

Given her lack of enthusiasm to move, I wasn't sure Betsy would be helpful, but I didn't share that.

"I'll call you next week after I've had a chance to talk to my wife about scheduling." I was anxious to get off the call and on the road to Toronto. I didn't want to be late picking Maddie up for dinner.

It was snowing even harder when I pulled out onto the QEW highway towards Toronto. I tuned the car radio to the all-news station to get an update on the roads. By the time I pulled onto Maddie's street, the roads were completely covered. If it wasn't for her station wagon in the driveway it would have been difficult to know where to turn in.

Maddie opened the front door and came outside as I came up the walk. "I'm sorry. I didn't get time to shovel the walk. You're getting your pants wet."

"Are you ready to go?"

Maddie turned, locked the door, and then came down the steps towards me.

"All set. Where are we off to?"

"It's a surprise."

"How mysterious."

I drove us across town to The Prince Hotel and then led Maddie through the hotel lobby to the adjacent restaurant.

"We're going for Japanese food?"

"I've been told this is very authentic."

"Wow. It's been years since I have had Japanese food."

"I wanted to pick something a little different. When I read about this place, I had a feeling you might enjoy it."

Maddie slipped her arm through mine and pulled me in closer beside her. "It's a great surprise."

When I made the reservation, I'd discussed the options with the hostess and had chosen for us to sit at a private table rather than at the communal dining around the stovetops and sushi bar. We opted for the chef's menu that included several courses that spanned their whole offering with sushi, grilled meats, noodles, and soup.

"This food reminds me of the restaurant at my hotel in Tokyo," said Maddie sitting back and taking a sip of her sake.

"I saw in your experience profile that you did a project in Japan. It stood out because I went there for work too."

"Of all the countries in the world we could have worked – we both had work in Japan. Incredible."

"Were you there more than once?"

"Just once for several weeks, about 10 years ago. How about you?"

"I've been several times. My first trips were for a month at a time. But more recently, I've gone for shorter trips."

"If any of them were in the spring of 1966... we were there at the same time."

"I was. I'm sure I would have noticed you."

"Because I'm a woman?"

"Well... yes. A lovely Canadian woman would have stood out. Maybe that's why you seem so familiar."

"You've never said I seemed familiar."

"It might have been creepy to tell you."

"It would explain some things."

"Like what?"

"Like why we get along so well. We have shared experiences that we didn't realize we shared."

I picked up the sake carafe and drained the last few drops into Maddie's glass. "Looks like we've shared all the sake. Shall I order more?"

"We're on the last course. Do we need it?"

I nodded to the waiter to get his attention. "Another sake please."

"Small or large?" he asked.

"Small should be enough," said Maddie.

"Very well," said the waiter, "a small sake. Are you by chance hotel guests?"

"No. Just here for dinner," I replied.

"The roads are quite terrible. If you have far to drive, you might consider getting a room for the night. I can bring a phone for you to speak with reception."

Maddie looked at me. "I can get a taxi home if you decide to stay."

"It may take a while to get one, Madam. But I can get the bell captain to request one for you."

I looked at Maddie and shook my head. "I don't want you heading off into a snowstorm alone."

"I'll get your sake," said the waiter. "Just let me know if I should bring you the house phone."

CHAPTER 12

I tried to convince Nate to take the waiter's advice. "I think you should get a room. I'll get a taxi."

Nate shook his head. "I won't sleep knowing I've sent you out into a snowstorm alone."

"I'll be fine. You shouldn't drive back to Oakville." I didn't want our evening to end with us going our separate ways, but it was the safest option.

"I've driven in snow."

"This is Canadian snow. If they're saying the roads are bad, they are."

Despite my protests, he insisted on driving me home.

I regretted giving in from the get-go. Nate had to make two attempts to get his car out of the parking lot and once on the street, we found ourselves plowing through snow almost a foot deep. The car fishtailed several times as Nate tried to accelerate through the larger drifts. By the time we made it down the ramp onto the Don Valley Parkway, I was deeply concerned about him attempting to drive me home, let alone to Oakville.

The highway was clearer than the city streets, but it was snow-covered and slick. We passed stranded cars perched on the piles of snow on the shoulder and others with their nose or tail jammed against the guardrail. I leaned forward in the car and peered through the crescent-shaped opening left by the windshield wipers. I saw the sign for Eglington and realized how little progress we'd made. The radio DJ repeatedly implored listeners to get off the roads and from the few cars we encountered that were moving, it appeared most Torontonians had heeded the warning.

It would normally have been less than a half-hour drive, but it was almost an hour and a half by the time we crawled off the highway and onto Parkside Drive. At this rate, it would take Nate hours to drive to his apartment, if he made it at all. I knew the right thing was to convince him to wait until morning.

"I can make up the couch for you," I suggested.

"I don't want to impose…"

"No imposition. I insist. I won't sleep knowing I've sent you out into a snowstorm alone."

Nate chuckled. "That's my line."

"It worked on me, so I figure it'll work on you."

"Will your husband be ok with it?"

"I've made up the couch countless times for his friends. And he's away at a ringette tournament with Anne, so he won't be inconvenienced in the least."

"I'm inclined to accept. I'm not sure I'll even get out of your street."

His words sent a little shock wave of excitement through me, and I realized I was more than just relieved he wouldn't be driving home in a snowstorm. I was happy he was going to spend the rest of the evening with me.

The snow was deep. I knew it wasn't going to be easy to get Nate's car off the street and into my driveway. As we approached, I could see my car was just a lump under the white blanket that draped over my yard and driveway.

I pointed to my house. "I'm the next driveway. You're going to have to take a run at it."

Nate attempted to speed up as he turned the car but only managed to get the first third of the car into the driveway. I didn't want to suggest what he should do next. It was his car and he'd made such a gallant effort to get me home safe. He made a couple of attempts to go forwards and backwards to get the car to move either in or out, but it wasn't budging.

Nate sat back in his seat, his head fell back onto the headrest, and he let out a big sigh. "Ok Canadian. Now what?"

"I'll get out and push and you try to get it rocking."

"You're not getting out to push."

"Then I'll drive, and you push."

Nate pulled his coat around him and got out. I slid across the front seat into the driver's seat. I closed the door but rolled down the window so I could call back to him.

"When I go, you push."

"Ok."

"Ready?"

"Go."

I could barely see Nate in the rear-view mirror, but he thumped on the trunk, so I took that as a sign he was ready. I put the car in gear and gave a short but hard stomp on the accelerator and then let off. I could feel the car shifting. I did it several more times until finally, the wheels caught, and the car lurched ahead just enough to get it completely off the road before coming to a sudden halt in a whoosh of snow.

I looked for Nate in the rear-view mirror, but I couldn't see him, so I called out, "Are you all right?"

I didn't hear an answer, so I jumped out of the car. I found Nate getting up from all fours at the base of the driveway. He was caked in snow. He tried to brush it off, but he only managed to paste the wet snow even more completely to his trousers and coat. He looked like a snowman.

I started to laugh. "Sorry about that."

Nate grumbled. "I should have let you push."

"Come on Frosty. Let's get you inside and thawed."

I opened the front door, kicked off my boots onto the tray in the hall. I expected Nate to follow me in but he was still on the front porch stomping, shaking and brushing at his clothes trying, unsuccessfully, to dislodge the snow clinging to his pants and coat.

I opened the screen door. "Give it up. Just come in."

Nate let out what I think was a grunt, but came in. I tried to shut the door, but he'd planted himself dead center on the mat just inside the door.

"Move," I said. "As my father always said, we're heating outside."

"I'll get your floor wet."

"Won't be the first time or the last."

Nate took off his galoshes and dress shoes. I watched him hold them in his hand while looking down at the tray with my boots on it. He shifted his weight from side to side and tilted his head, generally looking uncomfortable.

"You can just put your shoes there. Make yourself at home."

He reached down, stood up my boots and moved them to one side, and then added his footwear to the tray.

I smiled at how precisely he arranged them. "Nice job organizing the shoes. Now, give me your coat."

Nate handed me his coat. I slung it over the banister and started upstairs. "I'll hang it and your pants where I put Anne's snowsuits to dry. I'll get you something of Will's to wear."

I looked back from halfway up the stairs.

Nate was just standing there looking up at me. "I'll just wait here?"

"You can't change in the front hall. Come with me."

Nate followed and waited at the top of the stairs while I went into our bedroom and got a pair of Will's sweatpants and a sweatshirt.

I took them to him and pointed to the bathroom. "You can change in there and then put your wet things with your coat. I'm just going to change into something comfy too and then I'll hang everything up to dry."

Nate went into the bathroom, and I went back to my room. I figured since Nate was going to be wearing sweatpants, I could put on my flannel PJs and we'd be similarly dressed. He'd not feel like he's underdressed, and I'd be cozy.

Nate was standing in the living room looking out the window when I came downstairs. I could see his face reflected in the glass and he was frowning.

"It's still really coming down out there," he said.

I scooped up his coat and pants from the banister. "Good thing we're in here and not stuck out there. Make yourself at home. I'll be right back after I hang these up."

I took Nate's wet things down to the laundry area in the basement. It was right beside the furnace. Will had installed a series of hooks into the floor beams overhead to dry his hockey gear, but the hanging points had expanded to accommodate Anne's ringette gear and also a line for me to hang clothes. I hung Nate's coat on one of the empty hooks. I noticed his trousers were of fine wool. I couldn't just hang them from a hook, so I got a pants hanger and carefully hung them upside down to best preserve the crease.

Despite my invitation, Nate looked uncomfortable and not at all at home. He was still standing with his arms crossed, scowling out the window.

"What can I get you?" I asked.

"I don't want to put you out any more than I already have."

"What's the fun of getting snowed in without someone to share it with?"

"It's not the evening I had in mind. I was hoping to treat you, to thank you for all you've done helping me find a house, not having me invade yours."

"Then I have just the thing."

I went to the kitchen and fished out the bottle of champagne that had been sitting in the bottom of the fridge for the last couple months. Will and I had never gotten around to opening it. It still had the ribbon on it. On my way back to the living room I grabbed two champagne glasses from the china cabinet in the dining room.

Nate turned away from the window as I set everything on the coffee table. "Champagne?"

"The partners gave it to me to celebrate my promotion."

"Are you sure you want to open it tonight?"

"We can toast your new house. Unless you don't like it."

Nate picked up the bottle and examined the label. "Shouldn't you serve this at a more … elegant occasion?" Nate tugged at his sweatpants and raised his eyebrows.

I smiled. "Champagne goes with everything. Even flannel and fleece."

Nate's face broke into a big smile. He plucked a tissue from the box on the side table and placed it over his forearm and then draped the bottle over it like our sommelier had presented our bottle of sake earlier.

"Would Madame allow me to open the wine for us?"

"But of course, Monsieur."

The phone rang, and I pointed to the kitchen. "I'll just get that."

I hurried back to the kitchen and answered the phone. It was Will.

"I hear things are pretty bad there," he said.

"It was a brutal drive back from the restaurant. I invited Nate to stay the night because the roads are really bad."

"His wife OK with that?"

"I would think she'd be happy he wasn't going to get stuck in a snowbank and freeze to death."

"He hasn't called her?"

"She's in Boston, but I should offer to let him call home. How's the weather there?"

"It's not snowing here. Once we got past Oshawa it was clear."

"I'm glad you didn't have a difficult drive. Is Anne asleep?"

"She conked out after dinner. She was really revved up on the drive and at practice, but she hit a wall and has been out for an hour or so."

"Tell her good luck from me tomorrow."

"Hopefully, we won't get knocked out. But if we do, we'll be home tomorrow night."

"I hope the snow lets up. I'm not sure I'll have the driveway dug out before tomorrow night. It's already about three feet deep."

"I'll call you tomorrow to let you know."

"Ok. Good night."

"Bye."

CHAPTER 13

I'd taken the foil and basket off the top of the champagne bottle, but waited to pull the cork until Maddie came back from her phone call.

She waved a bag of potato chips. "It's not caviar…"

I twisted the cork, and it gave way in my hand with a solid pop. "But they're salty. I think they'll be perfect."

"Music? Should I put on the radio?"

"Sure."

Maddie opened the top of a long wood cabinet and flipped a couple switches. She bent over and leaned on her elbows. I could hear the warble from the speakers as she tuned the radio. I held the bottle suspended, not pouring the champagne into the glasses because I found myself admiring the way her back arched and the way her hair was swept to one side exposing her neck.

She looked back over her shoulder at me. "We need something upbeat. Don't you think?"

The radio warble morphed into a pop song.

I looked away, pretending to not have been staring at her and poured the wine. "Whatever you like."

Maddie grabbed one of the throw pillows and placed it behind her back and settled with one leg tucked under her at one end of the sofa. She looked so different from the tightly wound and serious professional I'd spent so much time with. It wasn't just the loose plaid flannel bottoms and white t-shirt that made her look relaxed.

Maddie picked up her glass from the coffee table and held it up. "To finding you a new home!"

I picked up mine and touched the rim of my glass to hers. "To the most brilliant and delightful house-hunting-consultant-friend a guy could ask for."

Maddie grinned. "Here here to that!" She took a big sip of champagne. "So when is the big move?"

"We haven't set the exact date with the movers, but it won't be until June. Although I'm going to move in after we close, but just with the furniture from my apartment."

"That'll give your wife time to make any changes."

"I'm going to get it painted throughout before we move in."

"I would leave the color choices to her. Men are so often colorblind…"

"I'm not colorblind, but if she wants to choose, that'll be great."

"I can't imagine she'd not want to."

"She's still not particularly enthusiastic. Did I tell you she's insisted on keeping the Boston house?"

Maddie took a sip of champagne and her face suddenly shifted to analytical. She pressed her lips together and looked up and away from me. I'd seen that look in meetings. It's what she did when she was considering the answer to a question. "Well, that might pay off. Given that real estate is a good long-term investment and if you can rent the property…"

I didn't want her to worry about it, so I cut off her verbal deliberation. "That's the plan. I met with a property manager that is a member of our club. He's assured me there's a market for what he called executive homes."

"They would be the experts," she said with a big smile. "I'm glad things are coming together for your move. It's a big change."

I noticed as we talked that her face was more animated and expressive than I'd ever seen it. And she was so pretty. It's not that I hadn't noticed that she was attractive, but tonight I found myself fascinated by her face. I watched how her lips moved and the way her eyes flashed when she teased me. Like when she had taunted me earlier about my precise placement of my shoes on her doormat.

Maddie leaped up off the sofa. "This song makes me want to dance."

She started to sway her hips. She drained the last of the champagne from the glass in her hand, set it down and then reached her arms out towards me.

"Come dance." She grasped my hands and pulled me to my feet.

There was no resisting. I almost tripped over the coffee table but caught myself in time.

"You want to dance to this?"

"Oh yeah. I am the Dancing Queen." She sang along to the lyrics of the song while swaying her hips.

She grinned at me, threw her arms above her head, and did a twirl. "Come on, go with it." She took my hands and spun us around.

I sighed and tugged her in close, putting one hand on her hip and holding out my other arm, trying to take the lead.

Maddie tilted her head and, with a devilish gleam in her eye, flung both her arms around my neck. "Let's do it like the kids do," she purred and pressed her body into mine, our hips pressed together in rhythm.

"Big finish," she said sliding her hands down my arms and twisting around so we ended up with her back to me and her arms crossed in front of her. She leaned back and laughed and let her head fall back onto my shoulder.

It felt good to hold her. Her bare neck was exposed just below my chin. It was so inviting I couldn't help but kiss it.

I stopped myself, expecting Maddie would pull away. She didn't. She let out a happy little moan and swayed to the rhythm of the slower song that had begun to play.

She had such a lovely neck. I reached up with one hand and traced my fingers from her ear, down her neck to the collar of her t-shirt that had slipped aside and exposed her collarbone and part of her shoulder. I was just about to lean in to kiss her shoulder when she twirled out of my arms to face me.

Her brows furrowed, and her eyes squinted. "You shouldn't be doing that."

I felt my chest tighten. "I'm sorry. I…"

In an instant, her face transformed from annoyed to a mischievous grin. "I said you shouldn't. I didn't say you couldn't." She slipped her arms around my neck and leaned in, pressing her entire body against mine.

Her head tilted back, and her eyes were locked on mine. I searched then for any hint of what she was thinking. I could barely breathe looking into them. She was gorgeous. I wanted to trace every detail of her beautiful face. I slid my hands up her arms, over her shoulders, and up her neck to cradle her face between them.

I hesitated. I wanted to study every detail of her face with my fingertips. I worried she'd pull away if I did. My heart was pounding so hard I thought she might feel it. I floated my fingers along her jawline and behind her ear. I noticed how small and pretty her ears were. Then I traced the contour of her cheekbone.

She closed her eyes and let out a little sigh. I took that as a cue I could continue. I traced her eyebrows and then carefully brushed the ends of her eyelashes with my fingertip. I ran my forefinger down her nose and onto her lips. My fingers trembled with excitement as I traced her upper lip.

Maddie's lips puckered, nibbled at my finger, and then curled into a grin. Her eyes sprung open and looked directly into mine. "Do you have any idea the effect you're having on me?"

"It's just an innocent caress," I said, brushing a wisp of her hair off her forehead and then trailing my fingers across her cheek and back to her lips.

"I like your kind of innocence. What other innocent things are you thinking of doing?" Her voice was lower. Sultry.

"I suppose I could innocently kiss you?"

"I think innocently kissing would be ok." She brought her face very close to mine with her lips slightly parted.

I leaned in and kissed her. At the first touch of her lips, I felt a sizzle like an electric shock run through me. Our kiss deepened and Maddie's tongue flicked across the edge of my lip.

"Maybe not such an innocent kiss," I whispered.

"I'm not having an innocent reaction."

"What sort of reaction?"

Maddie turned so her back was against my chest. "Give me your hand."

I was puzzled but complied. She placed her right hand on mine and guided it to the waistband of her pyjama bottoms.

She looked up over her shoulder and asked, "Are you sure you want to know?"

All I could do was nod.

Maddie slid my hand under the fabric. I could feel her skin and then soft fuzz as she moved my hand lower to between her legs. I involuntarily gasped as she pressed lightly on my fingers, and I felt warm, soft wetness surround them.

She pulled both our hands out and spun back to face me. "See. Told you it wasn't innocent," she cooed softly.

"You're an evil woman," I said pulling her back into my arms.

"Nooo." Maddie made the cutest pout.

"Beautiful, smart, funny, and evil. And you were right. We shouldn't be doing this."

"I usually like to be right…"

"I'd like to prove you wrong…"

"I dare you to try." Maddie leaned into me and brushed her lips over mine, sending a shiver through me. I just had to kiss her again. With both hands, I held her head as I touched my lips to hers, but to my delight, it was Maddie who kissed me hard and hungrily, knocking me off balance. I stepped backwards to steady myself and bumped into the wall behind me.

Maddie giggled, seemingly proud of herself for causing me to stumble and she was determined to keep me off balance. She leaned into me even more, kissing and pushing me back against the wall. She ran her hand up the inside of my thigh.

I grabbed her hand. "Oh no you don't." In one quick motion, I grabbed both her hands and spun us around so her back was to the wall. I kissed her nose and cheeks and lips then moved down her neck to her collarbone. She wiggled her wrists from my grasp. I stopped kissing her and took a step back.

"Don't worry," she said in a sweet soft voice. "I'm just going to get this out of your way." She grabbed the hem of her t-shirt, pulled it off over her head and tossed it onto the sofa.

I tried to look into her eyes, but I couldn't help but stare. Her breasts were lovely. I cupped one in each of my hands and stroked the soft outer curves with the tips of my fingers. Her eyes closed, she let out a little moan and she leaned back against the wall. I continued to stroke her breasts while I started to explore her with my lips. I kissed her neck and shoulder, then down between her breasts, then across her left breast.

She wiggled and giggled when I touched her nipple. "They're very sensitive. You need to be gentle with them."

But I was emboldened by the way she'd exposed herself to me. "I'll try. But they are just so delicious I want to devour them." I nuzzled her breast and made a humming hungry sound.

She tugged at the bottom of my shirt. "You're overdressed."

I pulled off my shirt. Maddie untied the string of my sweatpants and I in turn pulled at her pyjama bottoms.

Now both naked, I pulled her into my arms and kissed her on the mouth. Maddie's hands slid up my back and into my hair. I moved from her lips to her throat and then continued to kiss down the length of her body until I was kneeling before her. I kissed her thighs and between her legs. Maddie shifted her weight and I was shocked, in a good way, when she lifted her leg and placed her thigh on my shoulder, opening herself up. I kissed and explored her with my tongue. Her fingers were still in my hair and I felt her holding on tighter as I nibbled and licked her.

She let out a moan and then pulled my head away from her. She tapped me on the shoulder and pulled at my arm.

"Come here," she said as she moved towards the sofa.

She lay down, taking my hand as she did and pulling me on to her.

As much as I wanted her, I was shocked that this was happening. "Are you sure?"

"It wasn't what I imagined we'd be doing tonight. But yes."

That was all the encouragement I needed. I slipped into her, and we locked together. Maddie moved with me. It felt so incredibly good. I'd never been with a woman who was so active and alive while making love. It was amazing and I was left breathless and blissfully exhausted.

I rolled aside and Maddie shifted to lie in my arms but didn't say anything.

"Are you ok?"

"Yes. Are you?" She stroked my chest, dragging her nails gently across my skin.

"Better than ok."

"So a good evening?"

"It's not what I was planning. I just wanted to take you to dinner."

"Are you sure?"

I was taken aback. "How could you think that."

"You did pick a restaurant in a hotel. And you did consider getting a room for the night."

"I picked Japanese. I didn't plan on a snowstorm."

Maddie elbowed me. "But you've been making a lot of excuses to see me."

"Because I like you. A lot."

"I like you a lot too." Maddie twisted her head around and gave me a little peck of a kiss on my neck.

"That's a relief."

CHAPTER 14

My pencil lead snapped for the umpteenth time. I clicked to advance it, and grumbled, discovering it was empty. I pushed it, my notebook, and the map I was working on aside. I put my elbows on my desk and rested my face on my hands and took a couple of deep breaths. I was having a hard time concentrating on the cross-section I was drawing. My mind kept drifting back to the weekend.

Friday's snowstorm had stranded Nate at my house. What had started out as an innocent invitation to wait out the storm had turned into a wonderful, wildly exciting, and fun weekend together. It should be easy to let it be a one-time thing. Two friends, enjoying each other's company and nothing more. But it was more. Which was why I was so distracted.

Snippets of memories replayed in my mind. Nate's hands caressing me after we'd had sex on the sofa. Shoveling the driveway to free his car and the snowball fight that left us breathless and giggling and soaking wet. Showering together afterwards, and the thrill of his soapy hands gliding over every inch of my body. The day and a half we spent together were the best time I'd had in years.

From the moment we met, I had a feeling that Nate and I were destined to be friends. I'd tried to ignore it and keep things strictly professional. But the more time we spent together, the more I discovered how smart, funny and loyal he was. That and the way he just seemed to understand me eroded my resolve. And now, discovering that we clicked at a whole other level added to the strong attraction I felt towards him. I wanted more, but that wasn't something I was going to say to Nate.

I replayed our conversation from the morning before when I woke up to Nate, lying on his side facing me, watching me sleep.

He gently brushed the hair off my face. "You're remarkably pretty in the morning."

I closed my eyes again. "It's still pretty dark."

"Your loveliness shines bright."

"You're just saying that because I didn't make you sleep on the sofa again."

"I am grateful."

"It seemed only fair you get a good night's rest after shovelling my whole driveway. Twice."

"My back thanks you."

I opened one eye. "Just your back?"

Nate reached over and pulled me into his arms, wrapping his upper leg around mine until our bodies were tangled together. "A lot of my parts are very thankful we had this time together."

"It's been ok."

"Ok? Not great? Good thing I'm not planning on being snowed in with you next weekend."

"Where are you next weekend?"

"I'll be in Boston."

My heart sank and I pulled away from him. He'd said Boston but I knew that meant at home, with his wife. We both had families and commitments that were not to each other. My jealousy was irrational but boiled in my stomach.

"What's wrong?" he'd asked.

"Nothing's wrong. Just reality setting in."

Nate nudged closer and nuzzled my neck. "You weren't supposed to happen."

"Morning after regrets?"

"Never. I mean… you're perfect and I want you. And I shouldn't."

I choked down my disappointment because I knew he was right. "Then we shouldn't."

"Just the sex part. I don't want to stop seeing you. As a friend."

"Deal." I extended my hand. "Just friends from now on."

Nate pushed my hand aside. "Not so fast. You're still my consultant, aren't you? I've found your council on many matters invaluable." His voice was suddenly serious and professional which struck me as funny as he was naked in my bed.

I stifled my chuckle and mustered a serious tone to respond. "I'm counting on it. You have me on retainer for the next year."

"I'm not sure I can be in the same room as you and not want to kiss you." He leaned in and kissed me on the nose.

"I think you'll manage."

"I'm not so sure."

Nate started to kiss my neck and shoulder and I could feel my resolve melting. "Maybe once more for old time's sake?"

Nate grinned and rolled me onto my back while rolling on top of me.

I let out a groan as his full weight pressed down on me. "You're crushing me."

"I do kinda have a crush on you." He lifted himself up onto his hands and knees and kissed me on the lips before nibbling his way down my neck and collarbone and down between my breasts.

I closed my eyes and enjoyed the sensation of his hands and lips. It didn't feel wrong, it felt great. Nate seemed to know exactly what I wanted. He kissed his way down my body, and I was tingling and wet before he reached my belly.

He looked up at me as he slid his hand down between my legs and dipped his finger into me. "You turn me on." He moved his finger around.

I let out an involuntary moan. "You're doing a pretty good job of that yourself." I twisted, pressed my hip up and bucked him off me and rolled onto him.

He looked up at me with surprise and then grinned. "That's a new move. You've been holding out on me."

"Too bad this is the last time then," I said as I positioned myself so I could slide him inside me.

"Then we better make it a double," said Nate pressing up into me and placing his hands on my hips as I rode up and down on him.

About a half hour and three positions later, we were both satisfied and spent. We fell asleep, waking up when it was much brighter.

I got up, slipped on a robe, and went to the window to see what condition the driveway and roads were in. Nate looked disappointed, but didn't protest when I suggested we get dressed and go out for breakfast.

We picked a small table rather than eating at the counter of the little diner just a few blocks up from my house.

Nate topped up my coffee from the carafe the waitress had left on the table. "Glad to get me out of your house?"

"That's not why I suggested we go out."

"Why then?"

"Because I'm out of coffee. I didn't get to the store yesterday."

"You should have said something. We could have gone out."

"We were a little … occupied."

"But if you needed something…"

"I can get what I need at Kims."

"Kims?"

"Small grocery, variety store on the corner. They have a little of everything. I'll stop by this afternoon before Will and Anne get home."

I'd intentionally mentioned Will and Anne to see what his reaction would be.

Nate sat back and crossed his arms. For a moment he looked angry but then he sat forward again and started to look around, his eyes following the waitress as she delivered food to another table. "I'm pretty hungry."

I wrapped my hands around my coffee mug. "Shouldn't be long. Coffee's hitting the spot for me." I needed the caffeine to get me going. I felt tired, or maybe sad. I'm not sure which.

Our conversation over breakfast, on the whole, had been minimal. Nate had been noticeably quiet, and I hadn't felt like filling in with chatter as I'm apt to do.

I had an uneasy feeling about the way we left things on Sunday, but I couldn't spend all day fussing about it. I had a cross-section to finish and get into the drafting department. I checked my drawer for pencil leads, but I had none. I got up and grabbed my coffee cup to refill on my way back from the supply cabinet.

I'd just settled back at my desk when my phone rang.

I answered it without looking up. "Good morning, Ms. Cole speaking."

"Good morning, Maddie. Is this a bad time?"

My stomach did a flip-flop at the sound of Nate's voice. "Not at all."

"I just wanted to call… to see…," Nate hesitated. "Just to say hello." He sounded uneasy.

"Is everything all right?"

"That's what I was going to ask you."

"I'm fine. You?"

"Honestly, I can't stop thinking about you."

"Is that good or bad."

"Good question. A bit of both I guess."

"Dare I ask what you're thinking?"

"It was great spending time with you."

I wasn't sure where this conversation was going, so I reached behind me and closed the door of my small office so no one could overhear me from the corridor. "I take it you got home ok."

"Should I have called? I wanted to call you but I wasn't sure when …"

"I wasn't expecting you to. I just meant was everything all right at your place on account of the snow."

"Oh. Yes. Everything was fine. They'd cleared the snow around the apartment building before I got there."

"That's good."

I heard Nate take a deep breath before he responded. "I think we should talk."

"We are talking," I said with a cheerful tone, hoping to put him at ease.

"I mean about … what we did."

I chuckled and blurted out, "Several times in fact."

"I'm trying to be serious."

"I know. Let's not."

"But I must. I didn't expect… you're just so… uhh."

"I'm so what?"

"Irresistible."

"You're going to have to learn to resist. We can't be having wild weekends having great sex all over the place."

"That's not exactly dissuasive. It was great. You're amazing and the more I know you, the more I want to know."

"All the more reason for me to keep my distance."

"If that's what you want." He spoke slowly and softly and sounded sad.

"It's not."

"What do you want?"

I wasn't prepared for the question. I wasn't sure what I wanted so I gave the answer I thought he was looking for. "Can't we just let this be a lovely memory and continue being friends?"

"I can do that." Nate's voice was noticeably brighter.

"Then it's settled."

"I better let you get back to work."

"Hope your trip to Boston goes well."

"Meeting with the moving company and the management company to rent the house."

"I'm sure you've got it all in hand."

"Can I call you?"

"Of course. I'm on retainer remember?"

"I mean… outside of work."

"I know."

"I'd miss talking to you if I couldn't."

"You can call me. We're still friends. Right?"

"Friends. Yes."

There was a knock on my office door. "I gotta go, someone's at my door."

"Ok. Just one more thing. It was amazing spending thirty-nine hours with you… not that I counted."

My door opened and Dave poked his head in.

I waved him in. "Yes Mr. Jacobs, I'll follow up with you after you're back from your trip."

"You can't talk. Ok. I'll let you go."

"Bye for now."

"Bye Maddie."

CHAPTER 15

"I can take these to the door for you, Mr. Jacobs," said the limo driver pulling my bags from the trunk of the sedan.

"No need. Thanks." I handed him a twenty-dollar bill as I took my suitcase from him.

His face brightened into a delighted grin. "Thank you, Sir! Have a great weekend." He stood beside the car and waved to me as I turned to head up my front walk. It was a generous tip but, on the short ride from Logan Airport, I'd learned he was working full time, going to school and applying to law schools. He had no idea that I'd worked cooking and bartending to pay my way through school and I could appreciate how hard it would be for him to make it all the way to the bar.

I paused partway up the walk to look up at the house we'd lived in for almost ten years. The light snow falling had covered the lawn and shrubs with a white blanket, but the walk was salted and clear. The porch light was on and cast a warm glow over the front door and steps. The real estate 'for rent' sign with the smiling face of our agent was the only blemish on the picture-perfect landscape.

A blast of wind blew open the front of my overcoat I'd not bothered to button, giving me the incentive to hurry up and get inside.

I slipped off my galoshes and put them on the mat on the floor of the hall closet. I took off my fedora, brushed off the snow, smoothed the brim and gave the peak a squeeze to reshape it before setting it on the closet shelf to dry.

I could hear music coming from Ann's room, so I called up the stairs, "Hello. I'm home."

No one answered.

I left my suitcase at the base of the stairs and slid open the pocket door to my office. Other than the stack of mail on my desk, my office appeared untouched. Not a single footprint marred the vacuum streaks in the carpet. I set my briefcase on the desk and went to find Betsy.

I found a note on the kitchen counter.

At bridge club.
Dinner in crockpot - will be ready at 6:30.
Don't wait for me.

I was hungry. I peeked under the lid of the crockpot. Tuna casserole. At least it was something Ann liked. I looked at the clock on the wall over the telephone. I had time to change and unpack before it would be ready.

The music got louder as I climbed the stairs with my suitcase. I paused outside Ann's bedroom and knocked.

"I'm home." No one answered. I opened the door a crack. "Ann? Are you there?"

"Hold on Dad. I'm on the phone."

Only then did I notice the gray phone cord snaking from the telephone table, along the baseboards of the hallway and under Ann's door. How she could talk on the phone with the music blaring was baffling. I just shook my head and carried my suitcase down the hall and into the master bedroom. I set it on the bench at the foot of the bed and opened it. I took out my suit and shook it and then opened the closet and pulled out a hanger. It didn't dawn on me until I started to hang my suit in its usual position that none of my clothes were there. My first thought was that Betsy had started packing before I noticed that the closet was still full of her clothes and only mine were missing. I hung the suit and opened my dresser drawer to get out a pair of casual trousers to change into. All the drawers of my dresser were either empty or had Betsy's things in them. I was starting to clue in that Betsy had moved all my things out of our room.

She'd officially moved me to the guest room. Which is where I found my clothes, some in boxes and others hung in the closet and in the small dresser meant for overnight guests.

While Ann was away at boarding school, I often slept in the guest room, but this was clearly a message from Betsy. It's not the marital sleeping arrangements I envisioned as a young man. But if it kept the peace and made keeping my 'until death do us part' vow easier, I wasn't going to complain.

I got my suitcase from our bedroom and finished unpacking it in the guest room.

I knocked on Ann's door on my way back downstairs. "Come down for dinner. It's ready."

"Gimme a minute."

Betsy had left the kitchen table set for two, so all I needed to do was to go downstairs and get myself a few beers from the fridge in the rec room. I also brought up a couple cokes for Ann, who was in the kitchen scooping tuna casserole into a bowl when I got back.

She started to slink away with her bowl.

"Where do you think you're going?"

Ann rolled her eyes. "To eat in my room. Mom's not here."

"I'm here. Sit." I picked up my bowl and served myself.

Ann puffed her cheeks, huffed, and flopped into a chair at the table. "All right. But I have to get ready."

"Ready for what?"

"To go out."

"You're going out?"

"It's Friday."

"Where are you going?"

"To the movies. What's with the third-degree, man? Mom knows. She said ok."

"I'm not Man, I'm your father. It's well within my rights to ask you where you're going and with whom."

Ann just glared at me and looked into her bowl spooning tuna and noodles into her mouth.

This wasn't the start to the week home I had hoped for. Betsy out. Ann going out. We had a lot to get settled. Starting off at odds over dinner and going to the movies wasn't going to help move things along. It was time for Ann and Betsy to start preparing to move. I wanted to show them photos of the house I'd bought for us. We had to decide what would be going with us and what we would get rid of. We needed to set a schedule for packing and moving. I wanted everything settled before I had to go back to Canada.

I tried again to engage Ann in conversation. "What movie are you going to see? Anything good playing your old man would like?"

"You're not coming with me if that's what you're suggesting."

"I wouldn't dream of it. I was thinking I would take your mother while I'm home. Or we could go as a family…"

"Are you trying to ruin my life completely? I won't be seen at the movies with my parents."

"How could you think I would want to ruin your life? I work every day to make your life better."

Betsy dropped her keys with a clatter onto the kitchen counter behind us. "You think moving us to a foreign country is going to make our lives better?"

"That's one thing he might have done right," said Ann getting up from the table and putting her bowl and glass into the sink.

I was flabbergasted. And confused. "You're ok with moving to Canada?"

"Amy was bragging about going to college out of state and then Mel told her that I was considering going to school out of the country and Amy was positively green. I had to go with it, so I applied to the University of Toronto and Western right away."

"You've been accepted to Boston College. That's still an option." Betsy started to fill the sink with water and soap.

"Toronto has a solid Art History program and going to school in a foreign country… that would be the bomb."

Betsy pulled on her rubber gloves and started washing dishes. "Boston College has an excellent program. World renown."

I got up from the table and moved towards Ann with my arms open to give her a hug. "That's wonderful. I hope you get accepted wherever you want to go."

Ann let me hug her but was stiff and didn't hug back. "Can I go now?"

She left to get dolled up to go out leaving Betsy and me alone in the kitchen.

"That's great that Ann has found a program in Toronto that she's interested in."

"She hasn't been accepted yet."

I got another beer from the fridge. "Are you going to have some dinner?"

Betsy pulled off her gloves and dried her hands but didn't answer me.

I picked up my bowl to get a little more casserole. "I can serve you some while I'm in here."

"I'm not hungry."

"So, there were good snacks at bridge club. Jenny's house?"

"Yes."

"She's a good cook."

"No one leaves my house hungry either."

"I wasn't implying they did. Why must you take offense to everything I say."

"I don't. Just the offensive things."

I knew things were going downhill. "Please. I just got home."

"Whose fault is it that you're away all the time and I'm here taking care of everything?"

"I know. Moving is a lot. That's why I'm home now. To get things done."

"Your idea of getting things done is giving a bunch of orders then flying off and expecting us to do all the work."

"We're hiring movers. They are going to pack and move everything we tell them to. It's not like I'm conscripting you to hard labor."

"It's not that easy."

"We just need to make a plan and schedule…"

Betsy just glared at me then turned away and started walking towards the living room. "Wash your own dishes when you're done."

I stood holding my bowl and took a couple of deep breaths. The flicker of hope that Ann's enthusiasm had softened Betsy's resistance to moving was extinguished.

I grabbed my fork from the table and picked at the tuna and noodles while leaning against the counter. The tuna I'd shared with Maddie had been a much more pleasant experience. And it wasn't just because the tuna we ate was so much better than the gray flavorless flakes floating in milky white goo mixed with soggy noodles and sad little peas. I scraped the remnants from my bowl into the garbage. I wished Maddie was around to talk to. She made me feel alive.

CHAPTER 16

"You are one foxy mama in that dress," said Will as I came down the stairs.

"If that means you look fantastic, then I agree," said my Aunt Connie who was hanging up her coat in the closet.

"Thank you, both. Thanks again Aunt Connie for coming to stay with Anne tonight."

"Weeee Aunt Connie!" shouted Anne, running down the hall from the kitchen and throwing her arms around her waist. "I gotta show you this." Anne grabbed her hand.

Aunt Connie looked up at me and shrugged as Anne dragged her toward the kitchen.

Will peered through the cut glass of our front door. "The limo's here."

Aunt Connie called out from the kitchen. "You kids have fun. I got this."

I opened the closet and unzipped the bag with my mother's mink stole I'd borrowed for this evening. I pulled it out, turning to Will for him to help me drape it over my shoulders, but he was already on the porch waving to the driver. It was moments like this that reminded me that Will and I had grown up in very different worlds. You could put him in a tux, but he greeted the limo like it was a hay-filled truck he needed to direct down the laneway.

An evening like this was a rare event for us. I was stunned when Will handed me the elaborate invitation to attend a black-tie carnival ball. One of Will's business associates, a land developer who had hired him as his primary electrical contractor, had bought a table at a charity ball. Will was uncharacteristically enthusiastic about going to a formal event.

"Mario said he's taking care of everything, even sending a car to take us there and back."

It had been ages since I'd needed an evening gown. I had to get something suitable to wear, so I took my friend Claire shopping with me. She has impeccable taste and knows why something works or doesn't because, besides being a nurse, she was a fabulous amateur seamstress.

It was a stroke of luck there was a huge sale of winter formal wear at Holt Renfrew, left over from their New Year's Eve collection.

"I love the way it drapes, and the hint of cleavage is… ooh là là," she'd gushed when I came out of the dressing room wearing the midnight-blue velvet halter dress with a deep v in the front and a waterfall of velvet that flowed from the back of my neck to the floor.

"There's more than a hint of cleavage." I tugged at the front panels to draw them closer together. "How do I wear a bra under this?"

"You don't."

"Can I get away with that?"

"In this dress, you can get away with murder. Buy it."

There were two glasses and a half bottle of champagne in the back seat of the Lincoln Towncar Mario had sent to pick us up.

"It'll be about a half-hour drive. Help yourselves to a drink," said our driver, who'd introduced himself as Tony.

"I'm not partial to the bubbles myself," said Will.

I was worried about opening it and having it burst out onto my dress. "I don't need anything right now."

"If not now, maybe on the ride home," said Tony.

There was a biting wind blowing off the lake up Water Street in Oakville when Tony opened the car door and extended his hand to help me out. The mink stole covered my bare shoulders and was long enough in front and back, so I didn't freeze going from the car into the Oakville Club.

After checking our coats, an elegantly attired couple greeted us in the lobby; the gentleman in an impeccably tailored tuxedo and his wife in a shimmering empire-waisted, deep green floor-length raw silk gown with a breathtaking emerald and diamond necklace.

The lady looked at the invitation that Will produced, and she handed us a program. "Welcome to the Oakville Hospital Mardi Gras Gala. I'm Gloria Hartwell and this is my husband, Henry. Mario Sasso's party is at table five. Have a wonderful evening." She extended her arm to indicate we should head into the main part of the dining room.

The room was magnificently decorated. Purple, gold, and emerald-green satin banners hung from the high wooden beamed ceiling. The tables were elegantly set with tall silver candelabras, each holding seven candles. As the flames danced, they cast flickering reflections in the glasses and silverware. There were masquerade masks at each place setting. They were suspended on a rod that was inserted into the starched napkin that had been folded into a cone. There were white masks with bright feathers extending out from the top and black masks with sequins for eyebrows alternating around the table.

We wove our way through the tables, finding table five in the front row near a low stage where a trio of classical guitar players were playing. On one side of the stage, there was a small podium. Behind it and the guitarists, extending the entire length of the stage, were multiple sizes and styles of drums set up and ready for yet unseen musicians.

Only two seats were empty at our assigned table.

A large man bounced out of his chair and opened his arms to greet us as we approached. "Tobi!" He gave Will a bear hug. "Ya got here. Ok. Good. And this bella donna must be your wife, Madeleina." He took my hand and kissed it. "Finally, we meet you." He turned back to Will. "She's much too good for you, Tobi." He turned back to me and took my arm. "I will introduce you to everyone."

He proceeded to lead me around the table. The other guests stood up to meet us.

"This is Rocco Bruno and his wife, my sister, Lucia. Rocco, Lucia, Madeleina and Tobi."

I extended my hand to them. "Call me Maddie. Lovely to meet you." It was odd hearing him call my husband Tobi, presumably short for Tobias, but Will shook hands as if it was completely normal.

Next came Mario's brother Frank and his wife Rosa, whose name I would remember because she wore a rosy-pink sequin dress and had a diamond-crusted rose charm on a thick gold chain around her neck. Next, he introduced us to his son Daniel, who was a carbon copy of his father, except his hands were not as calloused and his diamond ring was much smaller, and to his wife Cindy whose dark hair was up in a large, braided knot that was very elegant but in stark contrast to the gold lame jumpsuit she wore that was more appropriate for a disco than a gala.

"Last, but first in my book, my wife Jeannie." Mario took her hand and leaned in and kissed her behind the ear.

Jeannie batted her long false eyelashes at him and then turned to me and rolled her eyes. "He's not always this charming." The aqua sequins of her dress rippled and flowed like the ocean as she retook her seat at the table. "Come sit beside me. The boys will sit together on the other side."

Cindy and Lucia took the seats to Jeannie's right, and I took the one on her left, leaving the four seats facing the stage for the men. Looking around at the other tables, which had rapidly filled up, the couples were seated together, as was clearly suggested by the alternating male and female masks at each place setting. I looked up at Will and patted the seat beside me to suggest he take it. He nodded, but didn't sit down. He and Mario appeared to be having a serious conversation while Rocco and Daniel had left to go to the bar.

Lucia leaned towards me. "You and Tobi have a daughter, right?"

"Yes, Anne. She'll be seven next month."

"At least you got a while until you have to pay for a wedding. We have three daughters and only one married off. Jeannie's only got one left now that

Danny tied the knot back in September."

Jeannie lifted her empty wine glass and tapped it with her long, painted fingernail while looking over at Mario. He immediately broke off his conversation and headed to the bar. Will followed him without asking if I wanted anything, but I hoped he wouldn't return without something for me. It was already feeling like it was going to be a long evening.

One consolation was that the dinner service began very soon after Will and Mario returned from the bar with cocktails for all of us. I was grateful for the rye and ginger that Will brought for me and for the glasses of wine that accompanied each course.

As the wait staff made the rounds with coffee and tea, the guitarists, who had continued to play throughout dinner, stopped and moved off stage. Mrs. Hartwell, who we'd met upon arrival, came up to the podium. She adjusted the microphone and cleared her throat. The chatter in the room quieted and there was the sound of chairs scraping as guests rotated to better view the stage.

"It is my great pleasure to welcome you all to this year's Oakville Hospital Volunteer Association Gala. As the chairwoman of the Gala committee, I am delighted to report that we have already met our initial goal of selling out every seat for this year's event." She paused while the audience applauded politely. "An event like this does not come together without the tireless efforts of many of our members, and the generosity of our local businesses and corporate sponsors." There was another round of applause and some celebratory glass clinking at what I assumed were some of the corporate tables. I sipped my coffee as she listed off a long list of volunteers, but then she started to introduce the next speaker.

"And now, I'd like to invite one of our corporate sponsors and newest member of our fundraising team to come up and give us some of the numbers. Mr. Nate Jacobs, President of Bond Canada."

When I heard his name, I felt my heart drop to my belly, grab my insides and yank them up into my throat. I took a long, deep breath to settle the churning inside me. Across the room Nate got up from his seat and strode up onto the stage. He looked very smart in his tuxedo. I turned my chair a little more towards the stage.

Nate began giving the financial information about the OVA fundraising and the goals for 1977, but I wasn't listening. Although we'd talked a couple of times on the phone, I'd not seen him since the weekend of the snowstorm. He'd not mentioned anything about working with the OVA, or the gala, so seeing him was a complete surprise.

I told myself there was no reason why I couldn't walk over and talk to him after the speeches were over. I rationalized it would be common courtesy to say hello to my biggest client. But still, the thought of making a move towards him made my stomach churn with excitement and uncertainty.

He finished his talk and turned the podium back over to Mrs. Hartwell. My eyes followed him back to his seat, but I didn't turn my head. I kept myself facing the podium and tried to focus on what the chairwoman was saying.

"In order to make our goals for the x-ray machine for our radiology department Mr. Jacobs was just telling us about, we hope you'll consider making a donation and take part in our silent auction. Please make your bids generous for the fantastic items donated by our wonderful local businesses. We have something for everyone, from vintage champagne to the most modern camera equipment. And for the ladies, there's a fabulous fur coat donated by Barrington's, alterations included, and a pair of diamond earrings generously donated by Birks."

Jeannie pointed to her chest and mouthed, "I want the coat."

"And… to sweeten the deal, every time you place a bid, you'll get a raffle ticket and you'll be entered to win one of our fun door prizes, like movie tickets at The Playhouse or a family pizza dinner at Mother's. So please make lots of bids everyone and let's get that x-ray machine! And now, to get you all in the carnival spirit, we have Tempo Brazilia here to get you up out of your seats and to the auction tables!"

The drum band came out and, as they played, eight impossibly tall women dancers wearing remarkably little with the exception of elaborate feather headdresses transported us briefly to a carnival in Rio. They spread out through the room and got everyone on their feet and moving around the room in a parade to the Samba music.

While we were all swept out of our seats, the staff shuffled tables to make space for a dance floor. When the music came to a stop, Jeannie pulled Mario to the auction tables, presumably to place a bid on the coat. Will volunteered to get us each a drink, and I excused myself to slip to the ladies' room.

I came face to face with Nate in the small corridor where the washrooms were located. I'd just exited the ladies' room and he the men's.

"Maddie? What are you doing here?"

I gave a little shrug and put on a coy smile. "Just going to the bathroom."

Nate laughed. "I didn't see DB on the sponsor list."

"We're here as guests of Sasso Construction. Will does a lot of work for them."

"Aha. I saw them on the list. Home builders?"

"Yes. Quite successful, I gather."

"So… you're here with Will."

"Yes. Is Betsy here?"

"Yes. And you know Len Edwards, our CFO, and Delores, they're here as well."

"I should definitely say hello to them."

"How about now?"

"I'll just grab Will and I'll come find you."

CHAPTER 17

I should have expected it, but I wasn't prepared. With her head high, shoulders back, and her dress rippling with her stride, Maddie crossed the room toward us arm in arm with a tall, broad-shouldered man with a thick shock of blonde hair. Maddie and her husband were an impressive sight. I lost track of what I was saying to Len when I saw them.

Len turned to see what I was looking at. "Hey, it's Ms. Cole. What a nice surprise."

Maddie extended her hand to Len. "Nate told me you were here. Len, this is my husband, Will Tobias."

They shook hands and Len introduced his wife to them. Dolores waved to Maddie from her seat.

Maddie waved back. "Hi, Delores. Nice to see you."

Betsy got up from her seat and stood beside me. Her gloved hands clasped at her waist.

I put my hand on Betsy's back and stepped us around Len so we were closer to Maddie and Will. "I'd like to introduce you to one of my top consultants. Ms. Maddie Cole, this is my wife, Betsy."

"Lovely to meet you." Maddie gestured towards Will. "My husband, Will Tobias."

"She's Mrs. Tobias tonight." Will grinned, simultaneously putting his arm around Maddie and extending his hand to me. "You're the guy who shoveled my driveway, eh?"

Betsy shifted to one side and gave me a questioning look.

"Least I could do for providing safe harbor in a storm." I turned to Betsy to explain. "This is the colleague who lent me their sofa when I got stranded in Toronto last month."

Betsy's mouth was pressed into a thin line. "I see."

I thought it best we get off the subject of my stay with Maddie. "Are you driving back into the city tonight or staying nearby?"

Will gave Maddie a squeeze closer. "We got a limo for the evening. Nothin' but first class for my wife."

"We're staying at the Holiday Inn," said Betsy. "Our house needs a lot of work before we can move in."

Maddie cocked her head and scrunched her face and looked at me. "I thought you had an apartment here."

Betsy sighed. "It's just not suitable."

Maddie looked at Will. "We should probably check on our bids. See if we've been scooped for that clock radio you want."

I wished them a lovely evening, and they turned to walk away. I watched Will's hand slide up from Maddie's waist under the folds of the scarf of material that flowed from her neck like a narrow cape over her bare back. Seeing her bare skin made me want to be the one touching it.

Betsy had retaken her seat at the table, and I took mine between her and Delores.

Delores leaned towards me. "What time will the auction close?"

"I'll need to announce the closing of the bidding at ten thirty. You still have time to hit the dance floor." I'd asked Delores to help me collect the checks and distribute the auction items at the end of the evening, but I still wanted her to enjoy herself as my guest, not as my assistant.

"I don't think I'm up for a tango. But they certainly are." She nodded toward the couple on the floor. The large man was strutting his partner in the glittery dress across the room. He spun her around and into his arms and kissed her, all in time with the music.

"They're putting on quite the show," said Betsy.

"They seem to be enjoying themselves." Delores turned to her husband. "We'll wait for something slower. Right, dear?"

We weren't the only ones watching the tangoing couple. There were only a few couples on the dance floor with them and several faded back to the sidelines to watch them. As the band finished with a triumphant blast from the horn player, the man pulled his partner in close and said something to her. She nodded, and they hurried off the floor to one of the tables.

The band started to play a slower-paced song, but still with a swinging Latin beat. I was surprised to see the large man return to the dance floor with Maddie on his arm and his partner, in the shiny blue dress, with Will. As they began to dance there were a few missteps, but both Maddie and Will were smiling and laughing with their partners, who seemed to be enjoying their roles as dance instructors.

Delores turned to her husband. "I think we can handle this Latin waltz, don't you?"

Betsy let out a sigh, "It's not a waltz, it's a rumba."

The music reminded me of the Cuban nightclub in St. Petersburg we frequented before we were married. "We used to do a passable rumba. Would you like to dance?"

Betsy nodded. "We might not get anything more suitable."

I was unphased by her lack of enthusiasm. The mere fact that she agreed to dance was a signal to me that the evening was going well. It didn't hurt that I'd pounded back a couple of manhattans before and after dinner. I led her onto the dance floor, took her in my arms, and did my best hip and shoulder sway to the sensuous rhythm.

Betsy stayed stiff in my arms. "Don't get carried away."

"I know you can. I remember you perched on a stool swaying to the drums and guitars, sipping rum and coke…"

"I was young and foolish."

"And fun."

"I'm not here for fun. I'm here as your wife." There was a flash of satisfaction in her eyes as she said it. I knew she was striking back at me because I'd insisted she spend that particular week in Oakville because it was expected that my wife would accompany me to the gala.

I looked around at the other couples on the dance floor. Over Betsy's shoulder, I saw Maddie grin as her partner led her in a twirl. "I think there are a few wives here having fun. You could try it."

"It's never enough for you."

I knew she wasn't referring to our dance or attending the gala. I knew it was about our move to Oakville. She was right. I didn't think she was doing enough. She wasn't being supportive or helpful or fun throughout the process. She was dissatisfied with everything; my temporary apartment, the house I'd bought for us, the wind off the lake. She was determined to point out every defect. So even though this was exactly the sort of fancy event she relished, tonight, she refused to enjoy herself.

The carnival atmosphere may not have softened Betsy's stance, but at least it was good for fundraising. Delores accepted the checks and kept the ledger of the donations, and I handed the items or gift certificates to the winning bidders.

I discovered the Tango couple was the Sassos who had invited Maddie and Will to the event. Mrs. Sasso was ebullient at winning the fur coat her husband bid on. She immediately tried it on and gave him a big kiss.

"It's dreamy. I'm going to be hot in this for you tonight." By the tone of her voice, I had no doubt she was implying something sexy.

"Happy wife. Happy life." Mario looked at me with a conspiratorial grin as he wrote out the check.

I thought about those words later as I waited for Betsy to come to bed before I turned out the lights in our hotel room. She'd been pleased that the room had two beds. My wife happy wasn't my idea of a happy life. She'd made it clear we weren't going to sleep in the same bed, as she'd turned down the covers of both before going into the bathroom to change into her nightclothes.

This was my life and wife. I was determined to be successful, but that meant making difficult choices. I wished Betsy could see the opportunities my new position afforded us. She'd be spending the next couple of days with the decorator. I'd given them a generous budget for new furnishings. Successful shopping always improves Betsy's mood, so there was hope.

CHAPTER 18

I was not pleased to be woken up by a strange buzzing, warbling sound. It was coming from the clock radio Will had bought at the silent auction. I'd told him not to set it up last night when we got home. He pushed buttons, but the noise didn't stop until he got out of bed and unplugged it from the wall.

I growled.

Will got his robe from the back of the door, put it on, and opened the door. "Anne's up. I heard her talking to Connie."

I pulled my pillow over my head. "I'll be right there."

I didn't hurry out of bed. I knew Aunt Connie would make sure Anne had breakfast. Knowing her, it might be cake and ice cream, but Anne would be happy.

Anne never needed convincing to stay with Aunt Connie for a night or two. She always came home bursting with enthusiasm for whatever new experience she'd had. Aunt Connie had a knack for making you feel special and grown up. She believed that children, especially little girls, should be heard and seen, be allowed to express their opinions, and choose their own path in life. This was entirely contrary to the viewpoint of her sister, my mother, who disparaged Connie for ending up a spinster and having to work to support herself.

I'd had sleepovers with my Aunt Connie growing up and she gave Anne the same sort of spoiling she'd given me. Sometimes she'd cook a gourmet meal and her longtime roommate Pat would decorate and set the table as if they were having a fancy dinner party and they'd toast Anne's accomplishments, however small, with sparkling grape juice served in champagne glasses. Other times they would take Anne out for dinner at a new or exotic restaurant and then they would write up a review as if they were critics. Aunt Connie would file it in her desk on equal terms with reviews she'd clipped from the Dining Out section of the Toronto Star.

But this morning, Anne had a ringette game, so Aunt Connie had brought the party to her. She had placed the toaster in the middle of the kitchen table and Will and Anne were both poised over it.

"Leggo my Eggo," squealed Anne as they both lunged for the waffles that had just popped.

"I declare Anne the victor," said Aunt Connie. "You may choose the toppings."

"I want peanut butter and chocolate chips."

"And for the loser?"

Anne scrunched up her face and gave Will a long stare. "He gets…"

Will put his hands together in prayer. "Please, please not the syrup."

"Syrup for you," shouted Anne.

"What's going on here?" I pretended to be annoyed.

"Just a little friendly waffle battle," said Aunt Connie, reaching for the coffee pot and pouring a cup of coffee she then handed to me.

I held the cup with both hands and inhaled the aroma. "It's a pretty loud battle for this hour of the morning."

Aunt Connie gave me a scolding look. "Someone need a little hair-of-the-dog in her coffee?"

I was still groggy. I probably should have skipped the champagne in the car on the way home, and the brandy nightcap. But I was more tired than hung over.

Will had been in a great mood after the party. Mario had taken him aside and told him about a major building project and Will was going to be the lead electrical subcontractor. They'd sealed the deal with a handshake and a shot of grappa.

Will kissed my cheek. "Tobias Electric is on easy street."

I was skeptical.

Will called out to our driver. "What say you, Tony? Is Mario a man of his word?"

"If Mr. Sasso says so, it is so," said Tony over his shoulder.

"See. Tony knows." Will grinned at me with that boyish grin that distracted me from thinking like a businesswoman and drew me into his gleeful mood.

I really liked happy, fun Will. It was that version of him I still found very attractive. His broad shoulders and strong farm-boy arms hadn't changed much in the years we'd been together. His eyes still had that mischievous gleam when he was feeling playful.

"You were smokin' hot tonight." He touched my leg and drew his hand back like he'd been burnt. "All the guys were giving you the eye."

"I don't think so."

"Oh yeah. They were."

"They might have been looking at Jeannie or Rosa. I was stuck between them for most of the night."

"You looked like you were having a good time."

"It wasn't bad, but their dresses were more scintillating than the conversation."

"Huh?"

"We didn't have much in common. And you left me with them for ages."

"We went to talk to your guy too."

"Who? Nate?"

"He was checking you out."

His words made my heart do a little twirl, but I didn't let on. I gave a little snort of disapproval.

"He was," Will insisted.

"Maybe because he's never seen me in a dress."

Will put his arm around me, pulled me closer, and whispered in my ear. "I can't wait to see you out of that dress." He brought his other hand up and ran it up my arm under my stole and he made a sneaky grab at my breast.

I stifled a giggle. "Soon enough, big boy."

After our nightcap, I'd peeked into Anne's room and both she and Aunt Connie were asleep in the twin beds. Mr. Fluff, Anne's cat, was the only thing that moved. He made a dash to escape the room before I closed the door. Will came up the stairs behind me and started to fumble around the back of my dress.

"How do we get you out of this thing?" Will shuffled me into our bedroom and closed the door.

"A couple buttons here." I pointed to the back of my neck under the scarf and Will undid the buttons. "And a zipper here." I undid the zipper at the side of the skirt.

Will peeled the dress off me. He ran his hands from my shoulders, over my breasts and down to my waist. "That's so much better." He started to pull at my stockings.

I didn't want him to tear them. "Let me do it."

By the time I got my stockings off, Will had tossed aside his jacket and pants and was struggling to get out of his shirt. He'd not taken the time to undo more than a couple of the studs and he'd pulled it over his head exposing his chest, arms, and shoulders. I couldn't help but watch in amusement as he contorted to free his head and hands.

"Ya need a little help?"

Will's head popped out of the collar. "No, I got it." He grinned as he tossed the shirt and dropped his boxers, kicking them aside. He put his hands on his hips and wagged at me.

"Proud of yourself?"

Will smirked. "Look what I got for you." He did another wiggle.

It was tempting. He was obviously in the mood for fun, and I was happy to play along. I reached forward and slipped my hand between his legs. I gave his balls a teasing caress and then I wrapped my fingers around his penis. He was such a nice size, perfectly proportioned for his large frame. He was hard and warm in my hand. I was ready for what I knew he wanted.

Will reached around me and scooped his hands under my bottom. I wrapped my arms around his neck and he pressed me backwards towards the window. Then he lifted me and perched me on the edge of the waist-height ledge. He wrapped one arm around my back and his other hand pulled at my right leg.

Him standing and me perched was a position that always worked well for both of us. I wrapped both my legs around his waist, and he slid into me letting out a too-loud grunt.

"Shhhh. They'll hear us," I whispered into his neck where I'd buried my face, inhaling the faint scent of his cologne.

"Ok. Ok. But, oh man, you feel so good." He thrust up and into me.

I clung tighter. Tilting my hips to manoeuvre his movements to the most pleasurable angle. I barely felt the hard edge of the window that was digging into my lower back.

I leaned back against the kitchen counter, watching Anne press chocolate chips into a neat checkerboard pattern in the peanut butter-filled squares of her waffle. A flash of pain made me suspect the window ledge had left a bruise.

Aunt Connie put a glass of milk in front of Anne. "That's almost too pretty to eat."

Anne picked up her waffle and took a giant bite. "No it's not."

I glared at her and shook my head. "Eating with your hands and talking with your mouth full. Did we forget all our manners?"

Anne scowled, put her waffle down, and started cutting it with her knife and fork.

"Now, if you put another waffle on top and called it a sandwich…" said Aunt Connie, passing Anne another waffle that had just popped from the toaster. "Then it would be acceptable to eat it with your hands."

Anne took the waffle and mashed it onto the other one, and then grinned at me triumphantly while she picked it up and ate it.

"Your Aunt Connie lets you get away with too much."

Aunt Connie stepped away from the table and came to lean against the counter beside me. "Knowing how to get what you want within the rules is an important life skill."

Aunt Connie had mastered it. She had impeccable manners and was a consummate lady. But, now in her 60s, unmarried, and still working full-time, she'd broken a lot of the social rules. She was the only female relative that had supported my desire to have a career, and she'd been the only one to ask me whether I really wanted to get married. Everyone else assumed that I was relieved when Will and I got engaged because I was approaching 30 and still single.

Will got up from the table. "Time to get moving Annie Bananie."

"Just leave the dishes," said Aunt Connie. "I'll get them once you've all cleared out."

"Thanks," said Will.

Aunt Connie nudged me away from the counter. "You better go get dressed. You can't go to the arena in your nightgown."

"You don't need to come," said Will. "If you want to stay with Aunt Connie…"

"Pat's picking me up in a little while. I'll just clean up these and she'll be here. You go on," said Aunt Connie.

The girls were playing the Whitby team, so we had a bit of a drive to get to their arena. As we headed out the door, Aunt Connie handed me a full cup of coffee and a peanut-butter-waffle sandwich wrapped in foil.

"For when you're ready for breakfast."

I put the sandwich in my purse, thanked her for it and for taking care of Anne, and gave her a big hug.

The old arena where the girls were playing wasn't too uncomfortable if you got a seat near one of the overhead heaters. While Anne was getting ready with her team, I got a cup of coffee from the concessions and found a spot in the stands near center ice. I picked a row high enough so I could easily see into the visiting team bench.

Anne and her teammates were hopping around with excitement when they came out of the dressing room. They did their warm-up routine, skating around their stuffed animal team mascot they'd placed at centre ice. At least they'd be warm on the bench. It was apparently pretty chilly because their coach looked like she was cold in her team sweater. She had her arms crossed and was rubbing her hands on her upper arms and shuffling from side to side. She leaned in closer to Will. He said something to her and then turned up to point to me in the stands. When he saw me watching them, he waved and then moved to stand at the far end of the bench, leaving the coach alone in the centre. There was something off about the way she looked up at me. I wondered what he said to her.

CHAPTER 19

The weekly meeting with my director of facilities was running long. There were a lot of moving parts to building a new corporate headquarters for Bond Canada. I had big plans for the Canadian division, and this was a major infrastructure project that would set us up with space to grow.

"Are we on schedule?" I needed him to get to the bottom line for this meeting.

"In fact, we're running a little ahead. DB is wrapping up the site investigation. The senior project engineer is on site today and they plan to move all their equipment off site by the end of the week."

I wondered if Maddie was the engineer on site. She'd overseen the investigation and removal of the underground storage tanks she'd identified during the audit process. Now she was managing the soil stability project, but there were other engineers on the team.

"Thanks for the update. Let me know if anything significant changes between now and next week."

Delores opened my door a crack and peered through it. I nodded to her. My facilities manager stood up.

Delores swung the door open and stepped aside to let him leave. "I need to leave shortly. Do you need anything else?"

"No. Thank you. Please give my condolences to your sister."

"I will. Thank you."

Delores had left to attend her brother-in-law's funeral and I didn't have any meetings scheduled for the afternoon. So, I thought I might as well go see for myself how things were going with the new office building project.

I couldn't help but feel a little disappointed when I saw the DB engineering van parked outside the trailer that was their temporary site office. I'd hoped to see Maddie's car. Nonetheless, I was there, so I opened the door to the trailer and let myself in.

Maddie and another person had their backs to me and were bent over a map that was spread out on the desk. They didn't look up when I came in. Maddie was wearing dark blue coveralls and rubber work boots. The way her back arched as she reached across the desk… she made them look sexy.

Maddie pointed to several locations. "I'd like to have samples from boreholes 3, 7 and 12.”

“Whatever you say, Princess,” said the man beside her.

I was shocked to hear him address her that way. I cleared my throat to get their attention.

Maddie glared over her shoulder, looking annoyed that I’d interrupted, but seeing it was me, she stood up and smiled. “Mr. Jacobs. What brings you here?”

“Sorry to interrupt your work. I had some free time this afternoon. I understand you’ll be finishing up this week?”

“I’ll get those samples in the van, Ms. Cole.” said the man heading for the door.

“Thank you, Barry.” She waited until he’d left to answer me. “I’ve got a few more logs to review, but it looks like we’ve got what we need. I expect we’ll have all our equipment off site by Friday.”

“Did I hear right? Princess?”

Maddie laughed. “Yes. He’s the only one on the planet that can call me that. It’s a long story.”

“Perhaps you can tell it to me over drinks? When you’re done here.”

“Sometime, but not today. I’ve got to get the samples into the lab.”

“Lunch then?”

“I forgot my day planner at home. Why don’t you give me a call tonight and we can find a date that works.”

“You’re sure it’s ok to call you at home?”

“Why not? It’s a work thing and… we’re friends. Right?”

“Yes. Right.”

“You still have my number? From our stormy weekend.” Maddie’s voice was low and sultry.

“I do. It’s been hard not to call it.”

“I gave it to you so you could.”

Barry came back into the trailer.

Maddie stiffened. “I can give you a preview of what we’ve found.” Her voice was cool and professional. “The subsurface conditions were as expected, clayey silt till overlaying the Georgian Bay Formation shale bedrock. We’ll provide recommendations in our report with regard to foundation design. But based on what I’ve seen, the site is suitable from a geotechnical viewpoint for the structure you’ve proposed.”

“That’s good news.”

“We’ll have the final report to you by the end of the month, as promised.”

Barry was stacking up long wooden boxes at the far end of the trailer. I wished I could be alone with Maddie so we could talk freely.

“I’ll give you a call, as we discussed, to set up our next meeting.” I gave

Maddie a little wink.

She smiled and winked back. "I better get back to it. I want to get the samples to the lab before they quit for the day."

I waited until after seven that evening to call her. I was glad Maddie was the one to answer the phone.

"Hold on, let me get my day planner," said Maddie.

I heard her put down the phone and I could hear her speaking to someone else.

"It's Nate Jacobs, from Bond. We need to set up a meeting."

I heard a man's voice muffled in the distance.

Maddie picked up the receiver. "Ok, when were you thinking?"

"Is this a bad time? I can call you at the office tomorrow."

"Will wants to know if you curl."

"Curl?"

"Curling. The sport."

"Never tried."

I heard Maddie muffle the receiver and call out to Will. "He's never curled."

Maddie came back on the line. "Do you want to try?"

"I suppose so."

"We need a fourth for our St. Patrick's Day Bonspiel."

"What's a bonspiel?"

"A tournament."

"But I've never curled."

"It's mostly a fun event. Fundraiser and fun. If you pay the entrance fee. You can curl."

"When is it?"

"Next weekend, Saturday. The 19th."

"If you don't mind having a complete novice on your team."

"Everyone starts somewhere. Hold on I'll tell Will."

Maddie called out to Will that I was going to curl with them.

When she came back on the line, we set up a time to have lunch on Wednesday the following week. She joked that the update on the project was included in their fees, but the curling training would be extra.

"I'll buy lunch to compensate."

"From what I've seen, you have nothing to compensate for." Her voice was softer, lower. It was clear she wasn't referring to curling instruction.

"You're making it hard to not want to compensate you again."

"It's the hard things that are worth doing." Her voice was slightly breathy, and she emphasized the word hard.

Her insinuating that she might want to be with me that way again gave me a thrill. I felt a shiver of excitement. I was just about to concur when she continued talking but in a cold professional tone.

"We can discuss it further over lunch."

"I understand. You can't talk freely right now."

"That's right."

"I'll make the reservations and give you a call at the office with the particulars."

That Wednesday I had a meeting later in the city, so we agreed I'd pick her up at her office. Their receptionist called Maddie to let her know I'd arrived. I didn't take a seat to wait because I was brimming with nervous energy. I was excited to see her and share my latest perk. I escorted Maddie outside as soon as she joined me in the lobby.

She looked around as we came out of the door of her office building. "Where's your car?"

"Right here." I opened the rear door of the black sedan that was idling at the curb.

"You arranged a limo?"

"This is my car. And driver."

"You have a driver?"

I closed Maddie's door and I got into the opposite side of the car.

"It's very efficient given my schedule. It was actually Delores that suggested it. She knew the previous president kept a driver on staff. She informed me it was already approved in the budget. I think she worries about me driving in snow."

"She's right to."

"I managed to get you home in the worst snowstorm in decades."

"I didn't want to tell you at the time, but I would have preferred to drive."

"Well now neither of us must."

"At least not today." Maddie settled back into her seat, her back into the corner so she was angled toward me. "I presume you still drive yourself around on weekends?"

"Yes. Of course. Except for business functions. I can arrange it for that. I don't know how much I'll use it. I'm still new at this having a driver thing. I usually ride up front with Chuck." I tapped the front seat. "Back me up on this will ya?"

"Yes Sir. Mr. Jacobs. This is the first time you've ridden in the back."

"You're pretty lucky to have found Delores," said Maddie.

"I can't even take credit for that. She found me."

Maddie looked at me quizzically.

"She came in and started assisting while I interviewed assistants. Like she knew she was the right one for me. And she was right."

Maddie tilted toward me and in a low voice said, "Sometimes you just know."

I felt a warm rush at her words. The first thought that came to mind was I knew Maddie was right for me. I wanted to slide across the back seat and kiss her right then and there. I looked towards the front of the car. I saw Chuck glance in the rearview mirror. I turned myself toward Maddie and looked into her eyes. "This time, I do."

A smile spread across her face. The way her eyes locked onto mine made me believe that she was trying to tell me she knew too.

She sat back in her seat. "We got in the final lab data this morning. I didn't see anything concerning, so I can give you a preview of what you'll see in our final report." Her voice was cool and professional. She tilted her head towards Chuck in the front seat and I understood she was being cautious about what she said in the car.

I'd had Delores make us a reservation at Bardi's. The maître d' ushered us to our table.

Maddie looked around the room. "Didn't we sit in this booth the last time?"

"Memorable evening for you too?"

Maddie didn't answer, just gave me a sidelong look.

"It was for me."

"You had exciting news to share. Your imminent promotion."

"Sharing it with you was the memorable part. You made quite the impression."

'We've gotten to know each other a little better since then."

"I submit it's a lot better."

"And that's nice. Eh?"

"Nice? You're the best thing that's happened…"

"I'm a thing?"

"You like being difficult, don't you?"

Maddie winked. "You should have said that we are a thing."

"You are something else."

"You said best before. Now I'm just some? Make up your mind, man."

"You messed up my mind when we made love on your sofa."

"Not just on the sofa…" Maddie broke off speaking as our waiter appeared with menus.

We ordered drinks.

Maddie opened her menu. "Once we order lunch, we can get back to business."

"Didn't you cover everything on the way here?"

"I brought some notes." Maddie nodded at her satchel.

"I can wait for the final report. I prefer our other topic."

"You mean sex?"

The two businessmen sitting at the next table stopped talking and simultaneously looked over at Maddie.

Maddie either didn't notice or ignored them. Her eyes focused on her menu as she spoke. "We probably should talk about it. Clear the air before spending the whole day together Saturday."

"How could I resist time with you?"

"We should probably go over some basic rules."

"I know the rules. No touching, no kissing, no sex…"

Maddie tossed her head and laughed. "Those are very important. But I meant curling rules."

"I'll need more than a few rules."

"How much do you know?"

"Nothing."

"But you still agreed to it?"

"I'd agree to almost anything to spend time with you."

"Good to know. But we agreed to keep things cool."

"Can't get much cooler than on ice."

"At least you know curling is an ice sport. That's something. You'll want to wear something warm but not confining. You'll need to bend and crouch."

"You crouching and bending might heat things up."

"We won't be alone."

"True. Your husband will be there."

"And Claire. You're taking her husband Theo's spot. He's got a medical conference this weekend. He didn't realize the conflict until this past week. We thought we might have to play as a threesome."

"Lucky Will."

"No. In a threesome, I skip. He doesn't like that."

"This curling thing is sounding better all the time."

Maddie rolled her eyes. "You better behave on Saturday."

"Ok. On Saturday. Maybe I misbehave another day?"

Maddie looked down, picked up her drink and swirled the ice cubes in the glass. "I wish it wasn't so… complicated."

I reached over and placed my hand on hers, holding the glass.

She lifted her gaze and looked into my eyes. "You're married. I'm married."

"It was pretty simple. And then you happened."

Maddie frowned. "We can just forget it ever did."

"That's impossible. I want to remember every second with you. Sitting, here, at this exact table last August I knew...". I stopped talking because Maddie pulled her hand away.

"Knew what?" she said.

I almost blurted out what I was feeling. That everything just felt right when we were together. But seeing her frown, I was worried I could drive her away. So, I held back and gave her a safer answer. "I didn't want you to leave."

Maddie sat back and looked up towards the ceiling, exhaling. "We're in so much trouble."

"Because it's complicated?"

Maddie nodded. "It would be simpler if things were just one-sided."

I felt a tightening in my chest and my heart was pushing into my throat. I didn't want to assume anything. I wanted to know if she was feeling what I was feeling. "Am I to take that as you didn't want to leave either?"

"Let's just say I want to spend more time with you than I should."

I couldn't help but grin. "I want you more than I should."

"Then perhaps we should focus on your curling lesson." Maddie began explaining the game using our plates and moving the salt and pepper shakers to demonstrate the game.

"So it's like shuffleboard, on ice?"

"It would be easier to explain watching a game."

"I'm getting a general idea."

"Too bad you're not around later, you could come by the club."

"What time?"

"I should be done by 8."

"I could arrange that."

In the car after lunch, I asked Maddie to give Chuck the address for the High Park Curling Club.

She did but added. "Are you sure it's no trouble being later tonight than planned?"

"No trouble Ma'm. I'm available for Mr. Jacobs twenty-four-seven if he needs me."

"It won't be much later. It gives me an excuse to get away after dinner with Franklin. He's kept me late at his club on many occasions. "

"All right then.' Maddie got out of the car, bent over and poked her head back in. "See you tonight."

I was buoyed all afternoon by the knowledge I'd be meeting up with Maddie again. I was restless and checked my watch often, calculating in my head how long it would be until I was supposed to meet her. It amazed me that every time I saw her; it made me want to be around her even more.

I spotted Maddie at one of the tables as soon as I entered the curling club.

She saw me too and waved me over.

All the ladies at the table stood as I approached. All but Maddie and one other lady remained while the others gathered up their things and left.

"Your timing is perfect," said Maddie.

"I'm Claire." Claire extended her hand. "Pleased to meet you, Nate." She spoke with an accent that sounded French.

"Nice to meet you, Claire. I understand I'll be replacing your husband this Saturday."

"No one could replace my Theo." Claire winked at me and smiled mischievously.

"I hope I don't let you down."

"I'm not worried about that. Theo is a terrible curler but a wonderful husband." Claire patted my arm. "I'm glad you'll be joining us." She turned to Maddie. "You teach him well." Claire gave a little wave as she turned to go. "À la prochaine, mes amis."

"Let's go sit by the glass where we can see the sheets better." Maddie pointed to several chairs lined up along the windows. We sat and Maddie launched into pointing out the parts of the playing area. I remembered some of the terms from our lunch table lesson.

"Are you with me so far?" she asked.

"Got it. Start in the hack. Throw the stone. Let go before the hog line and hope it lands in the house."

"Yes. Unless your skip wants a guard or a takeout."

"What's a skip."

"The team captain or fourth. Will is skipping Saturday." She pointed to one of the stones in the lane in front of us. "See that red one that's out in front of the rings? That's a guard."

"I thought the idea was to be in the rings."

"A guard is there to protect stones in the house from being taken out by your opponent. You need to think strategically, think ahead to the different possibilities, and decide what shot to call. That's the skip's job."

"You haven't explained all the slapping."

"Sweeping."

"It looks like slapping."

"You need to learn how to sweep. That'll be your main job."

"I thought throwing was."

"You'll throw the first two stones. Claire and I will sweep yours. Then you'll be sweeping for the rest. Either with me or Claire depending on who's throwing."

Maddie suggested we watch a few ends of the men's league. She explained what each player was doing and pointed out how the teams decided what the score was after each end.

After about a half hour, Maddie got up. "Now I better show you how to sweep. I'll go grab a club broom."

Maddie came back with a straw broom that looked like it was made to carry a small witch at Halloween.

"How come the guys out there are playing with orange and yellow brooms?"

"They have their own brooms. The club brooms are the old-fashioned straw kind."

"What do you use?"

"I have a rink rat. It's an orange one. Now watch." Maddie demonstrated the slapping motion with the broom on the lobby floor. "Now you try."

It was a lot harder than she made it look.

"You better take that broom home and practice. But wear gloves."

I looked at my hands and I already had red welts forming on my palm.

"You'll need to bring a pair of shoes that are a bit grippy but very clean on the bottom. We'll make you a slider from tape."

"Slider?"

"Proper curling shoes have one foot that is normal and the other has a slider." She lifted her left foot and slipped off the woollen slipper that I hadn't noticed before. "See the bottom is smooth on this one. We can put tape on one shoe so you can slide."

"Do you have rental shoes, like a bowling alley?"

Maddie laughed. "No. But you certainly won't be the only curling virgin on Saturday so there will be other people needing tape."

"I should let you get home."

"Is Chuck waiting for you?"

"Yes. He said it was no problem. I think he's part cat. He naps while he waits. I think he's slept at least 8 hours today already."

"Then I'll see you back here Saturday morning. 8am."

"I can walk you to your car."

"No need. I have to run up to the locker room first anyway."

"I'll wait for you." I waved her off with my hand.

Maddie left the lobby. While I waited, I studied the trophy case. There were photographs of past club champions and I found Maddie in a couple of the photos. I felt a mix of pride I knew her but also dread that I'd look foolish alongside her.

Maddie reappeared. "I'm ready to go."

I pointed to her picture. "You didn't tell me you were a champion curler."

"I've been in the business girls league so long it's statistically unlikely I wouldn't have been on a winning team at least once."

"You mean rink." I grinned with pride at my new curling lingo.

"I knew you were a good student."

We walked together out of the club.

"Where's your car?" I asked.

Maddie pointed to it on the far side of the lot. She rummaged in her purse for the keys as we walked toward it. She opened the front door.

"You don't lock your car?"

"There's nothing to steal."

"There could be someone hiding in the back waiting to grab you?"

Maddie laughed. "Who'd want me?"

"I can't imagine any man not wanting you."

Maddie turned to me and leaned against the car.

I took a step closer and put one hand on her hip.

Maddie looked around the parking lot. "You're the only one dangerously close to me."

"I shuffled a little closer."

A smile crept across her face. "You're getting perilously close to crossing the friend line."

"Just trying to stay out of the wind. It's cold."

"You should go. I'm safely at my car."

I didn't move. I wanted to kiss her. I leaned closer.

She put her hand on my chest. "Chuck might see us."

"So if no one is looking…maybe?"

"We said no more…"

"I think you said it…"

"You agreed."

"Because it's what you wanted."

"It's more about what we shouldn't want."

"So you want me to kiss you?"

Maddie leaned forward and gave me a fast peck on the cheek and spun and slid into the front seat of her car. "Go home Mr. Jacobs before you get us both in trouble."

"You mean more trouble?"

"See you Saturday."

"I can't wait."

CHAPTER 20

Will and I arrived at the curling club and we each headed to our respective locker rooms to change into our curling shoes. Claire was already sitting on the bench in front of her locker when I entered.

She waved her gloves at me. "Bonjour Maddie. Ready to sweep up some prizes?"

"Without Theo, maybe not."

"He called from Montreal last night. He wishes us luck."

"We can just have fun. Not worry about winning."

"Winning is fun too. We can try for both." She picked up her broom and led the way down to the main room.

Will and Nate were standing by the table where the coffee was set up. Nate was holding a cup and Will was pouring liquid into it from a small glass pitcher labelled "aiming fluid".

I shook my head at Will. "Are you sure you should be starting so early with that?"

Will looked at me with feigned innocence. "Just making sure Nate gets the full bonspiel experience."

Nate took a sip of his coffee. "A little liquid courage can't hurt."

Nate was dressed in dark slacks, a white shirt, and a dark blue heavy cardigan. I gestured to his outfit. "You look ready to curl."

"Thanks to Mr. Corbett. I went into his sports shop and he advised me. I might never wear these shoes again, but at least I don't need to be taped up."

"You needn't have bought all that just for today."

"If I look the part…"

Will put his arm around Nate. "You'll look great in our team picture. Now let's get you out there for a few practice throws."

Nate gave me a "help me" look.

I waved to him as Will led him down to the sheets where the organizers were giving the intro to curling lessons for all the first-time curlers.

Claire poured herself a coffee. "Café?"

I nodded and she poured a second cup for me.

Claire leaned in and spoke quietly. "Nate did not want to leave your side."

"It's good if he gets to know Will."

"You've been spending a lot of time with him."

Even though Claire was my dearest friend, I chose my words carefully. "We get along well."

Claire pressed her lips together and looked at me skeptically. "Sometimes we meet the right person at the wrong time and it gets complicated."

"Nothing complicated. He doesn't know a lot of people and he's on his own until his daughter finishes high school. Then his wife and daughter will move into the house he bought in Oakville."

"It would be nice to add another couple to our supper club. Perhaps once his wife comes, we can invite them."

The beginning of the first game was announced. Claire and I headed to the sheet assigned to our rink. Will and Nate were already there with our first opponents. We introduced ourselves and all shook hands and then tossed a coin to see who would have the hammer first. We lost the toss.

Will patted Nate on the back. "No pressure. But you're throwing first." He turned and started gliding down the ice, facing back towards us. "Just aim for my broom and don't hog it."

Nate looked at me. "Hog it?"

"Come up short. Get it past the line down there." I pointed down the ice to the line Will was just gliding past.

Nate crouched down into the hack and I slid his first rock over to him. I looked down the sheet and Will tapped a spot at the front of the rings and then stood holding his broom in front of him and his arm out.

I interpreted the signals for Nate. "He wants you to throw a guard. Aim for his broom. When you let go, turn the handle so the rock spins clockwise."

Nate wobbled a bit as he slid forward but managed to release the stone along the right line. I could tell immediately it was light. Claire and I got on it right away and did our best to sweep it, but it came up just short. Claire pushed the stone out of play, and I slid back to Nate.

"You're making us work too hard this early," I teased.

Nate pressed his lips together. "Is there a penalty for not getting it there?"

"Just the right to mock you if you do it again."

Nate shook his head. "And I thought you were a nice girl."

Glenda, the other team's lead, was settling into the hack to deliver her stone. Their skip made the same motions with their broom as Will had done.

"Watch Glenda," I said to Nate.

Glenda delivered a perfect guard.

Will tapped his broom on Glenda's stone and motioned that he wanted Nate to take it out. I explained what he wanted.

"I need to throw hard?"

"Yes. But not crazy hard. Imagine you're throwing it hard enough to get your rock all the way to the other hack down there. Not into the parking lot."

Nate looked determined as he squatted to deliver his stone. He came out fast and Claire and I had to scoot down the ice to keep up with it.

"Off! Off!" yelled Will. "Leave it."

Claire and I stayed with the stone as best we could, poised to sweep if Will called for it.

Nate's stone made contact with a crack and the guard rock slid toward the back of the house. Will was on it the whole way. His powerful sweeping carried it to just biting the back ring.

"Way to go, Nate!" Will waved his broom in salute.

Nate was beaming as I slid back to stand with him while Glenda took her second shot.

"Get ready to sweep." I pointed to where Nate should stand while Claire settled into the hack and did her pre-throw routine. Will signalled for a draw in behind Glenda's guard and called for an in-turn throw. I knew Claire preferred out-turn, but it was too late to suggest it. Claire was already delivering her stone.

"I'm light," she said as she let it go.

"Sweep," bellowed Will. "Hard!"

Nate wobbled and tried to match my pace beside the rock. I was the only one doing any sweeping so Will slid down to meet us and maneuvered himself between Nate and me. With his help, we managed to carry Claire's stone into the rings and counting.

Nate shuffled beside me as we returned to the other end of the ice sheet. "You make sliding along look so easy."

"You'll get the hang of it. Think about only lifting your grippy foot off the ice and using it for pushing. Keep your slider on the ice."

"Now you tell me." Nate was focused on his sliding.

"Watch how they sweep." I pointed down the sheet. "Look we might get lucky."

The takeout their second had thrown was light, and only nicked Claire's stone, burying it further behind the guard. Will signalled for Claire to throw another guard to try to take away their option to knock out her counting stone.

I moved into position while Claire gathered up her stone. "Ok get ready."

Nate slid, somewhat more gracefully, into place beside me.

Claire threw.

"Off. Off," called Will

"Don't sweep," I told Nate. "Just stay with it."

The rock was running very straight.

"Wait for it," called Will.

We had only slid another few feet down the sheet when Will bellowed, "Sweep!"

Nate at least got a few brushes in and when Claire's rock came to a stop I gave him a thumbs up.

"Good job."

Nate grumbled. "I think that was all you."

The first few ends were difficult for him. I could tell he was getting frustrated. I tried to encourage him and to reassure him we were just here to have fun and the outcome didn't matter. As a team, we made a lot of our shots and at the end of the first match, we had only lost by one point.

"Sorry about dragging you down," said Nate as we gathered on the walkway at the end of the ice sheet.

"Don't worry about it," said Will. "They buy the first round, so it's all good."

I explained to Nate that we congratulate the winners with a handshake and then it's customary for your counterpart on the winning team to buy you a drink and then we reciprocate for the second round.

As if on cue, Glenda came up to Nate. "Good game, Nate. What can I get you to drink?"

'I'll have what you're having," said Nate.

Claire took Nate's arm and led him to our designated table. I heard her reassuring him that he was doing great for his first time and giving him one of her favourite consolation lines. "Half the teams out here also lost their matches, so we're in good company."

I hung back with Will as they walked away. "I'm not sure he's having fun."

"Don't worry about him. He doesn't like not being good at it. It's a guy thing."

"Maybe it was a mistake to invite him." I felt guilty that I'd wanted to spend time with Nate, but he looked miserable.

"He'll be fine. We don't need him to do much. And if we were only a threesome, we'd have to buy a lot more drinks."

We joined the others at our table just in time for their lead to propose a toast to Nate for surviving his first curling match. We all drank to Nate. He smiled more as the guys on the opposing team told him stories of their mishaps, some from when they were beginners and some from the past week.

After two rounds of drinks, we all stood up to stretch our legs.

"What's next?" Nate asked me.

"Once the B-group matches are done, we go out again. We play one of the teams that won their first match. Then after the B-group plays their second game, the top four teams from each group will play in the finals. After the finals, there will be dinner and prizes."

Nate was much better during our second game, but we still lost.

When we'd finished our drinks after the second game, Claire suggested we find seats by the glass to watch the finals.

"You might have made the finals if not for me," said Nate.

"If you want to take the blame, then you can buy us a couple dogs and we'll go watch some Wide World of Sports in the TV room. You've probably seen enough curling for your first day."

Will led Nate to the TV room and Claire and I sat by the glass overlooking the ice sheets.

"Your plan for Nate is working," said Claire.

"They may be getting along too well."

"Jealous Will might steal your new friend?"

"I think I have more to offer."

Claire turned and looked at me with one eyebrow raised and a knowing smile.

"I just mean we have a lot more in common."

"Such as?"

"He's well educated, ambitious. He understands me."

"More than Will does?"

"In work matters."

"Will is doing well with his company. No?"

"Yes. But when it comes to my career…"

"Perhaps if you worked with him?"

"I know. Like you and Theo. But you worked for him as his nurse…"

Claire chuckled. "You would only be satisfied if he was working for you."

We both had a quiet laugh at the impossibility of it.

"Nate's very encouraging. Working with him has been good for my career."

"You've never let Will hold you back."

"But I've never felt like he wants me to succeed. Nate does."

"Nate's not married to you. He has a wife at home to take care of him."

"He will. Once she moves."

"In the meantime, he's here alone?"

"I met her last month at the Mardi Gras ball. She's here some of the time."

Claire got up. "I'm going to the bar. Want anything?"

"A Tab." I nodded at Will and Nate laughing together at the bar. "Will's drinking enough for both of us."

It was a couple more hours before we were seated for dinner. We were assigned to the table with the rink we'd played for the first match. They'd finished just ahead of us in the ranking. Will and Nate were both very giddy from their afternoon of beer drinking.

Claire sat down beside Nate. "When does your wife join you?"

"Moving day is June 10th. But they will be here for Easter break."

"Once you're settled, you should join our supper club."

"I like supper," said Nate slurring his words a little.

"Does your wife like to cook?" I asked, knowing where Claire was going.

Nate snorted. "She's capable of cooking."

Claire explained how we take turns hosting dinners. "Maddie makes an appetizer and I make dessert and whoever hosts also makes the main course."

Nate straightened himself up and declared, "I will make my crab cakes."

I was surprised. "You cook?"

"I'll have you know… Missy… I'm a darn good crab cake maker." Nate was leaning a bit to one side, and then he hiccupped. "Excuse me."

"Buddy, you never admit that," scolded Will. "Cooking is a pink job."

"Then it's settled," said Claire. "You can do the main course."

"Can you get crab here? It's not like there's an ocean nearby. Like Boston."

Claire chuckled. "I'm sure we can. I can discuss it all with your wife …"

"Betsy," said Nate.

"I look forward to meeting Betsy," said Claire.

The bonspiel chairman started announcing the winning rinks and calling them to the prize table. We were well down the list and when it was our turn to choose; the pickings were slim. Will and Nate picked matching red baseball hats with the logo of some business I'd never heard of. They were giggling together about being twins. It was clear neither was in any condition to drive home.

I pulled Will aside. "I think Nate should stay with us tonight."

"Why?" He looked confused.

"Because he's too drunk to drive all the way to Oakville."

"He hasn't had more than me."

"He hasn't had any less either."

Will looked puzzled.

"You aren't driving home either. I'm driving."

"I'm fine."

"You are very fine. But also drunk."

"You mad Maddie?" Will giggled and elbowed Nate. "Mad Maddie sounds funny." He leaned like he was sharing a secret with him. "But it's not, trust me."

I pointed to the stairs to the locker room. "Ok, you two. Go. Change your shoes and get your coats."

Claire and I headed to the ladies' locker room to drop off our brooms, shoes, and curling sweaters. When we got back to the lobby, Claire gave me a hug before leaving. "See you Wednesday. Take care of them."

I waited for my tipsy passengers.

CHAPTER 21

Maddie didn't look happy as she took the car keys from Will and got behind the wheel. She was quiet on the short drive to their house. Will seemed oblivious to her displeasure.

I'd had fun with Will at the bonspiel. It's been a long time since I'd hung out with the boys. Sure, there was time with Franklin at his club, but that was business, and I still felt like I was pretending to belong in those circles. Will was a guy's guy. Like the men I looked up to growing up. Men who worked with their hands, in a trade, not behind a desk. Men like my father.

"Sorry to inconvenience you," I said to Maddie as she unlocked the door to let us into the house.

"Not a problem. Make yourself at home."

"Do we have any snacks?" said Will.

"I can look after I make up Anne's room for Nate."

"The sofa is fine." I didn't want Maddie to go to any trouble.

"Mads doesn't mind fixing things up for you."

Maddie started up the stairs, and I followed her. "Just give me the sheets and I can do it."

Maddie didn't answer me. She opened a closet at the top of the stairs and took out a set of sheets, then headed into the room I knew was Anne's. It reminded me of my daughter's room when she was younger. There were stuffed bears and a flowered bedspread that Maddie pulled back to start changing the bed.

"I'll just put these back on in the morning," she said, dumping the pillow out and folding the case.

She pulled the sheets off and handed them to me while she remade the bed with the fresh set. Her bent over reminded me of watching her digging her hands into the bedsheets as I slid into her from behind while standing at the edge of her bed. I stood there staring, holding the sheets but imagining tumbling her onto the bed and kissing her. I felt a shiver of excitement just thinking about touching her.

"I'll leave it turned down for you." She finished tucking in the sides and folding back the top corner.

"You're not going to tuck me in?"

"It's a bit early for that." Maddie moved towards me and looked into my eyes. "Maybe later."

I could feel myself leaning toward her. She reached out her hands and I reached for her, dropping the sheets I had forgotten I was holding.

We both leaned over at the same time to pick them up and we bumped heads.

Maddie rubbed her head and pouted. "Trying to knock me out?"

"I thought… no." My head hurt and I was a bit dizzy. I leaned over to get the sheets and wobbled.

"I'll get them. You're dangerous."

"You're dangerously close."

Maddie grumbled. "You better go downstairs before we get into trouble."

I didn't move.

Maddie picked up the sheet. "At least be useful." She handed me one end of it. I stepped back from her to help her fold it. When it came to the part where we bring both sides together, we paused. I knew I shouldn't kiss her. Standing so close, face to face, it was impossible for me not to want to. As my mind fumbled with thoughts of what to do, Maddie just looked at me. I was mesmerized by her lips. Her tongue brushing across them and the way she sucked in her lower lip.

"Maybe just one kiss," Maddie whispered and leaned in.

My heart pounded. I dropped my end of the sheet, put my hands on her waist and pulled her in and kissed her. Her mouth parted and her tongue darted across my lower lip, sending a shiver of electricity through me.

She pulled back. "Now we'll have to start all over."

I was confused.

"The sheet. You dropped it."

"I could do that over and over."

She took a long deep breath and shook her head. "We can't."

I felt a tugging in my chest. I wanted to take her in my arms, hold on to her and never let her go. I leaned towards her.

She put her hand on my chest and gently pushed me back. She picked up the sheet and loosely folded it with the other bedding, and put it all on the dresser. "We should get back."

I felt lightheaded and I needed to pee. "Can I use the bathroom first?"

"You know where it is." She gave me a wink.

I knew she was thinking of what we'd done together in that same room.

Standing at the sink in the bathroom, thoughts of her naked, soapy body flooded into my mind. I held on to either side of the sink and closed my eyes as I remembered kissing her in that very spot. The curls of steam from our long shower together still hung in the air. I kissed her neck and shoulder and down to her breast lapping up the drops of water that clung to her skin. Her fingers tangled in my wet hair as I continued down her body, past her breasts and her belly until I buried my face between her legs. I felt pride in how I'd made her pant and moan as I tasted her. I felt myself getting harder, remembering how she'd pushed me down onto the bathroom floor and straddled me.

But we'd been alone then. Tonight, we weren't. I had to splash cold water on my face and take a minute to let my chubby subside before I could leave the bathroom.

When I got downstairs, Maddie was sitting on the sofa.

Will was flipping channels on the TV. "Hockey ok?" Will looked at me.

"I vote for whatever Maddie wants."

"Hockey it is." Will flipped the channel and flopped into his barcalounger and popped up the leg rest.

Maddie looked up at me and patted the sofa beside her. "Come. Sit."

"Want a beer?" asked Will.

"Sure." I pointed towards the kitchen. "Where…"

"Mads will get it. Another one for me too, Babe." Will wagged his half-empty bottle at her.

"I can… Just tell me where." I put my hand on Maddie's shoulder to say she needn't get up.

Maddie sloughed off my hand and got up. "I'll show you."

She led the way towards the kitchen and down the back stairs to the basement.

"Beers are in here." She pulled the lever opening the door of the battered fridge at the bottom of the stairs.

"I know. From last time. I could have got them."

"But you shouldn't know."

"Does he always order you around like that?"

Maddie didn't answer. She grabbed three beers and closed the door with her hip. She popped off the tops using the rusty opener screwed into the side of the fridge. She handed me one then turned and started up the stairs. I wondered if she was mad at me for asking.

"Thanks, Babe." Will grinned up at Maddie and patted her bottom as she handed him his beer. "Do we have any chips?"

Maddie set her beer on the coffee table. "I'll check." Maddie took Will's empty bottle and headed back to the kitchen. I sat down on the sofa.

It was hard for me to imagine Maddie was with someone like Will. She was a different person with him. Where was the woman who demanded to be taken seriously, treated equally and not ignored? How did she put up with Will's chauvinistic ideas and treatment of her?

I felt myself getting angry, so I focused on the hockey game. Toronto was down by four goals, and it was only the middle of the second period.

Will frowned at the TV. "Guess it's one of those games."

Maddie set a bowl of chips on the end of the coffee table closest to Will. She settled on the couch beside me and curled her legs under herself just as Toronto scored their first goal.

She slapped her hand on the arm of the sofa. "That's a start."

Will popped up from reclining. "Yes. Nice shot." He leaned forward and grabbed a handful of chips and grinned at me. "You aren't cheering for the Leafs?"

"I don't have a horse in this race."

"Bruins fan?"

I nodded as I took a swig of my beer.

"I suppose that's allowed. Original six and all." Will grabbed another handful of chips and flopped back into the recliner and propped up his feet."

The Leafs came alive in the third period. I enjoyed watching Maddie cheer for her team. I was shocked at how much she applauded the big hits. Her attitude toward the roughness was delightfully unladylike. The way her breasts moved as she wiggled with excitement watching the players on the screen was decidedly feminine and equally enthralling.

Several beers and five unanswered goals by the Leafs giving them a win over Atlanta had us all in good spirits at the end of the game. Will got up from his chair as the evening news came on.

"I'm in too good a mood for news," he said. "I'm going to bed."

"I'd like to watch a bit." Maddie reached up to touch Will as he passed her.

He reached down and ruffled her hair. "Don't keep Nate up too late."

Maddie looked up at him. "He can go to bed anytime he likes. I'll be up soon." Maddie looked over her shoulder as Will went upstairs. Once he was no longer in view, she shifted around to face me.

I stifled a yawn.

"You're tired too?"

"No," I lied. I was exhausted and sleepy from drinking all day.

"Do you have to leave first thing in the morning?"

"I will. I don't want to impose on your Sunday."

"Don't worry about that. Anne won't be back from my aunt's until suppertime. So you can sleep in if you like."

"I'll be up."

"If you're hungry and I'm not up. Help yourself. There's cereal and bread for toast…"

"I could take you both out to breakfast."

"Let's play that by ear." Maddie unfolded her legs from under her and reached for the empty beer bottles.

I picked up the empty chip bowl. "Let me help clean up."

She took the bowl from me. "No need. Go on up."

I didn't want to go up to bed. I didn't want to miss my chance at a few moments alone with her. I'd spent all day sharing her attention, and I wanted some time with her all to myself. And it meant going to bed alone. I didn't want to think about Maddie in the next room, with Will. I couldn't help feeling like she should be with me not him. Yes he was handsome and fun but he didn't treat her like I would.

I took the bowl back from her. "It's the least I can do."

Her hand was still on the bowl as I pulled it toward me. She smiled and leaned in and gave me a soft lingering kiss on my lips. "I liked spending the day with you too."

I had that wrenching feeling in my chest. She knew what I was thinking and feeling almost before I did. The connection we had was undeniable. I knew then I loved her. Being just friends was no longer an option.

CHAPTER 22

I knew it was Nate calling even before I picked up the phone.

"I'm sorry about this weekend." Nate sounded more upset than I thought was warranted.

"It's not your fault. You didn't make it rain."

"It was a disaster."

Nate had invited us to go to the Blue Jays game. They were playing their first home game hosting his Boston Red Sox and he'd bought tickets for the six of us; Will, Anne and myself and Nate, Betsy, and their daughter Ann. After sitting through a cold, soggy rain delay, the game was postponed and the plan for the first get-together for our families was derailed.

I tried to lighten his mood. "It wasn't all bad. We still had fun."

"It was good seeing you."

I'd been looking forward to seeing Nate but also dreading seeing him with his family. "Betsy and Ann get home ok?"

"Yes."

"Your daughter made a big impression on Anne. She couldn't stop talking about her. How cool she was, how groovy her jeans were and that she'd been on a plane and gone to Europe…"

"How did she find out all that?"

"Apparently, she told her about London and Paris while they were waiting to get hot chocolate."

"I'm surprised."

"Anne's asked if she can have a trip for her birthday next year. Because you took Ann on a trip for hers."

"At the time it was like we were torturing her. Keeping her from having a party with her friends on her actual birthday"

"You should be pleased she's changed her tune."

"The girls seemed to get along."

"And Betsy?"

Nate sighed. "She didn't have much to say."

I could tell Nate wasn't being forthright. "So… I've got my work cut out for me if we're all going to be friends?"

Nate chuckled. "I can't hide anything from you. She did say Will was very strong."

I wondered what gave Betsy the impression that Will was strong. He hadn't lifted anything heavy or made any obvious show of strength. All I could think of was the streetcar ride from Exhibition Stadium.

The car was crammed with soggy and sullen baseball fans, and we were forced to stand in the aisle if we didn't want to wait for the next car to arrive. Will reached up to hold on to one of the loops above his head and then he tucked his other hand into his front pocket.

"Here's your hand-hold Annie," he said, rotating his elbow out for her to hang on to.

Anne wrapped both her hands around her daddy's arm as she always did when we rode the streetcar standing up. I held on to the corner of the seat beside me and placed my other hand on Anne's shoulder.

As the streetcar lurched forward, Betsy wobbled.

Will leaned towards her. "You can hold on to me too."

Betsy reached up and held on to Will's bicep. "You're strong."

Will puffed up his chest and stood like a sturdy tree. He grinned over his shoulder at Ann, who was standing by Betsy. "You too, if you like."

All three of them hung on to Will as our streetcar lurched through the downtown rush hour traffic.

Nate was standing behind me as he'd been the last to board. The streetcar was so crowded that no one noticed that he'd slipped his hand under the edge of my jacket, hooked his finger into the waistband of my slacks and pulled me closer to him. His finger caressed my skin and sent a shiver through me that wasn't from the cold. I turned slightly so I could give him a scolding look.

He batted his eyes innocently and shrugged and I stifled a giggle.

Nate's concerned voice interrupted my daydream. "Are you still there?"

"Sorry. Just thinking about our streetcar ride."

"Best part of the day."

"You've got to be kidding."

"Closest I got to you. So, yes. Best part."

"Touching was unavoidable."

"We should do that again."

"Ride the streetcar?" I knew what he meant, but I wanted him to be the one to say it.

"No." Nate lowered his voice to a whisper. "I want to touch you and press myself against you. But with less clothes on."

"So no rain slickers?"

"Things might get slick. If I do it right."

I felt myself grin and a rush of warmth travel from my heart to my knees and I clenched my thighs together under my desk. "That would necessitate time alone. That seems unlikely going forward."

"Are you saying it's impossible?"

"You're impossible."

"Ms. Cole. You have put a spell on me and I can't stop thinking of you."

"The novelty will wear off."

"That's not going to happen. The more I spend time with you, the more I want to spend time with you."

"Betsy and Ann will be moving here soon. Time together is going to get hard to come by."

"I do get hard around you."

"Stop. I'm being serious."

"I don't want to stop, and I am serious."

"At least we can get together socially."

"I can't see Betsy and Will becoming best friends."

"I did overhear her telling Will that being so strong must come in handy on job sites. Speaking of job sites, how are the renovations coming?"

"Maybe the next time you're out for a meeting, I could show you in person."

"I have a meeting tomorrow afternoon with your Health and Safety department."

"What time? Perhaps we could slip over there once you're done."

"My meeting is at one. I should be done by three."

"I'll get Delores to clear my schedule from three on."

"I need to go now. I have a meeting to get to."

"OK. See you tomorrow."

I hung up with Nate and opened up the report on my desk that I'd prepared to discuss with Dave. I had hurried Nate off the phone because I wanted a chance to run through the pitch I was planning to make. Working with Bond Chemical had opened my eyes to new services we could be offering to our clients.

The idea was born out of working with Bond Canada's Director of Health and Safety, who was on the project team overseeing the facility expansion project. He had attended a meeting in Boston of all the health and safety officers from across the Bond organization. The topic of the meeting had been environmental assessments of facilities to determine if there were health and safety risks. He told us about several facilities that had undergone assessments which had included sampling around and under existing facilities. He made an offhanded remark to me asking if I'd ever drilled through a factory floor to sample under it. I had to be honest and say I hadn't, but that we did have drilling equipment to sample through concrete and asphalt and I'd done that on many occasions.

I was sufficiently intrigued, so I made some inquiries with a few colleagues. None of them were doing environmental assessment projects. They did, however, put me on to a manager at the Ministry of the Environment and a couple of professors at the University of Waterloo. After speaking with them, I was convinced there was an opportunity, but it would require an investment. We'd need some new equipment, and we'd have to recruit people with the specialized training that these new investigations would need. That was the pitch I was making to Dave.

"You've been doing a great job building your list of new clients," Dave said. "I think you should stay in your lane."

"If we do this, clients will be calling us because there's only a handful of firms who can do this kind of work."

"There's only a handful because there's not a lot of work."

"But it's growing."

Dave acknowledged that I'd put together a compelling story, but he didn't think it was worth the risk. DB Engineering was growing and profitable and investing in a new line of work would cut into the partners' profits.

"You wouldn't want to have lower profits," he'd said. "It'll take you a lot longer to pay off your share purchase and cut into your bottom line too."

I was disappointed. Without Dave's support, there was no way the other partners would vote for a change in direction. They were barely on board with me being a partner, let alone side with me.

I was even more disappointed after my meeting at Bond. They had invited the senior people from their health and safety, construction, and engineering contractors. It was an opportunity for them to share some of their five-year plan with their consultant team so we could assist them in scoping and budgeting for future projects. Their desire to conduct an internal audit of the health and safety of all Bond facilities was the perfect opportunity for me to suggest environmental assessments. But I didn't.

After the meeting, I checked in with Delores to see if Nate was available.

"He's expecting you," she said, motioning for me to go in.

Nate must have sensed my irritation. "Meeting not go well?"

"The meeting was fine. Your people did a great job and all the consultants played nice."

"Then why the mood?"

"I'm sorry. It's got nothing to do with Bond. Or you."

Nate stood and took his hat and trench coat from the hook on the back of the door. "Let's get out of here. You can tell me on the way."

In the car, on the way to his house, I told him about the pitch I'd made to

Dave and that I wanted to be able to expand the work I was doing for Bond with these new services.

Nate pulled the car up to the front door of his house. "Sounds like a solid idea. But can you do the work?"

"I'd need to bring in some experts. But there's a lot of exciting research being done in Waterloo, so there are people."

"Interesting. Shall we go inside?"

Nate unlocked the front door and swung it open to let me enter.

We had to step around a scaffold that was set up in the centre of the foyer.

Nate pointed to a hole in the ceiling above the scaffold. "They're supposed to install the new chandelier tomorrow."

I could smell fresh paint and the floor was covered in drop cloths. Nate stopped me from taking off my shoes until we'd crossed to where the drop cloths ended at the bottom of the elegant staircase that swept upwards to the second floor.

"They finished painting today. The foyer was the last. I'll be glad to stop living in a construction zone."

"I didn't know you'd moved in?"

"It seemed like a waste to pay for an apartment once we closed. I didn't have much to move, as you can see."

I couldn't see any furniture from where we were standing.

"I'm sure what I brought won't be staying once the girls move from Boston. What do you think of the new colour scheme?"

"It's much brighter. Seems bigger. More open." I'd not been fond of the heavy velvet and foil wallpaper that had darkened the foyer and apparently, Betsy agreed. But now the foyer was completely white and felt very cold and harsh.

"Come see the kitchen." Nate led the way.

The only thing the kitchen had in common with the foyer was its brightness. It was a riot of yellow.

"It looks completely different." I walked around the island in the centre of the kitchen. The stovetop was surrounded by a yellow, tiled countertop that extended out on two sides with enough space to put at least six chairs. There was a giant side-by-side fridge, two wall ovens, a dishwasher, and a trash compactor. Yellow tile covered the counters that ringed the room and extended up the walls to the base of the upper cabinets.

"They just finished it this week. New everything."

"This will be a great kitchen to cook and entertain in. You could serve the whole meal around the cooktop if you wanted."

Nate smiled. "Maybe if we join your supper club, we'll do just that."

"Ah yes. Your crab cakes. I'm looking forward to that."

"I can't offer you much now. I haven't had a kitchen for the past three weeks. But I do have a bar." Nate pointed to the doorway that led from the kitchen to the family room.

It had also been freshly painted white but it didn't feel as cold as the foyer because of the thick dark wood beams in the ceiling and the brick fireplace with the floor-to-ceiling wood panelling and shelves on either side of it. Unlike all the other rooms we'd walked through, this one had some furniture, but it was minimal. A small brown sofa, a tall lamp with a large round turquoise shade, a set of tv tables, two folding chairs, a cheap-looking tv, and a bar cart.

Nate picked up the ice bucket from the bar. "Please have a seat. I'll fix you a drink." He waved the ice bucket. "Just need to get some ice."

I sat down on the sofa and waited for Nate. I smiled at how he'd used the set of tv tables as substitutes for end tables, coffee table as well as dining table. I surmised these were the furnishings he'd been using for months at his apartment. I'd thought Betsy had been very snobbish to insist they stay at a hotel rather than Nate's apartment, but I now was a little more sympathetic.

Nate came back with the ice bucket.

I got up and perused the bottles on the cart.

He took two glasses from the rack under the bottles. "Your order Ma'm? Gin, vodka or whiskey, on the rocks or with soda, or I could muster a Manhattan without the cherry, or a martini without the olives…"

"I don't know. Surprise me."

Nate set the glasses down. I thought he was reaching for one of the bottles but instead, he reached for my arm and turned me to face him. He pulled me closer and kissed me.

I didn't even think of stopping him. I leaned in as he ran his hands across my back and wrapped me in his arms. My brain went blank, and all I felt was a boiling desire.

Nate unlocked his lips from mine. Without saying a word, he took my hand and led me upstairs. My heart was pounding. He led me into one of the rooms and took me in his arms again, and we kissed. Kissing him unleashed an avalanche of desire that was unstoppable. Our lips were hungrily devouring each other while we struggled out of our clothes.

Nate pulled back the covers on the bed and then guided me onto my back. He hovered over me and looked into my eyes. He paused as if he was asking permission.

I reached up and scratched my nails lightly across his chest and then down his torso to his thighs. I felt his penis wiggle, and I grinned up at him with satisfaction at his reaction to my touch.

Nate lay alongside me. He started kissing my neck and shoulder. He languidly worked his way down my body, kissing and stroking my skin. It felt like he delighted in every kiss and stroke. His excitement was palpable, but I felt worshipped, not just desired. The pleasure he gave as he buried his face between my legs made me gasp for breath and involuntarily moan. As I shivered with an orgasm, he crawled up and slid into me. I closed my eyes as I felt my hips rise to meet him. He pressed in and out of me and I buried my face in his neck. I kissed his chest and shoulder. I wrapped my legs around his waist and moved with and against him. He pressed into me harder and faster. I felt waves of heat flowing up my body and I ground my hips in a circle as his pace peaked. My insides were pulsing as he gave a little yelp and pressed deep into me one last time.

We stayed tangled together and panting for a few seconds, and then Nate slid off me and lay on his back beside me.

I grabbed the edge of the sheet and rolled up in it onto my side, facing him. "So… What were we talking about before we got carried away?"

Nate rolled over and kissed me. "You should start your own firm."

CHAPTER 23

I was surprised to find Betsy seated at the kitchen table in her silk robe and nightgown.

"Coffee's ready." She didn't look up from making notes on the pad of paper in front of her.

"Can I get you a cup?"

She nodded.

I poured a cup of coffee and set it on the table beside her. "You're up early today."

"The boxes aren't going to unpack themselves." Betsy's tone made it clear she was accusing me of not being helpful enough.

"The crew will be back today. All you have to do is tell them where to put things."

"There's only one of me and three of them. I'm run off my feet."

"Ann can help you."

"Do you think our teenage daughter knows where everything goes?"

I gave up trying to make suggestions. I knew they'd be met with resistance. I poured myself a coffee. "Chuck will be here soon to pick me up. I've got a meeting in the city this morning."

"Does that mean you'll be home for dinner?"

"We can go out."

"I'll see what Ann wants to do."

I agreed to let them decide. I took my coffee and went to collect the paper from the front stoop. Slipping it into my briefcase, I waited in the hall, sipping my coffee, for Chuck to pull into the semi-circle drive in front of our house.

I read the paper in the back seat while Chuck drove me into the city. It was our usual routine, as he wasn't a big talker in the morning, and I had more room to open up the paper. He was considerably more chatty in the afternoon, so I sat in the front seat when he picked me up after my meeting at Dominion Bank and lunch with Franklin and John.

"According to the schedule Delores gave me, we're running ahead. Any stops before I take you to your office?"

"No. Just to the office."

"Need a shoeshine? A shave? Haircut?"

"Are you suggesting I need them?"

"No Sir."

"Would you tell me if I did?"

He shook his head and grinned. "No Sir."

I flipped down the visor and looked at myself in the mirror. My sideburns were a bit bushy, and I had a few curls of hair poking out behind my ears. "Maybe stop at my barber. I'll see if he can squeeze me in."

"Righto."

A few minutes in the barber's chair with his scissors flying as fast as his chatter had me not only looking better, but well informed about his other clients. I wasn't that interested in the gossip, but he did mention going to the grand opening of the new car dealership up the street from his shop. The way he described how their long-time customers brought plants and gifts gave me an idea.

Later, when Betsy, Ann and I were seated at Olivers Restaurant waiting for our drinks, I shared my idea with them.

"You've done a great job with the house, and I have an idea for the perfect way to show it off. A housewarming party."

"I've barely finished unpacking and now you want me to organize a party?"

"I'm not asking you to do it all on your own. I'll help."

"Besides a couple of neighbors, I don't know anyone to invite."

"Delores can help with the guest list."

"So, this is going to be all about you and your business acquaintances."

"That's not what I meant. We'll invite wives and families. I thought you'd like to get to know more people."

"It takes time to build a social circle. I don't think we're established enough to throw a party."

"The whole point of a housewarming party is to be welcomed and get established in the community."

Betsy frowned and picked up her menu.

"We had a lovely evening with Franklin and Diana, and we promised to get together again with Maddie and Will…"

Betsy turned to Ann. "What do you think?"

Ann shrugged.

I tried to get Ann on my side. "You could make some friends too."

Ann didn't look at me, but answered her mother. "I'm going to be in the city. What do I need with friends out here in the sticks?"

"So, you're not interested either." Betsy looked at me, shook her head, and looked back down at her menu.

I was perplexed at Betsy's resistance. "You've always stressed how important it is to cultivate a social network."

Betsy didn't look up, pretending to study the menu that hadn't changed in the week since we'd last dined at Olivers. "Let me think about it."

I suspected Betsy was resistant because it had been my idea. When we'd moved into our previous two houses in Boston, she'd wasted no time. She organized afternoon tea for the ladies of our neighborhood, set up dinner parties so that I could meet their husbands, and threw Ann a massive birthday party just weeks after we'd moved in. I hoped that if I let the idea sit with her, she'd come around. I let the subject drop.

After dinner, Betsy and Ann decided to watch the late movie on TV. I went to my study, ostensibly to catch up on some work I'd put off while out of the office most of the day. I flipped through the stack of documents and correspondence I'd brought home. I made a few notes, but nothing was so urgent it couldn't wait.

I got up and poured myself a bourbon from the decanter on the ornate side table Betsy had added to fill in space in my new, larger study. I stood sipping it in front of the bookcase, trying to decide if I wanted to read one of the books that had been expertly arranged by size and color interspersed with my miniature boat collection, just as they had been in my Boston study. I'd just picked The Money Changers and settled into my wing chair to read when Ann knocked on my door.

"Dad?" Her words had that lilt that told me she wanted something.

"What's up, Sweetheart?"

"I wanted you to know that, on further consideration, I think making some new friends might be beneficial."

It was uncharacteristic of her take my side in a family vote. "You're on board with having a housewarming party?"

"I could be."

"You aren't sure?"

"I'm open to making new friends ahead of starting the semester. I could do that if I signed up for the summer trip run by the art faculty. It's open to undergraduates in the art history program."

"What has this got to do with the housewarming party?"

"If you let me go, I'll convince Mother that your housewarming party is a good idea."

I had to admire her ingenuity in putting this scheme together. "Where would you be going on this trip?"

"London, Paris and Florence."

"That sounds expensive."

"It's about the art, Daddy. Not the money."

"Maybe next summer, after you've actually learned a bit of art history."

Ann tilted her head and leaned in conspiratorially. "So, you don't care that much about having a housewarming party?"

I didn't like the idea of my still teenage daughter taking off to Europe on her own. But I did want to have the party. There were several people I wanted to get to know better and build some alliances, and this was an opportunity to bring them all together socially.

"Tell me more about this trip."

CHAPTER 24

"It's hot," whined Anne from the backseat of the car. "Why do we need to warm their house?"

I twisted around in my seat. She was scowling and flapping the hem of her dress to fan herself.

"A housewarming party is about welcoming your friends to their new home."

"Or an opportunity to show off your big fancy house," grumbled Will.

"You're as bad as your daughter. I'm sure it will be a lovely party. We don't have to stay too long if you're not enjoying yourselves."

The Jacobs' driveway was filled with cars, so Will parked on the street. I handed him the large potted orchid I'd been holding in my lap, and he followed Anne and me to the house.

The front door was open. I could see Nate and Betsy standing inside in the foyer.

Nate saw us and gestured for us to come in.

"I'm so glad you could make it." He extended his hand.

The gesture felt overly formal, given that just the day before we'd made love in his office.

I followed his lead. I shook his hand, fighting the urge to give him a hug. "Thank you for inviting us."

Will shifted the pot and held it with one arm so he could shake Nate's hand. "Nice digs."

"It was quite the endeavour to make it suitable," said Betsy, who'd turned from greeting the guest who'd arrived ahead of us. "But we made the best of it, given what I had to work with."

"It a lovely home." I pointed to the orchid. "This is for you."

Anne tugged on my arm. She was pulling me toward Nate's daughter, Ann, who was walking down the staircase toward us.

"Ann, why don't you show Anne where the children's area is?" said Betsy.

Ann nodded and then leaned down to talk to Anne. "Do you want to see my room first?"

Anne's face lit up, and she nodded. "Uh huh."

Our daughter took off up the stairs behind Ann and didn't look back.

Nate nodded in the direction of his study, where I could see several men had gathered. "You really should have a chat with Franklin while you're here."

Betsy took Will's free arm. "If they're going to talk business, I'll show you where to put that and make sure you get to the bar for some refreshment."

I could tell Will liked the idea of finding the bar. He smiled at Betsy. "Lead on."

When they had moved down the hall and out of sight, Nate pulled me into the dining room that was across the foyer from his study. I looked around to see if anyone had seen us. I thought Nate wanted to steal a private moment where we could touch and maybe kiss. I started to protest that this was too risky.

"I told Franklin about your business idea and he's very interested."

I was annoyed. "Why would you do that?"

Nate looked dismayed. "Because you need funding. Just talk to him." He put his hand on my hip and turned me towards the study. I glared at him, but he pretended not to see and took my arm and started walking.

I was irritated by his insistence, but I didn't want to cause a scene, so I went along with him.

Franklin saw us approaching, and he broke off from the group he was talking with. "Nice to see you again, Maddie. Nate mentioned that you might be here today."

"Hello Franklin." I extended my hand. "Nice to see you too."

"Can I get you a drink? Nate has some good whiskey tucked away in this study."

"It's a bit warm for whisky."

"Then you'd like it on the rocks?"

I shook my head. "Water down the good stuff? Sacrilege."

"How about I leave you to talk, and I'll get you something cold from the bar?" Nate gave me an encouraging nod I hoped wasn't obvious to Franklin.

Franklin motioned for us to move out of the study and across the hall to the empty dining room. "So Nate tells me you have an idea for a new business."

"I do. Environmentally focused engineering that DB doesn't currently offer. There's a need to investigate chemical releases into the environment, whether accidental or intentional, and it seems to be increasing."

"Have you discussed this with Dave?"

"I proposed the idea to him. I suggested we expand DB's service offerings. He passed."

"That's a mistake on his part. I think you might be on to something."

I felt energized by his words. "I know I am. I was hoping that I could build a new division within DB."

"Why do you need them?"

"We are established with an excellent reputation. The business infrastructure is all there. We'd just need to add some additional personnel with expertise in hydrogeology and we'd need some new equipment...."

"How much to do it all yourself?'

My stomach churned, and I felt a wave of both fear and excitement. "I honestly don't know. I've not given it serious consideration. It's more than I could do alone."

"Perhaps the more important question is, if funding were not the issue, would you want to do it?"

My mind raced to grasp what Franklin was asking. Was it a leap I would be willing to make? I'd worked so hard to claw my way up to be a partner at DB. I'd be taking a big chance. But, on the other hand, I really believed there was an opportunity. It was as if I was hit by a bolt of lightning in that moment.

I answered Franklin emphatically. "Absolutely."

Franklin extended his hand. "Then let's make it happen."

I shook it.

"Let's find a time next week to meet and discuss the details. Call me Monday and we'll compare calendars."

Nate came into the dining room. "There you are." He handed me a glass wrapped in a napkin to catch the condensation.

Franklin patted Nate on the back. "Smartest thing you did on that acquisition was hire Maddie. I thought her good looks charmed you... but she's the real deal." Franklin pointed back at me as he turned to leave. "We'll talk next week."

"Your talk went well, I take it?" Nate was grinning with satisfaction.

"I'm still mad at you."

"Don't be. I just planted a few seeds. I want to help you."

"I don't need help."

Nate put his hands on my shoulders and leaned his head closer to mine. "I didn't think you needed help. Just a little... encouragement."

"You ambushed me. You could have warned me. I would have been more prepared."

"You were prepared. You already pitched it to DB."

"But he asked questions I couldn't answer."

"He's sold. He wants to learn more. You did great."

Betsy came into the dining room. "Sorry to interrupt your... meeting... but Nate, you have other guests."

I pulled away from Nate and looked over his shoulder at Betsy.

She looked annoyed.

I stepped around Nate toward Betsy. "I'm sorry. We shouldn't be hashing out business today. I'm going to go find Will."

I left Nate and Betsy in the dining room and crossed the foyer. Ann and Anne were coming down the main staircase. Anne had been transformed. Her hair had been in braids and now it was loose and curled up at the ends like feathers and she had on peacock blue eye shadow and pink cheeks. She was beaming and clearly delighted that Ann had replicated her own hair and makeup on Anne's little face.

I put my hands on my hips and pretended to be confused. "Who are these twins? I don't think we've met."

"I hope you don't mind Mrs. Tobias. Anne said she liked my eye shadow. I figured she'd like to try it on."

"She's a little young for this look." I motioned to Anne to come closer to me and I tilted her head up so I could get a better look at her face. "With such fancy hair and makeup, you'll put your mother to shame."

"Ann has a curling iron in her room. Can I have a curling iron?"

"We'll see."

Ann was standing at the bottom of the stairs, leaning against the railing.

"Thank you for keeping an eye on Anne."

"I didn't mind. It was fun to be the one teaching."

"Are you planning to be a teacher? Your father tells me you're going to U of T in the fall."

"No. I want to be an art dealer."

"Interesting. How did you decide on art dealer?"

"My great uncle owned a gallery in Florida. I used to love going there when we visited my grandparents. I would sneak into the back room and I would imagine I was a famous art historian discovering a lost master in the racks."

"Ann's going to Paris and London and…" Anne looked to Ann for help.

"Florence," said Ann. "A trip with the art history club at school."

"To see the great masters' works in person. That sounds like an excellent opportunity."

"I've been before." Ann started looking around. I could tell she'd rather be somewhere else than chatting with me.

"I hope you have a great trip. Come on, Monkey, let's go find your father."

CHAPTER 25

Maddie opened the screen door, held it with her back, and waved us in. "Welcome."

She looked great. I had to struggle to keep my eyes from wandering to the deep v of her halter top.

"I've brought Strawberry-Pretzel Salad," said Betsy.

Maddie took the dish from Betsy. "I've never had pretzel salad. Thank you. Come through to the backyard. Will's getting the grill started." Maddie led us through the house, and we went outside through a back door from her kitchen onto a covered porch.

Maddie's backyard reminded me of the neighborhood parties of my childhood in the shared lot behind our Baltimore row house. There were three portable picnic tables set up in the shade of a big tree that extended over Maddie's lawn from the yard next door and a scattering of mismatched lawn chairs. I regretted not asking if we should bring our own chairs.

Several guys holding beers were watching Will fan a stack of charcoal with a newspaper.

He waved to us and pointed to the cooler at the bottom of the steps just below where we were standing. "Grab yourself a beer."

There were beers and sodas on ice inside the cooler.

Betsy peered over my shoulder into the cooler.

"Would you like a beer or something else?"

Betsy sighed. "A Tab, I suppose."

I fished out drinks and opened them. I handed Betsy her bottle.

"No cups?"

"I think everyone is drinking from the bottle."

Betsy reached into her purse and pulled out her handkerchief to wrap around hers.

Of the others in the yard, I only recognized Claire. I led us over to where she was seated.

Claire popped out of her chair when she saw us approaching. "I've been looking forward to meeting your better half." Claire gave me a hug and then put her hand on Betsy's arm. "I'm Claire and over there is my husband Theo." She linked her other arm with mine and whisked us across the yard to where

Theo was pacing along the back fence carrying big yellow hoops.

"Theo. Stop that and come meet Nate and Betsy."

"Enchanté," he said to Betsy with a bow of his head as his hands were full of hoops and a big mesh bag was slung over his shoulder. "And good to meet you Nate. Maddie told us you were coming."

"Nice to meet you both." Betsy smiled at them and then asked me, "How do you know Claire?"

"He filled in for me curling," said Theo. "If you'll excuse me, I'm setting up the lawn darts."

"Can I help?"

Theo handed me two hoops.

Claire led Betsy back to the lawn chairs and the other women.

Theo leaned closer to me and said in a low voice, "Some people think children throwing heavy pointed objects is a good idea."

I got the sense that Theo was making a comment about Will and I liked him immediately. "Depends on who's children, I'd think."

"Take those to the edge of the garden. I think we should have all throwing away from the rest of the party."

"At least we have a surgeon on site."

"Let's hope my services aren't needed."

I placed the hoops and Theo lined up the two sets of darts in the grass a few paces away.

I saw Maddie come out of the house. She looked right at me and smiled and I thought she was going to come over to us but she turned as she stepped onto the grass and headed towards Will and the group around the grill.

Theo brushed his hands on his shorts. "That should do it. Shall we see how Will's doing with those coals?"

Betsy was seated between Claire and another woman. Both were listening intently to what she was saying and Betsy was smiling so I followed Theo.

Will had stopped fanning and had pushed the pile of ash-covered charcoal into a flatter arrangement and was setting the wire grill over the BBQ base.

Theo nudged Will. "Have we got heat yet?"

"Almost ready for Maddie to cook."

Maddie held her hand out over the BBQ. "Might need to let it go a little longer."

One of the guys I didn't know shook his head. "That's just wrong. Man makes fire. Man cooks on fire."

"Give it up Benny," said one of the others. "He ain't never gonna change."

Theo put his arm around Maddie's shoulders. "Why don't you let us do it?"

"I'm happy to relinquish the tongs to a qualified operator."

"Do you trust us?" said Benny.

Maddie's mouth curled into a mischievous grin. "You, never. The rest of you I'm not sure are sober enough." She leaned into Theo. "You're in charge. Come with me and I'll give you the burgers and dogs."

While me and the boys supervised Theo grilling, Maddie and the other women arranged the rest of the food on one of the picnic tables. They then herded the children and got them plates of food. The kids ate sitting on the porch steps and the adults sat at the other picnic tables that had been pushed together to make one long table.

I'd had a chance to meet everyone by the time we all sat down. Besides Claire and Theo, Maddie had invited the entire staff of her new company, Barry and Farley. Barry was on his own, but Farley was there with his wife and daughters. Benny, Carl and Don played hockey and baseball with Will, and they were there with their wives and children. The conversation was lively, fueled by plenty of beer and good food.

There was a transistor radio in the grass beside the picnic table.

Carl picked it up and shook it. "Does this thing play anything but Elvis songs?"

"Put that down," said his wife Janet. "It's an all Elvis tribute weekend. He died you know."

"Such a big loss," said Betsy.

"Huge," said Maddie.

"That he was," said Benny.

"Like you should talk," said Don.

"Maddie was pretty bust up about it," said Will.

"I'm glad I got to see him one more time," said Betsy.

"We saw him in Las Vegas last year," I said.

"Lucky you. I only saw him once. And almost missed that chance," said Maddie.

"Now she'll never get rid of that car," said Will.

"What car?" I asked.

"That's not why I've still got it," said Maddie.

I looked at Maddie and then Will. "There must be more to the story."

"I almost missed seeing Elvis on account of car trouble," said Maddie.

"And you still have the car? I'd think that would be a good reason for a new car."

"It wasn't my car at the time. It was my grandfather's car."

"You have your grandfather's car?"

"He gave it to me that same year."

"When was this?"

"Ages. At least 20 years."

"It's a rust bucket taking up most of the garage," said Will.

"It's a classic," said Don. "It'll be worth something someday."

"Did you see him here in Toronto?" asked Betsy.

"No. In Florida, St. Petersburg."

"Can I see the car?" I asked.

"You can't see much. It's under a tarp and other stuff."

"Go check it out," said Will. "Convince her to ditch it while you're at it."

Maddie stood up. "Anyone else coming?"

I was elated to be the only one to follow Maddie to the garage at the back of the yard. We entered it through a side door.

It took a few seconds for my eyes to adjust to the dim light. Maddie moved a couple of bicycles, a toy baby carriage, and a milk crate with rolls of used electrical wire to clear a path to the gray hulk at the back of the garage. As she pulled up the tarp from the front bumpers, a cloud of dust billowed into the air, flashing in the sunbeams that filtered through the small windows of the garage door.

"Here she is. 1955 Glass Top Vickie."

"You called your car Vickie?"

Maddie snorted. "It's a Crown Victoria, but this model, the Skyliner, was commonly referred to as a Glass Top Vickie."

"It's blue."

"Well, it was. Now mostly rust color." Maddie tugged at the tarp again to reveal a rather large rusty hole in the passenger side door.

"And you had a dead battery and it wouldn't start and you were going to miss your show."

Maddie stopped tugging the tarp. She looked at me with the scrunched-up face she always made when she was thinking carefully about what someone had just said.

"You were with a friend."

"How do you know that?"

"Because it was me that gave you a jump."

Maddie dropped the tarp and turned to face me. "You? What?"

I reached for her arm and pulled her close to me. She studied my face as if she was searching for something.

"I looked all over St. Petersburg for the girl in the blue Ford. And now I've found you."

Maddie shook her head. "It could have been someone else."

"I know it was you. It all makes sense now."

"How so?"

"Why I couldn't stop myself from wanting to be with you. You enchanted me back then and I've been waiting for you to show up ever since."

Maddie smiled. "So, you were my good Samaritan. I never did properly thank you."

"You can do it now."

"How would I do that?" Maddie's voice was a soft coo.

"You've been taunting me with that sexy outfit, and I've been wanting to kiss you all afternoon."

Maddie grinned and threw her arms around my neck and pressed her lips to mine.

I felt the warmth of her skin through my light shirt, but I felt a shiver run through me as her tongue flicked along my lower lip. I pulled her closer. Kissing her made me feel slightly dizzy and reckless. I couldn't think. I just wanted to touch every part of her. I ran my hands up her back and slipped one under the edge of her top to caress the curve of her breast.

Maddie pulled back. "We can't. Someone might…"

The side door opened, and Will's silhouette filled it. "Convince her it's junk?"

I quickly stepped backwards and tripped over the doll carriage.

Maddie grabbed on to me to steady me. "Watch out."

"Sorry I didn't see it there," I said.

"We'd have more space to move in here without it," said Will.

I was still trying to get myself sorted. I brushed at my shorts as if I was dusting myself off, trying to dissipate the bulge that had emerged with Maddie in my arms.

"He thinks it's a special car too." Maddie righted the baby carriage and then turned to pull the tarp back over the front of the car.

"Nuts," said Will, turning and leaving the garage doorway.

I took a step towards the open door so I could see out of it. Will was already back at the house, rummaging in the cooler getting beers.

I took Maddie's hand and gave it a quick kiss. "You know this means we were always supposed to meet."

"Should we tell them you were my hero?"

"Maybe not. Our secret."

"One of many." Maddie winked and walked past me out into the sun.

CHAPTER 26

The reception clerk handed me a key. "Welcome to the Waterloo Inn, Ms. Cole. Do you need help with your luggage?"

"No. Thank you."

"Your room is on the second floor. Please let us know if you need anything."

I didn't expect to need anything tonight except some quiet time to read. I'd had an early dinner with Anne before making the two-hour drive there. I had a stack of papers in my briefcase I wanted to review before attending the meeting at the university the next morning.

I unpacked my bag and hung up my outfits for the next two days and couldn't help feeling a little proud to be there. It was a real coup for our nascent company to have landed a seat at the table with the Ministry of the Environment task force developing guidelines for site investigations. Making the most of this opportunity was important to me, although, much of the credit for getting it belonged to Farley.

It was his wife, not my hiring savvy, that was the reason Farley Bolden became my partner. She desperately wanted to move back to Canada when Farley finished his post-doctoral work at the University of Illinois and pushed him to find something in Ontario near her family rather than move back to his hometown of Calgary.

A chance meeting at a Bond Global sponsored event on best practices for environmental health and safety was our first connection. He was a speaker, and we kept in touch after the event. He graciously provided advice and pointed me to research publications. Over the span of a few months, we became good friends. When I mentioned starting a firm focused on environmental assessments and monitoring, he'd come right out and asked me if I'd consider him for a partner.

I'd told Barry Bonville, the field technologist I'd worked closely with for years, I was considering leaving DB to start my own firm. I asked him if he would consider joining me. To my surprise, he'd said yes. It had all happened so fast. The ink was barely dry on the funding agreement with Franklin's bank, and Cole Civil Environmental Engineering already had employees two and three hired.

Farley and Barry were an incredible team. Barry knew everything there was to know about sampling, drilling, blasting, and earth moving, and Farley was an expert in the little-known field of hydrogeology. Whenever they were together, they couldn't help discussing ideas for some new gizmo or method to get better samples and data.

It helped that the Deputy Minister of the MOE was impressed by Farley's credentials. He'd worked as a petroleum geologist in Alberta before doing a master's and PhD studying hydrocarbons in groundwater. But we'd earned our place at the meeting because of the innovative work we'd done for our first major client. An introduction from Franklin led us to investigate sites with underground storage tanks across the province for a major chain of gas stations. We'd investigated more than two dozen locations and had discovered petroleum products in the subsurface at every one. Even though my company was less than a year old, we'd garnered the attention of the MOE staff because they'd seen the reports we'd submitted on behalf of our client. They'd been impressed with the way we'd documented our findings and our proposals for site remediation.

Work and projects were plentiful. Referrals from MOE staff were the only advertising CCE Engineering needed. We needed to hire at least one more geologist just to keep up. I planned to ask the University of Waterloo professors at the meeting if they had any promising students looking for a job in the Toronto area.

I was a bundle of nervous energy, and I needed to do something before I could settle in to read. I called home.

Anne answered the phone. "Hello, this is Anne Tobias speaking."

"Hi Monkey. Everything ok?"

"Ya."

"Where's your father?"

"Outside."

"It's time for you to be getting ready for bed."

"He said I could watch...."

"It's past 8:30. Bedtime."

"I was waiting for Daddy to come in."

"What's he doing?"

"Talking to someone."

"Who?"

"I don't know."

"Go tell him I'm on the phone."

"K."

I heard thumping, and I envisioned the cord stretching as the receiver dangled and swung where Anne had abandoned it to go summon Will.

I heard her voice in the distance. "Dad. Mom's on the phone."

I couldn't hear Will's response, but I did hear the front door bang.

"He's coming," said Anne.

"I guess you should run up, brush your teeth, get ready for bed."

"Ok."

"Don't forget you're going to Rosa's after school tomorrow and she'll bring you home and make dinner."

"I know."

"Love you, Monkey. Sweet dreams."

"Love you Ma. Here's Dad."

Will came on the line. "What's up?"

"I called to say goodnight to Anne."

"She's gone up now."

"Who were you talking to?"

"A friend dropped by."

"Who?"

"Keeley."

"Who's Keeley?"

"You know. Anne's ringette coach."

"Why was she here."

"She wanted to ask me a question."

"And she couldn't call?"

"She was in the neighbourhood."

"What about?"

"Huh?"

"What did she ask?"

"She has a broken light."

It wasn't unusual for people to ask Will about electrical things, but this was a bit odd.

"Sounds like an excuse. What did she really want?"

"She did ask if I could run practice this week. She has some couples thing with her husband."

"You were going to be there anyway." I wasn't surprised. Keeley struck me as a bit ditzy.

"Ya."

"Make sure you remind Anne to go to Rosa's after school. Her lunch for tomorrow is made, but you'll have to make her one for Thursday."

"Can't Rosa do it?"

"I think you can manage."

Will grunted. "Ok. See you Friday."

I said goodnight to Will and hung up. I wasn't feeling any more settled, but I forced myself to sit down at the desk and start reading. I started with the recommendation report Farley had prepared to present tomorrow. I rehearsed my sections. I would talk about our phased approach to site investigations and Farley would present the recommended sampling protocols and discuss the mistakes that could result in unintended contamination pathways. To make sure I had all the facts handy, I skimmed the abstracts for the papers we'd referenced and underlined the key points.

I was as prepared as I was going to be, so I decided to quit. I put on my pyjamas, brushed my teeth, put on the TV, and propped myself up on the bed. The silliness of Three's Company was just what I needed to let my mind relax, and I started to doze.

The hotel phone startled me awake. I answered it.

"Did I wake you?"

My heart did a little somersault at the sound of Nate's voice. "I don't think so. But I am in bed."

"Our favourite place."

"I thought your favourite was the parking lot behind the Country Squire?"

"That's a favourite too."

"And Coronation Park?"

"Also a favourite."

"I'm starting to think everywhere we do it is your favourite."

"Because you're my favourite."

"There really haven't been a lot of beds lately."

"That's why I'm calling."

"Because you have a bed in mind?"

"Yes. The one you're in now."

"But I'm alone in this bed."

"Would you prefer to not be?"

"That depends."

"On what?"

"On who."

"Me?"

"That seems unlikely. Unless you're calling from the lobby."

"What if I was?"

"I'd unlock the door."

"Then maybe you should."

"You're here?"

"Is that ok?"

"You can explain when you get here. Room 207." I hung up and hopped out of bed. I brushed my hair before going to the door to peer out the peephole at the hallway. When I saw Nate, I opened the door.

"Hello, Gorgeous." Nate pulled me into his arms and kissed me. His overcoat was damp and I could feel how cold his hands were through the thin cotton of my pyjamas.

"You're soaked."

"It's nasty out. Freezing rain."

"You shouldn't be out."

"I'm in now."

I took Nate's coat and hung it up to dry. "But why are you in Waterloo.?"

"I had a meeting in Guelph. I told Betsy I would get a room because at the last minute, my plant manager invited me to dinner and it's freezing rain and the roads are nasty."

"So you drove here?" I shook my head and gave him a scolding look.

"I took a chance you'd let me stay."

"I have a big meeting tomorrow. You can't be keeping me up all night."

Nate took my hand and led me toward the bed. "Then I'll just tuck you in and be on my way."

"I don't think so." I spun around. Catching him off guard, my tackle knocked him onto the bed and I pounced on him.

Nate grinned up at me. "I guess I'll stay then."

I rolled off him, snuggled up beside him and kissed his cheek. "Good idea."

"I know tomorrow's important. I just didn't want to miss a chance to see you."

"You're just randy."

"We can just talk."

"We talk every day."

"We can just sleep then."

I reached for his tie and tugged at it to loosen it. "You should get undressed. You'll get all wrinkly."

Nate sat up, took off his shoes, and then got up and placed them near the door. I scooted myself back to where I'd been propped up on pillows and watched him take off his jacket and tie like I'd watched the TV. Nate undressed down to his briefs and undershirt. He hung everything in the closet and then reached into the pocket of his overcoat and took out a Shoppers Drug Mart bag.

"I stopped to buy a toothbrush. Can I use your toothpaste?"

I nodded. "It's in the bathroom."

While I waited for him to brush his teeth, I got up and shut off the TV and the overhead light and put on the lamp on the nightstand. I fluffed up and rearranged the pillows on the bed, and turned down the bedspread. As thrilled as I was to have some time with Nate, the timing wasn't great. I needed to be up and out first thing in the morning. I remembered I hadn't requested a wake-up call.

Nate came out of the bathroom. "What time do you need to be up tomorrow?"

"I was just about to call for a wake-up call. I was thinking 6:30."

"I'll need to leave by 6:30. Better make it 6."

I picked up the receiver and dialed.

Nate came up behind me. His hands slid over my hips and around my waist and started kissing the back of my neck while I was giving the operator my request.

I hung up and turned to face him. "I thought you said we could just sleep?"

"Then let's get into bed." Nate pulled back the covers and slipped into the bed.

I stood over him with my hands on my hips. "You're on my side."

Nate slid across the bed to the far side and lay on his side looking back at me. He patted the mattress. "Get in here."

I crawled in and, with my back to him, melded my body into his.

He ran his fingertips along my thigh and up my side until he got to my shoulder. He tugged it and I twisted so my face turned up toward his.

He leaned in and brushed his lips over mine. As many times as we kissed, it never ceased to make me tingle. It's like my skin came alive. His slightest touch magnified, sending shock waves to my core.

I rolled over so I could get more leverage to kiss him back. Our lips were simultaneously hungrier. His moving from kissing my lips to along my jaw and under my chin. I gulped for air as he buried his face in my neck.

I wrapped my leg over his and clung to him. "This is so much better than making out in a car."

He made an affirmative sound that vibrated on my skin as his mouth nibbled along my collarbone to the top button of my pajama top.

I reached for the button and tugged it open.

His lips lifted off my skin. "Just one?"

A brief scramble out of our clothing and I was on my back, and he was draped over me. Our full bodies kissed as our naked skin connected from our lips to our toes. I could feel his hardness against my thigh and the wetness between my legs intensify.

Nate slithered downward until his face was over my breasts. He cupped them in his hands and ran his thumbs over them and around my nipples.

"Magnificent," he said.

I couldn't help but chuckle. "Are you talking to my breasts or to me?"

He looked up. His eyes locked on mine. "You are, they are, being with you… all magnificent."

"This feels magnificent."

"Then I should continue." His mouth curled into a grin. "To explore this magnificence."

He gave my breasts an appreciative fondle, and he took my nipple between his lips and gave it a gentle flick with his tongue. His kisses then followed his hands down my body. I closed my eyes so I could feel everything clearer: his lips tasting my skin, the prickle of his sideburns on my thighs, the flood of warmth as his tongue swirled and probed. He had me twisting with pleasure. I reached down and ran my fingers through his hair as the burst of energy engulfed me and released the tension, but intensified my desire to feel him inside me.

He needed no instruction. He rose onto his knees and patted my thigh. I flipped over and backed myself onto him. His hands were on my hips, but he stayed quite still letting me take control of the pace and depth until I was gasping once again.

I looked over my shoulder at him. "Take me."

With that he rolled me over again. He grabbed my wrists and held my arms against the mattress. His desire for me was palpable. I could feel him reaching his peak.

"Oh God. I love you."

His outburst made me smile.

We stayed tangled together. My heart was boiling with the closeness of that moment. My mind still unable to focus, flooded with the intense sensations from every nerve in my body.

Nate began to unwind from our embrace. "You know I didn't come for amazing sex."

I laughed. "Of course, you did."

"Ok, I didn't just come for amazing sex."

"Really? What did you come for?"

He was lying on his side, and he wiggled closer to me and put his head on my shoulder. "So I can wake up beside you."

His words were sweet, but he wasn't divulging what I wanted to know. "Why do you want that?"

He walked his fingertips up the midline of my body, up over my mouth, and tapped me on the nose. "Because it feels right to."

It did feel right when we were alone together, but we had to maintain two different versions of ourselves. The one that was all right and the one that felt right. It was all right to be respected colleagues who became friends and now share a social circle. It felt right when we could talk and touch without holding back.

Nate brushed a strand of hair from my forehead. "That beautiful mind is buzzing. You have a big day tomorrow."

"It's not that."

"Then what?"

"How long can we keep doing this?"

"You don't want to stop. Do you?" Nate sat up and his eyes searched my face for understanding.

"No. It's more like… I want us to be more. But…" I sat up and pulled the bedsheet to cover myself. "You aren't free."

"I'm not the only one. But we'll make it work. We have to."

"How can this ever work if we have to stay in the shadows."

"Because I love you."

I felt like a giant rock had been dropped on my stomach. He'd used the word love before. He'd signed "Love Nate" in a letter he'd sent me from Paris while on a business trip and he'd exclaimed it on occasion during sex. But this was a different profession of it. He was looking into my eyes, and I could feel that he meant it in the most profound sense of the word.

I leaned into him and kissed him. "We are in so much trouble."

He looked confused.

"I love you too. It's a problem."

A smile spread across his face. "A troublesome problem with only one solution… Make the most of times like these."

I rolled my eyes and shook my head at him. "And how do you propose we do that?"

Nate pushed me back down onto the bed. "I'll show you."

He kissed me hard, and I didn't want to think. I just wanted him to make love to me.

And he did.

CHAPTER 27

I couldn't help myself. I turned into the parking lot to check for Maddie's car. It was there; in the first space beside the plain-looking door of the square industrial building on Speers Road, where she'd rented space for CCE Environmental. I parked beside her car and sat there for a moment debating whether I should go in. It was just a little after six and it was possible some of her staff would still be there since she was. If they were, I'd need a plausible reason to be stopping by. I took my briefcase with me to the door so it would look like I was there on business.

The door was unlocked. The lobby lights were off and the desk where Ruby, the gal Maddie had hired as both her secretary and the company receptionist, was empty. I walked towards the glow coming from Maddie's open office door.

Maddie was sitting at her desk writing.

I knocked on the doorframe of her office. "Good evening, Ms. Cole."

Maddie jolted and sat up abruptly. "Oh my God! Don't sneak up on me like that."

"Are you here alone?"

Maddie nodded. "I have a proposal to finish."

"You should lock the door."

"I haven't budged from my desk since everyone left."

"I wouldn't want strange men sneaking in here."

"You mean like you?"

"I'm not a stranger."

"You said strange." Maddie flashed that mischievous grin that I found so irresistible.

"So now I'm strange? Hmmm. Do you treat all your clients with such disrespect?"

"Only the ones I really like." Maddie got up from her chair and put her arms around my neck and leaned in to kiss me.

I was glad that I continued to have access to Maddie professionally. I'd been pleasantly surprised at how amicable Maddie's departure from DB Engineering had been. As she'd explained it, they recognized that they had passed on her idea because they didn't want to take on the risk of a new business line but were interested in partnering with her for projects for DB clients who needed environmental services.

I put my arms around her and hugged her closer. "I like the personal service you provide."

Maddie pulled away and sat back at her desk, and pointed to a chair. "What brings you to my office today Mr. Jacobs?"

"Personal business only. I saw your car and I thought I'd stop in."

"Always a pleasure."

"I didn't think you'd be here. I was surprised to see your car."

"I'll be here for a while. I've got three proposals to write so Ruby can type them up and send them out tomorrow."

"You don't have time to go for a drink?"

"Not tonight. I'll be here for a while. Likely raiding the office snacks for dinner."

"I could bring you dinner. Pizza?"

"There's pizza at my house right now for Anne. I might get a cold piece later."

"So not expected home for dinner?"

"I knew I'd be late today."

"How about you work, and I'll get us dinner and bring it here?"

Maddie agreed and I rolled into action. If I'd known ahead of time, I would have planned something. I'd told Maddie that Betsy would be in Florida visiting her parents this week, but she hadn't suggested we plan to see each other. I'd assumed that meant she had obligations, not that she would be working late at her office only two miles from my home.

I was delighted her business was taking off, but the more successful she was, the harder it was for us to find time to be together. We still talked every day. Sometimes more than once. But I wanted her in my arms. I wanted to kiss her and touch her skin. For that, we needed time alone together, and there was never enough of that.

I pulled into our driveway and hurried into the house. I got out the phone book and dialed the number for Shelley's. I ordered and then went to the cellar to get a bottle of wine. I packed the wine, plates, cutlery and glasses and headed out to pick up the food and get back to Maddie.

I let myself into the office with the key Maddie had given me so I could lock the door behind me. I set up dinner for us in the small breakroom that also functioned as their conference room. I was just opening the wine when Maddie appeared in the doorway.

"You didn't have to go to this much trouble."

"There's nothing I wouldn't do for you."

Maddie sat down at the table, shook out her napkin, and placed it in her lap. "Nothing? I know that's not true. But thank you for bringing dinner. I'm starving." Although she smiled at me and I knew she wasn't angry, her words stung.

"If you weren't so independent, I could do more to help."

Maddie took the lid off the container of chowder and dropped in a few crackers. "I don't need more help."

"So, more sex?"

Maddie grinned. "That would be good. But no."

"Tell me what you need."

Maddie looked down and stirred her soup and gave a little snort.

"Are you upset with me?"

"No. I'm more upset with me. I don't like needing anyone for anything. And then you happened."

"I'm here, aren't I?"

"Only because Betsy is away."

"I'm not the only one with… complications."

"I know. That's why I'm not upset with you." Maddie was still focused on drowning oyster crackers in her bowl.

I took a big gulp of my wine. "You know I wish I could be with you always."

"Do I?" Maddie's voice had a bitter edge that made my heart ache.

"What do you want from me? From us?"

"I don't know. Sometimes it just hits me. How good it feels when I'm with you."

"I know that feeling."

"Then why do you stay with Betsy?"

There wasn't a simple answer to that question. I'd made the decision to marry her and at the time, it seemed like the right thing to do. Giving up on that commitment would disappoint everyone and make a god-awful mess of all of our lives.

Maddie didn't wait for me to answer. "I'm just so frustrated at how impossible our situation is."

"But we can make the best of the time we have."

Maddie let out a noisy exhale. "Ok. Let's start over. Thank you for bringing dinner. The chowder is great."

I lifted my glass. "To us. To you. To the best of times."

We ate our dinner, avoiding the topic of our relationship. Maddie told me about her plans to expand her staff and the negotiations with her landlord to modify the garage bay at the back of her unit with an insulated workshop and storage area. I updated her on the latest acquisition she'd done some assessment work on and let her know that we had more work coming her way.

"I'll make sure to put my best person on it." Maddie got up and started clearing the empty takeout containers from the table.

"I think as client number one, we should expect nothing less." I poured the last of the wine into our glasses.

Maddie sat back down and took a sip of her wine. "Ah, but you've slipped. You're no longer our biggest client."

I got up and moved to stand over her. "Longest standing client status mean anything?"

Maddie looked up and raised one eyebrow. "Shall we see about that?" Maddie reached for the buckle on my belt and pulled me closer as she tugged the leather through and undid it.

I gripped the back of her chair to steady myself as I watched her open my fly. Her touch had my full attention, and I felt the rush of anticipation of what she might do next.

She leaned her face closer to my groin as she freed me from my briefs. She looked up at me and grinned as she brushed her cheek against my skin and hovered her mouth near my tip.

"Is this what you meant by longest standing?" Her voice had changed to a sultry purr, and she flicked her tongue.

The sensation of wetness on my tip made me gasp and my knees tremble. I wanted to feel her mouth on me, and she knew it. She wrapped her fingers around me and guided me in. I reached down for her hair and tangled my fingers in it as she toyed with me, sucking me in, then releasing me and running her fingers and tongue along my shaft before taking me in again. I tried not to force myself into her mouth, but I couldn't help but lean in. She had me slick, and her hand and mouth worked in unison. I could feel the tension peaking. As I released, she sucked and swallowed, sending even greater shock waves through me.

I was still gasping as she looked up at me and licked her lips. "I thought I'd have a little dessert since you didn't bring any."

I pulled her up from her chair and kissed her. "You're something else."

She pressed her hip against me and her eyes sparkled with mischief. "Isn't that the service you wanted?"

I shook my head. "My goal was to do something nice for you this evening." I reached for the top button of her blouse.

"Dinner was great." She reached down and tucked me back into my pants. 'Now put that away. I need to get back to work."

As much as I wanted to keep touching her, I obliged and straightened myself up while she gathered up the dishes and carried them to the small sink.

I followed her. "I'll clean those up. You get back to work."

Maddie turned and threw her arms around my neck. "You know I'd rather be making love to you right there on that table."

"You're an evil temptress. I will if you don't stop being so… irresistible." I pinned her against the counter and kissed her.

She answered with her lips nibbling and tugging mine. I could feel my heart pounding and blood rushing from my brain, making me forget about dishes or work. In seconds, she'd cast her spell on me and the only thing I wanted was more of this.

She moved her hands to my shoulders and pried us apart. "We can't."

I swallowed my disappointment. "Ok. You work. Me dishes."

Maddie left, and I washed and dried the items I'd brought from home and packed them up. I wiped down the table and crushed the takeout containers into the trashcan so the lid closed properly. With the breakroom tidy, I put on my jacket and went to say goodbye to Maddie.

I watched her work for a few seconds from the doorway of her office. She was tapping on the calculator on her desk and writing down figures.

"Do you think you'll be much longer?"

She put down her pencil and stood up and walked towards me. "I'll be a while. I still have one more proposal to finish up."

I took one of her hands and pulled her closer. I ran my other hand across her cheek and through her hair. Brushing it back over her shoulder. "Will you call me tonight to let me know you got home ok?"

"I probably won't be able to talk. I could call before I leave here."

"I don't want you to stay later than you have to. Just call. We don't have to talk. I just want to know you're safe."

Maddie agreed, and she followed me to the front door so she could lock it behind me.

I stepped back and blocked her from closing the door. "You know I could stay and just watch you work."

"You'd be distracting." She gave me a little shove to move me through the door.

I pushed back. "Maybe I could help."

"Do you type?"

"Slowly."

"Then you won't be much help. Get going."

"Can I just say one thing?"

"Just one."

"Time with you is always the best part of my day. I wish I didn't have to leave."

"That's two things."

"Both true."

Maddie gave me another playful push. "I love you too. Now go."

148

CHAPTER 28

Theo took our coats, and Claire ushered Will and me into the living room. Claire's Christmas decorations were always elegant and abundant, but for her New Year's Eve party, she'd added a whole new dimension. The room was sparkling with dozens of candles in tall holders that reflected off a huge drape of gold lamé fabric that hung from the ceiling, over and behind her enormous grandfather clock that she'd placed prominently at the front of the room. On a table by the door, there were fancy hats, tiaras, and boas for the guests to wear should they want to embellish their outfits.

She'd been planning this party for months. Back in September, when our supper club was gathered at her house, the conversation had drifted into a discussion of the messes around the world of the past few years. We bemoaned the oil crisis, the mess in Vietnam, Watergate, the Beatles break up, Three Mile Island, and wage and price controls... just to name a few.

Claire didn't like all the negativity. "Enough. We need to start the new decade off right. We need to have a farewell party."

We all agreed that the seventies should have a proper send-off and Claire insisted on hosting a party to usher in 1980.

The living room was already quite full. Claire and Theo had invited friends from the curling club, Theo's medical colleagues, their bridge club and, of course, our supper club. I knew most of the guests, but I noticed Nate and Betsy were standing by the bar with a couple I didn't recognize. A server dressed in black was making drinks.

Will pointed to them. "Shall we get in line for a drink?" He didn't wait for my answer but made a beeline for the bar.

He put his arm around Nate. "Happy New Year, Jacobs." He turned to Betsy and gave her a peck on the cheek. "You too, Bets."

Betsy slid her gloved hand through Will's arm. "It seems you're everywhere we go these days." She was referring to the fundraiser for the Oakville Art Society that she had organized with local artists exhibiting holiday-themed artwork.

"Betcha didn't think my kind swam in the same ponds as you folk, eh?" Will played up his Eastern Ontario accent.

I didn't hear Betsy's answer, but she was smiling, so I figured they were playing out their usual rich girl, poor boy banter.

That they got along so well made it easier for Nate and me to do things together. They'd even rented a cottage alongside ours last summer. I'd worried they'd be uncomfortable because we'd rented the same cottages with the same group of friends for several years in a row. But, as it turned out, Betsy had more in common with the other wives than I ever did, and she masterfully assumed the role of queen bee before the week was over.

Nate gave Will a pat on the back and then turned to me and gave me a hug. As he did he whispered in my ear. "You look yummy."

As I pulled back, he slipped his hand up my side and under my breast. It could have been an accidental touch, but I knew it wasn't. I checked to make sure Will and Betsy were still facing the other way and then I looked at Nate and mouthed, "Behave."

Nate grinned and gave a nod that made me think there would be more misbehaving before the night was over. I couldn't help but smile because I too wanted to misbehave with him. Being near him had that effect on me.

Nate turned and nodded toward the couple he and Betsy had been speaking to when we'd arrived. "Do you know Mike and Joan Williams?"

"I don't."

"Then let me introduce you."

He introduced us. They had met before because Joan and Betsy both volunteered with the Oakville Arts Society. Mike was a hand surgeon at St. Michael's Hospital; thus, they were also friends with Claire and Theo.

"Small world, eh?' said Mike after I'd explained our connections to both Claire and Nate.

Our conversation was interrupted by the sound of a bell. It came from the front of the room near the grandfather clock. Claire was standing on a chair trying to get everyone's attention.

"Welcome everyone. I hope you have a lovely evening as we bid farewell to the seventies and welcome in a new decade. I encourage you all to eat, drink and be merry. But Theo and I would like to suggest that this evening is also a time to think about the year ahead and to make promises to yourself about the things you want to add to your life and the things you want to leave behind. You are all our dear friends, and we hope you will encourage one another to live your best year yet by sharing with each other the things you're looking forward to in the coming year." She waved to Theo to come stand beside her.

Theo raised his glass. "We want to propose the first toast. To the last night of the year and the first night of the next and best one for all of you."

There was a chorus of "Here, here," and glasses clinking. The rumble of conversation picked up again as two waitresses appeared with large trays of hors d'oeuvres.

Will handed me my drink. Betsy introduced him to Joan and Mike and then the six of us helped ourselves to the passing canapés and stood in a group nibbling and drinking.

"I know what's going to make my year," said Mike. "We're going to the Winter Olympics."

Joan hip bumped her husband. "He's been determined to go to a Winter Olympics after we went to the Montreal games."

Mike shrugged. "I caught Olympic fever."

"We're taking the whole family," said Joan.

"No plane tickets needed. It was the ideal scenario," said Mike.

'It's not a bad drive to Lake Placid," said Will.

"That's the plan. Pack the kids in the car and drive straight through," said Mike.

I knew that drive well. "I've got a project going in Cornwall. I'm practically there every month."

"Our daughter Anne loves watching sports. She's my little athlete," said Will.

"You should definitely take her," said Nate. "You should all go. Especially since Maddie has to be out that way anyway."

I wasn't sure how I felt about Nate suggesting family vacations for us. "Are you planning on going too?"

Betsy wagged her index finger back and forth. "No. No. No. Getting through the winter is bad enough."

"Betsy gets cold watching on TV." Nate looked at Betsy and she gave him a nod.

"Lots of events are inside; skating, hockey…" said Mike.

Betsy shook her head. "I had to endure hockey games when he had season tickets in Boston."

"You only went to a few games."

"A few too many."

"Maddie's folks have Leafs tickets." Will nudged me. "I wish your mother didn't like hockey. We might get'em more often."

"The stadiums are so cold." Betsy wrapped her arms around herself as if she was cold.

"Mother wears her fur coat," I said.

"I did too. But that didn't help my feet," said Betsy.

"Sounds like you're a solid no for Lake Placid," said Joan to Betsy. "So, what are you two looking forward to for next year?"

"Ann completes her bachelor's degree, and we are taking her to Europe," said Betsy.

"Oh yes. You've mentioned it. The trip to all the great cities and galleries."

"Of course, we've all been before. But now she has her art history degree, so we'll both be prepared to appreciate it."

I felt like Betsy was bragging and it irked me. "Graduating already? Just a three-year degree then?"

"Yes. And she has excellent grades."

"What does one do with a three-year art history degree?" asked Mike.

"She's met a nice young man, Brandon. He's from a good family. I think she'll be fine." Betsy's answer wasn't a surprise to me. I knew Nate had been troubled that Betsy was more concerned about Ann marrying well than preparing her for a career.

"We're going to have dinner at his parents' home next weekend before the kids go back to school," said Nate.

"Is this your first time meeting them?" I knew it wasn't, but I asked the question anyway.

"We've met socially on a number of occasions. Gloria and Henry are active philanthropists and major donors to the Art Society." Betsy couldn't resist name-dropping. I knew Nate was irritated by it.

"The first time we've been invited to their home. It's a family dinner for Brandon's birthday," said Nate.

"Sounds like things are getting serious," said Will. "Start saving for that wedding."

Nate frowned and downed the last of his beer. "I hope that's not it. Anyone need a refill?"

While Nate was getting another beer, Mike went back to talking to Will about their plans for the Olympics and making suggestions about things that we should do if we went. I got pulled into a conversation with Claire and several of the ladies from the curling club and I ended up in the kitchen with them, looking at Claire's copy of our schedule.

When I returned, I saw Will talking with Theo, but I didn't see Nate or Betsy. Betsy would never leave a party without properly thanking the host and hostess and I'd been with Claire, so I didn't think they'd left. My first thought was that they'd slipped away to be alone together. I was envious that she had the option. It's what I would like, a few minutes alone with Nate.

As our relationship intensified, so had my conflicting emotions whilst spending time together with our spouses. We got to see each other more often than we would if we only met privately, but we had to endure seeing each other with someone else.

On occasions like this, we had to pretend we were nothing more than friends. In private, we could openly express our true feelings without restraint. We could touch. We could say, "I love you." We allowed ourselves to believe that we belonged together. That sparkling crystal vision of what we were to each other would shatter whenever Betsy placed her hand possessively on Nate's arm and gushed about her husband's success or their dazzling daughter.

I'd initially disregarded Nate's assertions that we were destined to meet. He'd been adamant that, from the first time we met, he knew he wanted to get to know me, and the more he did, the more he wanted to know. I don't remember the exact moment when things changed for me, but my secret wish for the new decade was that somehow, we'd find a way to be together.

CHAPTER 29

We were dwarfed by the large white pillars that framed the entrance to Gloria and Henry's home. Although I'd passed the Lakeshore Road estate many times, I was astonished at the size that wasn't evident until you'd passed through the front gate and approached the house.

Ann skipped up the front steps and reached for the doorknob.

Betsy pulled her arm back. "We can't just walk in."

"They're expecting us. And it's cold." She gave a disgruntled snort but rang the bell and stood back with us and waited.

A uniformed woman in a black dress and white apron opened the door.

"Good evening. Please come in."

"Hi Greta," said Ann. "Mother, Dad this is Greta. Greta my parents Nate and Betsy."

"Pleasure to meet you, Mrs. Jacobs, Mr. Jacobs," said Greta.

Ann popped off her boots and slipped past Greta just as Gloria came toward us from the rear of the house.

Ann held open the bag she was carrying. "Where should I put these?"

"We'll do gifts in the library after dinner," said Gloria.

Ann disappeared off to the right.

Gloria motioned us in. "Welcome. So lovely you could join us."

Betsy handed her fur coat to Greta but looked at Gloria. "Thank you for inviting us. These are for you." She handed her the yellow and blue wrapped box of candy.

Gloria looked pleased. "Ann spreading rumors about my Laura Secord addiction? You needn't have brought anything, but thank you." Gloria looked behind Betsy at Greta and her face clouded. She reached for Betsy's coat. "I'll take that. Thank you for getting the door for me, Greta." Then she turned to me. "Give me yours too. Come through, we're in the kitchen."

Gloria headed towards the rear of the house, stopping to hang our coats in a closet tucked under one of the pair of staircases that coiled up to the second floor. She turned and called up toward the walkway over our heads. "Henry. They're here."

The kitchen was swarming with activity.

I spotted Brandon. He was lifting a blender out of a cupboard.

He waved. "Hello Mr. Jacobs, Mrs. Jacobs. Hollandaise emergency."

Ann's head was in the fridge, and she emerged with a carton of eggs and a lemon. "Birthday boy wants Hollandaise."

I'd never seen Ann cook anything that didn't come from a can or a box, so I was concerned she was attempting Hollandaise. I was even more surprised when she handed the eggs to Brandon, who started separating them and dropping the yolks in the jar of the blender like a pro.

Henry came in behind us and patted me on the shoulder. "Welcome to the Hartwell Zoo, Nate, and you too, Betsy."

I handed him the brown paper bag with the top-shelf bottle of bourbon I'd picked up at Duty Free the last time I'd been in the States. "This is for you. Ann told me you liked whisky, so I thought I'd supply some of the Yankee version for your collection."

He pulled out the bottle. "Thanks Nate. This is super. Shall we crack into it?"

"I'm more of a beer guy."

"Then a beer it is. Betsy, can I get you a drink?"

Betsy declined. I followed Henry around the corner to a large butler's pantry between the kitchen and dining room.

He opened a large glass-fronted refrigerator. "Molson, Labatt's or my favorite, Henninger."

"I'll try a Henninger if you can spare it."

"Anything for AJ's dad."

Hearing Henry refer to my daughter by a nickname I'd never heard before was a little disturbing.

Back in the kitchen, everyone was busy doing something except Betsy. She had that soft smile and she was clutching the handle of her purse with both hands. It was a stance that meant either she was uncomfortable or disapproving, or maybe both.

Ann was watching Brandon pour melted butter into the blender. Gloria was peeling boiled potatoes and Greta was mashing them. Charlotte, their youngest daughter, was arranging fruit on a tray and Audrey, the eldest, was putting out serving dishes.

I set my beer on the counter. "What can I do to help?"

Greta pointed the potato masher at me. "You take over mashing. I'll start the gravy."

I rolled up my sleeves and took my place beside Gloria.

She plopped another potato into the bowl. "I hope you like Beef Wellington."

"Sounds wonderful."

"Brandon's choice. We always let the birthday boy, or girl, choose what's for dinner on their day."

Brandon came to the sink beside us. "As it should be. It's only one day a year." He filled a pot with warm water and set the blender jar with the Hollandaise in it.

"Do you have any family birthday traditions?" asked Gloria.

Birthdays were the same as other days. Ann and Betsy decided what we would do, and I didn't get a say. I didn't say that, just answered, "Nothing in particular. It changes with my girls' whims."

We all finished up our tasks and hovered around the large island in the center of the kitchen, chatting.

"Ok. Everyone, out," said Greta.

I watched Brandon take Ann's hand as we all moved to the dining room, and he led her to a seat beside him.

"Where would you like us to sit?" Betsy asked Gloria.

"Anywhere you'd like."

Betsy didn't move.

Henry pulled out the chair next to where he was standing at the head of the table. "How about here Betsy?"

Betsy sat, and I slid her chair in before taking the seat beside her.

Henry made the rounds of the table, pouring everyone but Charlotte a glass of wine. He poured ginger ale into her wine glass instead. Then he stood by his chair at the head of the table.

"We must first have a toast to the birthday boy. Twenty-two may not be a major milestone year in the traditional sense, nonetheless, today we all wish you an extraordinary year ahead. Happy Birthday, Brandon. Cheers."

We toasted and as soon as our glasses hit the table, Greta appeared with a large tray filled with salad plates. It was a Waldorf salad served in a cup made from a lettuce leaf and it was delicious.

We had just finished our salads when Charlotte began teasing Brandon.

"I guess you won't be hanging out with the princess in St. Moritz this year since AJs coming."

Brandon glared at his little sister. "Really Charlotte. Now?"

"What's this about St. Moritz?" I asked.

Ann looked at Gloria and then at Henry.

"We've invited Ann to come with us skiing during reading week. With your permission, of course," said Gloria.

Ann leaned forward in her chair and looked back and forth between Betsy and me.

I looked at Betsy to gauge her response.

"This is the first we've heard of it," said Betsy.

"We don't mean to put you on the spot," said Henry. "We've reserved an extra room, just in case AJ will be joining us."

"Where will you be staying?" asked Betsy.

Charlotte answered. "We always stay at Badrutt's Palace."

I'd never heard of it, but it sounded expensive. I was already putting aside a small fortune for our summer trip to Europe. I made a good living, but funds were not unlimited.

"We'd cover Ann's trip and accommodations. She will be our guest."

"And ski lessons," said Brandon. "We know an excellent private instructor, if you're worried about that."

Betsy stiffened. "That isn't necessary. If she goes, we wouldn't expect you to pay for her."

I didn't want to get into negotiations about who was paying for what at the dinner table. "Would it be alright if we had a chance to discuss this as a family and get back to you?"

"Why can't you just say yes? It's only a week." Ann's face was slightly flushed, and I got the impression we were embarrassing her.

Gloria raised her hand slightly towards Ann and then looked at us. "Whatever you decide is fine. Know that we will take care of her as if she was one of our daughters."

"That's very reassuring," said Betsy. "I think it's a wonderful opportunity for Ann. Don't you, dear?" She looked at me and I knew she had decided to take Ann's side.

I gave in. "If Ann wants to go skiing instead of going to Florida to see her grandparents, then I'm alright with it."

Ann's face burst into a big smile. "Thank you."

Brandon put his arm around her and pulled her sideways into him. "Best birthday present. It's gonna be a blast."

Later, on the way home, Ann leaned forward from the back seat of the car. "Didn't I tell you they're super neat."

"You're blinded by your infatuation for Brandon." Betsy's tone was condescending.

"I'm not."

"So you didn't see how they let the help boss your father around? Telling him to mash the potatoes."

"Greta's not the help. She's been with them forever. They love her."

"They shouldn't let the staff talk to guests like that."

I knew I shouldn't comment, but I did anyway. "I wasn't offended. I wanted to help."

"See. Dad gets it."

"With his upbringing, he doesn't know any better."

Her words stung, but I said nothing.

"Mother! You sound like a snob."

"Me? All that business about paying for you. Do they think we're poor?"

"The Hartwells are super kind and generous. That's all."

"We don't need their generosity. We'll pay your share. Won't we?"

I nodded, but I wasn't sure what that would mean and how I was going to do it.

"You just let us know the travel plans and we'll buy your tickets."

Ann sat back and huffed. "You can't buy a ticket on their plane."

"What do you mean, their plane?"

"I mean we're flying to Switzerland on their plane."

I wondered how rich you needed to be to have your own plane. It would be wonderful to be able to just fly away anytime you wanted. I wanted to fly away right now, but I'd settle for just getting out of this car and away from the claws that were flying between my wife and daughter.

CHAPTER 30

Claire and I were long overdue for lunch together. Before I started my business, we used to meet at least one Saturday a month after our hair appointments. With all that had been happening, I really needed someone to talk to, and Claire was the only one I trusted. I'd suggested we treat ourselves to La Chaumiere. It was small, the food was excellent, and the service was as French as the cuisine.

I arrived a few minutes early, but the maître d' seated me while I waited for Claire.

She came up behind me and fluffed the back of my hair. "The new colour, *très jolie.*" Claire always looked fabulous, but today she was sporting a new hairstyle.

"Thank you. Love the new do."

"I wanted something a little rad, as the kids would say." Claire turned her head to show off the asymmetrical line of her cut.

Hearing Claire use the word rad made me chuckle. "You're always rad compared to me."

"I don't know. You're pretty radical. Ms. I'm too busy running my empire to have lunch with my best friend."

"I'm sorry. It's a lot. I…"

Claire flapped her hand to stop me from talking. "First, we choose our wine and then I'm all ears." Claire picked up the wine list. "Sauvignon Blanc?"

We ordered the wine and then I asked Claire, "What have I missed while I've been neglecting you?"

Claire smiled. "A lot. André was accepted into medical school."

"That's exciting."

"I'm not sure who's more excited, André or Theo."

Even when André was little, he aspired to be a doctor. When he was about five, he would wear one of his father's white shirts as a lab coat, put his toy stethoscope around his neck, and perform health checks on us when we were at their house.

"He's been so focused. You must be proud."

"I hope he isn't too focused."

"Most parents worry about their children's lack of focus."

"I worry he won't take time for the most important things; beauty, wonder, fun, friendship, love… the things memories are made of. But especially, love."

"You just want everyone to find their Theo."

Claire and Theo met when she was just eighteen. She went to see Duke Ellington at Café St. Michel. She saw Theo across the room, and she knew they were supposed to meet. So, she walked up and introduced herself.

I'd always thought Claire was excessively optimistic, with her unwavering belief in the existence of soulmates. But that was before I'd met Nate. The way Claire had described seeing Theo for the first time was eerily similar to what Nate had admitted to me.

It wasn't until the waiter rolled away the appetizer cart and we had begun fishing buttery escargot from their shells that I brought up the subject I was hoping to discuss with her.

"You know Nate and I are… close."

"I've noticed." Claire lowered her voice. "You love him, don't you?"

I was taken aback, and my first instinct was to deny it. "I… I wasn't going to say that."

"But you do." Claire's brow was furrowed. I thought she looked concerned.

"I don't want you worrying." I looked down, focused on the morsel of bread I was using to sop up the garlicky butter from the nooks of the escargot dish.

"Have you just realized this?"

"No. It's been a while."

"Is it mutual?"

"I think so."

"Think or know?"

"Sometimes I know, but then other times… it's confusing."

"Does Will know? Or Betsy?"

"I don't think so. We've been careful."

"Then what's upsetting you?"

"I feel… unstable."

"Do you want to be together? That would be… messy. But not impossible."

"When we're together, that's all I want."

"Have you talked about it?"

"About a million times. He says he knows he should be with me. That we belong together. That he should have got my name and number when he jump-started my car."

Claire squinted at me. "Your car?"

Up until then, I'd kept my word to Nate and not told anyone, even Claire, that we'd met when I was 18. I told her the story. I also told her we'd been in Japan at the same time just before Will and I were married.

"And you didn't realize you'd met before?"

"He says he knew from the first evening he wanted… no… needed to get to know me."

Claire pressed her lips together and looked at me sidelong. "And you don't believe you're supposed to be together?"

"My heart says yes, but my head tells me I'm foolish."

"Why?"

"Because he's in Europe on a family vacation with his wife and daughter."

"You go on family vacations. You said you had a fantastic time at the Olympics."

"We did. We enjoyed it very much."

"So, how is that different?"

"He's not jealous. I am."

"How do you know?"

"He encouraged us to go. He even helped with scheduling meetings at their facility in Cornwall to make it easier for me to balance work and vacation."

"He was being helpful. It doesn't mean it didn't eat at him too. You're rationalizing."

"None of this is rational. If I'd been rational, I'd never have allowed things to go this far."

"This far?"

"For this long."

Claire leaned forward. "To be clear, we're not talking about a one-time indiscretion?"

"No. we've been lovers for years."

Claire sat back in her chair and let out a little huff. For the first time in the conversation, Claire looked surprised. Then curious. "So, what's changed? Why tell me about it now?"

"I don't know. I just…" I paused and studied Claire's expression.

There was no disapproval or judgment.

There was a tightness in my throat as my emotions boiled up from my belly. "Sometimes I feel like I'm going to burst."

She leaned forward and put her hand on my wrist. "Don't keep it all bottled up. Your secrets are safe. Your happiness is what's important."

"That's just it. I'm happiest when we're together. He gets me. But I can't have it all the time."

"Why not?"

"Because he's married."

"Have you asked him to leave her?"

My chest clamped. "Of course not. I couldn't do that."

"Why?"

The frustration and sadness in my chest intensified, and I felt tears forming at the edges of my eyes. I hated to admit the reason, even to myself let alone Claire. "Because he might say no."

"And that scares you."

"It proves he can be loyal to his commitments, but it also portends that failure is inevitable. It makes me want to break things off and it makes me want him more."

"Only you can decide what's right for you."

"I don't want to need him."

"You don't need him. You are my fierce, successful, beautiful friend and you are perfectly capable of taking care of yourself. But if he is your destiny, you shouldn't waste the time you could be sharing."

CHAPTER 31

I was relieved to hear Maddie's voice on the phone. "You're a hard woman to get a hold of."

"Sorry. It's been hectic." Her voice was distant. She sounded distracted.

"Is this a bad time?"

"No. Hold a sec."

I heard her put the phone down, her chair rolling and a door closing before she came back on the line.

"I'm all ears. What can I do for you?"

"I wondered if you'd like to have lunch or dinner. Whichever is more convenient for you."

"I see. When were you thinking?"

"As soon as we can. We haven't had any time for us lately."

"You were away. In Europe. A bit far to meet you for lunch."

"You were never far from my thoughts."

"How was the trip?"

"Seen enough art to last a lifetime."

"Sounds educational."

"We had some excellent guides."

"Ann enjoy it?"

"Seemed to."

"That sounds lukewarm."

"She impressed our guides with her questions and knowledge."

"That art degree is good for something after all."

"Mostly I was either superfluous or refereeing."

"Since when do Betsy and Ann disagree?"

"Our daughter has a mind of her own now."

"Not always two against one now?"

"I'm still the bad guy most of the time. I'm used to it."

"How was Paris and the Le Maurice?"

"I should have booked the Ritz."

"Was it bad?'

"I thought it was great. Good enough for royalty and celebrities but not my wife."

Maddie was sympathetic. "That's unfortunate. I know you were looking forward to staying there."

The vacation had drained me. I'd done everything I could to please Betsy. I'd booked the best hotels, arranged for private tours, endured endless shopping, and spent more than I'd budgeted on clothes and jewelry. I'd even made reservations at a romantic restaurant for the two of us the evening Ann was meeting up with her friend in Paris. But there was no romance to be had. We barely spoke.

Our conversations were nothing like the easy flowing exchanges with Maddie. Maddie always had something to share or a story to tell, and she expressed genuine interest in my thoughts and opinions. I even liked the way she challenged and teased me. It stimulated my thoughts and ideas. I got pleasure from replaying our conversations and imagining what I would say and do the next time I saw her.

There were many occasions over the past three weeks when I imagined how different it would be sharing the experience with Maddie. I'd surreptitiously sent a few postcards, addressed to her office, but devoid of any overly personal message, because I wanted her to know I was thinking of her.

I wanted to look across the table into the eyes of someone who really saw me, who made my pulse quicken and made me feel more alive just being near her. Maddie made me feel that way.

This was the longest we'd gone without talking in ages, and I didn't want to wait any longer. "So... About lunch? We could try The Omega. It's close to your office."

"Anne's home from camp. Staying with my parents during the day. I'm working through lunch to get home early."

"All week?"

"I have a meeting with your workplace safety team later next week. I could stop by your office afterwards."

"I hope you do." I didn't say that I wanted to see her away from the eyes and ears and distractions of the office. I didn't want to give the impression that I was desperate for sex. I was, but I didn't want to let on. "But you've no time this week?"

"I'm really jammed. I've got to go to Sarnia Wednesday too. Meeting a new client."

"Just for the day?"

"Overnight. Meeting is Thursday morning first thing."

I paged through my day planner to look at Wednesday's and Thursday's schedule. I could clear up Wednesday afternoon enough to get to Sarnia for dinner and if I left at five in the morning, I could be back for my first meeting Thursday.

"Could we meet for dinner Wednesday?"

"I'll be in Sarnia."

"I know. Are you free?"

Maddie didn't answer.

It occurred to me that maybe she didn't want to see me. I felt a churn in my stomach, but I didn't want her to feel pressured. "If you can't, I understand."

"We should have dinner."

Her sudden acceptance quelled my concern, and I could feel myself grin. "That's great."

"They tell me the restaurant at my motel is good. I'm staying at the Sahara Motel if you want to get a room there."

We'd often gotten separate rooms when we've met up during business trips; to keep up appearances when there were others around. We would request interconnected rooms whenever possible, so we could stay together without anyone noticing we were entering the same room.

I assumed that was the case. "You won't be alone?"

"I'll be on my own."

Her words sent my heart back to my stomach. I didn't want a room. I wanted to be in her room, to hold her, touch her, feel her skin against mine and wake up beside her. But I would book a room even though I hoped I wouldn't need it.

I circled the meetings on my calendar I would ask Delores to reschedule. "What time do you want to meet?"

"I need to stop at a site in London, but I expect to be there about five."

We decided to meet at six so that Maddie had a chance to change before dinner.

As soon as we hung up, I buzzed Delores. "I need you to reschedule a couple meetings, please."

"I'll be right in," she replied.

She came in carrying the schedule book she kept on her desk and opened it on mine. "Which meetings?"

"I need to block off Wednesday afternoon from two thirty on."

"No problem. What should I categorize it as?"

"Off-site meetings."

"Do you need me to arrange the car?"

"I'll be driving myself. Thank you."

Delores picked up the book but didn't leave.

"Is there something else?"

"I wondered if you wanted to give me a more specific story. In case your wife calls."

Although we never discussed the details, Delores knew that I had a personal relationship with Maddie. Fortunately, she was wholeheartedly supportive and infinitely discreet. She liked Maddie very much and was not Betsy's biggest fan. Betsy had never shown her much respect, so she had no problem bending the truth to facilitate me spending time with Maddie.

"That's a good idea. I'll let you know. And could you please book me a room at the Sahara Motel in Sarnia and a reservation for two at the restaurant if they take them."

Delores nodded. "I'll get right on it.

Everything was falling into place, but I felt uneasy. Maddie had seemed reluctant to find time for us to meet and the suggestion of separate rooms was perplexing. I couldn't think of anything I'd done that would have upset her. She'd known about the trip to Europe for months. We'd talked about the itinerary. She'd asked lots of questions, so I'd assumed she wanted to know the details. I wondered if that's what had upset her. I'm sure I told her I wished I was planning the trip for us, but maybe I'd only thought it.

It was just part of our reality. She had Will and Anne and I had Betsy and Ann. Our relationship had blossomed despite the shadow of those obligations. For me, it was another indication that we were supposed to happen. Not ideal. But I wanted whatever we could have. It was precious. And ours. And I treasured every moment.

CHAPTER 32

All the way to Sarnia, I rehearsed in my head what I would say to Nate. I was so engrossed, I almost missed the turn for the motel. My conflicting desires were the conundrum. My heart and my head were providing vastly different guidance. My heart wanted to hang on, no matter how much it hurt. Experiencing our powerful connection was worth any pain. My head told me I needed to terminate our relationship because there was no endgame that wasn't catastrophic.

My relationship with Will wasn't bad. I didn't have a good reason to leave him. He was still fun to be around, he made me laugh and he did what he thought a husband should do. For him, that meant he would provide for us. But that's not what I lacked. I could provide for us. I wanted an emotional and physical connection with someone who believed in me and my endeavors, who understood how I measured success and who empowered me to achieve my goals. I wanted Nate.

Our relationship was an addiction. I craved how I felt with him. Nate instinctively gave me exactly what I needed. I could be the best version of me when we were alone together. When he looked at me with adoration and awe my heart soared. But the high was fleeting. After each clandestine meeting we reluctantly parted and resumed our separate lives, and the contrast between who I could be with him in private and the public version of me became more evident.

Despite the countless times Nate had told me he believed we belonged together, he never once suggested that he would leave Betsy so we could. His unwavering commitment to his vows was both commendable and exasperating. While they'd been away in Europe, I'd made up my mind; it was time to break myself of the habit of needing him. It was the logical thing to do. If we couldn't take this relationship to the next level, then it was time I put it behind me. However, hearing his voice on the phone the past couple of days left my heart screaming for more time with him. The only thing my heart and head agreed on was that I loved him.

There was a note for me from Nate at the front desk when I checked in at the motel.

I requested for us to have interconnected rooms and they informed me the one adjacent to mine is available. I'm in room 114. Call me when you're ready to have dinner. I made a reservation for 6:30 but they aren't busy so we can go any time we like.

My heart had me ask the clerk for the adjoining room. Head kept me from unlocking and knocking on the interconnecting door until I'd gotten out of my field clothes and showered. It had been a scorching day, and it felt good to stand naked beside the air conditioner. I knew Nate wouldn't mind if I invited him in before dressing. But I knew where that would lead, and I wouldn't want to stop once we started.

I got dressed and then knocked on Nate's door.

He opened it so fast I wondered if he was standing at the door waiting for me.

"I thought I heard someone next door. I was hoping it was you." He stepped back from the door. "Please come in."

The room was cool, and the curtains were drawn. Nate had shuffled the furniture in his room to make space for a small folding table and two chairs. There was a candle in the center of the table and a bottle of champagne in a bucket of ice and two glasses on the desk adjacent to it.

"What's all this?"

"It's not Paris. But I brought a little bit back for you." He handed me a tissue paper wrapped parcel. "While you unwrap that, I'll open the wine."

A single gold sticker held the tissue paper together. Inside was a beautiful scarf. The silk slithered through my fingers as I unfurled it. Concentric navy and red on a white background with a crisscross pattern of black lines and brass rings that suggested an equestrian harness. It was beautifully made, the edges hand rolled and the texture of the material flawless. I looked closer at the sticker still clinging to the paper. It was embossed with a horse and buggy and the name of a company I instantly recognized. It was Hermès.

"It's lovely. But you shouldn't have."

"I wanted you to know I was thinking of you."

"I got a postcard today."

"Only one? I sent several."

"Just one. This is too much."

"I wish I could have brought something more. But this was the best I could manage without drawing undo attention."

"How did you get this by Betsy?"

"I went out shopping by myself. Ostensibly to get something for Delores as a thank you gift for the extra work she put in before I went away."

"What did you get Delores?"

"A scarf as well. But much smaller."

"You could have brought me the small one."

"The lady in the shop told me this one could be worn as a top. When she demonstrated how to tie it on a mannequin, it made me think of the halter top you wore the day we found out we'd met before."

"You remember what I wore?"

"I'll never forget the moment I realized it had always been you I was supposed to be with." Nate picked up the champagne bottle, poured, and handed me a glass. "Let's drink to that."

"I'm not sure."

"Not sure you can drink or not sure we're supposed to be together."

"Because we're not together."

"We're together now." Nate stepped towards me and tried to take me into his arms.

I stepped back to avoid his embrace. Nate's expression was either confusion or annoyance. I wasn't sure which.

"Physically in the same place. But our other attachments make it impossible to be truly together."

Nate again moved closer to me. "It's been like this all along. Nothing has changed."

"That's exactly the problem. Nothing has."

Nate sat down on the edge of the bed. "But we've talked about this. We agreed that we would keep our relationship just between us. It's what you wanted."

"I wanted to keep feeling how good it feels when I'm with you. And keeping us a secret is the only way that could work."

Nate patted the spot beside him on the bed and I sat down.

Nate put his arm around me and nuzzled my neck. "Being with you is the best thing in my life."

"But not good enough for you to want only me."

"I do only want you."

"Then why are you and Betsy still married?" It surprised me that I blurted out the question that had been plaguing my thoughts. I couldn't stop myself from continuing. "I don't think you even like her. You say you love me, but you don't want to be with me. It's an impossible situation and I'm not sure I want to be in it anymore."

Nate was silent. Inhaling deeply, he looked into my eyes with a pained expression.

I felt a tremor in my chest, and tears start to form. I clenched my jaw and took a deliberate breath. But my emotions were boiling over and I couldn't stop the tears. They spilled over and dribbled down my cheek.

Nate pulled out his handkerchief and gave me a playful nudge and smiled. "I don't want you to blow your nose in your new scarf."

I took it and wiped my face. "I'm sorry. It's just… Why are we doing this?"

"We can stop if that's what you want."

His words sent a wave of panic through me. He suggested it so easily while I'd agonized over the thought of breaking up. My heart felt like it was imploding. I put my elbows on my knees and my head in my hands and tried to think.

Nate ran his fingers through the ends of my hair. He leaned down, trying to see my face. "I don't want you to be upset. What can I do? Anything."

I knew his concern was genuine. There was a tremor in his voice. I could feel the slight tremble of his fingers as he tucked my hair behind my ear and brushed the length of it back over my shoulder.

I took several deep breaths as I regained composure. Then I sat up and swiveled towards him. "What do you want?" I leaned in. Looked him squarely in the eyes. "Besides all the great sex?"

Nate grinned. "It is great sex."

I frowned.

He put his hand on my thigh. "We could never have sex again, but it won't change how I feel about you."

I shook my head and grumbled. "What does that even mean? If your feelings are so enduring, why haven't you ever asked me to be with you? For real… not for a rendezvous when it's convenient."

Nate chuckled. "You know you've never been convenient."

"Stop trying to be cute."

"But if cute works…" Nate winked and leaned his head towards mine.

I stood up. If I stayed close, I was going to kiss him. Being near him muddled me. I could clearly see all that was wrong with us when he wasn't around. But then and there, him looking at me, into my eyes with that adoring look, I felt wanted and needed in the most delicious way. I wanted to feel that more. To never stop feeling it. I wanted to encourage it by throwing my arms around his neck and kissing him so hard he would fall back on the bed, and I would pounce on him. I had done the exact thing more than once and we'd always ended up naked and making love.

I fought the urge by walking over to the champagne bottle and spinning it in the ice. I avoided looking back at him.

"Say something." There was longing in his voice.

"Why are you here?"

"I wanted to see you and give you your present."

"But why?"

"Being with you feels right."

"It's not… we wouldn't have to keep it a secret from almost everyone."

His back stiffened. "Does someone know?"

"I told Claire that we were… involved." I peeked at his face to see his reaction.

He pressed his lips together. "Hmmm." He shook his head and sighed.

"I needed someone to talk to."

"You can always come to me."

"Not when you're with your family, in Paris, having romantic evenings." I regretted how petty and jealous it sounded.

"It was a trip for Ann."

"Right." My sarcasm was clear.

"Nothing has changed. Why is this particular trip a big deal?"

"Straw that broke the camel's back."

"I thought we were happy. Did Claire talk you out of … us?"

"As a matter of fact, she said that if you were the one, nothing should stop us from being together."

"Then why are you pulling away?"

"Because you don't want to be with me."

"I do. I just… can't."

"Why not?"

"We made other commitments. It would be messy for both of us."

"If we'd just made the mess when we first started, it would have been cleaned up and forgotten by now."

"But we decided not to. The timing wasn't good."

"Is now a better time?"

Nate downed his whole glass of champagne. He pointed at the bottle.

I filled his glass and topped up mine. "I guess that's a no."

"Ann is engaged."

"Congratulations. What does that have to do with it?"

"Rather inappropriate to ask for a divorce while planning our daughter's wedding."

I understood. I admired and loved his character and devotion. Nevertheless, I was angry his devotion didn't benefit me. "You probably should go home and plan then."

"Why don't we have some dinner. We can talk."

"We're talking now. Do you think I'll be more reasonable in public?"

"I never said you weren't being reasonable."

"When is the wedding?"

"Next June."

"After that will the timing be appropriate?"

"You know it's not that simple."

"Then it really is that simple. There is no point in us continuing to see each other."

Nate put his hands on either side of my face and gently turned my head and pulled my lips close to his. "How can you say that? We're good for each other. We're friends. We're more than friends. We love each other. You can't give up on us."

I pulled away. "I can't do this anymore." I pushed past him to the connecting door to my room.

"Don't go. Please." Nate's voice was soft and pleading.

My back was to him. I knew I should take two steps forward through the door, close it behind me and not look back. But I was frozen. My heart had been wrung out. I wanted to escape to keep it empty and hard, but his words flooded it with warmth and desire. My stomach twisted in knots as my thoughts and feelings pulled me in opposite directions.

I felt Nate's hand on my shoulder.

"Please. Stay."

I couldn't deny his request.

CHAPTER 33

I didn't want to imagine my world if Maddie hadn't turned around. I knew I'd come perilously close to losing her. When she pulled away, it felt like the good that held my life together started to crumble. Without her, I'd be lost. She was the moonlight that guided me through the dark times and the blinding light of the sun that brought more heat and passion than I ever could have imagined. We never had enough time together, and I wanted to make the most of every moment. I didn't want to waste time second guessing our choices or fighting about what we couldn't change.

"Now what?" She put her hands on her hips and stared at me with a blank expression.

I knew I needed to say the right thing. Do the right thing. Or she might pivot and go.

"Maybe I could buy you dinner?"

Maddie nodded. I pocketed the room key, and we left through the main door of my room and walked along the parking lot to the restaurant at the front of the motel near the road.

Maddie's client hadn't steered us wrong. The food was good. Not fancy, but homey and comforting, and just the remedy for the emotional drama of the previous half hour.

We talked over dinner, but I avoided mentioning anything about the trip or Ann's nuptials. Maddie talked about her office expansion plans and other business topics. By the time we finished eating, it felt like things were back to normal.

I reached for her hand as we walked back to my room, and she placed hers in mine. That simple touch sent a ripple of excitement through me. Before everything blew up, I'd imagined our reunion quite differently. I'd imagined my mini-Paris setting with the champagne and present would be the precursor to undressing her and making love. I still wanted that. Wanted her. But I didn't want to derail the tenuous détente we'd achieved over dinner.

I unlocked the door to my room and held the door open for Maddie.

"I left my key in my room. I'll need to go through from yours."

I followed her inside. The scarf I'd bought her was in a bundle on the bed. I picked it up. "Maybe you'd like to try on your scarf?"

Maddie smirked. "You're just trying to get me to take off my top."

I extended it to her. "Always a pleasure when you do. But this would be for educational purposes. To show you how to tie it."

Maddie took the scarf from me. "I need to call home. But how about I model it after I'm done?"

"Ok. Sure."

Maddie went through to her room. I wasn't surprised she closed her side of the interconnecting doors for privacy as she called home. I left mine open and sat on the bed waiting for hers to reopen. I could hear her muffled voice as she talked on the phone. Then quiet.

I waited, but nothing happened. I stood and paced the room. I considered knocking. I considered calling her room. I know it was only a few minutes but each one that passed made me more apprehensive that she had decided not to reopen the door. I finally decided I should knock and as I reached for the door it opened.

Maddie was wearing the scarf. At least partially wearing it. She had it draped over one shoulder and was holding the ends to keep it from slipping off. She'd left her skirt on but was naked from the waist up.

I wanted to kiss her exposed neck and shoulder. I wanted the scarf to slip and let me see the curves that rippled the surface of the silk. I was already hard.

"Are you going to show me how to tie it or just stare at me?" Maddie fluttered the material of the scarf with her hands.

I reached for the edge of the scarf. "I need it to show you how to fold it."

Maddie smirked and tugged one end of the scarf, so the material slithered over her shoulder, slowly falling away, to reveal her breasts.

Just the sight of her nipples made me want to press my lips to them and run my tongue over them. I wanted to suck them.

Maddie waved the scarf in front of my face like a matador taunting a bull with his cape. "Hey there. Focus."

"Can I help it if you mesmerize me?"

"Scarf tying time. Here. Take it." She took my hand and placed the scarf in it.

I held the scarf by two corners so if was fully open. "The lady in the store did it so fast…"

"Do you remember what she did?" Maddie leaned against the door frame and her lovely breasts taunted me.

I wrenched my eyes from her and focused on the scarf. "She folded it in half to make a triangle. Then she wrapped it around…. You'll need to stand still while I try this…"

Maddie stretched out her arms and held her head high and let me walk around her.

"You take the folded end and wrap it around and tie it under those delicious breasts. Then you take the triangle points and cross them and…" I couldn't resist pausing to look at her breast and how, with her arms raised, they were pointing up at me. "Unfortunately, cover up those delicious breasts."

Maddie lifted her hair as I tied the scarf ends at the back of her neck.

"There." I stood in front and examined my work. "Maybe needs a little adjustment." I ran my hands down from the knot and shifted the silk to drape more evenly. I couldn't help but let my hands skim over her chest and I felt her hard nipples through the material.

She put her hands on her hips. "Done?"

I nodded.

Maddie stepped away to look in the mirror. "Not bad. Maybe if we tried this." She undid the knot at the back of her neck. Her hands moved quickly and she crossed over and twisted the material and retied it into a perfect top. Then she turned to show me.

"Yours looks better."

"It feels like I'm barely wearing anything it's so soft."

"Really? How about we experiment with that." I reached for the tied ends and undid them.

The scarf slid down and dangled from her waist.

"Oh yes. It definitely feels like I'm barely wearing anything." Maddie's eyes were locked on me and her mouth had an evil grin.

I had to kiss her. I slipped my arms around her, drew her closer and pressed my lips to hers.

She let out a little moan and her lips parted and she kissed me back while letting her body lean in to me.

Our kissing was hungry, breathless, and our tongues danced over each other's.

I kissed her chin, her jaw, and down her neck. I paused at her neck to run my nose across her collarbone and feel her skin under my lips and cheek. I noticed the faint scent of the perfume she liked and I searched her neck with my nose for the source, finding it just behind her ear.

Maddie's hands moved to my face, and she kissed me hard and then pulled away.

I didn't want to stop.

She turned her back to me. I held my breath, waiting to see what she was doing.

She reached behind her back, untied the scarf from her waist and trailed it behind her as she moved towards the bed. She placed the scarf on the nightstand and without turning around, undid the button and zipper of her skirt and stepped out of it.

It was an explicit invitation, and I zealously accepted it.

Her back was to me. I kissed the back of her neck while reaching around to cup her breasts in my hands. I slid my hands down while running my lips down her spine. When I reached the top of her panties I pulled them off her hips and down to her knees, kissing her backside as I exposed it.

She twisted and leaned over the edge of the bed.

I got down onto my knees and continued kissing along the curve of her bottom. She let out a little moan as my nose pressed upward between her legs. I could feel her wetness on my face, and I wanted to taste her. She bent over further, her legs parted, and she opened up.

I ran my tongue over her lips. She pressed backwards onto my face, so I wrapped my hands around her thighs and pulled her in. She responded by tilting her hips even further, giving me more direct access. She rocked against me as my tongue caressed and my lips sucked her into my mouth. Her wetness excited me. Her apparent pleasure delighted me.

She twisted around, pulling away from my face. Her voice was something between a growl and a purr. "You're going to have to fuck me now."

I got out of my pants as fast as I could while she slipped off her panties and got on all fours at the edge of the bed. I slid into her, and she pushed back against me driving me deeper inside her. I grabbed her hips. I let her lead. I timed my thrusts to meet her rocking backwards onto me until I could feel her grinding and hear her gasp, so I knew it was my turn to let go. I was certain we'd climaxed together as I felt her clamping onto me as I burst inside her.

Maddie scooted further onto the bed, and I crawled up beside her and slid my arm under her head. She rolled slightly towards me and clung to me by throwing an arm and a leg over me. I felt pride seeing the contentment in her eyes. Reaching for her face, I ran my fingers over her cheek and jaw and brushed the stray hairs away.

Maddie nibbled one of my fingers as it brushed over her lips. "Why are you doing that?"

"Don't you like it?"

"I like it too much."

"That sounds like a good reason to keep doing it."

"Or a reason to never do it again."

I didn't know what to say. I stroked her cheek again instead.

Her eyes pulled away from mine and she focused on my chest hair where her fingers were gently scratching through it. "Tell me again why you're here?"

I could sense that she was slipping back to her earlier mood. I wanted to reassure her. "Everything is just so right when I'm with you."

Maddie sighed. "Ya think we're the two wrongs that actually make a right?"

"This doesn't feel wrong. The only time I'm completely myself is when I'm with you."

"I promised myself that this wouldn't happen again."

"And yet…" I pulled her closer and kissed her forehead. "You let me in wearing nothing but a scarf."

"I just wanted you to know I liked your present." Maddie squirmed away and pulled the scarf off the nightstand and ran it through her fingers. "To thank you."

"An excellent thank you."

Maddie sat up in the bed against the headboard and draped the scarf to cover herself.

I tugged at the end to pull it down. "Don't hide the goods from me now."

Maddie held fast to the edge of the scarf so it didn't budge. "They are not your goods."

"I think you like the way I handle your goods." I ran my hands over her thighs through the silky material.

She let out a soft moan then pushed my hand away. "That's not the point."

"I don't understand."

"You've never asked me to leave Will and be with you."

I was taken aback by the statement. I didn't know what she wanted me to say. She'd never suggested she was considering leaving Will. I didn't want her to leave him for me.

Maddie closed her eyes and leaned her head back against the headboard. "I can only conclude that means you really don't see anything more for us than just this."

"This is not nothing. You're the one I should be with. But it's not the right time."

"Will it ever be our time?"

"You know I love you. Isn't that enough?" I slid up beside her and put my arm around her.

Maddie rested her head on my shoulder. I felt her relax into me. "I can't love you this much and not want more."

"If circumstances were different, we would be more."

Maddie yawned.

I slipped off the bed and started pulling back the covers. "Maybe we should sleep on it."

Maddie crawled under them. I slipped my arm under her head and pulled her in close. Maddie wrapped a leg around me and nuzzled her face into my neck.

I stroked her hair and hoped that my touch would convey how much I adored her. Holding her in my arms I knew she was exactly where she was supposed to be. Her breathing slowed and I could tell she'd fallen asleep.

My mind was still processing the evening. Maddie had put an option on the table we'd never let ourselves consider. We leave our spouses and be together. Of course, I wanted what she wanted, but it just couldn't be. I imagined the consequences. Our families, our friends and our reputations mangled and permanently damaged because we couldn't keep our relationship just between us.

I fell asleep hoping that in the morning Maddie would see that keeping things the way they are is our best option.

CHAPTER 34

Betsy and the groom's parents had just been seated when Brandon, the groom, and his best man followed the priest from the vestry and stood at the front of the church. A vibrant burst of chords from the organ brought everyone to their feet and swiveling to the rear of the church where the double doors were being opened by two dark suited attendants.

Ann stood centered in the doorway, flanked by her bridesmaids. She looked like royalty in the elegant gown and long veil that draped from a tiara on her head.

Nine bridesmaids in voluminous lavender taffeta dresses, carrying bouquets of pink and white roses, slow-walked one at a time up the aisle. Following behind were a ring bearer and two flower girls, who sprinkled pink rose petals on the white carpet that had been rolled out down the aisle.

Nate came forward and stepped to the side as Ann moved through the doors and onto the carpet. The two attendants fluffed and arranged her train. Nate extended his arm to his daughter. She nodded to him and smiled, and they started down the aisle.

Ann looked straight ahead, her eyes fixed on Brandon, her expression serene and confident. Her long train flowed behind her like a luxurious white river dotted with pearls. As Nate approached our pew, he smiled and nodded to us as he did for many of the guests who were seated on the bride's side. I turned to the front as they passed. Brandon looked delighted by the vision he saw walking towards him.

The church was dripping with flowers. There were sprays of roses on every pew and six large standing arrangements flanking the altar. Ann handed her cascading bouquet of white roses and ivy to her maid of honour. She bobbled it, almost dropping it, apparently not expecting it to be so heavy.

I needed to take out a tissue to dab my eyes as the couple exchanged their vows. They had memorized them and spoke to each other with an earnestness that was touching and inspiring. I wasn't the only one who felt their connection because the church burst into spontaneous applause when the priest announced them as man and wife.

The traditional wedding mass concluded with the jubilant couple walking out of the church to the triumphant strains of Jeremiah Clarke's Trumpet

Voluntary, complete with two trumpet players amplifying the organist's performance.

Nate and Betsy were standing near the bride and groom on the sidewalk outside the church. The small area at the base of the steps was jammed with people.

Will tugged at my arm. "We got some time to kill. Let's go grab a drink."

"I wanted to say hello." I craned my neck to see if we could manoeuvre ourselves to where Nate was standing.

"We'll see them at the party. Know a good place nearby?"

"The Hearthside is close. How about that?"

"Do they have beer?"

"It's a pub."

"It'll do."

It was a hot day, and I was enjoying the cool of the pub even though we'd only walked from the parking lot. The reception didn't start until six, so we had a couple of hours to wait before heading to Le Dome. Nate had told me that they would be taking pictures outside at Gairloch Gardens if the weather was nice. I wondered how Nate was faring in his black tuxedo in the sun.

Will had taken off his jacket and left it in the car, but he was obviously still hot because he loosened his tie and unbuttoned the collar of his shirt. He took a long sip of his beer. "Not looking forward to having to give our little Annie away one day."

"We've got a few years left before you've got to worry about that."

"I don't know how old Nate looked so calm."

"Probably because Ann and Brandon are crazy about each other."

"Doesn't hurt he's a gazillionaire."

"I think that matters more to Betsy than Ann."

"You're just saying that because you've never liked her all that much."

"I like her."

"You tolerate her. You think she's a silly spoiled kept woman."

"She is spoiled."

"You wouldn't let me spoil you."

"I won't be a silly kept woman for anyone."

"I hope our Anne finds someone to take care of her. Even if she doesn't want it."

"I hope she marries her one true love and lives happily ever after."

"You sound like a fairy tale."

"I don't mean it that way."

"Fairy tales are nice."

"They are unrealistic, misogynistic, and full of gender stereotypes. Not exactly the world I want my daughter to believe in."

"Lots of big words to say you don't want our Annie to find her prince?"

"She doesn't need a prince. She needs a partner." I didn't tell Will everything I was thinking. Instead of waiting for a prince to bring her happiness, I aimed to instil in Anne a strong sense of self-belief and self-reliance.

My mother didn't set that example for me. She encouraged me to find a man who would provide for me as my dad had for her. I didn't see the point in that. What I did see was how she had to find subversive ways to put aside money for herself, while he could spend and do whatever he wanted because he earned the money and controlled the finances. And it wasn't just about money, it was about being able to choose your own path and not be limited by other people's expectations. I didn't marry Will to have him take care of me. It was for practical reasons, and to satisfy my mother's desire to not have a spinster for a daughter. I don't entirely regret marrying him, but I do feel like I failed to be true to myself, and that, I do regret.

I didn't want Anne to settle for someone suitable. If she was going to marry, I hoped she'd find her soulmate. The person who'd encourage her to be her best self, support her pursuits and understand her. Being with Nate had given me a taste of what that would be like. I hoped she'd have better timing finding her person. Not find them too late, when the rest of her life got in the way of them being together.

We finished our drinks and headed for the reception. Will looked over the heads of the mass of people waiting outside the entrance. "I said we had time for another drink."

We had to wait outside for a few minutes before it was our turn to go through the receiving line. Betsy was the first in the line. "We're so glad you could come. Will, Maddie, these are Brandon's parents Gloria and Henry Hartwell."

I tried to pause and say something to Nate, but we were handed off to the Hartwells, and Betsy was already introducing Nate to the couple behind us.

"Thank you for coming," said Gloria.

Henry extended his hand to me. "I'm delighted to finally meet the Maddie that Ann's been talking about."

I must have looked surprised.

"You didn't know she's a big fan of yours?"

"I'm not exactly a celebrity."

"She says you've inspired her to be her own boss."

Will chuckled. "She is bossy."

I knew Will was trying to be funny, but Henry didn't smile.

I redirected the conversation away from me. "We're delighted to see Ann and Brandon so happy."

Henry looked across the room to where the couple were standing, and he looked very contented. "We're delighted to officially welcome Ann into our family."

Gloria had turned to greet the next couple, and we worked our way through the line of bridesmaids and groomsmen until we finally got to Ann and Brandon. Despite the large number of people they'd already greeted, they showed no signs of tiring.

Ann threw open her arms to give me a hug. "I'm so glad you could come."

I hugged her, but was careful not to crush her dress. "Best wishes for a lifetime of happiness."

Will shook Brandon's hand. "Congratulations."

"Thank you, Maddie," said Ann. "I hope you'll share your secrets to juggling career and family."

I thought it was sweet of her to insinuate I was good at it. "I'm sure you'll be much better at it."

Brandon put his arm around Ann and grinned. "She's got great ideas and I promise not to get in her way."

I didn't want to hold up the line, so we thanked them for including us and we moved to the table with the place cards and seating chart. We found the card with our names and assigned table. Table 50. We were surprised at the number until we entered the round banquet hall with the ornate dome in the center. There were two concentric rings of tables interspersed between white columns around a large circular dancefloor. Our table was the last one at the far end of the room.

Will pointed to the bar located directly behind it. "Best table in the house."

Franklin stood as we approached. He must have heard Will's comment. "At least we won't have anyone scrutinizing how we eat our soup." He extended his hand to Will. "Good to see you, man." He put his arm around me. "And always good to see my favourite engineer."

"And female entrepreneur of the year," said his wife, Diana. "Congratulations. Franklin showed me the article in the Journal.

Franklin pulled out the chair next to his and I sat down.

Will pointed to the bar. I nodded and he trotted off to get us both a drink.

I looked around. The room was lavishly, but elegantly, decorated. The chairs were draped in lavender covers with white bows and there were sparkling candles ringed with roses on every table.

Diana touched the petals of the lavender rose in front of her. "Aren't the flowers just spectacular?"

"Everything is lovely."

She swivelled towards the head table. "I've never seen anything like that garland. I think there are little holders for the bridesmaid's bouquets because the loops are in front of every other chair and there's a little space…"

I hoped we weren't going to talk about the décor all evening. I looked up at Franklin.

He turned towards the entrance. "There's Delores. I bet they're relegated to the business associates' table too."

Indeed, they were and a few minutes later Chuck, Nate's driver, and his girlfriend arrived. It was an interesting cross-section of people that had been lumped together at our table. I wondered if Betsy had intended it to be an insult. If she had, it backfired because I was grateful. I was acquainted with and liked them all, which is not always the case when attending a wedding where you don't know most of the guests.

At the end of the meal, Brandon's sister Audrey stepped to the podium and introduced herself and her role as Master of Ceremonies. She was sharp and funny and promised to yank the mic away from anyone who went over their allotted time, which garnered a hearty round of applause, and a few heckles from the head table. Sticking with tradition, Nate was the first to be summoned to the podium.

He started with the compulsory thank-yous to the guests, wedding party, officiant, venue, and wedding coordinators. His speech was perfectly delivered, but every time he said "Betsy and I" or "we" I felt uneasy. I shouldn't have been bothered seeing Betsy join him to welcome Brandon to their family or by the way she clung to his arm and looked at him so approvingly. I should have been happy for them and for Ann that her parents were both supporting them.

I felt discouraged. Watching them, I saw no signs of the distance in their relationship Nate portrayed when he described it to me. His commitment was admirable, but it prevented us from fully realizing what we could have been as a couple. It highlighted the futility of our relationship.

The thoughts that danced through my head were utterly inappropriate for his daughter's wedding. I fantasized about him pulling me aside and kissing me and then telling me that now that Ann was married, he would leave Betsy. Even if I was still with Will, he would be there for me.

I looked over at Will. He was whispering something to Chuck and the two of them were snickering. Did I regret marrying him? It hadn't been bad. It was comfortable and we fit in with our social circle of stable married couples. We didn't fight, much, and we still enjoyed sex. Thirteen years of marriage had taught us how to be together, but we'd not gotten closer. We'd settled more and more into our individual lives. As the years passed, we devoted more time to our separate pursuits. His to sports and time with the boys and mine to my career and business and, whenever possible, Nate.

Would I leave Will for Nate? I had competing voices inside me with their answers. One that urged me to take the leap because pacing back and forth along the edge will never get you to the other side. The other voice holding me back warning that if you jump, it might be off a cliff and you'll hurt yourself or worse, drag Anne with you into the abyss.

The speeches were over and a live band was setting up on the stage behind the head table.

Delores stood. "Ladies room anyone?"

I nodded, picked up my evening bag, and followed her.

CHAPTER 35

The band leader waved at me. It meant he would announce the next song was the father-daughter dance. Ann and I had poured over all the songs in the band's repertoire, and we'd finally selected How Sweet It Is (To be loved by you) as the one they would play for us. It was one of the few decisions I'd been permitted to have an opinion about. To Betsy's credit, it was a beautiful wedding. It had run far over the budget I'd given them. But, in that moment, as Ann held my hand and led me onto the dance floor, I didn't care because I saw how happy she was.

I twirled her and she landed perfectly facing me just as we'd practiced.

She grinned. "We got this."

Her dress swished around my legs as we danced and I held her further away. "I don't want to step on your dress."

Ann squeezed my hand. "Don't worry. I'm only going to wear it once."

She looked like a princess, but I saw a flash of determination in her eyes that told me she was saying more about her commitment to Brandon than about the dress.

I was so proud of her. "How did you get so grown up?"

"It took a while. But I got there."

"For me, it happened so fast. One minute you're playing with dolls and the next you're buying a house."

"You're forgetting about my spoiled brat years."

I thought to myself that those weren't entirely her fault. Betsy both modeled and enabled her bad behavior. But living away at university and Brandon had changed Ann. She wanted to do things for herself. She'd accepted the Hartwells' help in financing the gallery she was planning to open in September, but she'd had me structure an agreement such that the money was a loan, not a gift.

I wanted to encourage her in both love and life. "It was all worth it now that you've turned out ok."

Ann chuckled. "Ok? Just Ok?"

"I can't wait to see what you'll do next." I sent her for a final twirl as the song drew to a close.

She leaned in and kissed my cheek. "I love you, Dad." She said it with such sweetness I felt my face flush and a pang in my throat.

I kissed her on the forehead and then reached into my pocket for my hankie and dabbed my eyes.

Ann scooted away and grabbed on to Brandon and then she yelled, "Ok people. It's time to party."

The band leader urged everyone onto the dance floor. They started to belt out Hall and Oats' song You Make My Dreams Come True, that was a big hit on the radio, and got everyone up and moving.

I returned to our table and sat down with my parents. Dad's knees were too bad for him to get up and dance, but he swayed to the music with his arm around Mom.

I sat beside Mom. "Just let me know if you need a dance partner."

"I've got mine right here." She patted Dad's leg and then nodded at the next table. "Betsy needs you."

Betsy was motioning me to join her.

I kissed Mom's cheek. "You kids behave."

Betsy looped her arm through mine as I came to her side. "The photographer is taking reception pictures. Don't wander off."

"Sitting with my parents is not wandering off."

"We need to make the rounds." Betsy gave my arm a subtle tug to indicate where she wanted to go.

I led her towards the table nearest us where Brandon's aunts and uncles were seated.

I saw Betsy nod to the photographer, and he moved into position across from us so he could photograph us speaking with the guests.

We thanked everyone and they bestowed the customary compliments; how lovely everything was, how beautiful Ann looked, et cetera, as the photographer snapped candid pictures. Then we moved on to the next table with the photographer in tow to repeat the process.

As we made our way around, I kept an eye on the far end of the room, on Maddie's table. It was empty. I hoped that they would return before we got there. I hadn't had a chance to speak to her all day, and I desperately wanted to at least say hello.

We made it about halfway through the tables when Betsy's brother Beau tracked us down.

It was clear he'd been taking advantage of the open bar. He put his arm around Betsy's waist. "Come on Dolly, it's time to dance with your big brother."

Betsy rolled her eyes but didn't protest.

I looked around to see if I could spot Maddie. She was also on the dance floor. With Will. They looked like they were having fun. I tried to feel glad, but I would have preferred they didn't look so happy together. I needed a drink.

Turning away from the bar, I saw Delores standing by her table. She waved to me.

I joined her. "Are you enjoying yourself?"

"How could I not. It's a fabulous party."

"I'm glad."

"Have you seen Maddie?"

"Only briefly. We haven't spoken. Why?"

"Just wondered."

"What aren't you saying?"

"She seemed…" Delores shrugged. "Off?"

"Angry? Sad? What?"

"You should talk to her."

"Did she say something?"

Delores raised her eyebrows and gave me a look that told me she knew more than she thought she should say.

"Is she upset with me?"

"Let's just say your devoted-husband-happy-family routine may be a little too convincing."

I looked away towards the dance floor where Maddie was now dancing with Franklin. "She doesn't seem upset."

Delores leaned in as if to tell me a secret. "Perhaps she's also putting on a show for someone's benefit."

Beau and Betsy were headed my way. "I'll talk to her if I can get free."

Beau patted my shoulder. "Where'd you bury the bourbon? I think it's safe to break into it."

I must have looked confused.

Betsy laughed. "He's a northerner. He doesn't know what you're talking about." She turned to me. "Bury the bourbon, best you have, top to bottom, fair weather you'll have."

I had never heard that saying before. I turned to Beau. "I might've missed that, but we've got lots of bourbon at the bar. Shall we get you one?"

Betsy waved us off. "I'll go check on Mother and Father. Join me there."

I saw Maddie leave the dance floor and Will head towards us.

I patted Beau on the back. "Get us both one. I'm going to hit the head."

I left him at the bar and followed Maddie into the corridor. She went into the ladies' room. I lingered outside.

I caught her by the arm as she came out. "Hello beautiful stranger."

"Hi." Her voice was flat and her smile thin.

I led her into the manager's office at the end of the hallway. I knew it was open because we'd been given permission to use it to store gifts that had been brought to the reception.

She stood just inside the door with her arms crossed. "What do you want?"

I reached around her and closed the door. "To be alone with you. To tell you how gorgeous you look and to kiss you."

She pulled away as I leaned in. "Probably shouldn't."

"What's wrong?"

She pressed her lips together and sighed.

"This was the first chance I've had to get away."

"Maybe you should get back to your wife then."

"I needed to see you."

"Why?" Her eyes were cold and I could feel her putting up a wall between us.

My stomach twisted. "Because I can never see enough of you."

"You've been busy."

"Never too busy to find time for us. I need you. Love you. You know that. Right?"

"So you say."

"It's just been crazy with all this wedding stuff. It was for Ann."

"I understand."

"I don't think you do. You're mad."

"No."

"Then what?"

"Disappointed."

The word landed like a punch in the chest. That was worse than mad. "What can I do?"

"Nothing. It's just the way it is. We're stuck."

"What do you want from me."

"I want more for us."

"I want that too but…"

She interrupted me. "That's exactly the problem. There's always a but." She turned and reached for the doorknob.

I held her arm. "Don't go." I hated feeling as if she was pulling back from me. It was like a part of me was being torn out.

She leaned back into me and I wrapped my arms around her. She took a deep breath and let it out slowly. I reached up and brushed the hair from her neck and ran my fingertips from her ear to her shoulder. I wanted her to know how much I cared for her.

She tilted her head to the side and back and relaxed into me.

We stood like that for a few seconds, and then I turned her to face me. "We'll figure it out." I touched my lips to hers and kissed her as lightly as

I could.

Her eyes closed and she sighed. "That's not fair."

"Can I kiss you again?"

"You better."

The way her body pressed into mine gave me permission to pull her closer and kiss her deeply. Running her tongue across my lower lip, she ignited that familiar excitement within me. Her hands clawed at my back, and I pressed her backward and pinned her to the door. I could have made love to her right then and there.

She put her hands on my shoulders and pried us apart. "We have to stop." Her chest rose invitingly as she took in several deep breaths.

I knew she was right, but I didn't want to let her slip away from me for fear she would start building up the wall that I'd just broken through.

She straightened her dress. "We should get back."

CHAPTER 36

I knew Will was back from the store. l heard him on the back porch. He repeatedly dropped the bag of ice to break apart the cubes before emptying it with a clatter into the cooler filled with beer. I imagined not all the guys' wives were happy they'd signed up for yet another baseball tournament this month, but I didn't mind.

Will used to invite me to travel with him to tournaments, but that was before we had Anne. I suppose now that she was spending the entire month of July at Camp Nibi Nagamo, I could go. But he hadn't suggested it, so I didn't either.

I was looking forward to some time for myself, an afternoon of pampering, thanks to a birthday gift from my partners, Farley and Barry. The note had said:

Happy Birthday Maddie

We appreciate how you're never afraid to get your hands dirty, so we thought we'd get you a manicure and a gift certificate you can use for whatever work you'd like to get done while you're in the shop.

The way they described it made me sound like an old car being taken in for service, but I appreciated their efforts to get me something I could use. My plan was to spend a couple hours at the office finishing up a report before heading to my appointment. At least my hands would look ladylike for my Sunday brunch with Ann, who was just back from her honeymoon.

Some would question my sanity for befriending my lover's daughter, but it had come about quite naturally. She'd interviewed me for her journalism course back in her first year of university and ever since, she'd reached out for advice. It started with the occasional phone call to ask my opinion, morphed into her visiting me at my office and then, most recently, going out for lunch or dinner. Over the past couple of years, I'd become a hybrid mentor-aunt-friend, and I'd grown very fond of her. Getting to know her also made me feel more integrated into Nate's world, and I wanted that.

I think it made Ann more comfortable discussing topics one wouldn't normally share with a mentor because she knew her parents were my friends and I had worked closely with Nate for many years. But there were times I had to tread carefully, and not let on that I had prior knowledge, because I'd already heard about a particular incident from Nate.

The hardest part was trying to be objective when she described her problems with Betsy. As far as she knew, Betsy and I were friends, and she was looking to me to help her navigate their relationship, not to pile on my own grievances. I'll never forget the first time she launched into an outright rant.

"She can be such an embarrassment. She thinks she's the perfect lady, but there's this ugliness just below the surface. She has no respect for people she deems below her and she's borderline racist."

I'd done my best to help her deal with the situation without condoning Betsy's abominable behaviour. But on the inside, it further fueled my frustration with Nate that he was committed to their relationship.

Ann and I pulled into the restaurant parking lot just seconds apart. She greeted me with a big hug.

"Hugs are so much better than air kisses."

I presumed she was making a reference to her new family, but I didn't ask, just hugged her back.

We were seated at a table near the window with a view of the river below. There was a pack of skiffs from the rowing club skimming along and several large boats and sailboats maneuvering out of their slips to take to the lake for a Sunday sail.

"This place feels so different in daytime," said Ann.

"This is my first time here."

"We've been here to see bands. Different scene at night."

"Their brunch is supposed to be good."

A waiter came up to our table with a pitcher. "Mimosas for you ladies?"

"Certainly," said Ann.

I nodded. "This is perfect to toast the new Mrs. Hartwell."

"Jacobs-Hartwell. I've decided to add to, not change, my name."

"Then to you, Ann Jacobs-Hartwell. May you have a lifetime of wedded bliss."

We touched glasses.

Ann took a sip and then winked. "So far so good."

"The brunch or married life?"

She laughed. "Married life. Jury is still out on brunch."

"I hope it's still good. You just got back from your honeymoon."

"Honeymoon plus family vacation."

"Was it ok?"

"It was amazing. We spent a week in Santorini, just the two of us, and then we got on board a yacht with the whole family and sailed around the Greek islands. You'd think being stuck on a boat with your in-laws would be the worst honeymoon ever, but it was so much fun."

"Hard to come back to reality after that."

"We were both looking forward to getting home to our new place after almost a month away. Don't get me wrong. It was incredible. We had guides and private tours and fabulous meals and parties with other yachties..." She broke off speaking and sat back and looked at me. "I must sound like I'm bragging."

"You don't. It's a whole different world I've never experienced."

"You're worried I'll get snobby like my mother."

"The thought never crossed my mind. You're your own person."

"I worry about it. It's why it's so important for me to have my own thing."

"Speaking of that, how's the gallery coming along?"

"Fifty-seven days until opening."

"Coming fast."

"The construction for the renovations is finished, but the fixtures, painting and furnishing are still not done."

"Will it be ready in time?"

"Better be. I've already ordered the invitations for the grand opening."

"Is there anything I can do to help?"

"Come to the opening?"

"Of course, but I meant to help you get ready."

"I appreciate the offer. Are you good at assembling and putting up light fixtures?"

"Assembling I can handle. Wiring is more Will's bailiwick."

"I couldn't ..."

"I'll ask Will. He's away this weekend but I don't think we've got too much going next weekend. I'm sure we could come out for a few hours to help you."

"That would be awesome."

Throughout the rest of our brunch, our conversation revolved around plans for her business. Her vision was to have a gallery shop that brought an eclectic collection of art to Oakville. She wanted to provide a service for those who wanted to purchase art to decorate or to collect, but also to provide a space where the community at large could experience art in the few minutes they had between running errands or going out to dinner.

For the opening, she would be exhibiting pieces predominantly from local artists through her and Betsy's association with the Oakville Arts Council. But the Hartwells had procured several pieces from some very prestigious artists and they had offered them to Ann to sell on consignment to get her inventory started.

Ann had been hesitant to accept their offer. "Initially, I was uncomfortable with the idea. But I remembered you'd told me that sometimes you were annoyed when people tried to help you. But you'd come to know that they weren't helping because they saw you as weak but rather they believed in your success, and were willing to invest in it."

I grinned. "Sometimes I am so wise. I should really take my own advice more often."

We hugged again in the parking lot, and I promised to call her after I'd talked with Will about coming by the shop to help.

The answering machine light was blinking when I got home. I played the message.

"Hey, Mads. Just giving you a heads-up, I won't be home tonight." His voice was jovial, he didn't sound drunk, but it was still early.

We'd long ago agreed he should stay an extra night and come home in the morning if he and the boys were drinking. So, his call made me think they hadn't run out of beer.

I pulled out the steak I'd bought for our dinner from the fridge, wrapped it tightly, and tossed it in the freezer. I'd had a big lunch and it didn't make any sense to cook it for me alone. I leaned against the fridge and looked out the back window.

I could see Rosa, our neighbour, in the vegetable garden that took up most of her yard. Maybe someday I'd have time for more than the little strip with herbs and a couple of tomato and pepper plants that Rosa had planted with Anne one week when I'd been out of town for work. I decided I'd better go water them so she wouldn't think I didn't appreciate all the little things she did while she was helping out with babysitting and meals.

Rosa saw me and waved. "Do you want some lettuce?"

"Only if you have extra." I didn't want to deprive her of the fruits of her labour but hers was lettuce I actually liked.

"Bring me a bowl."

I got the colander from the kitchen and passed it over the fence. She cut out several bunches of leaves with a muddy stub of a knife.

"That's plenty," I said. "Will's not here for dinner."

"I give you extra. For tomorrow." She cut a few more chunks and handed the now overflowing colander back to me.

"Thank you. It's lovely, but a lot."

Rosa wiped perspiration from her forehead with her arm. "If we don't eat it, the rabbits will. Enjoy while we can."

I finished watering and then used the hose to wash some of the globs of mud off the lettuce before bringing it into the house. I dumped it all into the kitchen sink and filled it with cold water and started the arduous task of separating and rinsing each leaf.

My mind wandered as I mechanically cleaned. I thought about my brunch conversation and about Ann. Her marriage to Brandon put her in such a different circumstance than the one I'd been in myself at her age. Not because she'd married into a wealthy family. That was the least of it. She had a partner who genuinely wanted her to follow her dreams and encouraged and supported them both emotionally and with the resources he had.

Will was supportive in his own way. I rarely cut grass or shovelled snow. But when it came to understanding what I really needed, he just didn't get it. When I was faced with a problem, he wasn't the one I turned to for advice. In the past, I'd turned to my father, grandfather, or business mentors like Dave. Later, when I needed to make important decisions, I sought input from my business advisors and partners to explore ideas and gain multiple perspectives.

The realization that Will and I rarely had a conversation that wasn't transactional made me feel sad. We didn't trade ideas that built on each other's. We didn't even argue much anymore. It dawned on me that I didn't miss him when he wasn't around.

In contrast, Nate and I talked a lot. Sometimes we had conflicting opinions, but our discussions were stimulating. I smiled thinking about the time we'd laid naked in each other's arms, and we'd debated the liability of the Watertown manufacturing site Bond had acquired. We'd laughed about there being something wrong with us, but it felt good and freeing to not have to compartmentalize myself into different personae. With Nate I could be lover, learner, professional advisor, and friend all at once.

I finished washing and putting away the lettuce. I considered going outside but it was hot and humid, and I decided to stick to the air-conditioned house. I put on a record and picked up the book I'd been trying to get through for the past couple weeks. Despite it being a thriller, it didn't keep my mind from wandering so I gave up and decided to give Nate a call.

I dialed the number for his home office. It was the private line paid for by his company, it only rang in Nate's office, and it had a separate answering machine. Betsy never answered it, but even so, I never left messages just in case she was within earshot when he played them.

Nate answered after one ring. "Nate here."

"But you should be with me," I answered in my sexiest voice.

"That might be hard to explain to Will."

"He's not here. Won't be home tonight."

"How convenient for us."

"So, you're going to jump in the car and come right over." I didn't actually think that was possible, but I was in the mood to tease him.

"That could be arranged."

"You're such a tease."

"You started it."

"Did not."

"Did too."

"Are you looking for an argument?"

We both giggled at the Monty Python reference.

"No definitely the other thing." Nate was referencing the same sketch that ends with an inquiry for a blow job.

"That could be arranged."

"I'll be there in an hour."

"Seriously?"

"Is that ok?"

I could feel my heart beating faster and that excited panic of a sudden change in plans. "Yes. Sure."

I tried to read while I waited for him, but I ended up pacing around the house and checking out the front window for his car.

He didn't pull into the driveway, but parked one house down across the street. He looked around as he walked back. I held open the front door and he jogged the last few yards up the walk and into the house.

"Hello Beautiful." He backed me up against the door I'd just closed and kissed me.

I pressed my lips onto his and gave his lower lip a little nibble, then wiggled out of his hold. "How did you get away?" I started towards the living room.

Nate followed me. "Major issue in Japan. Need to go to the office to prepare for a meeting in a few hours."

"And Betsy doesn't mind?"

"She's going to Ann's. Helping with wedding gift thank you notes or something."

"Ann didn't mention that."

"When did you talk to her?"

"We had brunch today."

"You didn't tell me."

"She called this week."

"Hmm."

"We had a nice time. Good talk."

Nate pressed his lips together. "Something I should know?"

"Nope."

"Secret woman stuff?"

"You know that's not my thing."

Nate grinned, grabbed my wrist, and turned me to face him. "And what is your thing? Why have you summoned me here?"

I answered his question by putting my arms around his neck, molding my body against his and pressing my lips to his. Nate wrapped his arms around me and we continued to kiss. He held me tighter and our kisses got hungrier until we both needed to come up for a breath.

Nate didn't release his arms, but tilted his head back to look down at me. "You just want to use me for sex?"

I shook my head no and winked. "Not just sex."

He kissed me again. "I'm ok with that."

I pulled us towards the sofa. I sat down while he was still standing. I reached up for the button on his pants and I looked up at him. "Since you're not here for an argument you should get out of these work pants."

He let out a little gasp as I opened his fly and tugged them down. I looked up into his eyes. He had that sweet excited adoring look that made me want to give him anything his heart or penis desired.

He stepped out of his pants and draped them neatly over the edge of the sofa and slipped off his briefs. His arousal was obvious, and I reached out to stroke it. I wrapped my fingers around his length and gently led him back to standing directly in front of me.

I brought my face closer, and I could smell the clean but musky scent of him. I scratched the nails of my free hand through the coarse curly hair of his groin while stroking him and running my fingers of my other hand gently over his head, and up and down his length.

Looking up at him I leaned closer and teased him with a flick of my tongue. A clear drop formed, and I licked that off too. He steadied himself by tangling his fingers in my hair. I took him slowly into my mouth and used the tip of my tongue to search for the notches and ridges that rippled as I passed over them. I felt him shudder and that sent a happy thrill through my heart.

His hands went from my hair to my shoulders, and he pushed back from me.

I was shocked. "What's wrong?"

He pulled me up from the couch. "Nothing. It feels so good."

"But why…"

Nate kissed me. "I can't explain it, but I just need to make love to you right now."

Now I was the one shaking.

I couldn't resist throwing my arms around his neck and kissing him hard.

His hands pulled at my shirt and our lips unlocked just long enough for him to pull it off over my head. We flailed out of the rest of our clothes while keeping our faces pressed together hungrily devouring each other's kisses.

Once we were naked, Nate pulled me down onto the couch. His left arm cradled my head while his right stroked my body starting at my collarbone, down my chest, with a detour to cup my breast and run his thumb over my nipple, then down between my legs. I felt him smile as he kissed me and I knew he was excited by the wetness his fingers had discovered.

He shifted on top of me and looking into my eyes he slid into me. He moved slowly and deliberately. I wanted him to thrust harder and I squirmed to press up into him.

He stroked my face, tilted my chin up and whispered, "Just look at me."

We looked deep into each other's eyes as he moved in and out of me. The connection between us so complete it was as if we had become one body. The intensity of emotion welled up in my chest and my heart felt like it would explode. We moved together until I felt my inner muscles spontaneously clasping and releasing, sending waves of hot pleasure washing over me. Nate responded by pressing deeper and harder for a final few thrusts.

We didn't immediately untangle. We stayed connected, looking into each other's eyes, breathless. My mind was floating somewhere far from my body because there was not a thought in my head other than how perfectly content I was. I had no words but every nerve in my body was firing at once. Like my every cell was clamouring to hold on to this feeling.

As I slowly surfaced from the emotions that had flooded over me, I had a moment of complete clarity. Together we were many times more than we could ever be alone. We amplified each other like constructive interference of two waves merging. Being with him didn't make me cancel out or lose part of myself, it made me stronger, more powerful and our joining created an intensity we couldn't achieve apart.

I tightened my grip on him. "I want this always."

Nate laid his head next to mine and kissed my shoulder. "You are incredible."

"I mean we shouldn't be married to other people. We should be together."

"If circumstances were different, or maybe in another lifetime, I'm sure we would be." Nate's lips brushed against mine.

I didn't want to break the spell that had me feeling so good. So, I squirmed to get leverage to kiss him firmly.

Nate moaned softly and we made love again.

CHAPTER 37

We were on the 17th hole before I figured out why Jack Sullivan, Bond's CEO, and Bob Martin, our CFO, had come into town. Our morning meeting could have easily been conducted by conference call. But they'd insisted on coming in person, and that I make a tee time at Glen Abbey, my country club, in the afternoon.

Jack climbed into the cart beside me after teeing off. "The way you've integrated Bond Canada into the organization over the last five years has resulted in some impressive synergies. We would like to restructure the US and Canadian divisions to create a Bond North America."

Restructuring could be business code for downsizing but I wanted him to know I was a team player. "Sounds like an exciting project."

"Don't worry, you're not going to be out of a job. We'd like you to build the North America division and then run it."

I was being offered an incredible opportunity. "I appreciate your confidence. Has this been approved by the Board?"

"In theory, yes. But the first step will be to come up with a detailed proposal, an organizational structure and transition plan we can present to them. We think you're the man to lead that effort. Of course, we'll need to keep things under wraps until it's time to pull the trigger."

It was going to mean a lot of extra work, travel, and negotiations, but this was an even better outcome than I'd imagined when I took over the Canada division. I hoped I'd be offered the top spot for the much larger US division, but this was a step beyond. Consolidating and reorganizing was going to be a monumental task, but I already had several concepts I was anxious to start working on.

I hated to break off the discussions we were having in the clubhouse after our round but, as I explained to them, it was the opening day for Ann's gallery, and I had to make an appearance. Thankfully, they understood. We decided I would meet them for dinner at Olivers, where I knew they would accommodate us. It was only a couple of blocks from Ann's storefront gallery on Lakeshore Road, so I would join them as soon as I could get away. I stopped at the phone booth in the lobby to call Olivers, then I quickly showered, changed and headed to Ann's event.

"Welcome," said the plain-clothed security guard who checked that my name was on the guest list. Even if Ann hadn't told me about the security for the event, his size would have suggested he wasn't one of the waitstaff.

The space seemed much smaller than when I'd last been there helping with the painting. There were at least 20 people clustered in small groups around the different pieces.

Ann waved to me from the back of the gallery. She was standing in the doorway of the small office that she had designed to process sales and other business transactions. Her in-laws Gloria and Henry were there too, along with Betsy and Brandon. I weaved my way back to them.

She opened her arms and gave me a hug. "I wasn't sure you'd make it. Mother said you had a business meeting at the club."

"I couldn't miss this."

She swung the wine glass she was holding in an arc. "It's a good turnout."

"Already made her first sale," said Henry. "And the wine's just started to flow."

Ann turned to me. "Can I get you something to eat? Some wine?"

"I'm fine. I've got to go to a business dinner later."

"That's too bad," said Gloria. "We were hoping you'd all come to the house afterwards to celebrate."

"I would…"

Henry stopped me by patting me on the back. "Don't worry about it. First of many celebrations, I'm sure."

I heard Claire's voice behind me.

I turned to greet her and Theo. "Glad you could make it."

Claire swept by me and took Ann by the hand. "This collection is inspired."

"That's very kind."

"I love the tulips. I could decorate a whole room around that one picture."

"Are you an interior designer?" asked Gloria.

Claire grinned but shook her head. "Oh, my goodness no."

"If you saw her Christmas decorations, you'd swear she was a professional," said Betsy.

"I could use someone like you to give me some ideas. Ours are getting tired," said Gloria.

"Gloria, Henry, these are our friends, Claire and Theo," I said.

"Lovely to meet you," said Gloria. "I'd like to hear more about your decorating ideas. I love the tulips too but I've no clue where I'd put it."

Betsy, Gloria, and Claire wandered off towards the far wall where a giant blurry yellow and orange painting was hanging. Only because they'd said so, I could see they might be tulips.

Henry must have noticed me staring at it. "I didn't see tulips either."

"Betsy and Ann have all the art knowledge in our family," I said.

"I'm sure you gave Ann her business sense. She's done a remarkable job getting this place up and running."

"I know she's grateful for the support from Brandon and you folks."

"If you'll excuse me, I see a friend of ours has just arrived, and I'd like to say hello." Henry headed towards a short man standing by the sculpture near the front window.

Ann came to stand beside me. "Maddie was here earlier. She dropped in at lunch time. She had to be home to get Anne after school. First week and all. She wanted to be there."

My heart sunk a little but I tried not to show it. "Too bad she and Will couldn't make the party after helping out."

"I gave her a private showing. The VIP treatment she deserves."

"That's good."

"You know you don't have to stay." She winked at me. "I wouldn't notice if you slipped out. I've a lot of other important people to talk to, ya know."

I gave her a kiss on the cheek. "You know how proud I am of you."

"I do. Now make excuses to Mother and get out of here."

CHAPTER 38

The public works director I was meeting with stood and reached across the table to shake my hand. "We'll finalize the RFP based on your input and send it out to you next week."

"I look forward to working with you on this project." I was happy that the meeting had gone well and wrapped up early. I had time to make it to Anne's ringette game after all.

There were only a few cars in the arena parking lot. Even for a game that would decide the final standings for the season, the girls' ringette games didn't have fans besides the parents who could make it to the 4:45 game. I parked beside Will's truck and made my way to the dressing room.

Most of the girls had, like Anne, been playing for several years and no longer needed their parents' help getting into their gear. Still, the room was crowded today with moms and dads joining in on the pre-game cheering ritual in support of their little athletes.

I looked around for Anne. She was in the far corner of the room lying on top of the goalie equipment. Will was just finishing strapping her into it. He pulled her up onto her feet.

The room erupted with the cheer usually reserved for the end of a game. "Holy moley. What a goalie."

Anne grinned and waved her stick triumphantly. "Go Dragonflies!"

Neither Anne nor Will had seen me yet. I made my way between the row of benches towards Anne.

Will still had his back to me. He was standing beside Keeley the team coach. He patted Anne on the head and then he put his arm around Keeley.

The way he touched her made my stomach clench into a fist.

Anne spotted me. "Mom. I'm goalie."

Will quickly dropped his arm from Keeley's waist and turned towards me.

I pretended I'd seen nothing and focused on Anne. "I see that. I can't wait to see you in net." I gave her a high five.

Keeley clapped her hands. "Ok ladies, time for warm-up. Let's go."

Anne and her fellow Dragonflies gathered their gear and their mascot, Wingo the Dingo, and filed out to the ice behind Keeley. The other parents followed the girls. I hung back.

Will didn't leave either. "I didn't think you were coming."

"My meeting finished early. I told Anne I'd come if I could."

"Last game and she's goalie."

"I know. Do you think I'm not paying attention?"

If Will read into my words that I meant more than just about Anne and her game he didn't let on.

"I better get out to the bench." He held up both hands with his fingers crossed. "Hope it goes well tonight. We'll have a daughter in the dumps if things go south."

I climbed up to a spot in the stands across from our team's bench. I wrapped my coat tightly around me before settling in to watch. As the girls ran through their pre-game drills my mind chewed on what I'd seen in the dressing room.

It wasn't surprising there was a familiarity between Will and Keeley. They'd been coaching Anne's team together for a long time. I didn't know that much about her, other than she had a daughter on the team and I was under the impression she was younger than me. Will didn't talk about her. I knew her name because he and Anne would refer to her as Coach Keeley. It had never occurred to me to ask about her.

Now I couldn't stop myself from watching her.

She was attractive. Definitely fit. She hopped on and off the ice with the graceful confidence of someone equally at home on either surface. Once the game started, she paced back and forth behind the girls, doling out encouragement and instructions while Will tended the door at the end of the bench.

Despite their separation, I couldn't un-know what I'd felt when I'd seen him touch her. Every nod or look that passed between them made me even more sure that their connection was something more significant than friendship.

Anne was doing marvelously in goal and I along with the other parents cheered as the girls pulled ahead with their first goal. At the end of the game Anne was at the center of the celebration and she was still wearing her big grin when I hugged her in the dressing room after the game.

Anne squirmed out of the goalie gear and grabbed a handful of grapes and an oatmeal cookie from the snack trays.

"Good cookies," she mumbled through a mouthful of crumbles.

I wondered if she played for the snacks rather than love of the sport.

Will picked up Anne's bag and nodded at the cookies. "One for the road?" It hadn't ever spoiled her dinner, so I just smiled as she grabbed another cookie.

The three of us started walking out to the parking lot.

"Shall we go for a celebration dinner?" I asked.

"We have to wait for Coach Keeley and Susie," said Anne.

"We carpooled," said Will.

"I suppose we could all go." I hated the idea, but I couldn't help suggesting it.

"I'll just run them home and then catch up with you and Anne," said Will. "Where shall we go?"

"Pizza," said Anne.

Will drove them home and then joined Anne and I at Frank Vetere's, her favourite pizza place. We toasted Anne with root beers and we shared a mountainous ice cream sundae for dessert before heading home.

It took a while to get Anne to go to bed. She was buzzing from the excitement of her team coming first in the league and a sugar high. She chattered on about the game and reenacted the shots she blocked. I didn't rush her. It was Friday night so if she slept in it wouldn't matter.

I joined Will in the living room where he was watching TV. He was sitting in his recliner, and I took my usual spot on the sofa. I pretended to watch the show because my emotions were starting to boil up now that I had stopped concentrating on Anne.

My brain scrambled to sort out what I was feeling. I was angry, but the reason for my anger was complicated. Was I angry at him for something I suspected he was doing? It was duplicitous of me to be angry at him, given my relationship with Nate. And I didn't have any proof that he'd done anything. Was I angry at myself for feeling like I needed to hold on to Will? I'd never wanted to need anyone, and throughout our relationship, I'd fought to maintain my independence. I needed to say something to Will.

I got up from the sofa and stood between his chair and the TV. "If you want a divorce to be with someone else. I won't stand in your way." I didn't wait for an answer. I went upstairs.

A few minutes later I heard Will putting on his coat and the front door closing. I looked out the window and watched his truck back out of the driveway.

CHAPTER 39

Sharing the exciting news with Maddie needed to take place away from my office. She suggested we meet at her house. It was unusual to meet there in the middle of the day, but I didn't question it. I parked my car a couple of houses down from hers, to not draw attention, as a precaution.

She was slow to answer the door. When she finally did, she was holding her phone in one hand and the receiver to her ear with her shoulder. She motioned me in, then held up one finger and mouthed, "one minute." She then walked to the far end of the hallway, towing the phone cord behind her.

I took off my galoshes and laid my overcoat over the top of a tower of boxes stacked in her front hall. The stereo was playing in the living room, so I settled in there. I couldn't hear her speaking over the music and I hadn't realized she'd hung up, so I jumped when I felt her hand on my shoulder.

She slid her hand up and ran her fingers through my hair. "Everything ok?"

"You snuck up on me."

"I tried to finish up quickly."

"I didn't mean to interrupt."

"You didn't. My lawyer. The fewer minutes the better."

"True enough."

"Can I make some coffee or get you a drink?"

I held up the brown paper bag in my hand. "I brought champagne."

"We are celebrating?"

"I wanted you to be the first to know. You're looking at the new president of Bond North America."

Maddie's lips curled into a smile, but her eyes didn't follow suit. "The board accepted your restructuring proposal?"

"Not only that. They've offered me a board seat." I pulled out the bottle, pulled off the foil, and unwound the wire basket holding the cork.

Maddie turned her back to me and crossed the room to the archway to the dining room while talking. "That's big news. Congratulations."

I could see her open the china cabinet and take out glasses. "A big win. I wanted to celebrate with you." I twisted the cork until it popped out of the bottle.

"No end to your crazy travel schedule. A lot more trips to Boston?"

"Lots of travel but the other way. I'll be based in Boston. But I'll be back here a lot."

"You're moving?" Maddie set the glasses down on the coffee table.

"I'll be part of the senior management team, at corporate, so it makes sense to be based there."

Maddie sat down on the sofa. I sat beside her and poured champagne into the glasses. I picked one up and turned to Maddie to hand it to her. She was biting her lower lip and staring across the room.

"I'll be back here a lot. Nothing has to change with us."

She didn't look at me. "How can you say that?"

Her tone cut into me. She was upset. I supposed she could have assumed I'd run the new organization from the Canadian headquarters, but that wasn't logical given the scope of the organization and role I was being offered.

I set the glass I'd poured for her back down on the table and put my hand on her thigh. "It might even make things easier. Whenever I'm here, I'll be on my own."

Her head turned just enough for her to glare at me. "Betsy agree to this? I would have thought she'd want to stay close to Ann."

"Frankly, I was surprised. As soon as I told her about it, she asked me to give notice to the tenants in our house as soon as possible."

"You didn't tell me moving was part of your plan." She slid away so my hand slipped off her thigh and she backed herself into the far corner of the sofa and crossed her arms.

"It will be one less complication for us if Betsy is in Boston."

"She'd be pleased to hear you call her a complication."

"You know what I mean. Will goes away, but she rarely does."

"Yes. He does go." Her voice was bitter.

"You're angry."

"I just wasn't expecting this."

I picked up the glasses. "Come. Have a drink. It's a good thing."

She took the glass and downed it. "A good thing would have been for you to tell me you had finally decided to leave Betsy. Not to leave the country with her."

"I promised her we'd move back someday when I took this job."

"Keeping your promises is admirable. But highly inconvenient."

"It's not like I can turn it down. I've eliminated my position in the restructuring."

"I guess you're getting everything you want." She put down her glass. "I think you should go." Her voice cracked.

I didn't want to leave her. "Not when you're upset." I felt like my lungs were collapsing and I couldn't breathe.

She closed her eyes and drew in a jagged breath as if she were trying to stop herself from crying.

I'd never seen her like this. "What can I do?"

"It's just a lot. All at once."

I didn't know what to say or do. We sat there for a long moment looking at each other. I searched her eyes and face for a clue.

This was not what I expected. She'd been on my side from the beginning. Making me look good from the early days of the acquisition through all the expansion to make the Canadian division the star of the Bond portfolio. We'd talked about the restructuring, and she'd been a sounding board for my ideas and had asked questions that challenged me and ultimately made the plan more robust. I was so proud to be recognized for the work I'd put in, and she'd been with me every step of the way. I wanted to share it with her.

I asked her again, "What can I do?"

"I don't know."

I slid closer and took her hands in mine. "We don't have to let this come between us. We'll still talk on the phone, just like we do now. I mean, we've gone weeks without seeing each other and that doesn't change how I feel about you. And we'll see each other. I'm still going to be your best client, right?"

She gave me a weak smile. "You do always pay my invoices on time."

"I hope there's an opportunity for you too. I'm not going to forget how much you've helped me."

"I'm sure you've got plenty of American consultants who can do what we do."

"But no one else will ever be you."

She scrunched her face up and gave me a playful scolding look. "I should hope not. That could get you into trouble."

I filled our glasses. "It's going to be good. You'll see." I handed her glass back to her.

"When is this all going to happen?"

"There will be a press release and an internal memo next week with an announcement but I signed my new executive agreement and so I've technically already started. Delores is setting up meetings with all my new and current direct reports."

"What's going to happen to her?"

"Her husband is retiring soon. She's thinking she might too."

"She probably doesn't want to train another boss."

"You're implying I needed to be trained."

Maddie raised her eyebrows and shrugged. "You'll have a hard time finding someone as good."

"I'd take her with me if I could."

"How about me?"

"You want Delores for yourself?"

She frowned. "Would you take me if you could?"

"I'm not leaving you."

"I beg to differ. Moving to Boston is leaving me." She looked at her watch. "Don't you need to get going?"

I supposed that Anne or Will were due home and she needed me to leave. "Wouldn't want to get caught here alone."

Maddie stood, downed the rest of her wine, set the glass on the coffee table, and then walked towards the front hall.

I followed her. I reached out and put my arm around her waist and tried to turn her to face me. She didn't. She picked up my overcoat, then turned. I leaned in to kiss her, but she turned her head, so my kiss landed on her cheek. She gave me a shallow hug and quickly pulled back.

I reached for her wrist. "I don't want to waste the time we have."

Maddie reluctantly let me pull her closer. She looked up into my eyes. They were the lovely eyes I longed to look into, but they were filled with disappointment I hated to see.

I ran my finger along the side of her face and brushed her hair back over her shoulder. "Just one more kiss goodbye?"

She pressed her lips together and just looked at me for a few seconds. Her eyes closed as she gently pressed her lips to mine, lingering long enough for me to nibble her bottom lip. Her mouth opened just enough for my tongue to slip between her lips. She took a deep breath, pulled back, her eyes still closed and turned away.

She opened the front door. "You should go." Her voice was soft. The tone made me unsure she wanted me to leave.

I sensed she was unsettled, wanting to be close but pushing me away. "I don't want to leave you like this."

"I'm fine. Just go." She swung the wooden door wider.

I put on my coat and slipped on my galoshes. "Will you call me when you can talk?"

Her mouth curved in a thin smile. "Sure. Be careful. The roads could be slippery."

I pulled my coat around me to block the wind and freezing drizzle that bit into my face as soon as I left the porch. I turned and waved. Maddie raised her hand and placed it on the glass of the storm door in response and then stepped back and closed the solid door. I couldn't tell if she was watching through the small window, but I waved back at the house one more time.

It was much earlier than I'd expected so I drove to the office instead of going home. I couldn't help but feel let down at the unusually short visit. I'd hoped we'd share the wine and celebrate. Since we would be alone and in private, I'd hoped to feel her skin against mine as we satisfied each other in the most intimate way possible. I'd cleared my calendar to be able to spend the afternoon with her and I'd assumed she'd done the same.

Delores wasn't at her desk and my office door was open, which concerned me, until I discovered she was inside, standing over Jerry, our telecommunications manager, who was sitting behind my desk. He was plugging cables into a bunch of gray boxes cluttering up my credenza.

Delores looked surprised. "I didn't expect you back today. Jerry is installing your new terminal."

At the past few management meetings, we'd discussed the plan to install a new system that would give division leaders access to up-to-date reports. I hadn't been notified that my equipment was going to be installed.

"Do you need me here for the installation?"

Jerry answered without looking up. "No. It'll be a while before I get it up and running. Do you need me to come back another time?"

"I'll just get some papers and work from my home office for the rest of the day." I looked at Delores. "Call me there if anything comes up."

"Will do." She reached into my in-basket and handed me several stacks of papers. "Anything else you need?"

I shook my head but pointed to Jerry and the chaos on my credenza. She smiled and nodded with understanding.

I slipped the papers into my briefcase. "Ok. I'll get out of your way."

"I can show you the ropes on Monday," said Jerry.

Sitting at the desk in my home office later that afternoon, I was distracted thinking of Maddie. I couldn't get the vision of her eyes out of my head. They looked into mine with the same intensity that had drawn me to her from the first moment we'd met. But the fire in them had been so cold it pierced my heart like an icy spike. Being on the same page, intellectually, emotionally, and physically was one of the delights of our relationship. To feel disconnected like I did today was unsettling, and I felt the tension knotting in the base of my neck.

She'd been excited for me, or so I'd thought, when we'd talked of the restructuring. It was true that my travel had kept us from seeing each other in person as much as we would have liked. But we talked on the phone almost every day, even if it was just a quick call. She must have realized moving to Boston was a possibility given how often I'd been at head office over the previous six months.

The promotion was a big deal. She had to have understood how much it meant to me. I'd come up in the world, without family connections or fancy school degrees, by working hard, and doing whatever needed to be done. The son of a bus driver from Baltimore was going to run an international division of a global company and I'd be making more in one year than he'd made in thirty. It was something worth celebrating.

I picked up the phone and dialed Ann's number.

"Elysian Fine Art."

"Hi Honey. It's Dad."

"Is everything ok?"

"Yes. I was just wondering if you and Brandon were free this evening. I'd like to take you to dinner."

CHAPTER 40

Barry's finger was poised over the alarm keypad when I opened the office door.

"Everyone else gone?" I glanced up at the clock over the reception desk. It was barely five. But it was Friday. I couldn't blame them for wanting to get their weekends started early.

Barry nodded. "Just heading out myself." He traded places with me in the doorway. "I'll lock you in. Have a good evening."

I grabbed the stack of pink message slips from my slot behind the front desk and flipped through them as I walked to my office. Nate had called three times.

I set them aside on my desk. Three stacks of reports were laid out on my table for me to review and sign. They could wait until Monday because they wouldn't go out until then. I decided to just check that they were complete and then I'd head home myself. It gave me an excuse to put off calling Nate.

I'd just finished going through the first stack when the phone rang. I answered it just in case it was Anne. Now that she was twelve, she didn't want Rosa babysitting her anymore, so she was home alone.

"Are you avoiding me?" Nate's voice was playful.

The truth was, I had been avoiding him. The day he'd told me he was moving away was the day I was planning to tell him that Will and I were getting a divorce and that I wanted us to be together. I wanted us to get closer and take our relationship to the next level. But, after all his professions of love and that we belonged together, he had chosen to put even more distance between us. If he'd asked me what he should do, I probably would have encouraged him to take the position. It would have been our decision, and I would know he valued us and our relationship. But he hadn't. The realization that I wasn't a factor in his choices, but Betsy was, had been the blow that shattered the illusion that we would be together.

I didn't want to admit how broken that had left me. "Just busy."

"Are you ok?"

"Why wouldn't I be?"

"That's what I don't know. You're not yourself."

"Maybe I'm just reverting to my real self."

"What does that mean?"

"Nothing. So, why are you calling?"

"I'd like to see you. Have dinner. Or something."

I knew the something he was referring to was for us to make love, but I was determined not to let that happen again. I'd been a fool to let myself fall in love with him. Believing that we were somehow destined to be together was irrational. It was that belief that made me think Will leaving was a sign that our time had come.

The more I thought about how easy it was for Nate to move on, the angrier I was with myself. I started to think I'd just been a crutch that gave him what he needed so he could tolerate his marriage. I wasn't going to be that for him any longer.

"I think we should get used to not seeing each other."

"Don't say that. We'll still see each other."

I could feel my emotions welling up. I didn't want to break down like I had when he'd left my house the last time. I'd sobbed like an idiot teenager, and I didn't want to dissolve into that. "I have a lot to do. Was there anything work-related you needed?"

"Can we at least have a drink? Talk?"

"I need to get home. Anne is on her own."

"What do you mean on her own?"

"She goes home after school and not to Rosa's. She says she's old enough to babysit so she doesn't need one."

"They grow up so fast."

"I still need to get home to make her dinner. I don't want her using the stove alone."

"I'm around all next week. Betsy will be gone to Boston. Is there a day that works for you?"

"I suppose we could meet for lunch."

"It would be nice to spend the afternoon together."

"I meant lunch."

"Don't you want to make the best of the time we have?"

I pulled my day planner out of my briefcase. "I can't do Tuesday. But any other day will work."

"I am free for a long lunch Wednesday. I'll block off the afternoon, just in case."

I pretended not to have heard the last part. "Alright. Wednesday lunch. Will you make the reservation, or should I?"

"I'll take care of it. I'll pick you up at your office at… say… 11:45. Ok?"

"Ok. I should go. I have a few things to finish up here."

"We could talk over the weekend if you have the chance."

"Ok. Have a nice weekend." It was impossible for me to come right out and say no to him. I hung up quickly. Avoiding him was a temporary fix. I wanted to talk to him, see him, make love to him. Holding my emotions in check was exhausting. I put my head down on the desk.

There were two different forces driving me forward. One was pragmatic, dealing with the details that need to be taken care of and the other was vulnerable, hurt, sad and feeling gullible that I'd let a man so deep into my heart that without him there was a gaping hole.

I'd let myself believe that I was first in his heart. Secretly first, but first, nonetheless. I'd rationalized that he'd stayed with Betsy because he couldn't be with me. There was a sort of balance to our relationship; Will and me and Nate and Betsy, with Nate and me in the middle, together.

Will leaving me had unhinged that balance. I was free to choose who I would be with, and I wanted it to be Nate. He had disappointed me, but the anger I felt was at myself. I'd let myself need him. I'd left myself vulnerable.

My life had changed dramatically in the past five years, and Nate had been a major force. I might never have started my company without his encouragement. He'd been the one to plant the seed and had encouraged me in a way that Will never would. I wondered if I would have fought harder to hold on to Will, not just for Anne but for me, if I hadn't found love, support, and companionship with Nate.

I'd let myself depend on him and he'd taken advantage of it. I was determined not to give him that kind of power ever again.

I grabbed a tissue and wiped away my sad and angry tears. I looked up at Anne's school picture in the cardboard frame, pinned to the corkboard over my desk. I'd made a mess of things. I needed to clean it up and minimize the drama for her sake. I didn't have the luxury of indulging in melancholy self-immolation. Survival was key. As was keeping up the appearance of strength, resilience, and independence I wasn't feeling, to set an example for her.

The best thing for both of us would be for me to wrap things up here and get home. I shoved my day planner back into my briefcase, shut off the lights, locked my office and left work behind for the weekend.

Anne had her art supplies spread across the kitchen table.

I put the Chinese food I'd picked up on the way home on the counter. "What's all this?"

"I'm creating. It's for Wallipop." Anne had always referred to my father by that name, a mishmash of Pop that had been what I'd called my grandfather and his name, Walter.

"For his birthday?"

"Uh huh."

"Can I see?" I leaned over the table.

Anne turned it around so it was right-way up for me. "It's not done. It needs more buttons."

Her work in progress was a variation of her favourite format. She had painted a picture that was clearly their house on a thick piece of watercolour paper. Then she'd embellished it with black, grey, and white buttons of different colours and sizes to create the road and sidewalk.

"It's great. I don't suppose we'll be able to eat at this table with all this creating."

Anne pressed her lips together and grumbled. Turned her picture around and glued on another button.

Deep down, I was happy she was into making things. "I guess we'll need to eat in the dining room."

Anne didn't look up, but she had a sneaky little grin. "Or a movie?" She knew that I preferred we have our meals at a table, but she'd been spoiled by my parents who often let her have dinner in front of the TV, so she didn't have to sit at the table with the grownups.

"You keep creating. I'll set up the TV tables."

I capitulated because I wanted to encourage her. Her creations were surprisingly good. She'd even come up with the idea of calling them creations. She'd always made drawings. First with crayons and then later with paints. She also liked to collect things, like interesting rocks, shells, or pinecones. Last summer at the cottage she'd started to glue found items to one of her pictures. It had been a floppy mess, but Will had cut a piece of plywood to hold it up and the first creation was realized. Since then, she's used heavier paper or cardboard and found lighter things to glue like leaves, flowers, ribbons, or painted macaroni.

The buttons were the latest addition to her collection of creation supplies. My mother had given her an enormous assortment of miscellaneous buttons that had been accumulated over a couple of generations in a box I remember seeing under my grandmother's sewing machine when I was a child.

I didn't want to discourage her creativity, but dinner would get cold. "You can finish later. Go wash up for dinner."

Anne grumbled, but put the lid on her glue bottle and went to the sink. I heard the water running as I got two TV tables from the stand in the corner of the living room. The edges were worn, but the yellow sunflowers printed on the metal trays were as gaudy as they had been the day Will bought them at a garage sale.

He'd just moved into this house and didn't yet have a dining table, or much else for that matter. He'd proudly set up the tables for our first meal in his new house; pizza we'd picked up on our way back to his house after going shopping. As his girlfriend, I'd helped him decorate, and we'd gotten engaged after one of the many shopping trips we'd made to pick out furnishings. Our décor had evolved, but the tables had remained. They've served us for parties, can't miss sporting events like the playoffs or Olympics and now the latest craze, movie night with the videotape player Will had bought as a Christmas gift for the family from Santa. He'd kept on putting 'Fom Santa' on surprise presents long after Anne stopped believing.

I snapped the trays into their legs, set both in front of the sofa and went back to the kitchen to get the food. I fixed a plate for Anne and got cutlery and a napkin from the drawer.

Anne scampered ahead of me, climbed onto the sofa, and slid one of the throw pillows under her to make herself taller.

I put the food down in front of her. "Milk?"

Anne nodded. "Can you start the movie?"

"Which one do you want to watch?" I turned on the TV and flipped it to channel 3, so I could connect the tape player.

"Herbie."

"Love Bug it is." I popped the movie out of its plastic case, put it in the player and pressed play.

Anne squirmed in her seat as the opening music played. "Daddy likes this one."

"He does." I didn't want to discourage her from talking about him but, whenever she did, I worried she would ask questions I didn't know how to answer.

"He doesn't have it at his house. Can he come watch it here?" Her little face was pursed with concern. Like she was afraid to ask the question or maybe afraid of the answer.

"If you want him to come watch it with you, we can ask him and arrange it."

"Can we call him now?"

I doubted he would be sitting at home on a Friday night. "Not now. We can call him after dinner."

Anne seemed satisfied. She stabbed a chicken ball with her fork and nibbled on it with her eyes glued to the TV.

I left her and went back to the kitchen. I poured a glass of milk and while I was in the fridge took out the bottle of wine I'd opened the night before. I poured myself a glass. I wasn't hungry. My stomach was knotted. I took our drinks out and sat with Anne, hoping the misadventures of the mischievous VW and bumbling driver would make me giggle as Anne was.

CHAPTER 41

I'd offered to pick Maddie up at her office, but she'd said she would be out all morning and would meet me at the Omega where I'd made a reservation. I requested a table with some privacy, because I wanted to really talk with Maddie and I didn't want to run into anyone we knew. They seated me at a booth in the farthest corner to wait for my guest.

I had a flashback to the first time we'd had lunch as I watched her cross the restaurant. She had the same determined stride, and her face was steely and aloof. But unlike the first time, I knew that beneath the professional shell was a passionate heart, a sharp sense of humor and a brilliant mind. She was the most captivating woman I'd ever met and my heart beat faster seeing her coming toward me.

Maddie slid into the booth across from me. "Been waiting long?"

"Just got here myself."

Maddie picked up the menu and opened it.

I didn't see any reason we should be in a hurry to order. "Should we get a drink first? Talk? Or are you hungry?"

She closed the menu and set it aside. "Sure. Let's talk."

The sparseness of her words was unsettling. Her usual frenzy of thoughts and ideas shared at lightning speed was absent.

"What's wrong?"

Maddie looked away and caught the eye of our waiter who hurried over.

"Can I start you off with something from the bar?" he asked.

"A manhattan, please," said Maddie.

"Make that two." I waited for him to leave. "Are you going to tell me what's going on with you?"

"How's the new job?"

"That can't be what's bothering you. I thought you'd be proud I got the promotion."

"Proud? Why would I be proud? You earned it. I'm happy for you."

"You don't seem happy."

"Things are going your way. Just not exactly working out for me. For us."

"I still want to see you. It's not like we're together all the time now. We'll talk. Every day if you want."

"It's not going to be the same." She paused while the cocktail waitress dropped off our drinks. "I know it. You know it." She took a sip of her drink. Then closed her eyes and let her head fall back against the padded wall of the booth.

I slid around the table to be closer to her. I put my hand on hers. "We can make it work."

"This isn't working for me."

The way she said it squeezed the air from my lungs and knotted my stomach. "What are you saying?"

"I can't do this anymore. I can't be your once-in-a-while when it's convenient lover."

"You've never been that. You're the one for me."

"If that were true you wouldn't be satisfied with the way things are."

"You make me completely satisfied. When we're together, alone, we're in our own world. Perfectly right. We can be everything to each other. We just can't be in our private world all the time. Circumstances being what they are…"

"You mean your circumstances. I was ready to make our private world the real world."

"What about Will?"

"We're separated. We're getting a divorce."

I was stunned. "How? When?"

"What does that matter? It's clear we're not on the same page. I let myself believe we were destined to meet and somehow, we'd find a way to be together. I was ready to take a step closer. To be more available for our relationship. You not only chose to move away but you left me out of the decision completely. You showed me what matters to you, and it wasn't me."

"Of course you matter to me." I moved closer to her and took both her hands in mine.

Maddie turned toward me in the booth. Her lips were pressed together in determination, but her eyes gave away that she was hurting. She took in a long breath but said nothing.

"I don't want to lose you."

She shook her head. "I've given you too much. I can hear my father's proverbial warning." She dropped her voice to a lower register to mimic a man's voice. "Why buy the cow if you get the milk for free? No more."

"I don't even like milk."

Maddie's lips curled into a grimace, and she gave a little snort. "It's a metaphor."

"I never wanted anything from you but to be close to you. It was you that moved us from friends to lovers."

"That was just sex."

I knew she was being contrary just to be difficult. I smiled and wagged my finger at her. "No, it wasn't, and you know it."

Maddie crossed her arms defiantly. "I thought I did. But I was mistaken."

"Maddie admits being wrong. Make a note. This never happens." I took my pen from my breast pocket and pretended to write a note on the cocktail napkin.

Maddie finally smiled. Our banter was breaking down the icy walls she'd been putting up.

I leaned over and whispered in her ear. "I love you. Don't give up on us."

"That's just it. I have to."

"I don't understand. Why now?"

"I need to be there for Anne. For myself. I can't be waiting around for you to have time for me."

I felt her pulling back, her resolve reforming and I searched for words to stop it. "I wouldn't expect you to. Haven't I been there for you? I'll always be there for you."

"From Boston. Married to Betsy. You can't."

Why couldn't she see that I hadn't had a choice. "I couldn't turn down this job."

"I know. Just like you can't leave Betsy. That's why this can't go on."

"What can't? We can still be friends, can't we?" I was clinging at anything that would keep us together.

"Not now. Maybe." She drank the last of her manhattan. Shook the glass and stared at the ice cubes. "I don't know if I can. I'll be reminded of what I thought we were, and it'll just hurt." She put the glass down, slid out of the booth and stood up. "I need to go."

I slid out and reached for her arm. "Don't. Please. Not like this."

The way she looked at me I knew this wasn't what she wanted but what she needed.

She lifted my hand from her arm. "Goodbye, Nate."

She walked away and I sank back down into the booth. I stared at the place where she'd been and the empty glass. I felt like a gaping hole had opened up in my chest. I wanted to go after her because she was the only thing that would make me feel whole. But I didn't.

CHAPTER 42

It was unexpectedly cold for mid-May in London, Ontario. I regretted not throwing in a coat when I'd packed to attend the Environmental Geochemistry short course and Geological Association of Canada 1984 meeting. I hustled from my car into the conference center.

My pager chirped. I recognized Will's number. I had a few minutes before the lecture on groundwater contamination started, so I headed down the hallway off the main lobby to the payphones.

I punched in my calling card number and then Will's office number.

He answered right away. "Glad I caught you before your meeting."

"I only have a few minutes. Is everything ok?"

"I got a call from the travel agent about our tickets. There's been a change to our flight, and I just wanted to check with you before I told her it was ok." Will was responsible for the flight arrangements for our trip to the Summer Games in Los Angeles. We were both making an effort to be agreeable, but I still wasn't sure it was a good idea for the three of us to go on this trip together. Anne had been asking to go to a summer games since we went to the winter games in Lake Placid. I'd agreed to take her, but then she'd added the request for Will to come too.

"What's the change?"

"We need to leave two hours earlier. Six am.

"I don't see any problem. Is that it?"

"Yup. Thanks."

"Everything OK with Anne?"

"I suppose. She's left for school."

Anne preferred to have Will come over and stay with her at our house when I had to go out of town. She wasn't old enough to stay alone for multiple days yet, but she was too old to be shuffled back and forth between our house and Will's apartment. Despite the drama of high school, teen hormones and dealing with having divorced parents, she was remarkably well adjusted. So I wasn't overly concerned that Will wasn't on top of things.

"Remind her she's got her English essay due tomorrow."

"Ok."

"And she's babysitting Thursday night for the Zimmermans."

"Got it."

"Alright. I have to get going."

"No worries. Talk to ya later."

I hung up and made my way into the lecture hall. It was packed but thankfully, Farley had saved me a seat beside him.

He pulled his briefcase off the chair to make room for me to sit. "Sleep in?"

"No. I had to call Will."

"Problems?"

"Just details for our LA trip in July."

"I still can't believe you're going on vacation with your ex."

The moderator introduced Dr. Cherry from Waterloo so I didn't have to explain again that I would have preferred to be taking the trip with just Anne, but that she wanted to share the experience with both her parents. I had initially agreed, thinking that Will wouldn't because he had a new girlfriend he seemed serious about. Fortunately, or unfortunately, depending on your point of view, he'd agreed.

It was especially important that, before we made any plans, Anne understood and could accept the situation. Just because Will and I had agreed to both go, it didn't change the fact that we were divorced.

One of the many conversations Anne and I had was over Dim Sum at Sai Woo, a Chinese restaurant that was a favourite of hers. Our family had been going there for years, all the way back to the fifties when I'd gone with my parents as a child. I let her pick the dishes and once she'd filled our table with plates and steamer baskets, she started asking questions about the trip.

"Do they have good Chinese food in Los Angeles?" Anne stabbed a dumpling with her chopstick and plopped it on her plate.

"We can visit Chinatown one day and check it out. "

"I'd like to go to the beach too. Dad would like that I bet."

"Maybe we can go to Chinatown and Dad can take you to the beach." I wanted to curb her expectations that we'd be doing everything all together.

"You don't want to go to the beach?"

"We've talked about this. I'm happy you don't want either of us to miss out on experiencing the Olympics with you again, but I don't want you to have delusions that your father and I are getting back together." I'd already explained to her that Will and I jwould have separate rooms and that she could stay with either of us and I would be ok with whatever she wanted.

"But you guys are getting along. You don't fight or anything."

"And I'd like to keep it that way." I took a scoop of rice and picked at it watching Anne for her reaction.

Anne scooped rice onto her plate, poured sauce on it, and stirred it. "But what if he wants to come back?"

"He doesn't."

"But what if…"

"You know he's seeing someone."

Anne gave a dismissive snort. "Third one this year."

"That's none of my concern. His love life is his business."

"But you don't have anyone."

I ignored her suggestion that I needed someone. "As long as you're safe, secure, happy and have a good relationship with your father, that's all that matters."

"But don't you miss him?"

"You don't need to worry about me. I'm sorry you're stuck in the middle. I'm trying to be as accommodating as I can, but if this trip is going to confuse things for you, I'll back out and let you go alone with your father."

"I don't want that."

"Ok then." I turned the lazy-susan in the center of the table to rotate the dishes around. "Now let's do some damage to these steam buns."

I'd reinforced that conversation multiple times over the past few months as we planned the trip to Los Angeles. Will looked to me to make most of the decisions, which was characteristic of most of our interactions over the past two years.

The initial shock of Will leaving had triggered my self-preservation instincts. It stung that he wanted to be with someone else, but that hurt spurred me to take action to protect myself, my business, and Anne. The possibility that I could be free to be with Nate had initially softened the blow, but that consolation evaporated when he made the decision to move back to Boston with Betsy.

Will agreed when I suggested we wait to tell Anne until we'd settled some of the details. We told her he was going to see his parents, which was partially true, but he was also looking for an apartment to rent because I'd insisted he couldn't stay with us.

He found a small place on the second floor over a pizza place on Dundas.

He'd taken me to see it before he signed the lease so I could approve. "Anne likes pizza, and it's close so it will be easy for her to visit."

"She needs to eat something other than pizza if she comes to stay with you."

"I know. I just thought it was a plus."

Will didn't feel the need to get his own attorney so I had my lawyer draw up the separation agreement and custody papers. I wanted nothing from his business but I wanted to make sure I could independently support myself and Anne. Will fought nothing. I got the house, my business, full custody of Anne and a commitment from him to provide support for Anne's future education. I agreed he could see her as often as he wanted as long as it wasn't disruptive of her attendance at school and that he could take her on vacations or travel with her to the sporting events she wanted to participate in.

To his credit, he made his leaving as stress-free for me as it could have been. He packed up his things in a half-dozen big boxes and left everything else behind. I was left with much more than half of everything. And he left me with a house full of memories embedded in the photos, furniture and possessions we'd acquired during our marriage.

Despite the lack of disagreements with Will, getting divorced was still a major disruption.

My mother was dismayed. "How could you let this happen? Did you even try to get him to stay?"

My father was pragmatic. "Just tell us what you need. I know a good lawyer."

Friends said they didn't want to take sides. But many did. Couples who'd long socialized with us were hesitant to invite me alone, so my circle of friends constricted.

My business partners had been solid throughout the whole process. Farley especially. They volunteered to take on more responsibilities and were there for me whenever I needed to leave to take care of things with Anne. And our business had flourished. We'd hired three more graduate students from Waterloo, and we were expanding our client base across the country. On top of that, there was so much happening in the field of groundwater contamination, it was exciting to work with experts like the ones presenting at the short course I was attending.

I had a few dents, but my post-Will life was on track.

CHAPTER 43

Ann had called to find out if we were going to spend the holidays with them in Oakville.

Betsy was insistent. "We have to go. It's Jake's first Christmas."

"He's only six months old. He's not going to know." It's not that I didn't want to go. I looked forward to getting to know my grandson and I missed spending time with Ann. But Ann and Betsy in the same house was just asking for conflict. We'd visited several times in the last couple years since we moved away and every time I ended up refereeing some dispute. I much preferred the solo visits I had arranged while in town on business.

"But we will know. Ann wants us there."

If it was what Ann wanted, I wasn't going to oppose it. "I'll call the travel agent."

The skies were grey but there wasn't any snow on the ground when we arrived at Ann's house on Christmas Eve. Despite the lack of snow, her house glittered. The enormous pine tree in her front yard was wrapped in lights so it looked like a giant Christmas tree and her long ranch house was awash with red and white spotlights that made it look like a giant peppermint stick.

Inside was decorated too, with the centrepiece being a big silver and white artificial tree with white lights and blue ornaments. Not my idea of a Christmas tree, but it was very sparkly.

"What a unique tree." Betsy's tone made it clear she didn't care for it either.

I tried to divert with something positive. "The decorations are super. I bet Jake likes the shiny tree."

"He sure does. I can't wait for you to see Brandon's parents' place. Claire's outdone herself again this year."

"Maybe you could get her to help you next year," said Betsy.

I looked at Brandon for help.

Brandon picked up our bags and started towards the guest room. "Let's get you settled in. Shall we?"

I paused at the door of Jake's room and Ann stopped with me. He was asleep in his crib with all the lights on.

"Amazing he can sleep with it so bright." I kept my voice low so I wouldn't wake him.

Ann put her arm around me. "He's amazing. We'll turn them out at six o'clock. We want him to get used to napping when it's bright, for when we're in the Bahamas next month."

Betsy stopped and turned. "You're taking a baby to the Bahamas?"

I cringed at her disapproving tone, but neither Ann nor Brandon seemed phased.

"He's going to travel the world," said Brandon. "No time like now to get him accustomed to it."

"And we'll not be able to travel in a few months." Ann put her hand on her belly and smiled.

"You're having another? Oh my. So soon?" Betsy's tone had switched to concern.

"It was a bit of a shock," said Ann.

"But we weren't planning on just one." Brandon grinned. "So… No time like the present."

Ann and Brandon left us in the guest room.

I closed the door. "You're not here five minutes and you've already tried three times to pick a fight."

"I've done nothing of the sort." Betsy pointed at our garment bag and suitcase, and then the bed.

I lifted the bags onto the bed. "Why must you be so critical?"

"Oh, come on. You didn't like that ridiculous tree either."

"Don't start. Nothing is ever good enough for you."

"There's nothing wrong with sharing motherly advice."

"When it's asked for."

Betsy turned away and unfolded the garment bag. She made a production of pulling out each of her dresses, shaking them out and hanging them in the closet. She was radiating righteous indignance, and I didn't have any desire to continue with the subject. I was getting more and more aggravated by her. At least at home, I could escape to my bedroom or my office. But here, we had to share the same space, and it wasn't worth the pain of pressing the subject further.

She pulled out my suit and handed it to me. "You'll need to change for dinner. Remember, we're going to Gloria and Henry's."

I hung the suit in the closet. "I remember. I'll change later. I'm going to wear my sport coat."

Betsy opened the suitcase, took out my rolled ties and shoved them towards me along the bed. "Ask Brandon if you need a tie."

"I'm not wearing a tie tonight." I put the ties in the top drawer of the dresser along with the briefs and socks that Betsy had unpacked onto the bed.

Every time we're invited to the Hartwell's, Betsy obsesses over what we're wearing. I'd capitulated on multiple occasions and put on a tie only to remove it because Henry was dressed comfortably in slacks and a shirt.

Betsy pulled all my clothes from the suitcase and set them on the bed in a pile. I separated out my folded dress shirts and put them on hangers in the closet. Then I put everything else into a drawer. She continued to unpack one item of hers at a time, shaking it out and either hanging or refolding it. She didn't look at me or speak, so I left the room.

I found Ann in the kitchen. Jake was strapped into his highchair and Ann was scooping green mush into a little bowl from a plastic container.

"You're making your own baby food?" I was surprised because Ann had never shown any inclination towards culinary arts.

Ann laughed. "You're kidding, right? This is from Greta. She insists on making it for him. She says we can't know what's really in those little jars. I have enough in the freezer to feed him until he's three."

"What's on the menu tonight?"

"Asparagus, parsnips and sweet potato for dessert."

"That doesn't sound like dessert."

"It is after parsnip. He's not getting fruit yet."

I put one finger under Jake's tiny hand and he gripped it. "Do you like parsnips? Your Grandpa Nate likes them."

"He does. He's not crazy about broccoli, but asparagus is a green he likes."

"He must take after his father."

"Asparagus has grown on me too. If we'd had hollandaise on veggies, I might have been more enthusiastic."

"That isn't in your mother's repertoire."

Ann sat in front of Jake with the dish of green, white, and orange puree. "Nor are vegetables that don't come in a can." She hovered a tiny spoonful in front of his mouth, which opened immediately.

I watched Jake gobble the veggies from the spoon. "Apparently Greta makes good veggies. You think they're better than your mother's Veg-All Casserole?"

Ann shivered and made a gagging noise.

"It's not that bad."

"Marginally better with frozen vegetables. But still nasty."

"When I was a lad, we couldn't afford anything but canned or the ones my mother put up. I suppose I acquired a taste for it."

"Well, I never did, and I hope he never does."

"Unlikely with Greta preparing his meals."

I leaned against the kitchen counter and watched Ann cooing and feeding Jake his dinner. We'd never had a baby in the house, but I'd seen my sisters cackle and make funny faces while feeding their babies. I wondered if it was something mothers learned or instinctive behavior. I couldn't help but smile, watching how she made Jake giggle.

The phone started ringing.

Before I could offer to get it, Ann called out, "Brandon. Can you get that? I'm feeding the baby."

He must have heard her because the ringing stopped.

A few moments later, he appeared in the kitchen. "Seven thirty still ok for us to be at Mom and Dad's?"

Ann looked at me.

I checked my watch. "I'm sure it will be."

Brandon picked up the receiver of the phone on the kitchen counter and pushed the lighted button that was blinking. "Seven-thirty is good." He paused, listening to the caller. "Yes. I will. Ok. Bye." Then he hung up. "Mom said to tell you it's casual. Come as you are."

I felt a little burst of vindication, remembering my earlier conversation with Betsy. "I'll let your mother know and that we should get ready to go."

Ann nodded and then looked at Brandon. "Can you get Jake's things together and watch him while I change?" She scraped the last few streaks from the bowl and popped them into his mouth.

Brandon reached in around Jake and unbuckled him. "Come on, little man. Let's get you ready to go see GeeGee."

"Gee Gee?" I asked.

"Mom decided Grandma Gloria was going to take him too long to learn, so she decided she wanted to be GeeGee."

"I didn't know we had options other than Grandpa or Grandad."

"There's still time to decide. He's only just started saying ma."

Brandon carried Jake out. Ann put away the baby food and put the dish and spoon in the dishwasher.

"Can I help with anything?" I asked.

"Mom and Dad have practically set up a nursery in Brandon's old room, so we don't need to bring much. You have time to relax before we go."

"Would you mind if I called Aunt May? Everyone should be at her house tonight so I can wish them all Merry Christmas. I'll keep it short."

"Talk as long as you want. Let's call now so I can say hi too, and then I'll go get changed."

Ann led me to the den, and I dialed my sister's number. We put the call on the speaker so we could both hear. My sister called my parents to the phone and Ann wished her grandparents Merry Christmas from her and their great-grandson.

"Did you get the package we sent for Jacob?" asked my mother.

Ann looked at me and shrugged.

I answered. "We brought it with us. We'll put it under the tree."

"Thank you," said Ann. "I'm sure whatever it is, he'll love it."

"Or eat the paper," said my mother with a snicker.

"Thanks for the heads up, Ma," I interjected. "Watch for paper eating. Any other grandparent advice from the experts?"

"Only that time flies. Enjoy every minute."

Ann said goodbye and left me to talk to the rest of the family. The phone on their end was passed around to everyone at my sister's house. Once I'd wished all the nieces and nephews, brothers-in-law, and the cat Merry Christmas, I rang off and went to see if Betsy was getting ready to go.

CHAPTER 44

Somewhere over the Atlantic Ocean, as we flew back to Toronto, I finally relaxed. The trip to London to celebrate Anne's 16th birthday had gone well, but it had been a whirlwind of activity. I'd spent the entire week managing our bookings and schedule and hoping Anne would like it. The destination had been a secret right up until we'd headed for the airport, so I'd had a nagging worry the whole time that she wouldn't be thrilled with her big surprise.

The best surprise for me was how well we got along. That wasn't a given during her turbulent teenage years. We had a constant tug of war between what she wanted to do and what I thought was appropriate for me to allow. Her persistent defiance of the guardrails I put in place to protect her made me lose my patience. She sulked and was moody and miserable when she didn't get her way.

There was a movie playing on the screen at the front of our cabin. Lifting the armrest between us, Anne leaned over and placed her head on the edge of my seat, allowing her to have a better view of the screen. We both had our headsets on, but I was only half watching the movie about a mermaid who comes on land to find the man she rescued from drowning when he was a boy. It had been out in the theatre a couple years before, but I hadn't been compelled to go see it then either. Romantic comedies where everything works out in the end just didn't have enough reality or comedy for me to justify spending money on them.

Anne seemed to enjoy it. She had kicked off her shoes and had her legs tucked up under her. She was wearing her favourite extra-long blue sweater and the new jeans we'd bought at Selfridges. Neither of us was particularly fond of shopping, but I'd still planned a mini tour of the famous stores: Harrods, Selfridges, and Fortnum & Mason. We'd purchased something at each store and were bringing home fancy tea, an umbrella, and Anne's jeans. I was sure Claire would be disappointed in our lack of fashionable acquisitions.

This was Anne's first real international trip. We'd been to the United States several times, for the Olympics as well as border towns like Buffalo and Niagara Falls that were only a couple hours from home by car, but that wasn't much of a culture shock given that at least half of our television stations were American. I wanted to open up her worldview and England was a natural first step, given the language was understandable. Seeing her experience a foreign country for the first time was a delight. From driving on the left side of the road to different vocabulary like jumper, crisps and lorry, I relished watching her discover and appreciate the differences.

I smiled, remembering our first dinner at the hotel restaurant.

"I can have wine?" Anne's eyes were enormous.

"Yes, Miss. Or a pint with your meal, although I'll defer to your mother." The waiter looked at me and I nodded.

I had no intention of letting her have more than one, but she was now 16 and it was legal in England for her to have it, so I let her choose.

Anne grinned at me and then looked up at the waiter with a serious expression. "What wine would you suggest to accompany the steak pie?"

"It is customary to pair red meat with red wine."

"Then I'll have that." Anne sat up tall in her chair with a Cheshire cat grin.

It made me happy to see her looking confident and proud of herself. There was hope I'd not messed her up completely by divorcing her father. It hadn't been easy on her despite my efforts to not let our grownup problems affect her.

In the beginning, Will had been around a lot. But, within a year or so Anne outgrew the need for a babysitter and so I stopped asking him to stay with her when I had meetings in the evening. And since she stopped playing sports and was spending more time on her art that didn't interest Will, her time spent with him had dwindled to special occasions or when she asked to see him. I never intentionally kept him from seeing her, but I didn't push him to either. He seemed to be more focused on his new wife than on us, and I was fine with that. I wondered if, when the next Olympics rolled around, Anne would insist on the three of us going as she had last time. I hoped not.

The movie finished, and Anne took off her earphones and unfolded her legs. "I need to pee." She wiggled forward in her seat.

I got up and let her out. She headed for the toilets at the back of the plane. It felt good to stretch my legs, and I decided to follow Anne and go myself while I was up.

There was someone in line ahead of her.

"Getting in the queue for the loo, too?" She had a goofy grin and appeared proud of her rhyme.

"How very English of you." I pretended to be serious, but I was, in fact, enjoying seeing her so gleeful.

"Has a nice ring, eh? Queue for the loo." She rocked side to side, repeating "queue for the loo" several times, adding a little sing-song rhythm and swaying back and forth.

"You're a nut-bar." I suspected she was wiggling around because her urgency to go was high.

The doors to both toilets opened and we all shuffled places.

Anne added, "Whoop dee doo," to the end of her rhyme and slipped into one of them.

The stewardess was handing out drinks when we got back to our seats. We both asked for a coke. Before the stewardess moved on to the next row, Anne asked, "How much longer?"

"About two and a half hours, Miss. We'll be around with a snack after we finish this beverage service."

Anne took her book out of the seat-back pocket. She was supposed to have it finished and have her assignment ready to hand in when we got back.

I could see from her bookmark she was a little more than halfway through. "You're going to have some catching up to do when we get home."

"I read this much in an hour." She fanned the book to show me. "I can finish it before we land. But these questions are weird." She unfolded the assignment paper she was using as a bookmark.

"Weird how?"

"Like, describe the meaning of the Beasts of England song and how that meaning evolves over the course of the novel." She shrugged. "I don't get it."

I'd read both 1984 and Animal Farm but it was years before. "Doesn't it start out as a revolution song and then it gets banned? It's been a long time since I read it."

Anne didn't look impressed by my answer. "Maybe I need to finish the book first." She folded the question sheet up and shoved it in the back of the book and started reading.

I pulled out my book. It was an interesting coincidence that we'd both brought dystopian novels to read on this trip. Although my choice of Margaret Atwood's The Handmaid's Tale was a more horrifying depiction of corrupted power with a patriarchal society professing high moral standards, but abusing that power and subjugating women.

We both read our books for the rest of the flight.

It was early afternoon when we got home from the airport, although it felt much later. We each carried our bags up to our rooms. I unpacked and started separate laundry piles on my bedroom floor. When I was done with my suitcase, I went to Anne's room to get her dirty clothes so I could sort them and start the first load.

Anne's suitcase was open on the floor, but still full. She was sitting on her bed flipping through her sketchpad.

"You haven't unpacked." I started to pull things from her suitcase. "I'm starting laundry."

She hopped off the bed. "Can you do my new jeans first so I can wear them tomorrow?" She wiggled out of them and tossed them on the floor beside me.

"Anything else?"

Anne knew from my tone that I wasn't pleased. She took a bundle of clothes from her suitcase. "I'll do it now."

I grabbed all her dark clothing and jeans, added them to mine, loaded them all in the laundry basket I'd pulled from my closet and carried them down to the basement. I'd just started the machine when Anne appeared.

"When will you get the pictures developed?"

"I can drop the films off tomorrow. We can probably go through them together on the weekend."

She pressed her lips together and glared.

I wondered if our getting-along period was about to end. "Why the scowl?"

"I want to start painting before I forget how it felt. I think I need the pictures."

"So, your mother actually had a good idea?"

Anne had scoffed when I'd suggested that we both capture the sights in our own way. Anne with her sketchbook and me with my camera. It had been such a long time since I'd had the time to take pictures that were more than just snapshots for the family photo album. I enjoyed having time to explore a scene from different angles and taking several shots with different settings while Anne sketched.

"I told Ann I would do a picture from London."

It was news to me, but I wasn't surprised. Ann's influence had spurred my daughter's interest in studying art. Ann had suggested she attend the summer art camp that the Oakville Art Society was organizing. So, when Anne returned from her month at Camp Nibi Nagamo, she spent two weeks learning new techniques from various local artists. She'd even spent some days off school helping Ann in her gallery. I would bring her to the office with me and then drop her off with Ann when she opened the gallery.

She was really good with Anne and still made time for her even though she had two little ones at home. She'd even found a collector to buy my old car when I converted part of our garage into a studio space for Anne.

My friendship with Ann had led to some uncomfortable moments in the first few months after Nate and Betsy moved back to Boston. Ann regularly mentioned that Nate had told her to say hello if she saw me. I would thank her but refrain from asking about her parents any more than polite conversation required. I'd transferred the Bond account to one of my junior associates, so I didn't have occasion to run into him at their offices either.

At first, I had to force myself not to think about Nate. Thinking of what we

could have had was torture. Gradually, with disuse, the memories of us blurred
and now, when I was reminded of him, it didn't hurt quite so much.

CHAPTER 45

Betsy was still in Florida, so the house was quiet and dark when I got home from the airport. I switched on lights as I made my way up to my bedroom to unpack. After stuffing my shirts and suit into the laundry bag for the dry cleaner, I carried it downstairs and put it by the door, ready to be set out for them to pick up.

I opened the fridge. As I suspected, all I found was beer and condiments and not much else. I'd had a breakfast meeting with the team in Denver, so I'd declined the meal on the plane. But it was almost seven, and I was in the mood for something solid and comforting. I decided to go to Marino's. It was small; I knew most of the staff, and the food was delicious. I could eat alone at the bar and chat with Franco, who presided over it with healthy pours and bad jokes.

The restaurant was half full, but there was no one sitting at the bar. Franco had the Bruins game on the small TV that was perched on the shelf beside the better bottles. I took the stool closest to the TV so I could watch the game while I had dinner. Franco didn't ask, he automatically poured me a beer and set it in front of me. I couldn't decide if I enjoyed being treated as a regular or if it was worrying that I'd become one.

"Just the beer or something from the kitchen?" Franco pointed to the board with the specials. "We gotta nice grilled fish tonight, with a side of shrimp and pea risotto."

"Does sound good. But I feel like a pizza."

"You got it. Pepperoni, mushroom, extra cheese?" Franco started backing away towards the door to the kitchen.

"Yes. Thanks." I took a sip of my beer and squinted to see the score of the game. The game was in Toronto, which made me think of Maddie. We hadn't spoken in over a year. Still, the most insignificant thing could trigger a memory of things we'd done or said. She'd have teased me for ordering the same thing and cheered against the Bruins even if they hadn't been playing Toronto just to be contrary. I still missed her, and I hoped she was doing all right.

Franco came back from the kitchen and dragged the stool he kept behind the bar over to where I was sitting. "The missus still out of town?"

"Helping her father, yes."

"Tough when the wife goes first. My Uncle Tony had to move in with his daughter because he woulda starved with my Aunt Angie gone."

I nodded to acknowledge, but I was certain that Howard Williams would not starve. Their longtime housekeeper, Viola, was still doing the cooking, cleaning, and laundry. She even went to the market to get what she needed to prepare his meals.

There was no need to give Franco all the details. Betsy had first gone to Florida six months ago when her mother had fallen and broken her hip. She was in the hospital and needed surgery. Betsy and her brother Beau took turns at the hospital, and Betsy stayed with her father in the evenings. She had booked a ticket to stay for a couple of weeks, but when her mother's condition deteriorated, Betsy, of course, had to stay longer.

Unfortunately, her mother developed a severe infection that proved to be fatal. I flew down to be with Betsy and Ann for the funeral. While I was there, Betsy told me she needed to stay with her father to sort out her mother's things and get him settled into a new routine. Ann had to get back to the boys, so I offered to stay and help. Betsy declined, saying she had Beau nearby if she needed help, so she didn't need me to stay.

It was only a minor inconvenience for me to have no one at home. I had a busy work schedule, and the months passed quickly. Our cleaning lady kept up the inside of the house and I negotiated a discount at our local cleaner for my laundry every week. Until the country club closed, I played a lot of golf and often had dinner in the club lounge. It's not that I minded cooking for myself but whenever I didn't have time to shop for groceries, I went out. My go-to place was Marino's. With winter approaching, there wasn't even much yard work to keep me busy on weekends so, I'd decided to use my time off at Thanksgiving to fit in a visit with Ann and my grandchildren.

Franco groaned as Toronto scored a second goal. He got up and went to the kitchen and brought back my pizza and set it in front of me. He pointed at my glass.

"Yes. Thanks," I said.

He poured me another.

The waitress came over and gave him a lengthy drink order. He moved off to the other end of the bar to fill it, leaving me to eat my pizza and watch the game.

The camera panned around the arena. The familiar stands of Maple Leaf Gardens reminded me of the first game I'd seen there. Maddie had asked her father for his season tickets for a game when the Bruins were in town. It was almost exactly nine years ago we were sitting in that arena. I remember how happy I was to have an excuse to spend the evening alone with her. And the Bruins had won. I felt my heart pressing against my ribs thinking of Maddie and how good it had once been between us.

That was the moment I decided I would try to see her when I was visiting Ann.

Ann had to work on Thanksgiving Day because it wasn't a holiday in Canada. She invited me to spend the day with her at the gallery. She didn't have a lot of appointments, and she said she'd be happy for the company. I agreed, even though I was tempted to go into work myself at our Oakville plant so I could touch base with my management team.

I held the coffees we'd picked up at Tim Hortons as Ann unlocked the door and turned on the lights. She led me back to the storage room and showed me where I could hang up my coat. Then we settled in her office while she waited for her first appointment to arrive.

Ann pulled the brown plastic lid off her coffee cup. "How's Pawpaw doing? Mother hasn't told me much."

"As long as she's there, he's not going to adapt."

"I don't see him as the adaptable type."

"He still goes into the office several days a week, even though your Uncle Beau took over the firm more than twenty years ago."

"It's good he has something meaningful to do."

"I'm not sure he does much case work these days."

"At least it gets him up and out of the house."

"He doesn't seem to be anxious to take over running the household."

"That's no surprise. But if he is capable of going into the office, he has Viola at home, and can afford to hire more help if he needs it, why should Mother have to stay and look after him?"

I didn't have a good answer to the question. "Speaking of helping. What can I do to help you? You might as well put me to work."

"I have a shipment that needs unpacking, and I'd like to install several new pieces in the showroom. But we can finish our coffee first." Ann sipped her coffee, and we chatted about the collection she had put together for the Christmas season. I was impressed at how strategic she was in focusing the gallery inventory on items that would make good gifts either for corporate gift giving or for personal collections as well as Christmas themed art.

Ann showed me the shipment and explained her unpacking, inspecting, and cataloguing procedure. She left me to work in the storage room while she went out to the showroom. I heard the gallery door chime and Ann greeting her client.

Ann had checked in with me between clients, but she'd had a steady stream of walk-ins that kept her out in front most of the time. Left to focus on the task, it only took me a couple hours to finish, so Ann set me up in her office and had me update her inventory log. She had a stack of invoices that needed to be matched up with the catalogue numbers and then recorded in her master ledger. It was tedious work, but it made me happy to help her out. I was pleased I got through the entire stack before the end of the morning.

"You can come work for me any day." Ann patted me on the back. "Maybe when you retire, you can be my assistant."

"I think I already am." I handed her two phone messages I'd taken while she was with her last client.

She looked them over. "You've made my actual assistant's job very easy. She'll be in tomorrow and won't have anything to do."

"What's next? You said you wanted to swap some pieces?"

"I think I should buy you lunch first."

We walked to Shelley's and had a quick lunch and then I spent part of the afternoon helping her hang several paintings and move the sculpture pedestals to accommodate new pieces. I got up on the stepladder and adjusted the lighting while she stood back and gave directions.

We finished in time to get everything in place before her last appointment. I waited for her in her office while she met with one of her corporate clients. I decided to try to give Maddie a call while I waited.

I dialed her office number, but the receptionist told me she was out of the office. I declined to leave a message, instead deciding to leave a message on her home answering machine.

I called her number.

A male voice answered the phone. "Hello."

"Is Maddie available?"

"Can I take a message?"

My heart sunk as I recognized the voice. "Hi Will. It's Nate Jacobs. I tried her office, and they said she was out, so I thought I'd leave a message at home."

"You in town or something?"

"Yes. Visiting Ann for Thanksgiving."

"Nice. Mads was in the shower. Let me see if she's out."

I heard Will set down the phone and call out to her, but I couldn't hear her response.

"She says she'll be in the office tomorrow morning if you want to give her a call there. We're in a bit of a rush to get to Anne's school."

"Is everything alright with Anne?"

"Yes. She's got a painting in the school art fair."

"That's wonderful. I won't keep you. Have a nice evening."

I hung up the phone just as Ann returned to her office. "I hope you don't mind, I used your phone."

"Not at all. Everything ok? You look weird."

I forced a smile on my face. "I called Maddie. She wasn't available, but Will told me Anne's got a piece in the school art fair."

"Anne's got several pieces in the fair. She's extremely talented."

"You're in touch?"

"Anne helps out here sometimes, and she gave me that painting." Ann pointed to a small picture hanging on her office wall.

"Looks like… London?"

"She painted it from sketches she made on her birthday trip. It's good, eh?"

I stood up and studied the picture more closely. Now that I knew to look, the Anne Tobias signature at the bottom jumped out at me. The picture had a recognizable Big Ben, blurry and gray, a rainy sky and vividly colored umbrellas in the foreground.

I was impressed. "Definitely talented."

"Maddie has really been encouraging her. I found a buyer for her old car, and she converted the back half of her garage into a studio for Anne."

My heart sunk for the second time. First Will answered the phone, so it seemed they were back together, and Maddie sold the car that we had discovered had a connection to me. As much as I wanted to call her and hear her voice, it seemed like she was putting us behind her and if that was what she wanted, I shouldn't insert myself again.

I decided not to call her at the office.

CHAPTER 46

The lobby of the Royal York Hotel was jammed. I wondered what percentage of Canada's geologists were currently roaming the hotel. The annual Prospectors and Developers convention brought them all out of the woodwork and the backwoods to party under the guise of educating, recruiting, and investing in the exploration industry in Canada. After more than thirty years of attending the PDAC, I was still amazed by the mix of people in everything from Armani suits to hiking boots, all part of the same organization.

I first attended, as a student, with my Pops. His company had booked the same suite for at least twenty years, and I'd always made that my first stop. He was so proud I'd become an engineer; I think even prouder than my father ever was. He never failed to introduce me to his colleagues as the brightest of the Cole engineers, and he took great glee at their shocked expressions. The year he'd retired, they'd gone all out and booked a live jazz band to play his favourite music until the liquor ran out in the wee hours of the morning. I wished my Pops was still around. I think he'd be proud as punch of what I'd accomplished so far.

I gave my name and graduation year to the woman at the door to the Queen's alumni reception and she handed me my name tag and drink tickets. I looked around and spotted Robbie waving to me. He'd come down from Ottawa to attend, and it was our custom to meet up at the PDAC each year.

Robbie waved, and I weaved my way across the room to where he was standing with a couple other classmates of ours. After exchanging the perfunctory pleasantries, Robbie suggested we redeem our drink tickets before the kids drank all the good stuff.

"Still a rye and ginger gal?" Robbie wedged himself into the crush in front of the bar.

"Please." I extended my drink tickets to him.

Robbie winked. "This round's on me." He held up his two tickets.

"Ok big spender." I stepped back into a clear spot and watched Robbie as he got our drinks. Although we only saw each other, at best, a couple times a year, it was never awkward. It felt like no time had passed since we'd been students together, working on assignments, studying for exams, participating in school social events, going to football games, all the while playfully debating just for the fun of it. Our classmates teased that we bickered like an old married couple, but our relationship was never romantic, nor were we a couple.

Robbie had several girlfriends over the years we were at school, and ultimately married one of them. No subjects were off limits for us, and he often confided in me when he was perplexed by their behaviour. I would try to help, but often I found their motivations to be so foreign to me I could only commiserate not elucidate.

I suspected that we'd be having one of those conversations later tonight. I'd asked what show he and his wife would be seeing because that's what they did each year when she came with him for the convention. He'd told me that he was coming alone this year because he and his wife were splitting up.

Robbie handed me my drink. "We're getting too old to fight the crowd for a free drink."

"Speak for yourself."

"At least we're not the oldest ones here. I saw Professor Banks when I came in. He must be a hundred by now."

"He was never one to miss a party."

"Maybe that's the secret." Robbie clinked my glass. "Here's to the fountain of youth being a cocktail party."

We spent the next hour catching up with the few classmates that were in attendance, and I met several recent graduates that were looking for jobs.

"You must go through a lot of business cards," said Robbie as I dug another stack out of my purse and put them in my jacket pocket.

"It's all about networking."

"So, it's not what you know, but who you know?" Robbie was clearly trying to goad me.

"We don't all have a cushy government job. Some of us have to hustle to get work in the door so we can pay the bills."

Robbie did a little dance step. "Do the hustle…doot doot doot…"

I rolled my eyes. "Don't quit your day job."

The reception was winding down, so we discussed where we wanted to go next. I had several mining companies I wanted to talk to, and he wanted to meet with some surveyors and geophysics companies. We decided to do our own things for a bit and meet on the mezzanine level at nine o'clock.

I managed to track down the people I wanted to see and had several interesting discussions about potential groundwater and surface water monitoring projects for tailings ponds and waste rock piles. I'd also had a few more drinks and was feeling like I needed to eat something more solid than the couple of hors d'oeuvres that I'd snagged along the way.

Robbie was waiting for me when I stepped off the elevator. "I'm about done here. But if you still need time, I can just tag along.

"I made my rounds. Do you want to go someplace and get dinner?"

"Oh yeah! I haven't eaten since lunch. I could eat a horse."

"Not sure I know anywhere nearby serving horse."

"Funny. What do you feel like?"

"If we can get a cab, we could try the Keg Mansion? It's later, so we should be able to get in."

Luck was on our side. We snagged a cab right away and when we arrived; we got a table all alone in one of the smaller rooms.

"I had no idea this was here. How come we've never come before?"

"It's a bit out of the way. Too far to walk from the Royal York. Especially in March."

"It's still winter in Ottawa. This is nothing."

"Speaking of winter, we had a blast in Calgary."

"I'm so jealous you went to the Olympics again. What is this, the third time?"

"Yes. Two winter and one summer."

"I don't know how you do it."

"You have to book everything really far in advance to get what you want."

"No, I mean going with your ex."

"Oh. That."

"Yeah. That."

"It can get interesting."

"Sounds like there's a story there."

I wasn't sure I should tell Robbie what had happened in Calgary, given what he'd told me about the status of his relationship. "Not one worth wasting our precious time on. You got more going on than I do."

That was just the opening Robbie needed to launch into telling me the sad saga of his separation and the bitter fight they were in. His kids were both married and so there was nothing to fight over there, but she wanted significantly more financial support than Robbie thought was fair. He was bewildered by her behaviour. She'd been the one to suggest they get a divorce, but she was the one dragging out the process with a shark of a lawyer. The legal fees alone were staggering, and Robbie was frustrated that the whole exercise was pointless as they'd eventually end up in court with a settlement that was essentially the same as the initial agreement his lawyer had drawn up.

I was sympathetic, but Will and my divorce had been far less adversarial. I gave him the only explanation I could think of for her actions; perhaps she didn't want a divorce after all.

He stared into his glass as he swirled the ice cubes around in the whisky. "That never occurred to me."

"Do you want it?"

"I thought I did."

"So you don't?"

"I don't know."

"You might want to sort that out and maybe ask her that question."

"This is why you're my favourite. You aren't all soft and romantic. You cut through the bullshit."

"I can be soft and romantic. Just not with you."

Robbie laughed. "That's a relief. Is that why Will's still sniffing around?"

"There's no sniffing." I was lying and I think he knew it, but he left it alone and we moved off of personal topics and on to talking about the convention and the meetings we'd had.

After we'd had a lovely steak dinner, and some Irish coffees for dessert, we shared a cab back to his hotel where we said goodnight and I carried on home.

It was late and Anne had already gone to bed, but she'd left a note that she'd saved a voicemail from Will on the machine.

The message was long and rambling, and it sounded like he might have been drinking. He asked about getting copies of pictures from our trip, which had me suspicious because he wasn't one for keeping photo albums or hanging pictures of us around his house, and he ended by asking me to call him. I got a strong sense that the reason he called had nothing to do with pictures.

It all started when we met another family from Ontario who had seats beside us at the hockey game. They had three daughters around Anne's age, and we got to talking as we cheered on the Canadian team. The girls had all played ringette and hockey and one of them was in her first year studying art at Sheridan College. The girls really hit it off, so part way through the game we shuffled seats so that the girls were all sitting together.

When the game ended, Anne asked if she could go to the outdoor concert at the Olympic plaza with them that evening. I wasn't keen on Anne going traipsing around Calgary on her own at night, but, as it turned out, they were staying in the same hotel and they would all come back together. The parents invited Anne to join them for an early dinner so they could get to the plaza early to get a spot. So Will and I headed back to our hotel alone.

I had to call my office to check on a few things, so I left Will at the bar in the lobby and went up to my room. Housekeeping had been in, so I put the do not disturb sign out so that they wouldn't come in for their evening service that we didn't need because we'd been out all day and hadn't messed up anything.

I was in the middle of reviewing the budget with Barry for a proposal that was due when someone knocked at the door. I ignored the first knock, but a few minutes later, someone was knocking again. I put down the phone and answered the door.

Will was just unlocking his room next door. "I tried to call, but the line was busy."

"You might assume then that I was busy…"

"Ya. Sorry."

"What do you want?"

"I just wanted to ask if you'd like to have dinner tonight."

"That's what was so urgent?" I sighed.

"I wanted to make a reservation."

"Ok. Sorry. Ya. Sure."

"What time?"

"I'll be on the phone with the office until about seven, so after that."

Will grinned. "Great."

I went back to the phone and apologized to Barry for the interruption. We went over the rest of the proposal and when we were done, I made several more calls to other staff to make sure their projects were on track and to provide direction as needed.

Will knocked on my door at exactly seven.

I opened the door. "Just need to get my coat." I noticed he had on dress slacks under his coat. "We going somewhere fancy?" I had dressed in one of my nicer outfits, but it wasn't much above smart casual.

"It's not a pizza joint. You look great by the way."

Will had booked us a table at Ceasar's Steakhouse. It was a safe bet. He'd wooed me with red meat and red wine, and we'd celebrated several anniversaries at the best steak houses in Toronto.

He jumped in to answer when the waiter asked what we'd like to drink. "We have to have a ceasar to start us off. This is where it was born."

I think we both enjoyed the dramatic table-side preparation of our cocktails. There was a silent moment when the waiter left and we both sipped our custom made drinks.

"Do you like it?" Will seemed uncharacteristically concerned about it.

"It's very good. How's yours?"

"Good." He appeared to be studying my face. "This is nice, eh?"

"A haven for the oil tycoons and cattle barons."

Will frowned. "I meant having a nice dinner. Just us."

I was surprised and felt a little uneasy that Will looked crestfallen. "Of course. It's nice. I hope Anne doesn't wonder where we are. I should have left a note." Anne was nearly eighteen, and I wasn't concerned, but I was attempting to divert the conversation.

"She's not a little girl anymore. I doubt she'll be home before us, and if she is, I think she'll be fine."

"You're right. I'm not worried. She's a good egg."

"It's the best thing we ever did. Make our Annie."

"She hates being called Annie."

"Not by her Daddy." Will had that sweet boyish grin on his face that he got when he was being mischievous. "Maybe she pretends not to like it because you're the one who doesn't like it."

I rolled my eyes and let out an exaggerated sigh. "I think we should order you some food. You're delirious."

We talked a lot about Anne over dinner, but Will was unusually focused on asking me questions. He asked about work and friends and if I enjoyed being on the board for the curling club. The conversation and the food were both very enjoyable. We ordered steaks and wine and split a giant slice of chocolate cake for dessert. It occurred to me, while we were waiting for the check, that Will had only talked about work and nothing about his personal life.

I was curious. "You haven't mentioned Susie once during this whole trip. Not even that you had to call home."

Will slumped back into the booth cushions. "There is no Susie any more."

"Since when?"

"Couple months."

"Does Anne know?"

"It hasn't come up."

I wasn't sure what to say. "I'm sorry?"

"It's ok. I'm not as upset about it as I should be."

"Dare I ask what happened?"

"I don't know. Just wasn't working."

"She left or you?"

"She packed up and moved out while I was on a big job up in Barrie."

The waiter stopped by our table and placed a silver tray with the check on the table. "Whenever you're ready."

I reached for my purse. Will and I had an agreement that we would split the expenses equally when it came to our joint vacations.

Will pulled the tray to him and plopped his credit card down. "Tonight's on me."

"That's not our deal."

"I want to. Don't be so bossy." He had a twinkle in his eye, so I knew he was kidding not being insulting.

"I don't want you to think I owe you something."

Will winked. "Don't worry, I ain't got no expectations you're going to put out."

"It'll take more than dinner." I was enjoying the playful banter between us.

"Oh really. What will it take?"

"More than one dinner."

"So… Two dinners then?" Will signed the credit card slip that the waiter had returned with.

I laughed and started to slide out of the booth. "Ready to go?"

Will raised his eyebrows and looked at me suggestively. "Always!"

"Ok Romeo, knock it off. We know this isn't going anywhere."

Back at the hotel, we ran into the parents of the girls Anne had gone out with in the lobby. They said they were going to have a drink in the lobby bar while they waited for the kids to get back and invited us to join them. I declined politely making an excuse I was tired because I really just wanted to have a long shower while I had the room to myself.

I'd just kicked off my shoes when there was a knock at the door. I thought maybe Anne had forgotten to pick up her room key at the front desk. It was Will. He was holding two drinks and asked if I'd like to have a nightcap with him before Anne got back.

I knew Will. I knew the look in his eye. I knew I should say no. "Ok. But in your room."

Will grinned and tilted his head towards his door. It was already propped open. I grabbed my room key, and we went into his room.

I was well aware the drinks were just a pretense. Will set them on the dresser and took my hand and pulled me closer.

"This is probably a bad idea." Despite my words, I leaned into his arms.

Wills hands slid around my waist and then down to stroke by bottom. "If you don't want to…"

My brain said no but my body was screaming yes, yes, yes.

"We shouldn't be doing this." My words didn't match my actions. I ran my hand between us and brushed over his groin where I could feel him growing under my touch.

Will responded by slipping his hand up my back under my sweater and unclasping my bra with a flick. His hand slid around under my shirt. I let out a little gasp as his fingers slid under the cup of my bra and brushed over my nipple.

"I think the girls need to be freed." He pulled away and started to pull up my sweater over my head.

In a flurry we undressed each other and then we tumbled together onto the bed. We didn't even bother to turn it down.

Will tried to kiss me but I turned my head and his lips landed by my ear. He didn't seem bothered, he proceeded to kiss down my neck, across my chest and down between my legs.

I closed my eyes and got lost in the sensation of his tongue and fingers licking and probing. Very quickly I felt the tingling that expanded into the warm waves of pleasure that made me rock and press myself onto his face.

He started to climb up onto me, but I rolled over and got on all fours. Will didn't hesitate. He slid into me. I moved with his every stroke. Pressing back to meet him with ever-increasing intensity. His hands grabbed my hips and pulled me harder onto him. Soon I felt the need to grip him with every muscle inside me and that caused him to grunt and gasp. He pressed in with a few more hard intense strokes that I knew signaled he was climaxing. He stopped moving, but stayed deep inside me and stroked my backside tenderly.

I slid away from him and rolled off the edge of the bed and went into the bathroom.

CHAPTER 47

"That's the last group, Nate." Bill, our VP of North American Commercial Operations, closed his folder.

It was only our largest customers that warranted me making an appearance at the SOCMA trade show. Our sales team had done a good job setting up appointments, and I'd had back-to-back meetings all afternoon. But it meant there'd be a backlog of things to deal with at the office in the morning and my day wasn't done. I had a conference call tonight at eight with the president of our Japan/APAC division.

Becoming President and CEO for Bond was the pinnacle of my career. I'd worked my way up to the top spot, and I didn't mind that work consumed about twenty hours of my day. If anything, I was energized by the demands of the position.

I would have liked to walk home, but it was drizzling rain, so I grabbed a cab back to my Back Bay apartment. I opened my mailbox and pulled out the bills and a small package. I looked at the return address. It was from Ann. I shoved both it and my mail into my briefcase and walked up the two flights to my unit. I could have taken the elevator, but I was trying to squeeze in a little exercise whenever I could to stay in shape, like taking the stairs or my morning sit-ups and push-ups.

I set my briefcase on the floor by my desk. I took out the mail, set the bills on the desk, and tucked the package under my arm. I walked through the kitchen, leaving the package on the kitchen table and turning the oven on to warm up while I went to the bedroom to change out of my suit. Even though I had one more meeting later tonight, it was a conference call, so they wouldn't know I was conducting it in my joggers and t-shirt.

Back in the kitchen, I put together the chicken dish I'd planned for dinner; a simple dump-and-bake chicken and rice recipe I got from the back of a Campbell's soup can. Once it was in the oven, I sat down at the kitchen table and opened the package from Ann.

Inside was a note.

Hi Dad,
Here are the pictures I promised from Jake's First Communion. I managed to get

one of him stuffing the money you sent into his pocket. You'll be happy to know that he's opened a savings account at the CIBC with it. He said you told him to save it for a rainy day – he thinks that means that he should use it for a Nintendo because it's a good thing to have on a rainy day.

I also included a couple of pictures from the Oakville Foundation Art Auction Benefit. I thought you might recognize one of the artists.

Jake and Eden are looking forward to seeing you when you come for their birthdays next month.

Love Ann

I flipped open the booklet of pictures. Ann had arranged them so that each photo was in a separate cellophane sleeve, and she'd written notes on the backs of some of the photos. Jake looked handsome in his dark blue suit and green tie and devout as he posed with the priest with his hands pressed together in prayer. There were pictures in front of the church with his parents and grandparents, including Betsy.

We'd agreed at the time of our divorce that we would take turns attending family events unless it was a significant event that we both wanted to attend. Because it was springtime in Oakville, Betsy was happy to travel to Canada and had requested she be invited. I had a prior commitment to be in Australia for the Asia Pacific Coatings and Chemicals Summit, so I was happy to accommodate her.

Our divorce had happened quietly, with a minimum of drama. Betsy had been living in Florida with her father for almost a year when she called me to let me know she was sending divorce papers for me to review. I was surprised because she'd never hinted that divorce was an option for us. The primary emotion I felt was not loss or anger, but relief. Our marriage had been an obligation and being released from it was good for both of us.

Because both her father and brother were lawyers, I was expecting her to ask for much more, but to my surprise, she only asked for half the value of the house and that she could choose whatever she wanted from the household furnishings and contents. It was settled quickly and within a couple of months, she'd come with movers and packed up her things and gone.

Soon after the divorce, I was promoted to the top job at Bond. The sizable stock grant and options that came with it more than offset the setback of selling the house to give Betsy her due. I purchased an apartment in a newly renovated historic building. Situated close to work and downtown and with easy access to the airport, it was an ideal location for me. It only had two bedrooms, one of which I'd made into my office and library, so when Ann and her family came to visit, I booked them into a hotel down the block. That didn't happen often, as I usually went to visit them.

I'd learned a couple of years later, from Ann, that the divorce had been Betsy's father's idea. It seems he didn't want me to inherit any of his estate and so he'd urged her to divorce me before he passed. When he did pass, he left his share of the law practice to his son and left Betsy the house and half of their substantial family trust. Betsy was a very wealthy woman.

In the photos, Betsy was dressed elegantly and stood proudly beside Gloria and Henry. I noticed she was wearing a large sapphire and diamond ring on her left hand I'd never seen before, and I hoped she wasn't squandering her money.

I flipped through the rest of the pictures; Jake opening gifts, cutting a huge white cake, and sitting with his legs crossed on their back patio with the other men, looking very grown up for a seven-year-old.

When I got to the pictures of the Oakville Foundation Benefit, a bolt of energy passed through my chest. Looking out through the camera was Maddie, dressed in a stunning deep blue dress. She was standing beside Claire, who was wearing a bright pink suit, and they were both holding glasses of champagne. On the back, there was a note.

Anne Tobias with her piece Streetlights that she donated to the benefit. Sold for $500. So proud of my protégé!

I turned over the photo and studied the picture. I barely recognized Anne. She was twelve the last time I saw her. In the nine years since, she'd transformed into a grown woman with a definite style of her own. Her dark hair was cut into a jagged pixie cut with blue streaks and she had on a leather jacket, short skirt, fishnet stockings and clunky boots. In contrast to her dark clothing, her face was radiant, and she had her mother's smile. She looked like a cross between a rock star and a supermodel.

I was drawn back to studying Maddie's face. The nine years since I'd last seen her did not show. If anything, she was even more beautiful. She looked proud and happy. I pulled the photo from its sleeve and studied the crowd behind her. I didn't see Will, but that wasn't surprising. He never really liked going to those sorts of events. It would have made sense for Maddie to bring Claire. Claire loved art and pretty things.

I'd been tempted to call her and tell her about Betsy and my divorce, but decided it wouldn't be right if she and Will were back together. I'm sure by now she's heard it from Ann. If she'd wanted to reconnect with me, she would have given me a sign. Any sort of contact, like a corporate Christmas card with a personal note, would have signaled that I should reach out to her. But there'd been nothing like that.

I took the photo with me and went to my home office. In the closet, I unlocked the small safe that was bolted to the floor. I removed my passport and the folder containing foreign currency that I always kept handy for international trips, then flipped through the packets under them until I found the small manilla envelope I was searching for.

The tape holding it closed was brittle and yellowed and crumbled a bit when I pulled the flap open. I shook out the Polaroid pictures of Maddie. I had locked them up, safeguarding them from prying eyes, but also locking them away like the memories that made my heart ache whenever I remembered them.

Seeing her evil grin looking directly at the camera instantly transported me to the night I took them.

I'd arranged to be in Cornwall at the same time as she was overseeing the site investigation at the plant. We were back in the motel room after going out for mediocre Chinese food.

Lying beside her after making love, I stroked her cheek. "I wish I could have this view all the time."

"Maybe you can have the next best thing?" She reached back and into her field bag that she'd tossed on the floor beside the bed and pulled out a bruised polaroid camera. "I've got a little film left."

My hands shook with excitement as I took the camera from her.

"Make sure you get my good side." Maddie tilted her head from side to side. "Which one?"

I tugged at the sheet, so it fell away from her breasts. "All of them."

Maddie's mouth curled into a seductive smile, and her eyes sparked with mischief. "I dare you."

There was no way I was going to miss the opportunity. I squinted to peer through the small viewer and wiggled backwards on the bed, making sure I had her face and breasts in the picture.

The camera churned out the square of film with a mechanical grinding sound.

Maddie snatched it off the front of the camera and turned it down on the nightstand. "No peeking for ten minutes."

"I only get one?"

"There's only one more in the cartridge. Don't you want to see how it turned out before you take another?"

It was a reasonable suggestion. I tugged at the sheet. "Maybe I should try for a little more of you?"

Maddie pulled it back, but rolled to one side and propped herself on her elbow. The sheet draped over the curve of her hip, her chin in her hand, and her sultry expression was too perfect for me to resist. I jumped off the bed so I could move back and get all of her in the picture. I set the film on the nightstand with the other one.

"Now all we can do is wait." Maddie pulled the sheet up and settled back onto the pillow.

I pulled the sheet off her and ran my hands down her body. "I can think of something we could do."

Maddie let out a playful growl. "Show me."

I crawled back into bed beside her. "I'm going to kiss every beautiful inch of you, especially the ones you didn't let me photograph."

Maddie took my face in her hands and pulled it to her belly. "You can start here then."

I stared at the pictures, remembering the excitement and desire of the night I took them. They were grainy and blurry compared to the photos Ann had sent me and they were both a little dark, but that just added to their sexiness. I felt a churning in my stomach. I wanted to reach out and touch Maddie's hand, her face, and have her eyes look into mine like they once did. There's no one else in this world that has the effect on me that she does.

CHAPTER 48

"Thank you, Wallypop." Anne cradled the bouquet of red and yellow roses tied with a blue ribbon with one arm and gave her grandfather a hug with the other.

I snapped another picture.

My father was beaming. "So proud of you. And delighted to add a fourth generation of Queen's alumni to our family."

It was a good thing we were alumni because we needed extra tickets so everyone could attend her convocation. Will and Janet had driven up that morning and I'd come the day before with one of our company trucks to help Anne move out of her student housing over the weekend. Will's parents had driven down from Verona for the occasion, and my parents had taken the train from Toronto.

We were all proud of her. Her delegation of supporters surrounded her as she stood on the lawn posing for pictures in her cap and gown. Everyone took turns standing with her while I took the pictures.

"I want one with you in it, Mom. Give the camera to someone."

"I'll take it," said Janet. "Let's get one with you and Will too."

I slipped the wrist strap off and handed my new compact camera to Janet. "Just point and shoot." I'd brought it so I could slip it into my purse, but I'd had it out constantly through the entire event. I had pictures of Anne walking in, walking to accept her degree, her shaking hands with the chancellor of the university, and a bunch more. I'd already put in a second roll of film.

"Enough pictures," said Anne after we'd exhausted every combination we could think of. "Time to go to Chez Piggy."

My father had insisted on taking everyone to dinner after the ceremony and Chez Piggy was Anne's favourite special occasion restaurant in Kingston. We'd gone there a few times when I'd been in town for a visit. We'd reserved a table a month in advance because it was small and very popular. And, despite its name, was sophisticated and had excellent food.

We started by ordering a bottle of champagne to toast Anne.

The waiter placed glasses in front of each of us. When he got to Janet, she waved him off.

"None for me. I'm pregnant." She said it nonchalantly, like we all knew.

Verna's mouth dropped open and if her eyes were any wider, they would have popped from their sockets.

Anne's face scrunched up and she turned towards Janet. "You're what?"

"I'm pregnant. What did you think? I was just getting fat?"

Will looked pained, like someone just stomped on his foot. "I thought we weren't saying anything yet."

"It's not like I can keep it a secret forever. I'm sure they're all happy for us. Right?" She looked around the table.

I felt a little sorry for her. She was obviously misreading the room as no one looked particularly happy, not even Will.

"Just one more thing to celebrate today," said Anne. "Nice we all found out together." She smiled and everyone relaxed a bit.

After that bombshell, I felt I needed to bring the focus back to Anne. It was her big day, after all, and I didn't want anyone to steal her spotlight. "Why don't you tell everyone about your new position at The Creative."

Anne launched into telling us about the company, an advertising agency in Toronto, and her new job. It was not a career path she'd ever thought of, but it was a perfect fit for her. She'd be using both her artistic talents and her newly minted commerce degree, and she was excited to get started.

After dinner, Verna and George drove my parents back to the train station to catch the 7:40 train back to Toronto. Will and Janet left to drive to Verona because they were staying at Verna and George's for the night. I was staying at the Holiday Inn on the waterfront, so Anne and I walked there from the restaurant. I'd booked a double room with a view of the lake and Anne had opted to stay there with me instead of her place while we disassembled and packed up her things from the house she shared with five other girls.

It was still early, so we changed into comfy clothes, walked over to The Toucan, a nearby Irish pub, and settled in to listen to some live music. While the band was playing, it was too loud to talk but, in between sets, we could. I probed Anne to see how she felt about having a step-sister or brother.

"It doesn't bother me that Dad's having a baby with her. I just think he's a complete idiot to be starting a family at his age."

I shook my head in disapproval, but she had a point. "That's not nice. He's not a complete idiot."

"So you agree. He's a bit of an idiot, just not a complete idiot."

"I didn't say that."

"Maybe it's Janet's way of keeping him from wandering off. Might be a good plan given his history."

"It would have been nice to not have it sprung on you today."

"It's ok. It's not like we've depended on him for… like… half my life…"

"I'm sorry."

"Don't be. I'm fine. Better than fine. We're fine." She looked at me and I had one of those dizzy feeling moments. Her words were familiar, and I felt like they were exactly the sort I would have said at her age.

It made me smile.

"Why are you grinning at me?" Anne's expression was suspicious.

"Just happy you turned out so great. I guess I didn't mess up too bad."

Anne shifted around the booth to sit beside me. "Better view of the band from here." She grinned, and I knew she was sitting close to me to make me feel better. She'd done the same thing on our sofa as a little girl whenever she noticed I was feeling sad.

I got a lump in my throat, and I could feel tears welling. Happy tears, but I did my best to contain my emotions by taking a deep breath. My daughter was a grown woman, a remarkable and talented one, but she was still my sensitive little girl who wanted to make things better for me in her own little ways.

She gave me a nudge and winked. "Maybe it's time you got serious about finding a new man."

I laughed. "Have I taught you nothing? We don't need no stinking men to survive."

She grinned. "There she is. That's my Mamma."

We listened to the band without talking for a while and my mind danced over the day and our conversation. Anne was moving into a new phase of her life. Launching from student life into the work world, she had her whole career ahead of her. There would be hard choices and challenges to overcome but there also would be triumphs. The years with the most potential for her to grow and thrive were ahead. I was excited for her, but I couldn't help but feel like it was a sort of ending. She was now fully taking the reins of her life. I would be there to support her, but the road she would take would be determined by her choices. That was as it should be, but it made me feel like I was being left behind.

Will was also moving into a new phase. Maybe not exactly new, but he was getting a do-over with a new wife and new baby. I still hadn't processed how I felt about it, but I found the situation more humorous than upsetting. Will was taking on a lot becoming a father when he's old enough to start taking his pension. My main thought was he really hadn't thought things through.

Thinking about their lives transforming contrasted with my life. It had been on the same path for some time, and I didn't see that changing any time soon.

It had been seventeen years since I'd started my company, and it had matured into a substantial organization. Our assessment services had expanded to include terrestrial and aquatic biologists, and we provided support to our clients for environmental planning and approvals. It had been intellectually stimulating to keep up with the fast pace of change in the science of contamination and hydrogeology and lead the expansion of the environmental industry. I'd been the one to suggest we hire our first full-time groundwater modelling specialist. I encouraged my partners to suggest new disciplines that we would need to add to stay ahead of the curve.

My life wasn't all work and no play. Since Anne had gone to university, I'd spent more time on social activities like making time to see friends, like Claire and I'd taken on volunteer responsibilities at the curling club as secretary. Those were good things and gave me personal connections outside of work. But most of my life centered around my company. It was my responsibility to take care of the business because it wasn't just for me, but for all my employees whose livelihood depended on it.

I realized that I had never considered that there could be a next chapter of my life. I was saving for retirement, but that was some nebulous time in the future when I was no longer working. What I couldn't imagine was what I would do if I wasn't working.

CHAPTER 49

The restaurant was glittering for the Mayors Millenium Party. Planning had started months before when the mayor's office had called to reserve the whole restaurant. The guests included local celebrities, business moguls and politicians. The who's who of Boston were mingling as our wait staff circulated, passing out cocktails and small bites.

The mayor's assistant came up beside me. "So, Nate, all these extra candles for ambiance? Or just in case the Y2K bug makes the lights go out?"

"I always have a backup plan."

She appeared concerned.

I realized my words sounded ominous. "Just kidding. Everything is going to be fine."

I was proud of what we'd accomplished. In only a couple of years, we'd become an epicurean magnet and much-coveted reservation. It all started when one of my golf buddies invited me to dinner. He'd recently remarried and his wife was the daughter of an Italian Marquis, from the Liguria region. She was an elegant woman, and they'd invited me to dinner while her cousin was visiting them. Their attempts at matchmaking were not fruitful, but the concept for Mare e Monte Osteria was born.

Her connections in Italy and culinary sensibility, our pooled financial resources, and my Rolodex of contacts, was our formula to launch a new concept in Italian cuisine. As the name suggested, the menu took advantage of our proximity to the ocean and the forests of the northeast to locally source ingredients. Our chef, recruited directly from a tiny town in Italy, created dishes inspired by his family's restaurant that had been in constant operation for over a hundred years. The combination was a hit. Although the first year was tough, once we got a few high-profile reviews and some loyal clients, we were sold out weeks in advance for most of the year.

The mayor's New Year's Eve party was an important event from a publicity standpoint, so even though I was a guest, I was hyper vigilant. That's why I excused myself from the people I was seated with and headed to the kitchen when I caught a glimpse through the service window of Chef Fabio waving his arms at the maître d'.

Chef Fabio's face was crimson. "This is *impossibile* situation!"

I quickly pulled the kitchen door closed behind me to obscure the kitchen drama from the restaurant. "What's the problem?"

The maître d' let out a huff. "Seems we're suddenly short a cook."

"It's your fault." Fabio stomped around in a circle like a caged tiger.

I looked around the kitchen. Gretchen, our sous-chef, looked like she was going to throw up and Paul the line cook was nowhere to be seen. "Where's Paul?"

"He took offense to his orders." Fabio pointed at the maître d'. "He needs to stay out of my kitchen."

I tried to diffuse the situation with reason. "He needs to be here. We can't afford to have anyone else leave. What do you need?"

Fabio snorted. "Someone to grill seventy-five filets."

I took off my jacket and rolled up my shirt sleeves. "Then get me a coat and an apron."

Gretchen laughed. "You're going to step in?"

"I'll have you know I was working a grill before you were born, young lady. Get me that coat."

Gretchen didn't move, but looked at Fabio.

"Go on. If he says he can grill… We don't have options."

"Please let my guests know I am fine and tending to some restaurant business," I said over my shoulder to the maître d'.

I washed up and Gretchen brought me a white coat and black apron from the laundry rack. I put them on, picked up the tongs and waited for Fabio to call out the first order.

Fabio looked dubious but picked up the ticket. "Two medium and one rare."

"Yes, Chef." I pulled two steaks and dropped them to sear.

For the next two hours, I sweated over the grill and the fryers. When it was time to serve dessert, Chef suggested I return to the dining room and rejoin my guests. I didn't want to sully our reputation by letting anyone know we'd had a meltdown in the kitchen during an important event, so I didn't provide any details about what I'd been doing, just simply said there'd been a problem that needed my attention.

The dinner service ended at precisely eleven, as scheduled. The guests bundled up to make their way to the First Night event where the mayor would be giving an address, and they would all view the fireworks over the waterfront from the reserved stands. I opted to stay behind at the restaurant with the staff to ring in the new year with them.

I pulled several bottles of Prosecco from the cooler and poured glasses for everyone. We put on the small TV in the office and all crowded in to watch the mayor talk and the countdown to midnight.

"Happy New Year, Nate." Chef Fabio gave me a giant bear hug. "You can be my cook any time you like."

"It was fun to get back on the line. I might just take you up on it." I realized how wonderful it would be to work in a kitchen purely for the enjoyment it brings, not because I desperately needed the money to pay for school and living expenses.

No one at Mare e Monte was aware of all the years I'd spent working in kitchens. I'd stuck to my role as the investor and man with the connections to bring in the high-profile guests. All the years of appeasing Betsy, by not mentioning my working-class upbringing and history, had made me reluctant to talk about my life before being a corporate lawyer and executive.

Gretchen pointed at my jacket pocket. She'd heard the sing-song electronic chime of my mobile phone before I had. I stepped out of the office and into the kitchen as I dug it out and answered it.

"Happy New Year." Ann and her boys were hollering in unison. I had to hold the phone away from my ear.

"Happy New Year to all of you." Just as I said it, the others came out of the office and started rummaging in the kitchen fridges and starting to pull together a midnight snack.

I could hear Ann talking but had trouble making out what she was saying over the clatter of containers on stainless counters. I blocked my other ear and concentrated on what she was saying.

"We're all at Harbourfront. We just watched the fireworks and we're headed back to the hotel, but it will take a while in this crowd, so I thought I'd call you now in case you're turning in soon."

"I'm still at the restaurant. I'm glad you called."

Gretchen waved her arms at the others and the clatter quieted down.

"How was your night?" asked Ann.

"My night was…" I looked around the kitchen. Everyone was watching me.

"He was a superstar," shouted Gretchen towards me.

"Three cheers for Nate," said Fabio and the others responded

I waved at them to get them to be quiet.

"What was that about?" asked Ann.

"I helped out in the kitchen tonight. We were short a cook."

"Oh my. And you saved the day?"

"I just did what I could, and it all worked out."

"That's awesome. You gotta tell me more. I'll call you tomorrow… I guess… later today, when it's less crazy. I gotta go. We're being swept along Queens Quay. I need to keep up with the boys."

"Be careful. Get home safe."

"You too. Bye."

Ann hung up and I popped the phone back in my pocket.

Gretchen winked at me. "Someone special?"

"My daughter."

"Daddy's girl. That would explain your grin."

It made me stop and think about how far Ann and my relationship had come over the past few years. "More now than when she was a teenager."

"All teenagers can't stand their parents. And if they do, they want something. I know. I have one."

"In no time you'll be wondering how they grew up so fast."

Gretchen held up her hands and crossed her fingers.

Chef Fabio banged a spoon on a big pot hanging overhead. "Time to eat."

We all gathered around the big counter and helped ourselves to the spread. We ate and talked and laughed until all the food was gone.

CHAPTER 50

Anne and I were both sitting in front of our computers while talking on the phone. We were trying to work out the final details for our travel to Torino. It had been eight years since we'd gone to an Olympics because I'd had to care for my mother, who'd moved in with me after my father passed away in 2000. Now she was gone too, and we were attempting to resurrect our family tradition.

Anne was hesitating to book her flight. "I can come home the day before, so we fly together like we always do."

I could tell from her tone she wasn't sure about my recommendation that she fly from Chicago, and I fly from Toronto. "It doesn't make sense for you to lose a day of vacation just to have one flight with me. Book the one that arrives at 8:05 and I'll get the one closest to that from here… arriving 8:25."

I understood her reluctance. This trip had a lot of new circumstances compared to our previous ones. I'd assumed Anne and I would be going to Torino without Will. He hadn't come on our last trip to Nagano, because his son Billy was only a toddler at the time. But Will had convinced Anne that now her step-brother was about the same age she'd been when we'd taken her to her first Olympics, she should be open to sharing the experience with him. So, Billy and his mother Janet would also be going.

Nagano was our first Olympic trip without Will and it was one of the most special for me. It was the first time I'd had no time constraints. I'd completed the sale of CCE Engineering to a large multinational consulting firm that was building its environmental capabilities by acquisition. At first, I'd resisted the notion of selling out of concern for my partners and staff. But the buyers were looking to keep the business largely intact and there were increases in benefits for my employees that, as a small firm, I could never have provided.

So, with a substantial nest egg and time to spare, I'd planned a trip for us that went beyond our usual fix of Olympic spirit. After the games, we travelled to Tokyo and stayed there for several days before flying home. It was fun to arrange for Anne to experience Japan when she was about the same age I was when I first went. She was impressed at my bravado, going so far to such a foreign place in the days before there was email to make arrangements or keep in touch with family and colleagues. I didn't confess to her that it was fearless naiveté rather than bravery that helped me survive the isolation and sexism of the culture at that time.

Despite being winter, not spring, as it was when I was there, being back in Tokyo, visiting the same temples and monuments, brought back many memories. As I walked the same paths in the Imperial Gardens, I thought about who I was then and the twists and turns of life that had resulted in being back in that place. The same person, but so different. A feeling that I had unfinished business in this city also nagged me. Maybe because there were things I could do now with Anne that I'd been excluded from in the past.

Anne was keen to experience the nightlife. So, we went out several evenings to different restaurants and nightclubs, something I'd done very little of when I'd been there. Another change was the explosion of karaoke bars that were nonexistent back in the 60s. We saw numerous places as we made our way home from dinner, so we asked our hotel concierge what it was and how it worked. He suggested a place close by and we got a tiny room just for the two of us. We sang to each other until we were hoarse. You'd think that would have been enough, but we were hooked, and we went back another night with some friends Anne had made on the train from Nagano.

Without Will, we'd been able to immerse ourselves in the art and culture of Japan, whereas on previous trips, we'd focused on just the competition with a little sightseeing between events. I'd hired a local guide who took us to visit artisan workshops, galleries and out of the way museums so we could get a more authentic experience than the usual tourist attractions.

Anne had said repeatedly how much she'd enjoyed that trip, and I hoped Will and his 'do-over' family wouldn't get in the way of her experiencing the art and culture of Italy while we were there. I wasn't worried for myself. I planned to stay on after the Olympics to go to a cooking school and travel around to see other cities besides Turin. But Anne had only been with her new agency for a few months, so she was limited in the amount of time off she could take, so we'd have to squeeze in everything we could between events.

Anne was waiting for me just outside the customs hall at Malpensa airport. We had decided that she would rent the car and drive and I would be in charge of maps and directions. There were a few confusing moments at the first toll booth for the autostrada, but we quickly figured out that the blue lanes took a credit card, and we were on our way.

Will, Janet, and Billy flew into Turin airport as they'd opted for a flight that connected through Frankfort. We met up with them at our hotel, the Hotel Dogana Vecchia, when they arrived later in the afternoon. Based on a recommendation from the hotel, we decided to have dinner at a pizzeria restaurant just down the block from the hotel.

Billy flipped through the menu the waitress had handed each of us. "They've got a thousand kinds of pizza."

The restaurant was prepared for the onslaught of foreigners because each pizza description was written in Italian, English, and German.

I flipped the pages doing a rough count. "More like fifty. Still, it's a lot."

Anne nudged Billy to look up from the menu and she nodded towards the next table where the waitress was placing a pizza in front of each person at the table. "And we each get to choose our own."

"That's so cool. Do they have pepperoni?"

"I don't know but here's one with hotdogs and french fries… called Wurstel." Anne pointed it out to him on his menu.

I couldn't resist a pun. "That sounds wurst to me."

Anne groaned. "No, the worst would be anchovies, or maybe this one with tuna and onions."

"That might not be bad," said Janet. "I like tuna and onion sandwiches."

Anne put her finger on one of the pizzas. "I think I'll go for something safe. Quattro formaggi. Cheese and more cheese."

The waitress came back and placed a large handful of packages of breadsticks on the table, and we ordered our pizzas and drinks.

We nibbled on the breadsticks and sipped our drinks while we waited for the pizzas to be made, and we talked about our plans for the next day. Anne had rented a car that would accommodate all five of us so we could drive to the mountainside venues outside of Torino. We wouldn't need it for the first few days as we had tickets for figure skating, speed skating and hockey that all took place in the city itself.

Our first event would be the pairs free skate, which didn't start until five o'clock, so we didn't have to worry about waking up early the first day. I knew from previous trips to Europe that I needed a long sleep to fend off jetlag. The Italians call jetlag *disritmia*, abnormal rhythm, which is a lot more descriptive of what I feel when I try to change time.

Our schedule allowed us to gradually work our way back to getting up early. Our day two tickets for the women's hockey game were for three thirty and the men's game the next day started at one thirty. We used the time before and after the events to explore the city and soak up the Olympic atmosphere. During our wandering, we found Canada House where we stopped to chat with other Canadians, and we visited the main broadcast square where the major networks from around the world were set up doing interviews of athletes and celebrities.

It wasn't until our fourth day that we ventured out of Torino. Other than the occasional snow squall and fog that made our trips longer than expected, we made our way to the venues for bobsled, skeleton, snowboarding and curling without incident.

We had tickets for twelve events, which was the most we'd ever done in a single Olympics. We'd witnessed Canadians win gold medals in women's hockey, men's curling, and skeleton. Will had been really disappointed that we couldn't get tickets for the men's hockey final, but as it turned out, Canada got knocked out of the finals, and it didn't matter that he'd be watching the last game from his own living room.

I got up early with Anne on Saturday morning. She was leaving to go home, as was everyone but me. They had to leave for the airport at six am so Anne could take them to the Torino airport before driving to Malpensa to catch her flight back to the States.

Anne put the last bag in, closed the trunk of the car, and came around to where I was standing on the sidewalk in front of the hotel.

"It's been great being together. I hate to leave." She put her arm around me.

"I'll email you pictures. I'll have lots of free time now that I'm alone."

Anne grumbled. "You're making me feel worse." She gave me a big hug.

"You're coming home for Easter, right?"

"Yup. And you'll make me all the dishes you learn."

I laughed. "We'll see."

Will, Janet, and Billy came out of the hotel lobby.

Will patted my shoulder as he passed us. "See ya, Mads." He opened the front and back doors of the car.

"Bye Aunt Maddie." Billy gave me a weak wave as he rolled sleepily into the back seat.

"Bye Kiddo. Have a good trip home."

"Ok. We got to roll." Anne gave me a last squeeze and headed for the driver's seat. She rolled down the window, stuck her arm out and waved.

I waved back and we continued to wave as she pulled away from the curb and down the street. I stood on the frosty sidewalk waving until she turned the corner and was out of sight.

CHAPTER 51

I'd just been handed my espresso when I heard a familiar voice saying, "Bon Gee-orno. I'm Maddie Cole. Here for the class." I was physically startled, and the tiny cup rattled precariously on its saucer as I spun towards the door to see if it really was her.

She wasn't looking my way. She was focused on collecting the class materials and pinning on the name tag the school had prepared for each of us. Her hair was slightly lighter, now streaked with gray, but her face was untouched by the years since I'd seen her. I was frozen, staring, barely able to breathe, waiting for her to look up. When she did, she looked around the large kitchen that would be our classroom and, seeing me, her face clouded with a look of confused surprise.

"Nate? What in the world are you doing here?" she said as recognition spread across her expression and she walked towards me.

"Cooking class," was all that came out of my mouth and then I sucked in a big breath of air but still couldn't take my eyes off her.

"Can I get you a coffee Signora," asked Sara, the woman in the white chef coat who'd been handing out nametags.

"Yes, please," said Maddie, following Sara to the coffee machine.

"You know each other?" said Sara.

"Yes. But we've not seen each other in years."

"Perhaps you can be partners? Because you're both here alone."

"That would be lovely," I said, having instinctively followed Maddie towards the coffee machine and then realizing perhaps she wasn't happy to see me, I added, "If it's alright with Maddie."

"Of course," she said, smiling at Sara and then turning to me. "I can't believe you're here."

When I'd read the list of possible cooking schools that my daughter Ann had researched, this one had jumped out at me. Given our history of crossing paths, it shouldn't have surprised me that it would happen again. I just didn't expect it would be halfway around the world, in Torino, Italy, in the teaching kitchen at il Melograno School.

"Were you here for the Olympics too?" I asked, recovering enough from the initial shock to formulate a question.

"Yes. We went to quite a few events. It's been fantastic."

"We?"

"Keeping up the family Olympic trip tradition. This is our fifth games."

"Where are they now?"

"They flew home Saturday. Anne had to get back to work and Will…"

"Cooking not his thing? Pink job."

She grinned and nodded. "You remember."

She launched into telling me about what they had been doing in Torino, the events they'd attended, the sights they'd visited. She was talking fast and continuously, the way she always did when she was excited or nervous. I listened, encouraging her to go on with a word or nod, because I just wanted to look at her, hear her voice, soak in that she was really there.

Then she interrupted herself. "Where's Betsy?"

"I presume in Florida."

"You don't know?"

"We're divorced."

"Oh. Sorry. I had no idea."

"I thought you'd heard. Through Ann maybe?"

"I've not seen her in a while."

Our catching up was cut short by our chef instructor calling us to attention. We gathered with the other students around the large work counters and did our best to follow her instructions for chopping, kneading, forming, and presenting the day's menu. Laughing and cooking together… it was as if we had flown back in time, to the sweetest days of our friendship. As we gathered around the large communal table with our classmates to share the meal we'd prepared, I found myself wishing we were alone so we could really talk.

After our meal, I asked Maddie if she'd like to meet for dinner or a drink.

"I have plans this evening. I'm going to a concert."

I silently hoped she'd invite me to join her, but she didn't.

"Perhaps another evening?" I waited for her to suggest something.

"Perhaps." Her unenthusiastic tone made my heart sink.

Seeing Maddie today, twenty-odd years later, turning and walking away, gave me the same churning in my stomach I'd felt the last time I'd seen her. I didn't want her to go. Unlike then, when I had no idea if I'd ever see her again, I knew I'd see Maddie the next day in cooking class. That kept me from following her, from pressing her for some time together.

Back at my hotel, I opened one of the beers I'd placed in the mini fridge in my room. I sat in the chair sipping it from the bottle, looking out the window at the sleet falling through the streetlights. I couldn't think of anything but her. My mind was flooded with memories that had been unleashed seeing her again.

CHAPTER 52

Mauro double parked his lavender Fiat Panda directly in front of my hotel lobby door. I waved to let him know I'd seen him, zipped my coat, and went outside.

He got out, trotted around the car, and opened the passenger door for me. "Did I make you wait?"

"You're exactly on time."

"It is not typical. But I thought you might be on time."

"Is it far? To the church."

"We go a little outside Torino. Maybe twenty minutes."

Mauro pulled into the flow of red taillights that filled the street in front of the hotel.

"Is it always this busy?" I could see a solid ring of lights, multiple cars deep, circling the roundabout ahead of us.

"It is normal." Mauro slipped the car into the circle, hung in the outside lane, and then zoomed out the first exit.

"Circles are very efficient. I wish we had more in Canada."

"You don't have them?"

"No. Most of our intersections have stop signs or traffic lights."

"I don't like to stop."

"We were honked at a lot the first few days until we learned not to."

Mauro zipped through three more roundabouts and onto a long, straight boulevard. "We will be out of the city soon and it will be much calmer."

I looked out the window as we drove. The buildings changed from large apartment buildings to smaller houses. The road narrowed to two lanes, and the houses gave way to fields on either side. It was dark. Mauro put on his high beams, but I still couldn't see the road well through the sleet and snow that streamed past us. I held on to the side of my seat as we careened impossibly fast through the turns.

I was relieved when we slowed to enter a village. There was a traffic light at the edge of town. It was red as we approached, but Mauro simply slowed down and didn't stop.

My momentary relief evaporated. "It was red."

"That light makes no sense. We just go." Mauro turned off the main road into a tiny street and then tucked the car into a parking spot in a small piazza.

He pointed to the building across from us. "The church is just there. Do you want I take the umbrella?"

"I don't think it's necessary. It's not that bad out."

There were several wide stone steps leading to a massive set of doors. Mauro opened a smaller door that was inset into one of the bigger doors, and he followed me into a small, dark vestibule.

He pushed open the door on the right side that led into the church. "This way."

The church was warmer than outside, but still very cool. I slipped off my gloves but buried my hands in my pockets.

The church was larger inside than it had appeared from the square. Six chandeliers hung in pairs down the center of the nave. Despite the many bulbs, the church was not bright. The way the light played on the flat faces of the pillars and the arches created the illusion they were carved, even though it was just painted decoration. Scenes with saints and angels covered the vault, and a ring of words in Latin ran around the perimeter at the top of the walls. The apse and chancel were brighter, lit by a single large chandelier and six enormous candelabras with seven large candles each. A gilded altar shimmered, reflecting the dancing flames of the candles.

The few wooden pews near the front of the church were already full. Rows of plastic chairs had been set up to add more capacity. I took a step towards an empty area.

Mauro put his hand on my elbow. "I have a good spot." He led me up the side aisle to near the front. He pointed to a single row of chairs set up a step in a side chapel. We took the first two chairs.

I was happy we had a clear view of the whole church. "The best seat in the house."

Mauro beamed and nodded. He didn't have to use words for me to know he was pleased by my remark.

Within a couple of minutes, the church was completely full, with people standing two deep all around the perimeter. There was a low rumble of voices that came to an abrupt end when a deep, sad chord reverberated from the organ. Then came a rippling melody that cascaded over us from the massive instrument whose rows of pipes lined the walls of the gallery at the back of the church. The music echoing off the stone walls could be felt as much as heard. The power of the sound made me close my eyes and take a deep breath. The smell of candle wax and the cool damp air made me think of the awe of the parishioners over hundreds of years taking in the same sights and sounds I was experiencing that evening.

Mauro leaned over and spoke softly in my ear. "You are moved?"

I smiled at him and nodded, and he grinned back at me.

After the organ solos finished, a choir of men entered wearing military uniforms and grey felt hats with round tops, flat brims in front and large black feathers on one side.

"Alpini," said Mauro.

I wasn't sure what he meant but I presumed it meant they were some kind of mountain military.

One man stepped forward and played a note on a pitch pipe. The choir hummed and harmonized on the tone he'd played and then burst into song in perfect multi-part harmony.

I didn't understand the words, but each song made me feel something different. The first was a march, determined and strong. The second was sad and made me feel a sense of longing and the last was happy and triumphant.

During the last song, four young boys weaved through the crowd with baskets collecting money. I dug a five euro note from my purse and dropped it in the basket when it came past us.

When the concert ended, we followed the crowd to the adjacent high school building. Mauro had explained that the evening was a benefit for church renovations, and he'd booked us for the fundraising dinner following the concert. When we reached the table at the door to the hall, Mauro gave his name to the person with a notebook. Mauro protested, but I insisted on paying the ten euros each for the dinner.

Inside the hall, there were five long tables that ran the entire length of the room, each with seating for at least fifty people. I followed Mauro to the second table where we found a slip of paper with his name and a two. At each place, there was plastic cutlery in a cellophane pouch, a bottle of water, plastic wine glass and a small hard bun wrapped in a paper napkin. Mauro explained that the dinner was prepared and served by volunteers and would start as soon as the hall was filled.

I sat down, but was soon again on my feet as people Mauro knew showed up and he introduced me. They were not the last. He seemed to know almost everyone who passed us.

I couldn't help asking him about it. "Do you know everyone here?"

"Most. I am from here."

"Do you still have family here?"

"Yes. My house is not far. My family has lived in that house for over two hundred years."

"Does anyone live there now?"

"I do. When I'm not working. And I stay often in the summer when the city is hot."

"I thought you lived in Torino."

"I do. My house is close to the bar."

"So, you have two houses?"

"It's quite normal to have a *seconda casa*."

"Second home?"

"*Sì*."

Once the tables were full and glasses of wine poured, an army of ladies bearing trays full of plates made their way down the rows between the tables. I was impressed at the meal we were served that included an antipasto of a few slices of different cold cuts, two rounds of polenta, first with mushroom sauce and then with gorgonzola and then for dessert a slice of crostata made with apricot jam on a short crust with a lattice pattern on top. Four courses, water, wine, and coffee for ten euros left me wondering how they made any money.

Mauro tried to translate for me, but the conversation at the table was impossible to follow. Everyone seemed to be talking at once and having more than one conversation simultaneously. Despite not understanding much, I enjoyed both the meal and observing the conviviality that rippled along the communal tables. I felt fortunate that Mauro was giving me a chance to experience some of everyday life in this part of Italy. And it had all happened because Anne needed one more coffee and Mauro's bar was right next door to our hotel.

Mauro had introduced himself to us the second time Anne and I stopped in at his bar for coffee. He suggested we come by in the evening for an *aperitivo*. We decided to take him up on it because we thought it would be fun to have a drink and watch the Olympic coverage on TV with the locals. We were confused when he brought a tray with slices of *salame*, bite sized squares of focaccia and tiny quiches, thinking it was ordered for someone else. He'd laughed and explained they were on the house. We devoured it happily. When he returned for the empty plate, he said if were still hungry he could serve us an apericena, a meal of small plates or make us panini.

We took him up on the offer and, in between serving his other guests, he parked himself at our table and chatted with us. His English was very good. He asked us lots of questions and we found out he'd worked in London for many years at an Italian restaurant before moving home to open his bar next door to the hotel run by his brother's in-laws.

"I think Mauro is sweet on you," said Anne later that evening, when we were back in our hotel room.

"You're imagining things."

"You're not too old to have a little fling. He's quite handsome for a man his age."

"I hadn't noticed."

But I had noticed his sandy brown hair and blue eyes, and the way his dress pants and crisp white shirt didn't hide his physique, even though he wore an apron the whole time. He was friendly, and I liked talking to him. So, after Anne left, I decided rather than watch the closing ceremonies alone in my room, I would go to Mauro's bar. It was then he'd invited me to the concert and dinner, and I'd seen no reason not to accept.

When he dropped me off at the hotel, he asked if I had plans for the rest of the week. I said I was busy with the class for the next few days. He looked disappointed, but I reassured him I would see him at the bar for my morning cappuccino.

He opened his arms and gave me a big hug and kissed me on both cheeks. "*Allora, buonanotte*. I'll be waiting for you in the morning."

I stopped at the front desk to request a wake-up call. As I walked up the stairs to my room, I started to think about the next day and cooking class, and I couldn't help thinking about Nate. I'd avoided thinking about him all evening, but now, alone with my thoughts, I no longer could.

CHAPTER 53

Maddie showed up for class just in time. I watched her as she tied on her apron and walked to join me at our worktable.

Rosalina our instructor, was already handing out the recipe sheets for the day's menu. "Today we will expand our pasta possibilities by making colorful pasta."

I leaned close to Maddie and whispered, "I was worried you weren't coming."

She didn't look at me but whispered back. "I never miss class. You never know what's on the test."

Rosalina continued to explain that we'd be making red and green pasta that required slight adjustments to the ratio of flour and eggs compared to the recipe we'd learned the day before, and we would be preparing two sauces that would complement the red and green pasta.

I skimmed the menu sheet. "Beet pasta? Have you ever heard of beet pasta?" I looked over at Maddie.

"Nope. But we came to learn new things so...."

Rosalina passed out the first recipe. "But first... We start with making our dolce because it will need time to cool after we cook it. We are going to make Bonet alla Piemontese. Although there are variations, we will prepare a traditional version using chocolate, caramel and amaretti. The creamy texture of this dessert is accomplished by cooking it in a *bagnomaria*, a water bath. You will start by making caramel. You have the ingredients and instructions." She waved her hand to indicate we should proceed.

Maddie began to weigh out the sugar while I got the pot of water going. Then she watched over the caramel while I got the loaf pan and set it in the deep dish that we'd use for a water bath. Rosalina oscillated between us and the other groups, monitoring if we were doing each step correctly and offering advice. We worked our way methodically through the steps and it didn't take us long to get our bonet into the oven.

"You work so well together," said Rosalina. "You have time to take a coffee while the other groups finish up."

Maddie and I went to the coffee machine. The little machine was capable of making two at a time.

I loaded the cups and pressed the button. "How was the concert?"

"It was interesting. First, there was a performance by the church organist and then a military choir. Both very good."

"It was in a church?"

"Yes. A small church just a little outside the city."

"How did you find out about it?"

"My new friend, Mauro. He invited me. It's his hometown."

"Is Will ok with you going out with some strange Italian guy?"

"I'm sure he's not bothered."

"So, he knows?"

"They weren't around when he asked me."

"They?"

"He and Janet and Billy… they did their own things some of the time, more suited to Billy's age."

"Who's Billy? And Janet?"

Maddie scrunched her face up and looked at me like I was being stupid. "Will's son, and wife."

"But I thought you were… you said you were still doing the family Olympics…"

"You knew Will and I got divorced. I told you."

My mind was still processing that Will was married, and it wasn't to Maddie. "You didn't get back together?"

Maddie looked confused and then laughed. "There's no way that was going to happen. We kept things civil, for Anne's sake, and it's worked out just fine."

The other groups in our class descended on the coffee machine so we moved away and back to our worktable. I felt a little dazed because my brain was swirling, calculating how many years had gone by, remembering how many times I'd kept myself from getting in touch with her, and feeling the wall I'd built, to keep myself from wanting her, crumble.

Maddie put her hand on my arm. "Are you ok?"

I realized my hands were gripping the edge of the counter and my eyes had been closed. "Yes. I… ahh…" I forced myself to smile. "Just realizing how much catching up I need to do."

"Do you need some water or something?"

"No. But I do need you to agree to have dinner with me."

Maddie bit her lower lip and let out a little sigh.

"Please."

She pressed her lips together and shook her head no.

My heart felt like it was falling through to the floor, but I took a breath and looked into her eyes.

"When?" There was hesitation in her voice, but her eyes had the determined fire I'd seen before, when she was facing a difficult choice and was determined not to give in to her fears.

"You look like you're agreeing to something painful."

"I just don't know why you want to."

"Because no one else is you." It was true, had always been true, but I regretted blurting it out.

Maddie responded with a big smile. "I was afraid you'd say something like that."

"Nothing to fear. Just dinner and conversation."

"That's how things start." Her eyes had the flirty twinkle that had always thrilled me.

Rosalina was tapping her wooden spoon on her pasta board to call us to attention. Maddie turned to face her and left me looking at her ear.

I leaned in and whispered. "We can only hope."

Maddie continued to look straight ahead at Rosalina, but I was delighted to see that she was grinning.

It was difficult to concentrate on Rosalina's lecture on creating different colored pasta. All I could think about was that Maddie and Will had not reunited. All these years, I'd operated under the assumption they had. She seemed unbothered by Will being remarried and having a son. But was that really the case? Then came a realization that made me feel queasy. What if she was ok with it because she had moved on and was with someone else? I needed more information.

Maddie turned to me. "What do you want to start with?"

Because I'd been so lost in my own thoughts, I didn't know what she was asking.

She was looking down at the recipe cards and didn't wait for my answer. "I think the beet." She looked up and at me. "Are you ok?"

"Yes."

"Yes, to beets or yes, you're ok."

"Both."

"You just look… off."

"Just thinking."

"About?"

"How much catching up we need to do."

Maddie looked down and shuffled the recipe cards. "So, we'll start with the beet pasta. Do you want to puree the beets while I measure out the flour?"

I got the message. Not now. "I'll do the beets."

We followed the instructions and made our red and green pasta. While the dough was resting, we moved on to the sauces. Rosalina wanted each group to make different sauces so we could taste more variations. She provided three sauce options for each color of pasta. One group had already selected theirs, so there were two options left for us to select from. I picked up the instruction cards for the spinach pasta and started reading them.

Maddie studied the options for the beet pasta. "I'd like to learn this one with gorgonzola."

I wasn't a big fan of blue cheeses, but I knew she was. "Ok. Then I pick butter and sage for the spinach."

We gathered the ingredients from the class pantry and fridge and took them to our work area. Both sauces would have to come together at the last minute while the pasta was cooking, but we did all the pre-work we could, measuring and chopping the ingredients so they would be ready in place when we needed them. Then we flattened, sectioned, rolled, and cut our fresh dough, following the methods that Rosalina demonstrated. She gave us several options of shapes we could make. We chose to make tagliolini from our spinach dough and stracci, irregular shapes cut with a zigzag wheel, for our beet pasta.

I held back from asking personal questions while we worked. I didn't want to do anything to make Maddie uncomfortable. We were getting along so well, talking and laughing, and it felt so right that we were working together side by side. And the food we made; it was really good.

When class was over, I followed Maddie into the hall where we'd left our heavy coats and boots.

I reached for Maddie's coat to hold it for her. "We make a good team. Our pasta dishes were the best ones."

"It's not a competition. It was a learning experience." Her voice had a scolding tone, but then her lips curled into a smile, and she lowered her voice. "But we kicked butt in there."

"There's just one thing we didn't get finished."

"The prosecco?"

"No, that was definitely finished. I didn't get your answer about having dinner with me."

"I don't think I'll need dinner tonight after eating this meal."

"Then maybe we just…"

"We could meet later for an aperitivo and have a bite to eat?"

I felt like I'd been given a boost of energy having her suggest we get together. "That would be great."

"Mauro's bar has good food. We could meet there."

"Sure. If that works for you." I felt deflated that she was bringing me to her friend's place, but I wasn't going to let that get in the way of seeing her. "Where is it?"

"Next to my hotel." Maddie sat down on the bench in the hall and changed from her shoes to her boots.

"Then I should see you back there now, so I know where it is."

"A not-so-subtle attempt to know where I'm staying."

"So that's a yes?"

She pointed to my shoes. "I was planning to walk. Work off some of this pasta."

I reached under the bench and pulled out my galoshes. "I've got my rubbers. You're not getting away that easy."

CHAPTER 54

Mauro saw us come in, and he came around the counter with open arms.

"*Ciao Cara.*" He put his hands on my shoulders and kissed both of my cheeks.

"Ciao Mauro. How are you this evening?"

"Not so good." His smile didn't match his sober words. He nodded over my shoulder. "You brought a date?"

"Just a friend." I took a step sideways. "Nate Jacobs, this is Mauro…" I realized I didn't know his last name.

"Missi. Mauro Missi. *Piacere*, Nate." Mauro extended his hand.

Nate shook it. "Nice to meet you." He didn't look that happy.

"We thought we'd come for an aperitivo and maybe some of those special panini you make?"

"Wonderful." He waved his arm towards the table Anne and I usually occupied. "*Accomodatevi.*"

Nate helped me off with my coat and draped it over the spare chair at the table and then placed his on top of it.

"He seems… friendly." Nate's voice had a bitter edge.

"Definitely. And constantly in motion." I tilted my head towards where he was coming around the bar with a tray of drinks in one hand and a platter in the other.

Mauro delivered the order to a table where four men were seated playing cards and then came over to us.

Mauro placed his hand on my shoulder. "I'm so glad you came in. It's been too long since I saw you."

I laughed. "Yes, so long. Since this morning."

Mauro looked at Nate. "You must agree that is too long to be away from this beauty."

"I do, but I was fortunate to spend most of the day with her." Nate looked smug.

Mauro clutched his chest. "I am wrecked with envy." He let out a hearty laugh and then put his hands into the pockets of his apron and looked at me. "For your aperitivo… Red wine for you?"

"Yes, please."

"I have the same one you had before. Was it ok?"

I nodded. "It was good."

"And for you?"

"I'll have the same."

I was surprised. "You can have a beer or something else?"

"I'm following your lead this evening." Nate's tone was playful, but his eyes looked into mine with an intensity that made my nerves ripple under my skin.

Mauro nodded. "Smart man. Wine for both. I will bring something perfect to accompany it."

I watched Nate's eyes follow him as he walked back behind the counter and into the kitchen behind it. His expression was studious as he took a good look around the bar before his gaze came back to me.

"Cute place, eh?"

Nate nodded. "Interesting contrasts. Marble, mosaics, a big chandelier and then a big tv, a neon beer sign…"

"Mauro tells me the place is packed for Juventus or Torino matches."

"That explains the big tv at least."

"I think it's great there's a place where everyone can gather."

"I'm not being critical. I'm just thinking how different a concept it is to the coffee shops or bars back home. This is both, but neither."

Mauro set an overflowing platter of food down in between us and then took our drinks off the tray he was holding in his other hand. "I bring you a little of everything tonight." He winked at me. "To make a good impression on your friend." He reached into the pocket of his apron and took out a paper sack of breadsticks.

I shook my head at him. "You know those are my weakness." I turned to Nate. "Watch out for them. They are evil. Once you start eating them…"

Nate looked over the dish. "It all looks very good. I'll have to tell our chef to rethink our antipasto board."

"Your chef?" I figured Nate had done well, but it didn't seem like him to hire a chef for himself.

"At our restaurant. Well, actually, three restaurants."

Mauro looked impressed. "You have three restaurants?" He grabbed a chair from the table next to ours and swung it around, and sat down.

"I'm part owner. It started with just one, but it sort of took off, so we expanded."

I'd assumed Nate was retired from his corporate position and would have kept busy, but I was still surprised. "What kind of restaurant?"

"Italian. At least our chef is."

"So that's why you signed up for cooking school?"

"I don't like not knowing how the sausage is made."

Mauro looked very confused.

I explained. "It's an expression. It means… you like to know how the process works, behind the scenes."

Mauro nodded and then grinned at Nate. "No *salsiccia* making here, but I will let you know my secret to success."

"Please do." Nate smiled at Mauro.

If I didn't know Nate so well, I would have thought he was happy to have Mauro's advice, but I could tell he was being patronizing in the hopes that Mauro would tell him and then go away.

Mauro leaned in over the table. "Make friends. They are more loyal than customers." He got up and put his hand on Nate's shoulder while looking at me. "And they will bring you more customers to befriend." He tucked the tray under his arm and left to check on the other tables.

Nate picked up his glass. "To friends, old and new."

I met his glass with mine. "Cheers to that." I took a sip. "Are you taking the class on Thursday?"

"And Friday. You?"

"Both, and then I'm going home on Saturday."

"Back to the grindstone?"

"Not exactly. Unlike you, I haven't started another business."

"You're retired?"

"I sold the company… eight years ago now. Time flies."

"What have you been doing since then?"

"I've stayed on as a board member, done some guest lecturing, got back into photography… I keep busy."

"No new Mr. Cole?"

It made me feel good that Nate seemed to be holding his breath, waiting for me to answer. "No Mr. Cole. No new Mrs. Jacobs?"

"No."

"Too busy building your restaurant empire?"

Nate shook his head. "Do you have plans for tomorrow?"

I was quite excited about my plans for the day the cooking school was closed. I launched into telling Nate that I planned to take the train to Milan and spend the day there, walking, visiting museums and famous landmarks and taking pictures.

"That sounds great. You wouldn't happen to want some company?"

"Don't tell me you didn't make plans."

"That was before I knew there was a chance I could spend the day with you."

"Well, I don't have a solid plan. I was just going to wander."

"I would like to wander with you. If you'll have me."

My heart did a little flip-flop. The way he looked at me made it impossible for me to say no. "I was planning to take the eight o'clock train."

CHAPTER 55

The Porta Nuova train station was busy. A steady flow of travelers streamed through the arch lined concourse. I wished we'd been more specific about a meeting place as I watched for Maddie in the lobby area in front of the ticket counters. I checked my watch. It was just seven thirty, the time we'd agreed to meet, but I felt like I'd been waiting for ages. I finally spotted her, and we went together up to the ticket window.

Maddie pulled a slip of paper from her pocket and read from it. "*Due per Milano Centrale alle otto.*"

The ticked agent smiled and answered in a mix of English and Italian. "The fare is twenty-two *euro* for *seconda classe.*"

Maddie started to unzip her coat.

I wanted to pay for the tickets and so I had the money ready in my hand. "I've got it." I handed it to the ticket agent.

Maddie closed her coat. "I'll get our tickets home."

I nodded, but I had no intention of letting her pay then either. I was grateful she'd agreed to let me join her for the day. I wanted to spend as much time with her as I could because we were both leaving on Saturday.

We found our train number and track information on the big board in the concourse, and we made our way to the platform to wait. When the train arrived, we boarded and found two seats across from each other by the window.

Maddie took off her gloves and shoved them into the pockets of her coat. She unzipped her coat and slipped her arms out of the sleeves, but left it draped over her shoulders. "I don't want to get too hot because when I go out I'll feel cold." She held the coat around her as she settled into her seat.

I'd thought her coat had looked very bulky, but I realized it wasn't the coat but the large camera and her purse that she had under it that made it look bigger.

She noticed me looking at them. "Purse close for security and keeping camera battery warm so it will last longer."

"That looks like a different camera."

"I've gone through a couple generations since you've been around. This one's digital."

I didn't know much about digital cameras or photography in general.

"Looks like a serious camera."

"One of the perks of retirement is time to get back into making pictures."

"Still have the darkroom in your basement?"

"Digital opens up a whole new realm of possibilities. I sit in front of my computer monitor instead of downstairs in the dark."

It was hard to hear each other and so we didn't talk much on the train ride. We leaned our heads close together when we wanted to comment on something we saw out the window and to go over the plan for what we'd do when we arrived in Milan.

From the train platform, we followed the signs to find the Metro. We each bought a day pass as Mauro had recommended, so we could use it as much as we wanted to get around, especially if the weather made long walks unpleasant.

We took the Metro to the Duomo Station and walking up we found ourselves in the big piazza with the gothic spires of the Duomo di Milano towering over us. Maddie dug her camera out from under her coat and took several pictures.

When she was done, she tucked it away again. "Too bad some of it's covered in scaffolding."

"Still impressive. I wouldn't want to be in charge of maintenance. Imagine the upkeep."

"It took something like 500 years to build. My guess is it's never ending. Shall we head there first?" She didn't wait for me to answer, but led the way across the square towards the massive doors.

When we got closer, we could see there was a sign indicating the entrance was through a smaller door within the huge door on the right side. Pushing it open, we accessed the cavernous church.

"Do you think they made it so big to make us feel small?" I'd become more skeptical about the intentions of organized religions in my later years, and it had tempered my enthusiasm for the magnificence of the grand cathedrals of Europe.

"You have to admire the ambition of it. The fifth largest in the world, I think." Maddie's head was tilted back to take in the towering stone columns and vaults, and then she looked down at the floor. "And this pattern is intricate. Imagine how much work it was to cut all those different colored pieces of marble."

We made our way around the perimeter slowly taking in the stained glass, frescos, paintings, and statues that decorated the small chapels that lined both sides of the main body of the church. When we got to the front, there was a sign indicating we needed a ticket to enter the crypt.

"Want to get tickets?" Maddie's voice was low.

I leaned close so my ear was nearer her lips. I got a whiff of her perfume and I had to stop myself from pulling her closer. I closed my eyes for a second.

Maddie repeated her question a little louder. "Should we go buy tickets?"

I hoped she assumed I hadn't heard her, not that I was being completely distracted by her nearness. "We're here. Might as well see it all."

There was a lady selling tickets and souvenir items at the back of the church. She suggested we might also want to visit the archaeological site below if we had time.

Maddie looked at me. "Sounds interesting. Want to?"

"Why not?"

As it turned out, visiting the archeological site was a good call. The crypt was more marble arches, stucco engravings along with the relics of saints and noblemen, whereas the archeologic excavations reveal the remains of ancient constructions that were on the site prior to the duomo that date back to the middle of the fourth century.

Fortunately, we were given a pamphlet in English that explained the site. We were the only people in the area, so Maddie read aloud the description for each of the numbered stations along the path through the excavations.

She read the section on the history of the archeological work and that the site was unknown until it was discovered in the 1960s. "I suppose it's easy to forget about what's underneath when it takes 500 years to build what's on top."

"I've already forgotten what I had for breakfast."

"You and breakfast. I bet it was eggs, bacon, and white toast. And a black coffee."

"So what if it was?"

"Some things never change."

"Some have. And that could be a good thing for us."

Maddie stopped walking. She turned to face me and took in a breath, like she was going to say something. But then she pressed her lips together like she was holding whatever it was back. Her eyes studied my face.

The last thing I wanted was to upset her. "I just meant…"

She interrupted me. "Now we're both unattached?" She looked annoyed.

"I shouldn't assume you are. I just meant… well … I am."

Maddie's face softened a bit and she exhaled. "I wish you'd figured it out twenty-plus years ago."

"Figured what?"

"How we could both be unattached at the same time."

"If I'd known you were…"

"You'd have turned down a promotion? I have my doubts." Maddie turned and continued along the irregular path that crisscrossed the exhibit and hit the button to illuminate the next section.

"Are you mad?"

"I stopped being mad at you at least a decade ago."

"I'm sorry."

"For what? Not leaving your wife? Having a successful career?"

"I hurt you."

"I allowed it. Learned my lesson."

I reached for her hand and stopped her from walking away.

She turned to face me and I could see her eyes were moist and her jaw clenched the way she did when she was fighting to hold back her emotions.

I had to make things right between us. "I was a fool. I never should have let you go."

"You're the one who went. Not me."

"I never stopped… my feelings … they haven't changed." I could see my words were not making her happy. She leaned away like they were landing like punches and she turned her head and wiped her eyes on the sleeve of her coat and then she pressed her fingers around her temples like she had a headache.

"Please don't be upset. I can't stand the thought of hurting you."

"More?"

"Why didn't you say something?"

"I wasn't going to beg. Why didn't you ask?"

"I thought you were happy. With Will."

She shook her head. "I was in love with you."

I took both her hands and turned her to face me. "I still love you." I looked around and we were still the only ones in the exhibit. I moved closer and reached one hand up to her face. "You're still the most beautiful, smart, desirable women I fell for in a blackout."

Just as I said the word blackout, the lights shut off over the excavation beside us.

Maddie looked over her shoulder at the now dark area. "Do you think that's a sign?"

"I hope so." I shuffled closer and put my arm around her.

Maddie didn't resist. She folded into my arms and we stood hugging for a long moment.

I whispered into her hair. "Can you forgive me?"

She nuzzled her face deeper into my shoulder. "I shouldn't." Her voice was muffled by my coat. "You really wrecked a good thing."

"Maybe we can still be good. Find some good?"

"Do you expect we can just kiss and make up?"

I grinned and gave her a peck on the cheek.

She wriggled out of my arms. "It's not going to be that easy. But as long as you're taking responsibility for the mess you made. I'm willing to put it behind us so we can have a good day together."

My heart was thumping in my ears and I suspect I had a ridiculous grin on my face. "Then lets move on and see where it takes us."

The rest of the day was terrific. We explored Milan all day; visiting famous landmarks, touring museums and art galleries, and window shopping along the luxurious fashion district. We made a few purchases along the way, but I think Maddie's favorite came from a large bookstore in the Galleria Emanuel that had a huge map book section. It was a pop up map of Milan that we used to find our way around.

The new map and the Lonely Planet Italy book that Maddie brought with her helped us get the most out of the few hours of daylight we had to see the city. We were both tired and hungry by the time we got back to the station to catch our train to Torino because we hadn't stopped for lunch, just a couple coffee breaks with pastries and a gelato, even though it was freezing out.

There was a snack bar in the station, and we bought two panini and bottles of water to eat on the train going home.

Maddie started eating hers even before the train pulled out of the station. "At least I'll have made room for our lunch tomorrow."

"I considered not signing up for the polenta class. Never liked grits."

"My neighbor Rosa makes it."

"The Rosa that used to babysit Anne?"

"And feed her supper. Anne insisted I sign up for all the lessons, including polenta."

"I might be hungry for dinner, if that's all we have for lunch."

Maddie caught on that I was suggesting we have dinner together. "I'm planning to go shopping tomorrow evening."

"You can't shop all night."

"I might be up for dinner on Friday. One last meal before heading home."

I was thrilled by her suggestion. "I'll find a place and make a reservation." My mind immediately started working on a plan.

Maddie refused my offer to share a cab back to her hotel, insisting she would take the streetcar. I suspected she was going to stop in to see Mauro, but I tried not to think about it.

CHAPTER 56

Anne was shocked when I told her I'd run into Nate at cooking school. "What a crazy coincidence. Nice you have someone to hang out with. You guys were good friends when I was a kid."

"We were." I wasn't going to give her any details about our more than friendship even though she was an adult and I doubted she'd be scandalized by anything I told her. She'd seen far more interesting behaviour from her father.

"Too bad we didn't know Ann was there. I'd have liked to see her. It's been ages."

"She and Brandon and the boys are skiing in Switzerland. Nate told me she closed the gallery for a month so they could do both that and the Olympics in one trip. They even brought a tutor for the boys so they wouldn't get behind."

"I bet that was popular."

"It sounded like it wasn't unusual. Nate referred to them as 'the tutor', like it was normal."

"Normal if you're the grandsons of a gazillionaire."

"I've got to get going. I need to be at class in half an hour and I'm still not dressed."

"You'll call me as soon as you get home tomorrow?"

"It'll be around dinner time. Will you be home?"

"Probably. But call my cell. I want to know."

"I will."

"Have fun at class and say hi to Mr. Jacobs for me."

"Ok. Love you."

"Love you. See ya." Anne rung off and I quickly got myself together to head out.

I could have told Anne that Nate and I had spent the day together on Wednesday and that we'd be having dinner together, but I didn't. Maybe it was out of habit, keeping the plans we made to be together a secret, or maybe I wasn't ready to admit to anyone, not even myself, how much I wanted to spend time with him.

I couldn't shake the nagging worry that I would get tangled up by all the old feelings I'd stashed away in a corner of my heart, walled off and deliberately ignored, until they stopped torturing me. Those walls were crumbling the more time we spent together, and I knew how hard it would be to put them back in place when we inevitably went our separate ways. The last thing I wanted was to feel the rejection and disappointment I'd had to muddle through when our relationship ended abruptly.

I had survived it, and I was happy and secure on my own. But, despite my efforts to stay detached, it was easy to slip back in sync with him. I knew it was hazardous, but the desire to be near him was stronger than my self-preservation instinct and willpower to keep him at arm's length.

It didn't help that he was so persistent. I could sense how much he wanted to be with me, and it reminded me of when we were great. That gravitational pull that drew us together that neither of us could resist, and the fiery passion that ignited when we touched. As much as I'd tried to douse that flame, it wouldn't go out and spending time together only made it grow stronger. I couldn't help but wonder how long it would be before I got burned.

CHAPTER 57

Maddie came down the marble steps and into the lobby, carrying her coat and purse. She was elegant, dressed in flowing black pants and a black blouse with a V-neck and long translucent sleeves. I saw the desk clerk give her an approving once over, but her eyes were on me, and I felt a swell of pride I would be escorting her.

I helped her on with her coat. "I have a car waiting for us."

The driver hopped out as we approached and opened the door for her.

"We're going in style," she said as she slipped into the backseat.

"Nothing but the best for you, my dear."

Making it a special evening had been a team effort. I'd called our chef Fabio to help me select a place based on the recommendations I'd gotten from the concierge at my hotel. He'd taken over the mission and had called a friend who was the chef at a small but exclusive restaurant outside of Torino and he'd given me the contact for the driver, Antonio, who would take care of transportation for the evening. I later found out that he was Fabio's cousin, who was a nurse, but drove people on his evenings off for a little extra cash to help pay for his passion for expensive cars.

"Thirty minutes and we arrive," said Antonio as he pulled away from the curb.

Maddie swiveled towards me as much as she could with her seat belt on. "So, what was your favorite lesson this week?"

"Learning that you were there."

She shook her head and pretended to be annoyed. "I meant the food."

"Ohhhh… that. I guess it was everything I got to make with you."

She ignored my comment, but I could see her suppressing a grin. "For me, the most interesting was the polenta. I bought a pot for it yesterday. Not sure how I'm going to pack it to get it home, but I'm going to make it for the next supper club."

"Our supper club with Claire and Theo? You're still doing it?"

"The world didn't stop revolving when you left."

"I bet you miss my crab cakes, though."

"Ya. The crab cakes. That's what I missed." There was more than a hint of sarcasm in her tone.

I knew I was pushing my luck, but I had to ask, "Is that all?"

"Of course not." Maddie's voice was sultry. "I missed everything about you, about us. But I got over it." She didn't give me a chance to respond. "Will you be bringing home some new ideas for your restaurants?"

"I leave the menu to Chef Fabio. But I'm going to suggest we offer an Italian style aperitivo, instead of our usual happy hour deal.

"That would be different. You might start a new craze. Maybe you should add an Italian bar to the restaurants."

"There's an idea. But we'd need one of those super shiny coffee machines with all the tubes and knobs and a lot more marble on the walls to make it authentic."

"I'd come for morning cappuccino if it were in my neighborhood."

"I'll work on it."

We chatted about my theoretical aperitivo menu and Maddie made several references to her and Anne eating at Mauro's and I couldn't help but feel pangs of jealousy that she'd enjoyed his company. It irked me we'd been in the same city for a couple of weeks before running into each other, and we'd missed out on spending all that time together.

Antonio turned off the main road. We both looked ahead as we were on a very narrow winding road, heading uphill. As we passed through each hairpin turn, there was blackness past the snow piles along the edge of the road. It made my stomach knot, thinking of what sort of sheer cliff might be in the darkness beyond the sweep of the headlights. I let out a sigh of relief when Antonio pulled the car off the road and into a parking lot.

Antonio stopped at the end of the walkway to let us out and came into the restaurant with us.

"*Signore Jacobs per due,*" he said to the lady about my age behind the counter.

"*Si. Si. Gli amici di Fabio.*" She took our coats, hung them on a rack, and then gestured for us to follow her to a table near an impressive stone fireplace.

"Welcome. My English, no good." She pointed to herself. "Sono Mariella." She pulled out the chair near the fire for Maddie.

"Thank you, Mariella." I positioned myself behind Maddie and slid her chair in before taking the seat opposite her. I pointed to Maddie and then myself and gave her our names.

"*Piacere. Vino?* Yes?" said Mariella.

"Yes. Please."

"I pick for you?"

I looked at Maddie to see what she thought.

She nodded.

"*Si. Grazie.*" I was pleased to see her face light up at my attempted Italian.

"You're learning Italian," said Maddie.

"Ann gave me a way to remember it. Sea like the ocean and grassy like a fairway. Sea grassy is yes, thank you."

We didn't need Italian to order our food, as the meal was preset. Each course was served with a description we didn't understand, and our wine glasses were filled with different wines throughout the meal.

After dessert, the chef came out with a bottle in one hand and a tray of tiny glasses. He made the rounds to each of the tables, ending with ours.

When I started to stand to shake his hand, he gestured to me to stay seated. "I hope you enjoyed the meal."

"It was magnificent," said Maddie.

"Superb," I agreed.

"May I offer a *digestivo*. A very special grappa. A small batch made from wine from my grandfather's vineyard. Very rare."

Maddie held up her fingers to show a tiny bit. "Just a taste."

He ignored her indication and poured us each a shot. "It is a great pleasure to have guests from America to our restaurant."

"It was our pleasure." I raised my glass to him.

"You have a beautiful place." Maddie took a tiny sip of her grappa as the chef poured himself a shot.

He raised his glass to me. "I hope you will tell Fabio that I am the better chef."

"I might need to keep that as our secret. It was an excellent meal for our last dinner in Italy."

"For this time. You must return and see us again." With that, he shook our hands and headed back to the kitchen.

No one brought a bill, but I saw people going to the counter where Mariella was standing and they were paying her, so we did the same. Before we'd even got our coats on, Antonio appeared, and he led us to the car, already warm and idling at the end of the walk.

"That was a really nice evening," said Maddie once we'd settled into the car.

"Nice? I was going for better than nice."

She smiled. "What were you hoping to achieve?"

"To make the most of every minute we have together."

Maddie looked ahead out the front window of the car.

I could tell she was thinking something. "Penny for your thoughts?"

"I'm conflicted."

I didn't want her to get upset. I wanted her to know how much she meant to me. I reached for her hand, and she didn't hesitate to weave her fingers between mine.

She tilted her head back, closed her eyes, and sighed. "I could so easily pick up right where we left off…"

My heart skipped a few beats and relief washed over me because I wanted to find that magical connection we shared, more than anything else I've ever wanted. "Wouldn't that be a good thing?"

"And then we go back to our lives and it's over. Again."

"We could just not go home?"

"There was a time I would have given up everything to be with you. But you didn't want me."

I could hear in her voice she was pulling away emotionally. "If I could go back, I would give up everything to be with you."

"We'd need a time machine."

"Then I'd go back. Way back. To that gorgeous doll in the broken-down car."

"That's pretty far back."

"You're still that gorgeous doll."

Maddie chuckled. "That's the wine talking."

"I may be emboldened by the wine, but there's nothing wrong with my eyesight. You are as beautiful today as you were then, and that day in your halter top in your garage when we discovered we'd met before."

"You remember what I wore?"

"Indelibly imprinted on my brain. So sexy. Irresistible." I tugged on her hand so she would look at me.

"When you look at me like that, I feel like we fell into that time machine."

"I don't ever want to leave this time and place."

Maddie sighed. "I don't either."

We rode in silence for a bit, still holding hands. It felt so familiar and good, yet my chest was tight, and my mind flashed with the memories of us that had been flooding back as I spent time with her. The way she had a quick response to everything, her laugh, the semi smile when she feigned annoyance, her eyes that made my knees wobble when she looked into mine with intensity and emotion. I felt a mild panic when I realized we had pulled onto the street for her hotel and in a few minutes, we'd be saying goodbye.

Maddie leaned towards the front seat. "Thank you, Antonio. You don't need to get out."

I wasn't going to let her get away so fast. "Can you wait while I see her inside?"

Antonio nodded. "No problem."

I walked to the door of the hotel and opened it for her.

I followed her into the lobby. "I guess this is goodbye, then."

Maddie hesitated and let out a long, slow breath. "Antonio's waiting."

"I can take a taxi later... if ... you wanted to... talk."

"I have a part bottle of Limoncello I will have to leave behind; if you want to have one."

"I'll take care of Antonio." I went out to the car and paid him for the evening and then returned to the lobby and followed Maddie up to her room.

It was a large double room by European standards. In addition to the two double beds, there was a desk and a small loveseat. One bed was completely covered in piles of clothes and a half-packed suitcase.

Maddie kicked off her shoes and hung her coat on the back of the desk chair. "Anne and I shared this room, but now I've spread out across it."

"I see you haven't gotten neater."

"Hey. You're the guest here. You can go..."

"I'm not criticizing, just observing."

Maddie scooped up a stack of books from the desk and a pile of clothes from the loveseat and put them on the bed beside the suitcase. Then she got out a long skinny bottle from a small fridge under the tiny coffee machine and set it on the desk.

"Are you going to keep your coat on?"

"I wasn't sure where to put it."

"Over mine will be fine." She held up two glass espresso cups. "Sorry, these will have to do." She didn't wait for me to answer, but poured the syrupy yellow liquor into them and handed me one.

The only seating options were the loveseat or the bed. Maddie sat on the loveseat. I decided not to squeeze in beside her, so I sat on the end of the bed across from her.

I leaned forward and extended my cup towards her. "Cheers."

"Cheers. Thank you for a lovely evening." She sat back and sipped her limoncello. A smile crept across her face.

"What are you grinning about?"

"Just thinking about how many times we've had a nightcap in a hotel room."

"The nightcap was rarely the reason we were there."

"True. We could end tonight the same way, I suppose."

A shiver of excitement went through me. "Are you suggestion we..."

"Well, we're old. But not dead... yet."

I wasn't sure if she was teasing or serious. "You haven't even let me kiss you yet."

She studied my face with a teasing grin, and she finished her limoncello in a couple of sips. She set her cup on the arm of the loveseat, stood, and then leaned down and kissed me.

I hadn't stirred the way she caused me to in so long I thought those days were behind me. "Oh my. Ms. Cole, you are naughty." I set my cup down and put my arms around her waist, and pulled her down onto the bed.

She giggled and rolled off me to lay beside me. I had that dizzying déjà vu feeling we'd been in that exact position before, our bodies pressed together, her arms and legs tangled with mine. It felt so natural to kiss her. She must have felt the same because her lips received mine with enthusiasm.

My lips tingled as I kissed her, and I was filled with emotion. The memories of so many kisses mixed with a desire to never stop kissing her. Maddie made a soft moaning sound. Knowing she wanted these kisses as much as I did, made it even more exciting.

Twenty years of time evaporated, and we caressed each other as we kissed. My hands moved from her face to her neck and shoulders and down her sides so I could feel her body and warmth and pull her closer. She stroked my arm and down my leg to my thigh.

Maddie wrapped her leg around me, thrust her hip forward, and flipped me over. I felt my back twist, but I ignored the pain because I was so delighted that she was on top of me looking down with a happy hungry expression that was so familiar, and I'd missed so much.

I put my hands on her hips. "You're making it impossible for me to not want to shag."

She was smiling. "Shag. Who says that anymore?"

"Old farts like me."

She laughed, rolled off me, and lay on her side facing me.

I rolled to face her. "I never stopped wanting you. There's never been anyone as special to me as you are."

"Show me." She ran her finger along her collarbone and pulled a little on the v of her blouse.

I reached and pulled the hem up a few inches and stroked the skin of her waist.

She pushed my hand away, and I regretted making a move and going too far. She twisted beside me and, to my surprise; pulled her blouse off over her head and tossed it aside. I didn't need any other encouragement. My hands found her breasts as my lips kissed hers. I slipped her bra straps off her shoulders and slid down the front so I could caress her breasts. They were still lovely breasts, and I couldn't resist kissing down her neck, along her shoulder to her curves while my hands cupped and stroked them. Maddie's head fell backward, and she breathed in and gasped as my lips brushed her nipple.

Her dress pants had only a stretchy gathered waistband so a slight tug and her lifting her hips slightly, was all it took for me to slide them off her. I ran my hand over the smooth top of her stockings and paused.

Maddie sat up. "I better get myself out of these. Spanx are no match for a novice like you." She stood up and wiggled and slithered out of her stockings and I was delighted to discover that she had nothing under them. She tugged at the bedspread. I got up, and she pulled back the covers and then she lay down on the bed.

Seeing her naked, I had to strip off my clothes and join her. Maddie's kisses made me forget my age, and I made love to her with all the emotion that had been pent up with nowhere to go since I'd last been with her. I kissed my way down her body and licked her and dipped my fingers inside her until I could hear and feel her orgasm.

Then I crawled up over her and slid inside her. I came almost immediately, as I was so overwhelmed with emotion and excitement.

"I love you. I love you. I love you." I whispered as I felt myself release into her.

Maddie's hips rocked and she made a happy humming sound.

I rolled off beside her and stroked her belly.

"Well, that was a surprise ending to the evening."

I moved my hand from her belly to her thigh and then across her body to her hip to pull her close against me.

"You're going to have to go now," she said in a soft voice.

"I don't really have to go." I didn't leave until later the next day, and I was already calculating in my mind how much time I'd need to get ready should she let me spend the night.

"I have to be up early, and I have packing to do."

"You're kicking me out? In the middle of the night in a snowstorm?"

She laughed. "Probably should have done that the first time, so we never got into that whole mess."

"It's your fault. You invited me in."

"It wasn't safe to let you drive home."

"So… You'll let me stay?" I put my hands together in prayer. I was being silly, but serious. I didn't want to leave. I wanted to hold her all night, and forever after.

Maddie got up from the bed and dug out the hotel robe that was tangled in the bedspread she'd dumped on the floor earlier. She put it on, tied the belt, and then threw the sheet over me. "I really need to pack." She left me there and went into the bathroom.

I wasn't ready to spring out of bed as Maddie had, but I also didn't want to overstay my welcome. I sat up slowly and collected my briefs and pants from the floor beside the bed. I put on the briefs and then stood up to shake the creases from my pants. I put them on awkwardly as my pockets were still full of my wallet and glasses and my belt had gotten twisted when I'd hastily removed them. I was still shirtless when Maddie came out of the bathroom, still in her robe.

She put her hands on her hips. "You're still here."

"I wouldn't go without saying goodbye properly." I put on my shirt and tucked everything in.

"Saying goodbye has never been my favorite part. But it's what we do."

"Maybe we should instead say *arrivederci*? Until we see each other.

"In another twenty years?"

"I doubt I have twenty years. How about tomorrow?"

"I'll be on a plane."

"You could change your flight. And I could. We could stay."

"I can't."

"I'll buy us both tickets home or anywhere. We could go to Rome or Paris or London…"

"I have to pick up my kittens on Sunday."

"Kittens?"

"Rosa's cat had a litter. She's been keeping two for me but I promised to take them off her hands as soon as I get back."

"Then I'll go with you."

"What about your restaurant empire?"

"You don't want me to fly to Toronto?"

"I'm sure you have obligations to get back to."

She was right but I didn't want to admit it. I had investor meetings scheduled the next week for our next expansion.

"Can I call you on Sunday?" I patted my pockets to make sure I had everything before I put on my coat.

"Do you need my number?"

"If your home number hasn't changed…"

"It hasn't."

"I've got it. I'll call." I reached for both her hands. "So, this is really goodnight, not goodbye."

She folded into me, her arms wrapped around me under my coat, and she was practically inside it as we hugged. She tilted her head back and I had to kiss those lovely lips. I felt tears welling at the corners of my eyes as the realization that I really was going to have to pull away from her.

"You need to go." She pushed herself back and zipped up my coat. "Before I change my mind."

"I don't mind if you do."

She patted me on the chest. "No. But we'll talk soon."

"Do you need a wake-up call?"

"I've got one scheduled and my phone alarm and my travel clock. If I don't get packing, I won't need any of them because I'll still be up when they go off."

I kissed her cheek. "Happy packing and safe trip tomorrow."

"Thanks." She opened the door and stood behind it out of view of the corridor.

I went halfway out the door and then peeked around it. "I need to say one more thing."

"Ok. Just one."

"I love you."

She smiled. "You're going to need to do more than say it for me to believe you."

"Then you should let me stay." I winked and her and she shook her head.

"Goodnight, Nate." She gave me a little push out the door and closed it behind me.

CHAPTER 58

First, I'd called Anne to let her know I'd gotten home safely, then I called Rosa. I assured her I'd be there the next day to pick up the kittens. With the time change and the lack of sleep the night before, I was knackered, so I went to bed early.

I made a quick trip to the store in the morning to pick up pet supplies and groceries for me. I set up a shallow litter box and a dish of food and water in the main bathroom upstairs. My plan was to keep them confined until I was sure they were using the litter box and eating, and they got used to me. I'd saved a sturdy banana box with a lid from my last trip to Costco to use as a makeshift carrier to bring them home from next door. I'd get a proper carrier for them later, but I didn't need it right away since Rosa had already taken them to the vet for their initial checkup and shots.

The banana box was enormous compared to the two tennis-ball-sized bundles of fur Rosa handed me. One was a golden yellow colour, and the other was brown and cream with patchy stripes. I probably could have put them both in a tissue box to bring them home.

I sat on the bathroom floor and opened the box. Their tiny voices that had been mewing constantly the whole time I'd carried them fell silent, and they huddled together in the corner of the box.

"It's ok boys. I know moving is scary, but you're home now." I watched them for a while and talked to them about nothing in a soft voice, so they'd get to know me.

After a bit, they started to stretch and move, so I took out the piece of heavy wool Rosa had given me. She'd said they couldn't resist playing with it, so I dangled it over the edge of the box.

"Anybody want to play?"

Both little heads followed the swaying yarn, but neither moved. I tried to coax them out of the corner by lowering the yarn into the box and pulling it along the floor. One yellow paw reached for it on my second fishing attempt. On my third pass, the brown and cream kitten pounced and pulled it away.

The yellow kitten didn't budge from the corner but looked up at me. I reached in and he let me pick him up without struggling. He was chubby and round, and he curled into a ball in my hand.

"Aren't you a cute little butterball?" I stroked his head with my thumb, and he purred. "Maybe I should call you Butterball. But maybe you'd think that's pejorative. I wouldn't want to give you a body image complex so young in life. Maybe just Butter?"

The kitten rolled over slightly.

"I think you like Butter." I repeated his name softly to him while I stroked his head and ears and the little furball started to fall asleep in my hand. I gently slid him from my hand into the cat bed I'd made with a cardboard box and some old blankets we used for picnics.

I looked around for the other kitten. He'd dropped the yarn and had jumped up onto the laundry hamper and was watching me from his perch. I slid closer to him, hoping he would let me hold him.

He leapt from the hamper lid to the vanity, back to the hamper and then to the edge of the tub, where he lost his balance and slid backwards into it. I couldn't help but chuckle because he looked like a cartoon cat, flailing as he tried to get a grip on the smooth surface of the tub but sliding, in slow motion, down into the tub.

I fished him out, but he jumped out of my hand and made another circuit of the bathroom, this time the hamper, vanity and the floor, avoiding the tub but still streaking around like a trapped wild animal.

"Aren't you an energetic kitty? What are we going to call a little streaky thing like you? How about Streaker?" I reached for him again.

He ran behind the toilet and then into the cat bed and pressed himself up against Butter.

"You just want to be near your brother, don't you? Everything is better with Butter, eh?" I kept talking to the kittens, thinking out loud about what to call them. "Maybe Bread and Butter? No, Bread is a terrible cat name. What else goes better with everything? Bacon does. You are sort of streaky and so is bacon. Butter and Bacon. Everything is better with Butter and Bacon."

Feeling satisfied that I'd come up with their names I left them to nap and slipped out of the bathroom to start unpacking in earnest. I'd not bothered to do any more than fish out my toiletries the night before. I had to at least dig out the gift I'd brought home for Claire because she'd be coming by to meet the new babies before dinner.

The Gianduiotto chocolates and small ceramic dish I'd bought for Claire were nestled between my heavy sweaters and they'd survived the journey as well as I could have expected. The outer package of the chocolates was a little crumpled, but I put both into a gift bag with some tissue paper and it looked acceptable. I didn't have Claire's talent for making bows, so I didn't bother with one. I just tied the strings of the gift bag in a simple knot.

I'd just finished getting her gift ready when the phone rang. I grabbed the handset from the cradle on my desk. I didn't recognize the number.

Unlikely that it was a business call on a Sunday, but I answered professionally just in case. "Hello. This is Maddie speaking."

"Hello. It's Nate."

"Hi. Your name didn't come up on my caller ID. Are you at home?"

"Yes. Got in late this morning. How was your trip home?"

"I got in last night. Uneventful trip. So, good in my book. You on a red-eye?"

"From London. Flew out of Torino yesterday afternoon."

"So, no early up for you then."

"No. Good thing. I got home quite late. Someone kept me out late."

"At least I sent you home at a decent hour."

"Funny story there."

"Oh?"

"I went down to the lobby after you shoved me out of your room…"

"Hardly."

"Unceremoniously kicked out, then."

"I had to pack."

"In any case, I went down to the lobby and asked the clerk if it was possible to get a taxi. He said it would likely be an hour. And I knew it would take me less time to walk."

"You didn't walk, did you?"

"He took one look at my shoes when I suggested it and he disapproved. He asked me where I needed to go. When I told him, he said he might be able to get me a ride."

"That was nice of him. So did you get a ride?"

"He told me to wait. A little while later, Mauro came into the lobby."

"Mauro from the bar?"

"He recognized me right away as your friend."

"He's good at remembering people's names."

"He asked if I was the person waiting for a ride."

"He drove you back to your hotel?"

"Apparently, he was just closing the bar, and he was on his way home. He said it wasn't out of his way."

"That was nice of him."

"I offered to pay him, but he declined."

"I'm glad you didn't have to walk."

"I suppose I could have gone back to your room and begged for shelter…"

"I might have taken pity on you. Maybe."

"You wouldn't be so cruel as to leave a man stranded in a snowstorm…"

"It wasn't a snowstorm. Just snowy."

"Did you pick up your kitten?"

"They are adorable little fluff balls."

"Until they scratch the upholstery."

"They're confined to the bathroom for now."

The doorbell rang. I looked at the clock. It was about time for Claire to show up. "Listen Nate, there's someone at my door. It's probably Claire."

"If you want to answer it. I can wait."

I hadn't expected he'd suggest that. "Ok. I'm just going to answer it." The phone was cordless, so I took the handset with and went to the door.

Claire bustled in as soon as I opened it. "Welcome home, dear friend." She gave me a big hug, almost knocking the phone out of my hand. "Sorry dear. You're on the phone."

"Just give me a second." I put the phone back against my ear. "Claire's here. I should go."

"Say hello for me."

"Ok I will." I looked at Claire. "Nate says hi."

"Nate Jacobs?" Claire's eyes were wide. "Hello back, of course." She gave me a look that told me she'd be asking a lot of questions when I got off the phone.

"Did you hear that?" I asked Nate.

"Yes. I'll let you go. Can I call you later?"

"You must be exhausted. I know I'll probably go to bed early again."

"Then tomorrow?"

"Tomorrow night I have a meeting."

"Sometime during the day then?"

"In the afternoon I should be home."

"I'll call you then. Have a nice visit with Claire. I'm glad you're home safe."

"Thanks. I'm glad you got home safe too. Bye for now."

When I hung up the phone, I turned to Claire.

She was standing with her hands on her hips, her head cocked to one side and her eyebrows so high they were pushing up her hairline. "You going to tell me why Nate is calling you?"

I told Claire I'd run into Nate at cooking school. She pressed me for details, so I described how we'd been partners in class and that we'd gone sightseeing and out to dinner. I told her that he was there on his own and that he and Betsy were divorced. I left out the part about him coming up to my room.

Claire nodded approvingly as I answered her questions. Then she offered her conclusion. "The universe has once again put you in the same place."

"Temporarily. He's back in Boston now."

"But there are no real obstacles to you being together."

"A thousand kilometers is a bit of an obstacle."

Claire gave a snort. "I meant you're both unattached. Physical distance is something you can easily overcome. You could drive there in a day, or fly."

"He was quite attentive all week. I'll give him that."

"You're not going to be stubborn and make it hard for him, are you?"

I hadn't planned to tell Claire about Nate before I'd had a chance to sort out in my own mind what it all meant. "Do you want to meet my new fur babies?" I started up the stairs.

Claire followed me. "When you're ready to talk about Nate, you know I'm on your side, no matter what."

CHAPTER 59

Tuesday had become my favorite day of the week. Although we occasionally spoke on other days, Tuesday was the day we both had the fewest obligations and the most time to talk on the phone. This was the third Tuesday in a row that we'd talked for over an hour.

Our conversations flowed naturally. That shouldn't have surprised me, considering the countless hours of intimate conversations we'd had in the past. Our clandestine relationship had relied on phone calls so we could spend time together and talk privately on an almost daily basis. There was a lot more distance between us now but, when we were talking, it felt the same as when we were calling each other from the same area code.

I'd wanted to broach the subject of us getting together in person. Instead, we'd spent most of the conversation talking about Maddie's plans for Anne coming home from Chicago for Easter.

"I've already been to the Laura Secord shop to buy Anne's favorite eggs and I can't wait to hide them for her on Easter morning." Maddie sounded like she was talking about a child rather than her grown-up daughter.

"Isn't she a little old for an egg hunt?"

"I'm going to make her work for them. Last year I mailed her some in a care package and she said the only thing missing was the hunting. So, I'm going to hide them really well just to get back at her."

"Hopefully the kittens don't get to them first."

"I hadn't thought of that. The big ones won't be a problem, but I might have to hide the little ones inside things, not just lying around."

"You'll be finding stray eggs until Christmas."

Maddie laughed. "Lucky me then."

"Besides egg hunting, have you other plans?"

"Claire, Theo, André, and his wife are coming for Easter dinner. How about you? Will you be visiting Ann?"

"She and the boys are going to Florida to spend Easter with her mother." I silently hoped Maddie would extend an invitation to me to join them for Easter.

"You just spent a couple weeks with them in Torino, so I guess that's fair. Do you coordinate with Betsy to decide on holidays?"

"Ann usually works that out with her mother."

"So, you don't talk to Betsy much?"

"There's no need. It's not like we go on family vacations together."

"She didn't like family vacations when you were together."

"Not the way you did. And you're still doing."

"I don't know if there will be many more."

"I thought you had a good time in Torino."

"We did. It's logistically complicated planning travel for two families and we've done summer and winter Olympics. Anne told me it was ok if we didn't plan on going to Vancouver with Will."

"That's a surprise."

"Not really. We've really enjoyed traveling, just the two of us. Who knows how much longer we'll be able to."

"You're giving up traveling?"

Maddie laughed. "Of course not. I meant Anne won't be single forever."

I almost blurted out that she shouldn't be either instead I asked about Anne and if she was seeing anyone. Maddie told me that Anne had become good friends with a few of her colleagues, and she had talked about going with her friends to clubs and shows in the city, but she hadn't mentioned anyone in particular she was more involved with.

"Sounds like you can count on her as a travel buddy for now. Have you got any other trips planned?"

"She used almost all her vacation days for Torino. There won't be anything big until next year. But we have ideas." Her tone was bright, and I could tell it was a subject she liked talking about because she started talking about some of the possible destinations. I knew from past experience she was thinking out loud the way she liked to do. In one breath she'd be selling the merits of a place and the next going through all the reasons why it wasn't a good idea.

I mostly just sat back and listened, asking the occasional questions to keep her going. The sound of her voice made me feel close to her and I was happy to be her sounding board if that's what would prolong that feeling. There was absolutely no clarity about where they would be going next, but I had gleaned that she had no plans to travel until at least after Easter, which gave me an idea.

CHAPTER 60

I noticed on the caller ID that Nate was calling from his mobile phone. When I answered, he said the connection was bad, and he'd call me back. While I was waiting for him to call, I went to the kitchen and rummaged in the fridge to see what I could pull together for dinner after we talked, or maybe during.

I'd enjoyed our long phone calls where we just hung out and talked. The week before, I'd put him on speaker and I'd managed to iron all my linen napkins that had been in no condition to use for at least a decade. I thought I would use them when I set the table for Easter dinner.

The doorbell rang, so I put the leftover rice I'd just found back in the fridge, and I went to answer it.

I was shocked to see Nate standing on my porch holding a bouquet of flowers and a shopping bag. "What are you doing here?"

"Surprise." He handed me the bouquet. "I come bearing gifts."

"That's why you asked if I was going out this evening?"

"It would've been a shame if I'd come all this way, and you weren't home."

"What are you doing here?" I was thrilled to see him but still processing that he was actually there.

"Are you going to invite me in?" The bright smile on his face dimmed, and he looked nervous.

"I'm sorry. Of course." I stepped back and let him pass me.

Nate set the shopping bag down and I took his overcoat and hung it over the end of the banister.

I caught my reflection in the hallway mirror. I ran my fingers through my hair to make it a little more presentable. "If I'd known I was getting company…"

"You look beautiful. I hope you're not upset."

"No of course not. It's wonderful to see you." I wasn't upset but I had yet to wrap my head around why he was there. And my mind was racing to figure out what I could offer him. Certainly not the leftover rice and miscellaneous vegetable remains I was going to throw together for myself.

"I just thought it would be nice to talk in person." Nate looked at me hopefully and then he picked up the shopping bag and shook it. "And I brought supplies. Wine, cheese, salame, olives and some focaccia my chef baked this morning. Would you have an aperitivo with me?"

My panic evaporated. "You've thought of everything." I led the way back to the kitchen.

Nate unpacked the food and wine onto the counter.

I handed him a bottle opener and wine glasses. "I'll just get a vase for the flowers. They are lovely. Thank you."

I arranged the flowers while Nate poured us each a glass of wine.

I raised my glass to him. "To very good surprises."

"Cheers. I'm glad you still like being surprised."

I set my glass down and got out a serving tray. "Friend on my doorstep with wine and cheese. I'll take that surprise any day."

"I'll hold you to that." Nate took a sip of his wine and watched as I arranged the food.

"You plan on surprising me often?" I picked up the tray, a couple of side plates and napkins and nodded towards the hallway.

"If you'll let me." Nate picked up the wine bottle and our glasses and followed me to the living room.

I had to set the tray on the sofa so I could clear the stacks of paper from the coffee table. I felt compelled to explain the mess to Nate. "I'm working on my taxes."

Nate looked skeptical. He had been in my office many times in the past and had criticized the stratigraphy of files and reports that covered most flat surfaces. But, wisely, he said nothing.

Once we were settled and we'd each helped ourselves to some food I had to get to the bottom of why he was there.

"So now you can tell me why you're really in town."

"I told you. To see you."

"You didn't come all this way to spend an hour talking to me."

"I'm hoping we can fit in more than an hour. I'm staying in town for a few days."

"Where?"

"I booked a room at the Royal York."

"You aren't staying with Ann?"

"I thought it would be more convenient if I stayed in the city."

"But you're going to see her."

"We're having lunch in Oakville tomorrow."

"She was in on this?"

"Sworn to secrecy in the event you happened to run into her. The boys don't even know I'm here."

"I'm sure they'll be delighted to see their grandpa."

"What really matters to me right now is if you're delighted to see me?"

I set down my plate and swiveled to face him. "It's a lovely surprise. And the wine is excellent. But why?"

He mirrored my actions and faced me. He looked down, took my hand with both of his and studied it. "Because life is too short to not spend every minute you can with the person you're meant to be with." He looked up and into my eyes.

A tsunami of emotion hit me. There was excitement and pain and fear rolling through me and I had to press my molars together to stop myself from gasping for air. I studied Nate's face. Older, but telegraphing the same passion and desire that had been my pleasure to bask in all the years we were together. It felt like nothing had changed and we were those lovers who knew we belonged to each other.

He answered my thoughts. "Nothing has changed."

"How can you say that with a straight face?"

"We may have been apart, but …"

"We're still apart." I pulled my hand back. Along with the delight of feeling his adoring gaze came the memory of how it felt to have it yanked away. I wasn't ready to let him off the hook for rejecting me.

His eyes stayed locked on mine. "We don't have to be."

My defenses were failing, so I forced my brain onto a rational track. "From what you've told me, I can tell you've invested a lot into your restaurants, and you've got dreams and plans for them. You're there, I'm here and I'm happy. Spending time together in Torino was fun. Talking on the phone and catching up has been good. But there's only so much we can be long distance."

"Hypothetically, if we were in the same place…"

"Then it might be a different story. But thinking about what-if scenarios could lead to feeling disappointed and I don't want to go there."

"I certainly don't want to disappoint you."

"Again." As soon as the word left my mouth, I regretted it because his face jerked like I'd slapped him. "I'm sorry. I know it's not fair to put all the blame on you for our affair ending. I shouldn't have let myself get so entangled in the first place."

"Calling what we had an affair makes it sound like it was wrong, something sordid."

"What would you call it?"

"Bad timing."

"Or the right time and we made all the wrong choices."

"By we you're implying me?"

I was but, in my heart, I knew it wasn't true. How many times had I wondered if I should have given him an ultimatum to leave Betsy or end things with me? The risk of losing him and the connection we shared had kept me from it. Then, when things ended with Will, I could have made an effort to stay connected instead of blaming Nate for leaving town. We might have found our way back together years ago. It was as much my choices, as his, that had kept us apart.

Nate was looking at me, waiting for an answer.

"If I'd asked you to leave Betsy and be with me, would you have?"

"In retrospect, clearly I should have."

My heart sank at his answer. "But you wouldn't have."

"I didn't say that. Honestly, I don't know." His lips were pressed together, and he let out a sigh. "Listen. It's water under the bridge. We made the choices we did, and we've ended up here. What matters now is what we decide next."

"What do you want to do next?"

Nate grinned. "I think we should decide where we're going for dinner."

"Seriously? We're talking about big life altering choices…"

"Which will take some time to implement. In the meantime, I don't want to limit this Tuesday chat to an hour, so I'm hoping you're free for the rest of the evening so we can have a little fun."

He was being charming and sweet and there was nothing keeping me from enjoying our time together except my own fears. I reminded myself of the life motto I'd so often repeated to Anne. Being afraid is not a good enough reason to say no to something.

"I'm free this evening. What did you have in mind?"

CHAPTER 61

Ann flipped off the neon open sign in the front window of her gallery while she held the door for me.

I stepped outside onto the sidewalk. "I hope closing isn't a problem."

She followed me out and locked the door behind us. "You're my only appointment this afternoon. Not much walk-in traffic in the middle of the week."

We headed west along Lakeshore Road to Paradiso, where I'd made a lunch reservation. The hostess showed us to our table, handed us menus, and left us to settle in.

Ann leaned in towards me and whispered. "Are we doing reconnaissance for your restaurants?"

I winked at her. "Always. Spot any hot trends, and you let me know pronto."

"Is that why you're staying in the city and not with me?"

"That would be a reason, but I'm also hoping to spend time with Maddie and it's easier if I'm staying close by."

"Quite the coincidence, you two in the same cooking class."

"It was a good surprise."

"You were good friends. I'm surprised you didn't stay in touch."

"It's complicated."

Ann sat back and looked at me sidelong. "Hmmm. That can only mean one thing."

I ignored her stare and read from the menu. "The red and white risotto looks interesting."

Ann leaned forward and whispered. "You were having an affair."

I didn't want to lie to her. "Whatever gives you that idea?"

She sat back again and nodded. "I don't know why I didn't see it before."

I wasn't prepared to discuss my past with Maddie with her, especially not in public. "A margarita pizza would be a good test of their pizza technique."

"I will say you two were far better suited than you and Mother ever were."

Her acceptance was reassuring. "We got along well."

"So, you were lovers…" Ann's voice had a teasing quality, and I knew she was fishing for details.

"This is not a conversation we're going to have."

She picked up her menu and pretended to read it, but she was peeking over it grinning. "Aww come on. Watching you squirm is fun."

"You're enjoying this?"

"How often can a girl get her father to blush."

"I'm not. What are you thinking you'd like for lunch?"

Ann continued to grin as she shook her head. "You're staying in Toronto to spend time with your ex-lover instead of with me. I need to know. How serious is this?" She was not going to let the subject go.

"I never said it was serious."

"You could do worse."

"I'm going to have the risotto."

Ann set her menu down. "You should go for it." Her expression was mischievous. "I'm going to have the Nicoise Salad with Ahi, and you're going to tell me what your intentions are."

There was no way I was going to let her provoke me into telling her anything more. "Are the boys looking forward to going to Florida?"

"Trying to change the subject?" She sighed. "Ok. But I hope you're going to let me in on what's really going on with you."

"There's nothing to tell."

"For now."

"What do you have planned for Easter break?"

"We've chartered a boat and we're going to do some sailing. The boys took lessons last summer and they're keen on it. We thought it would be fun to give them some experience on something a tad bigger than a sunfish."

"How much bigger?"

Ann grinned. "She's a fifty-foot catamaran. We've hired a skipper for the week, but he's ok with having the boys as his mates and showing them the ropes."

"I thought the point of going down was to spend time with your mother?"

"We'll be there for Easter weekend. Then we're outta there." The way she said it led me to believe she wasn't getting along with her mother.

"Any more than three days… Asking for trouble?"

"It's not that. Mother and Charles…" Anne paused and pressed her lips together. "Well… They have their ideas about things I'd rather not normalize for my boys."

She didn't have to explain, and I didn't want to put her in an awkward position by disparaging my ex-wife and her husband. I was well aware of the biases they'd cultivated growing up in white privilege in the south.

It was Ann's turn to change the subject. "These breadsticks are good. But nothing like the ones we had in Torino, eh?"

Talking about the food seemed like a safe subject. "The ones rolled in cornmeal at that place we stopped at after watching the downhill were the best."

"Were you keeping notes on all the places?"

"As a matter of fact, I did. And Chef Fabio has been very receptive to some of my ideas and we've started rolling out several new things across all our restaurants."

"Like what?"

"We've got a new happy hour menu inspired by the aperitivo I had with Maddie at a place she and Anne found."

"Seems Maddie is inspiring you a lot these days."

I frowned and shook the end of my breadstick at her.

She grinned and looked pleased with herself for getting a reaction from me. "So, in addition to stalking your ex-lover, what other plans do you have for this week?"

"There will be no stalking of anyone."

Ann rolled her eyes. "Anything else besides Maddie on your agenda?"

"I've got a meeting with a real estate agent. Going to do a little reconnaissance."

"For a new restaurant location? Are you thinking of opening a Mare Monte in Toronto?"

"No plans for that. Just getting the lay of the land."

"You could just relax and enjoy retirement. Focus on your hobbies."

"I thought that's what I was doing?"

"Maybe that was true with the first place you opened. But what have you got now? Three places?"

"The fourth opens this summer."

"That sounds like a lot of work. Don't you have other things you'd like to do?" Ann looked concerned.

"Honey, I'm doing exactly what I want to do.

She seemed to be satisfied, and we went back to talking about the boys. The opportunities for travel, the private education, the experiences they had were far beyond anything I might have imagined for my grandchildren. I was proud of the way Ann had made an effort to keep them grounded. She'd chosen to emulate her in-laws, instilling the same respect and responsibility she'd seen them demand of their children. And I saw more of myself in her now than I ever had when she was younger and more influenced by her mother.

CHAPTER 62

I checked my list. I'd forgotten the parsley. My phone started ringing as I pushed the cart towards the produce section. I rummaged in my purse with one hand to get the phone out to see who it was and if I needed to answer, because I didn't have time to waste. It was Claire's mobile number, so I answered just as the PA system in the store started announcing weekly specials.

"Did I catch you at a bad time?"

"At the grocery store. What's up?"

"Ha. Me too. Loblaws?"

"Fortinos."

"Just a quick question about Easter. How many will we be? I'm making the pastries and I want to make sure there's enough."

"I haven't invited anyone else."

"Nate leaving?"

"I haven't asked."

"Why not?"

"I haven't spoken to Anne."

It was a lame excuse and Claire wasn't buying it. "I can't imagine she'd mind."

She was right. I'd told Anne that Nate was in town and she'd mentioned it would be nice to see him. "I don't know if he's going to be in town."

"Well then, I'll just make enough for eight. Then if you and Anne both surprise us with companions, I'll have enough for all." Claire rang off.

I stared at the fresh herb display, distracted by Claire's question of why I'd not asked Nate. He'd gone out of his way to arrange his schedule around mine so we could spend time together. I picked through the bunches of flat-leaf parsley and selected a nice fluffy one. I wanted to have the best ingredients possible, just like our cooking school instructor had taught us.

I checked my list again. I felt scattered. Claire's call had stirred my conflicting feelings about Nate. We'd talked previously about his reappearance in my life, and she didn't see any downside to exploring where it might lead. But her heart wasn't the one on the line.

I hadn't forgotten the sting when what I'd believed was an unbreakable tie holding us together, broke. Like a rubber band stretched too far, when it snapped, it hurt. Nate was extending his end of the band to me again. It was tempting to want to grab on and never let go.

I'd enjoyed having him in town and we'd easily picked up where we left off in Torino. But I wasn't sure it worth the risk of stretching it again with a long-distance version of our relationship, knowing it might break once more.

He'd called that morning as he had every morning he'd been in town. "Just wondering if you had any free time this weekend."

"I'm going to be busy in the kitchen. Anne arrives on Thursday night, so I want to get a few things out of the way before she gets here."

"Perhaps I could help? We made a good team in Torino."

"Ravioli is on my to-do list. Anne challenged me to impress her with my new skills."

"It'll be faster with the two of us. Maybe leave time for us to go to a movie or something?"

I suspected the something he was referring to was more of what had happened on our last night in Torino. When we'd gone to dinner on Tuesday, he suggested we go to one of our old haunts, Bardi's. It was just a short walk from his hotel, and after dinner, he hinted I go there with him by suggesting the doorman could get me a cab. But I insisted on saying goodnight at the restaurant and hailing my own cab home.

The next day he rented a car and for all our subsequent outings he'd picked me up and driven me home afterward. He planned each outing and made it feel like every day we were going on a special date. There was a theme for each, something to do or see, and a restaurant to complement the activity.

We even kissed goodbye in the car like teenagers. The way it felt when our lips touched, sweet and exciting, and as if everything was as it should be. I'd been tempted to invite him in, but I'd held back.

When he offered to help me make the ravioli, I knew he was hoping to be there to eat them, and deep down, so was I.

I told him to come over any time after two. He arrived at my house precisely at two carrying a bag from Ashley's, a well-known china and gift store where brides often had their wedding registries.

He handed it to me. "I took a chance you could use this for your Easter dinner."

Inside was a small cut-glass bowl in a silver holder with a lid and spoon similar to the ones we'd seen in Italy that they used to serve grated parmigiano table-side and there was an electric grater.

"I charged up the grater last night, so you could use it today if you needed to." Nate unboxed the grater, set it up in the charger, and put the box back in the shopping bag.

"Easter presents early?"

"Just a little something to show you how much I appreciate you letting me spend time with you."

"You're just angling for an invite for Easter."

"Absolutely. But no pressure. I know you're looking forward to spending time with Anne, so I won't intrude on your weekend with her."

"It's not that…"

"Then what?"

I didn't answer. He didn't feel like an intrusion. That was the dilemma. It felt like he belonged in my life, but I knew it was temporary. He had another life, just as he always had. One separate and parallel to ours. The last time we'd tried to maintain a relationship and separate lives, I found myself wanting a version of my life I couldn't have, and I didn't want to put myself in that situation again.

Nate picked up the bag of flour from the table and examined it. "I guess we should get going on the pasta for your ravioli."

"Don't you have to be back in Boston soon?"

Nate set the bag of flour down. "Are you not getting the idea that the only place I want to be is here with you?"

His words were filled with love and devotion and penetrated me like water on dry sand. Soaking in and filling up the voids in me that had been empty for so long. As much as I didn't want it to feel that good, I wanted to feel that good.

But I wasn't ready to admit to him how much I was starting to want him there. "Even if I put you to work?"

"Yes ma'am. Where do you want to make the pasta? On the table?"

My angst over our relationship subsided as I focused on the task at hand. I pulled my mother's bread board from the space beside the refrigerator and the wall. "I knew I kept this for a reason."

"That's quite the board."

"My mother's." I hoisted it onto the table.

"She made pasta?"

"No, for bread. She didn't make it often because she didn't like doing it. Her mother forced her to learn and be the one to make it for the family. It was the depression. There was no money to buy bread from the baker, but they could afford flour, when they could get it."

"My mother baked bread. It smelled so good."

"The smell of baking bread makes me feel festive and full of anticipation because it was always a special occasion when she made it."

"If I'd know that, I'd have saved a lot on bar tabs for us." He gave me a nudge with his elbow. "Wanna hit a bakery later?"

I huffed at him. "We'll see how the ravioli making goes." Our playful banter was easy and fun. It was reminiscent of our best times together, so it wasn't a surprise it gave me that dizzying déjà vu feeling.

Nate examined the bag of flour. "Well travelled this is. Manitoba flour imported from Italy."

"Trying for as authentic ingredients as I could find." I got out my baking scale and a bowl and put them on the board.

Nate picked at the top of the flour bag with his fingertips, taking great pains to not tear the package while opening it. "How much are we making?"

I reached around him and tore open the bag. "I'm thinking two batches of 400 grams of flour would be easier to work with than one big batch."

Nate weighed out the flour and dumped it into a mound on the board. He formed a well in the center, just as our instructor had shown us in cooking class. I cracked eggs into a small bowl and poured them into the well.

I got a fork from the drawer. "You want to…"

Nate took it, whisked the eggs to break them and began pulling the flour into the center well to mix it into the eggs.

I was impressed. "Have you been practicing?"

"I might've dabbled a little in the kitchen since Torino." He grinned and added a dribble of water to the dough. It started to come together perfectly, and it was clear that he was underreporting his practice.

"You seem to have that under control. I'll start on the filling."

Nate continued kneading the dough while I got the ingredients from the fridge. I mashed the ricotta and an egg together in a bowl. I added freshly grated nutmeg and some salt and pepper. Then I cut off a chunk of parmigiano and used my new grater to stream fluffy ribbons of cheese on top of the ricotta.

"This new contraption works great." I gave Nate a thumbs up sign.

He gave a little shrug and looked pleased with himself.

I mixed in the cheese and put the bowl of filling into the fridge.

Nate, in the meantime, had moved on to making the second batch of pasta. I got out the plastic wrap and wrapped up the first ball he'd set under the mixing bowl and watched while he finished kneading the second batch.

Nate went to the sink to wash his hands. "We'll need to let it rest before we roll it."

I wrapped up the dough. "Gives us time to figure out my new roller attachment."

"We could use a rolling pin."

"And not play with my new kitchen toy? No way." I pulled my stand mixer from the back of the counter and set it on the table. Then I got the box of pasta attachments and pulled out the instruction booklet.

Nate pulled the roller from the box. He set it aside and took the round cover off the end of the mixer head. "Looks pretty straightforward." He inserted the roller and tightened the screw.

I read the instructions. "It says for ravioli we should go to number 6 or 7."

He turned the knob on the roller. "Bigger the number, the closer the rollers. Seven is the last number. Makes sense. Thinner is better for ravioli." He twisted the knob back. "What now, Chef?"

"Still should wait a bit longer." I got out a couple cookie sheets and wax paper to line them. "I thought once we make the ravioli, we could set them on these and in the freezer so they don't stick together."

Nate helped me line the cookie sheets and suggested dusting them with some flour, which I thought was a good idea.

We started rolling out a piece of the first dough and it was stretching well. We decided that Nate would work the dough and I would form and cut the ravioli. But he was much faster, so he alternated between rolling and cutting the ravioli apart.

I ran out of filling before we'd used up all the dough, but we'd made plenty.

Nate brought all the scraps and ends of pasta together into a ball. "What do you want to do with the extra pasta?"

"Do you want to eat it for dinner?"

"Are you inviting me?"

"Least I could do is let you eat what you made."

"Then how about the ravioli?" He looked so adorable with his eyebrows lifted and a hopeful querying expression.

"All right. You can come for Easter if you're still in town."

Nate's smile made it clear it was the answer he was seeking. "I can tell you right now that I accept before you change your mind."

I knew I could regret it, but it felt good to give in to what we both wanted, to be together. Nate worked the leftover pasta into fettucine, and I opened a bottle of wine. We went through my fridge and cupboards and came up with a plan to make a salad and dress the pasta simply with butter and Parmigiano Reggiano.

Nate congratulated himself on the gift as I used my new grater again.

I didn't disagree. "I've never questioned your taste in gifts."

"I still have the first thing you ever gave me."

I wracked my brain trying to think of what that was.

"You don't remember?" Nate reached into his back pocket and pulled out his wallet. He opened it and turned it on edge and dug a card out of the innermost slot. He handed it to me.

It was my DB Engineering business card. The edges were fuzzy, and the card had yellowed with age. I turned it over. I recognized Nate's handwriting.

Royal York Blackout June 24, 76

The fact that he'd saved it all this time and carried it with him was crazy, but I felt my heart melting. I'd convinced myself that it had been easy for him to move on from our relationship. That he'd clung to this tatty piece of paper was evidence to the contrary.

"How long has this been in your wallet?"

"I pulled it from my Rolodex when I was packing up my Oakville office. It had the date we met on it, so I couldn't throw it away."

I handed the card back. "It was a lifetime ago."

Nate slipped the card back into his wallet and then reached for my elbow and pulled me closer. "I've always felt we were supposed to meet. I messed up before, but not this time. Don't you think there must be some reason we can't avoid each other even when we're halfway around the world?"

"So, you were trying to avoid me?" I gave him a sidelong look and leaned away.

Nate pulled me closer. "Does this feel like I'm avoiding you?"

Our lips were so close. Mine tingled with the anticipation of touching his. It was an innocent embrace, but the emotional intensity of the moment made my skin shiver with tiny electric shocks running over its surface.

We kissed. It was unlike any kiss we'd had before. All the reasons we shouldn't be kissing had fallen away. My body against his made me feel like it had slipped into its most natural form and it was a perfect fit. Our lips parted and our tongues touching felt like a deep thirst was being quenched. Nate's arm slid up my back and over my shoulder and cradled my head. I let myself be supported by him as he kissed me even harder.

I don't know how long we kissed, but it was long enough for the pot of water on the stove to start to boil. The rattling of the lid brought us back to reality.

I pulled myself away. "I suppose we can pick this up after dinner?"

Nate gave me another kiss. "I'm yours for as long as you'll have me."

I shut off the stove. "The pasta can wait."

CHAPTER 63

It would be unthinkable to come to Easter dinner empty handed. Maddie had conceded that I could bring some wine. I closed the car door with my hip because both hands were full of Easter baskets and flowers, and I didn't want to set them down. I'd have to make a second trip to get the wine from the trunk.

The woman at the florist shop in the hotel lobby had helped me arrange and wrap the Easter baskets. She may have been taking pity on the nice old man who had paid far too much for the orchid plant, but I'd like to think that my plea, of trying to win back the love of my life that I'd let get away, had charmed her into helping me.

I'd spent the better part of the day on Saturday at the Eaton Centre trying to find the exact items to include in Maddie's basket. The shop woman's face looked concerned when I pulled everything out for her to wrap. However, after I'd explained each item, she said it was the most romantic Easter basket she'd ever seen. Anne's basket was slightly more traditional. I'd bought the Laura Secord chocolates that Maddie had mentioned were her favorites along with supplies to make her adult beverage of choice, margaritas.

Anne opened the door and called behind her. "Nate's here and he's come bearing gifts." She smiled and took the baskets from my outstretched hands. "You didn't need to…"

I passed her the flowers as well. "I need to get the wine from the car. I'll be right back."

Anne waited by the door and opened it for me when I walked back with the case of wine. "Mom is in the kitchen."

I slipped off my shoes without setting down the wine and carried it down the hall. Anne followed, carrying everything else.

I set the wine on the floor by the kitchen table because nearly every surface in the kitchen was covered and all four burners of the stove were occupied.

Maddie turned away from the sink and wiped her hands on a towel, and gave me a friendly welcome hug. "You brought the wine. Thank you." Then she turned back to the stove to stir one of the pots.

"That's not all he brought." Anne put Maddie's basket on the edge of the table but held on to hers. "Can I open mine?"

I was happy she was enthusiastic. "Of course."

Anne untied the bow from the top of her basket. "The Easter Bunny was already here this morning. I wasn't expecting a second delivery."

"He dropped it off to me. Said you were extra good this year."

"I thought Santa was the one with the nice and naughty list."

"Maybe they're in cahoots."

Anne let out a snorty laugh so much like Maddie's, it made me smile. "Looks like the rabbit is trying to get me in trouble." She poked at the bottle of tequila and the set of hand painted glasses filled with chocolates. "How did he know I like margaritas?"

I shrugged. "The elves?"

Anne tapped on Maddie's. "You going to open yours?"

"That's the biggest Easter basket I've ever seen."

"They're a tradition in my family. My mother always made us each one with items chosen specifically for each of us. I always had jellybeans because I liked them better than chocolate."

"Nothing's better than chocolate," said Anne. "And these are going back to Chicago with me. If there's any left."

Maddie looked back over her shoulder while moving something from the stove to the oven. "Can I open mine later?"

"I'll get it out of the way." Anne picked up Maddie's basket and carried it down the hall towards the living room.

I walked to Maddie's side. "What can I do to help?"

"Give me a minute. I need to get the ham back in the oven."

"Looks great."

"It's going to be a very strange menu. Mish mash of Easter traditions and by request favorites."

"Perfect way to celebrate with friends and family."

"Just warning you. It might be weird."

I could see Maddie was too focused on what she was doing to assign me a task. "Should I open the wine?"

"That would be good. Please and thanks."

I pulled two bottles from the box. "I'll open a red and a white, ok?"

Maddie didn't turn around but opened the drawer beside her and took out the corkscrew and put it on the counter. "Sure."

I was a little disappointed by her lack of enthusiasm for the Easter basket, but I could see she was preoccupied.

Anne came in and grabbed a couple of paper towels, wetting one at the sink. "Bacon just chucked up a hairball in the dining room."

The doorbell rang as she left to clean it up.

"I'll get it," I said.

Before I got to the door, Claire, Theo, their son, and daughter-in-law were in the hall, everyone carrying something.

"I'm so delighted you could join us." Claire hugged me with one arm as she had a large shopping bag in the other.

Theo shook my hand amiably. "It's been a minute, eh?"

Claire bubbled with all the enthusiastic charm I remember from our supper clubs and socializing. "You remember my son André? And this is his wife Monica and our soon to be first grandchild." She acted like it was completely normal for me to be there, and I wondered how much she knew about Maddie and my relationship.

Maddie and Anne joined us in the hallway and there were hugs all around. Monica needed the bathroom, so Anne took the box she was carrying and directed her up the stairs. Theo and André stood obediently waiting for Maddie and Claire to decide where everything they'd brought should go.

Once things were settled, Theo and André and I were left in the hall, and we drifted into the living room. We could see and hear Maddie and Claire in the adjacent dining room going over the table setting. Monica and Anne joined them and the four of them alternated going back and forth to the kitchen, bringing back and arranging platters on the sideboard.

"Best we stay out of the way," said Theo.

André grunted agreement.

Theo asked polite questions about Boston, retirement and the restaurants, and I asked André about himself and offered my congratulations on the new baby. No one asked about Betsy, and it dawned on me that they must know we were divorced and that it was possible that Maddie had told Claire everything.

I saw Anne bring the bottles of wine I'd opened and set them on the table. Then she came through to the living room.

"Can I get anyone a drink? Wine? Beer? Something stronger?"

"I'll take a beer," said André.

She looked at Theo. "And you?"

"Wine for me."

"Wine," I said when she looked at me.

"Then you take care of the wine for you and Theo while I go downstairs and get the beer. Grab glasses from the table."

I nodded.

Theo picked up two glasses and I poured us each some wine.

The Easter meal was soon underway, and it was, as Maddie had forewarned, eclectic. We started with hors d'oeuvres of multi-colored deviled eggs that Anne served while we had our pre-dinner drink. Anne said I had to have one because her grandmother had made them for her every year and had taught her to make them. The whites of most of the eggs were disturbing shades of pink, blue and green, so I selected a white one to be safe.

The eggs disappeared, and we all sat down for the first course, which was our ravioli with tomato sauce. Everyone raved at how delicious they were, and Maddie gave me credit for making excellent pasta.

"You're going to have to come make them every year from now on." Anne gave me a mischievous grin. "And bring the Easter basket too."

After the ravioli, I helped to clear the table while Maddie and Anne went to the kitchen to get the main course from the oven. They passed the pineapple glazed ham, lima bean casserole and scalloped potatoes.

"I never knew you could make lima beans into something good," said Monica adding a spoonful to her plate after eating the two beans she'd initially taken.

"It's the maple syrup," said Anne. "Grandma Verna made them with their own maple syrup and I think hers were even better."

"Ham and scalloped potatoes were our usual Easter supper, but we had green bean casserole with crispy onions on top."

"I thought green beans were Thanksgiving?" said Maddie.

"It's a multi-holiday dish," I said. I turned to Claire. "What were your family traditions?"

"We had lamb whenever we could get it," said Claire. "My father knew a man in Georgeville with a farm where they had sheep and goats and made cheese."

"We always had lamb too, but we got it at the Atwater market," said Theo.

"Maman makes the best rolled lamb leg with mint sauce," said André.

"Easter at your house next year, then?" said Maddie.

"You have to bring the ravioli or there will be a Poisson de Pâques for you!" said Claire.

André and Theo laughed, but everyone else looked confused.

Claire explained, "It's a family tradition, like April Fools, but at Easter and more mischief. Like hiding all the forks just before lunch and making everyone hunt for them so we could eat."

"Wallypop would have loved that game, but Grandma would have been livid," said Anne.

André chimed in. "One year, we made the mistake of starting on Saturday and Maman said the Easter Bunny had locked all our candy in a closet and she wasn't allowed to open it until we put everything right. We didn't do that again."

"I like the idea of the Easter basket rather than hunting," said Monica.

"I had to work for my chocolate this morning," said Anne.

"Butter and Bacon rearranged a few, making it a bit more challenging than the Easter Bunny intended."

"How do you know you got them all?" I asked.

"I count… I mean the Easter Bunny gives me a list." Maddie gave me an exaggerated wink.

"Of course. So he can send you the bill."

"He has my credit card on file," said Maddie, grinning. "Are there Easter traditions in your family?"

"We did the usual things; the Easter Bunny hid eggs and Ma made us Easter baskets, but my dad liked to come up with new ideas every now and then. Sometimes they worked out, like the year he borrowed a bus and drove all the kids in the neighborhood downtown for the city egg hunt. But they didn't always go well. One Easter, he got us each a live chick. They were in the middle of the kitchen floor in a large flat box lined with shredded colored paper. We thought they were the best Easter surprise ever and we were so excited to play with them. They were cute when they ran, so we chased them around the kitchen until one of them pooped and then Ma made us take them outside. The poor things were so exhausted they could barely lift their heads to eat and drink from the saucers we put in the box with them."

Theo stifled a chuckle. "I can see that."

"They only lasted a couple of days. Mother told us they flew away while we were at school. But I later discovered they'd expired, and she'd buried them in the garden."

Maddie pretended to be concerned. "Were you scarred for life?"

"Not me. But we never had live poultry in the house after that."

Claire got up from the table. "I think we should move on to a more civilized tradition. Easter dessert."

The good meal and easy conversation made me feel at home. "I'll help you."

Claire turned me down, and Maddie seemed content to let her take over. She served the desserts she'd made; an overabundance of miniature pastries and a towering stack of macarons in a rainbow of pastel colors.

With her part of the meal over, Maddie relaxed and was more engaged in the table conversation. I observed her as she talked with Monica about her pregnancy. It was a microcosm of all the things I knew and loved about her; she was curious and analytical, kind and supportive, and funny. Maddie caught me watching her, and she looked me in the eye with a hint of a smile. A warm wave flowed through me and I wondered if anyone else at the table could feel the connection between us.

After dinner, André and Monica were the first to leave, excusing themselves to make an appearance at Monica's parents' house. Claire and Theo stayed long enough to help clear the table and pack up the extra food. They offered to stay to do the dishes, but I said I would since I didn't have anywhere to be but my hotel room.

Claire gave me a big hug before leaving. "I hope we'll see you again soon."

I was sincere when I answered, "I do too."

Anne got a call on her mobile and she went upstairs to talk, which left Maddie and me alone for the first time all evening. I seized the opportunity to do what I'd been thinking about since I'd arrived hours earlier; I pulled her into my arms and kissed her.

Maddie's eyes closed and she put her arms around me in response. I felt her body against mine and I didn't want to let go.

She pulled her lips off mine. "What was that for?"

"Just wanted to thank you for the best Easter ever."

"Better than the time you got a live chick?"

"You're the best chick I ever got."

She gave me one of her disapproving snorts and wiggled out of my arms. "Well, this chick's got a lot of cleaning up to do."

"Ok then. Let's get 'em done."

We'd just started when Anne came back into the kitchen and the three of us worked together to do the dishes and clean the kitchen.

"You're kinda useful to have around," said Anne as we carried stacks of china to the dining room to put away in the sideboard.

"I'm hoping to be around more."

"Thinking of opening a restaurant in Toronto?"

"What gave you that idea?"

"Mom said you'd met with a real estate agent. We guessed you were scouting locations."

"That would be a reason to be around more. But so far, that's not the plan."

Anne looked at me sidelong with her lips pressed together. "Interesting."

"What's interesting?" asked Maddie, who'd followed us into the dining room with the crystal to put away.

"He says he's not opening a restaurant in Toronto."

"Didn't find any suitable locations?" asked Maddie.

"I think he's got something up his sleeve."

My sleeves were still rolled up from doing the dishes, so I held out my arms. "Nope. Nothing."

Anne patted her mother on the shoulder. "I'll leave you to beat it out of him. I've got some emails I need to answer."

"On Easter?" said Maddie, shaking her head.

"Client deadlines. But I won't be too long." Anne left us and went upstairs.

"I am curious," said Maddie. "Why…" She didn't finish the question but examined my face as if she was looking for an answer there.

"I came because I couldn't stay away, and I haven't left because I want to be near you."

"You say all the right things. It would be so easy to fall for you all over again."

"You mean you haven't fallen for me yet?"

"I'm resisting."

"Don't."

"You're going to leave, eventually."

"Temporarily."

"That didn't work out so well in the past."

"But this is our next time. Our second chance to get it right."

Maddie answered by pressing her lips together, scrunching up her face and letting out a little growl.

I reached for her arm and pulled her in for a hug. "You're so adorable when you're stubborn."

She growled again, but I felt her soften against me and she looked up and smiled, shaking her head.

"I know what you need."

"You do?"

"Your Easter basket." I took her hand and led her to the living room, sat her on the sofa, and then got the basket from in front of the fireplace where Anne had put it. I set it on the sofa beside Maddie and I sat at the other end.

"It's very pretty. I almost hate to mess it up." Despite her reluctant words, she pulled at the ribbon and detached the card that was taped to it.

I watched her face as she pulled out and read the card. It was a Royal York Hotel postcard, not an Easter card, because I wanted something to represent the place where we first met. I could see she was moved by my words by the way she took a breath and the look in her eyes when they met mine once she'd finished reading.

"You mean it?"

"Every word. Meeting you changed my life. I want to spend every holiday, special day, weekday, every day with you."

She reached over the basket jand hugged me.

"Open the rest."

She pulled back the red and pink striped cellophane. "A picnic basket?"

"Because life without you is no picnic… and I'd like to change that."

She grinned. "Cute." She opened the lid and pulled out the first item. "A ravioli form and pasta drying rack?"

"Something to make us more efficient next year."

"You're very presumptuous."

"Ok. How about it's because learning to make pasta is how I found you again."

She pulled out the next item, a snow globe with the Toronto skyline in it. "I'm getting the idea that everything in here means something." She shook it. "Hoping I'll generate a snowstorm, so you have to spend the night?"

I answered, "No." But my tone clearly said yes.

"You remember that night."

"Unforgettable."

She grinned and put the snow globe on the coffee table and dug back in and pulled out the bottle of champagne. "Always good to have on hand."

"You celebrated my successes and supported me like no one ever had."

"You did the same for me."

I nodded at the basket. "Keep going."

She pulled out the solid chocolate rabbit.

"I had to put some in."

She frowned. "Extra dark. A little bitter like me?"

"No secret message. You like dark chocolate."

"True." She pulled out the last item. A large plastic Easter egg. She shook it. "It rattles. Cat toy?"

"I should have got some. But no. It opens."

She squeezed the egg and the two halves popped apart.

The keychain I'd put inside slid out into her lap.

She held it up. "I ♥ Toronto. Is this for me or you?"

"I hope you'll accept a key for it. When I get it."

"Key for what?"

"A condo. Here."

"You're buying a second home?"

"It could become my first home."

Maddie closed her hand around the keychain and held it close to her chest. "You sure that's what you want?"

"Never been more sure of anything ever before."

Anne poked her head into the living room. "I'm turning in. Just wanted to say goodbye."

I got up from the sofa. "Great seeing you."

She walked towards me with open arms.

I hugged her. "Have a safe trip home tomorrow."

"I will." She reached down and patted Maddie's shoulder. "Night Mom."

Maddie looked up at her and smiled. "Night Monkey."

Anne turned and left. "You kids be good," she called over her shoulder as she went upstairs.

With Anne going to bed, the polite thing to do would be for me to leave.

"Guess the party's over. I should probably head out."

Maddie got up from the sofa. "You don't need to rush off. But you've probably been up since before dawn…"

"It's not that I want to leave." I pulled her into my arms. "And definitely not before I get a goodnight kiss."

Her eyes closed, and she leaned in and touched her nose to mine. "You could stay for a nightcap?"

"Tempting. But I have to drive."

"Maybe you don't."

"I could call a cab."

She opened her eyes and the edge of her lip curled into a sly grin. "That's not what I meant." Her voice was sultry and I felt my desire to hold her and touch her intensify.

"With your daughter upstairs?"

"Hmmm." Her grin was mischievous. "Perhaps you should go."

"No way, lady. No take backs. I'm staying."

A grin spread over her face. "So, a night cap then?"

"I'm already completely intoxicated by you." I ran my hand up her side, all the way to her face.

She leaned her head into my hand. The way she looked at me, I knew she wanted me to touch her as much as I wanted to touch her.

She turned away and took my hand, and I willingly followed her upstairs.

CHAPTER 64

Nate closed the bedroom door behind us. "You got new furniture."

I pulled the decorative pillows from my bed and tossed them on the floor. "About twenty years ago." My heart was pounding with anticipation, but I could sense that he was feeling nervous. "It's not our first time in this room." I finished pulling back the comforter and then moved in, sliding my arms around his waist in a gesture I hoped would reassure him.

He leaned his head forward and touched his forehead to mine. "Not our first time in this room." His breath was choppy, and I could feel a slight tremble in his hand that gave away his excitement.

"So, nothing new to be nervous about."

"You'd think that starting our tryst would have been scary. But I want to get it right this time, that's equal parts thrilling and terrifying."

I tilted my head back so our lips met, and we kissed. He slid his arm up my back. I instinctively melted into his embrace, letting him cradle my head and support me. My lips tingled as his tongue swept across my lower lip and our mouths opened to each other. Our tongues, stroking each other's lips as our hands held us together.

I felt him gently stroke my face with his fingers and I opened my eyes.

His gaze followed his fingers that traced the contours of my face. "You're so incredibly beautiful."

I knew he meant it, but I couldn't help deflecting the compliment. "You left your glasses downstairs, didn't you?"

He was undeterred. "And so sexy."

I rolled my eyes, but his words sent a warm ripple through me. "Mr. Jacobs, you always were charming."

"I promised myself that I'm going to get it right this time."

"We've had no trouble getting this part right." I reached for the top button of his dress shirt and undid it.

"I want to get every part right. I'll prove it to you if it's the last thing I do." His serious expression and the weight in his voice made it seem as though he was making a solemn vow.

I could feel his desire for me, the charged emotions between us intensifying with every touch. It made me feel both sexy and empowered. It felt good, and

I wanted more.

The worry of our happy bubble bursting had evaporated. "Then let's not make this the last then." I undid another button.

Nate grinned. "No wonder you terrify me. I can't tell if you're my irresistible sex kitten or the tiger that will tear my heart to bits."

"Guess you'll have to risk it." I growled, pulled him backwards, and we tumbled onto the bed.

"Dangerous tiger, definitely." He grabbed both my hands and pressed them into my chest as if to restrain me and kissed me firmly on the lips. "But I'll risk it all to be with you."

The way he held me was possessive but not dominating. He wanted me and I wanted him. Nestled together, I couldn't help but be amazed at how perfectly we fit, like two puzzle pieces that were destined to connect. Not just physically, but the way my heart felt like it had merged with his, and our emotions were intertwined.

As we kissed, he began to undo my blouse. His fingers brushed my skin as he moved down the line of buttons. I encouraged him with an approving moan. When he had them undone, he began kissing the skin he'd exposed, and I sighed with pleasure as his lips traveled from my neck to my navel. He then continued undressing me, kissing every inch of me as he revealed it.

He undressed me completely and then got up and stood over me while he undressed himself. Lying naked, with him looking down at me, I didn't feel vulnerable or exposed but cherished and admired.

When he slid into bed beside me, I was filled with desire for him to make love to me. I wanted to take our connection to its most intimate limit. No words were needed to convey that he shared my desire as he rolled me to face him and pulled my top leg over his hip. I continued to roll until I was on top, taking him inside me as I did.

He made a delighted moan and looked up at me with an awe filled expression. "Oh. I love you." His voice was a breathy gasp.

I leaned forward and kissed him and then sat upright dragging my nails down his chest as I did. His hands gripped my hips and I lifted myself up and down as he pressed up into me. Our eyes were locked on each other's, seeming to close the loop of our intense connection. We moved slowly at first, gradually building until he growled and twisted. Instinctively, we rolled together until he was on top. I closed my eyes as I felt him pressing against me and into me and my inner parts clutching him as he moved inside me.

"Look at me." His demand was gentle but determined.

I opened my eyes, and the oneness of our connection triggered a physical and emotional explosion that engulfed us both. There was no doubt in my heart that I was exactly where I was supposed to be. We were right, had always been right and will always be right as long as we're together.

326

heart that I was exactly where I was supposed to be. We were right, had always been right and will always be right as long as we're together.

CHAPTER 65

I called Anne in Chicago as soon as the plans I'd made for Maddie's birthday had started to come together. She needed to be in on it because I knew they always celebrated their birthdays together, even if they couldn't do it on the exact day.

Anne was happy to help. "What do you need me to do?"

"For now, I just need you to make sure she doesn't make any other plans for Saturday afternoon."

"No problem. I'll tell her to leave it open and she'll assume I'm planning something."

Since Easter, Anne has been wholeheartedly supportive of my relationship with her mother. Although the first morning was an awkward experience. Maddie was still fast asleep, but I'd woken up early, dressed, and gone down to the kitchen to make coffee. I'd planned to take one up to Maddie, say goodbye and slip away before Anne got up.

The pot was gurgling out the last bit of coffee when Anne strolled into the kitchen in her pjs.

"I figured it was too early for Mom to be making coffee." She nodded at my clothes. "I'm usually a lot more wrinkled making the walk of shame."

I couldn't tell if she was upset or teasing me. I felt like I'd been caught being naughty, so I tried to act like there was nothing going on. "Coffee?"

"Yes, please." She opened the cupboard beside my head, took out two mugs and handed them to me. "You want milk?" She opened the fridge and took it out.

I poured a cup of coffee and handed it to her. "Not for me."

She shrugged, poured some into her coffee, and put it back in the fridge.

"I thought I'd take a cup up to Maddie."

She sat at the kitchen table and glared up at me. "So, you know how she likes her coffee, eh?"

I sensed a trap. "Well, it was always black. I assume that's not changed."

Anne chuckled. "Relax. I'm just teasing. I have no problem with you and Mom knocking boots, if that's what you guys want."

I was relieved but also a little taken aback by her insinuation that what we had done was a casual thing. I joined her at the table and tried to reassure her gently that my intentions were good without delving into the details of what had transpired the night before. We ended up having a lovely talk while I made us both breakfast.

When Maddie finally came down, the first thing Anne said to her was that she was happy for us. Maddie looked at me with raised eyebrows, clearly wondering what I'd told her, but she didn't ask. Strangely enough, the atmosphere in the kitchen that morning felt so normal that we just moved on to planning the rest of the day.

In the months since, I've not seen Anne because her visits to Toronto have been few and have not coincided with mine. I don't know how much Maddie's shared with her about our past, but I know she was aware that, even before I'd found my condo, I was no longer staying at a hotel when I was in town.

I looked out my window at Lake Ontario. It was a glorious summer day and sailboats from the nearby yacht club dotted the blue green water. I was grateful for the perfect weather because the surprise I had in store for Maddie would happen outdoors.

Maddie had once again been by my side as I made the final selection for a place to call home in Canada. I wanted to pick a place she loved and felt comfortable. The condo she liked best was tiny compared to the house I'd had in Oakville. Perched high on the southwest corner of the building, it had an unobstructed panoramic view of Lake Ontario and the sunset, and met all my basic criteria, two bedrooms, two bathrooms, two parking spaces and a large enough kitchen and dining area to comfortably host a dinner party. But most importantly, it had a wrap-around balcony that Maddie found irresistible. She loved sitting out in all sorts of weather with a glass of wine, especially if there was a magnificent sunset. I always joined her, even though it was my least favorite part of the unit.

I couldn't help but feel anxious. After weeks of meticulous planning, the moment had arrived to put my plan into action. I headed to the bedroom and got my sport coat from the closet, picked up the gift bag from the dresser, and then got the car keys from the drawer in the kitchen. I was just about to lock the apartment door when I realized I'd left my phone behind. Going back in, I retrieved it and then hesitated, questioning if I had forgotten something else. I went over the plan in my head to make sure before heading out.

I left the car with the valet and went into the lobby of the Royal York. Today wasn't the day to try to save a few bucks by self-parking at a Green P lot. Maddie and Anne would be getting out of the movie theater shortly and Anne would be steering her this way under the guise of stopping for a drink before heading home. I quickly checked in with the restaurant and then headed back to the lobby to wait.

My heart rate doubled when I saw Anne and Maddie come through the revolving doors. "Showtime," I thought to myself as I straightened my jacket and walked towards them.

CHAPTER 66

There was no way it was a coincidence that Nate was in the lobby of the hotel when Anne and I walked in. I'd been somewhat suspicious that she was trying to get me out of the house when she'd suggested we go to a matinee showing of The DaVinci Code, seeing Nate, confirmed it.

Anne steered us toward him. "Hi Nate. Fancy meeting you here." There was no doubt from her tone that she was in on whatever was going on.

Nate gave Anne a one-armed hug and kissed me on the cheek. "Hello ladies. How was the movie?"

I put my hands on my hips and looked back and forth between them. "What are you two up to?"

Anne shrugged. "I don't know. I'll leave you with Nate to find out."

I was surprised. "You're leaving? I thought you said this was my birthday day with you?"

"I'll see you at home later." She gave a little wave as she pushed the revolving door and walked back out onto Front Street.

Nate extended his arm to me. "I believe you were brought here under the pretense of stopping for a beverage. Perhaps you'd permit me to buy you a drink?"

"No sense standing around in the lobby when there are perfectly good seats in the bar." I had one of those fuzzy déjà vu feelings as the words came out of my mouth.

Nate led me to the Library Bar. The hostess nodded at him and pointed inside as we approached her. I pretended not to notice. I was enjoying the suspense of not knowing.

The restaurant was full, but there were two seats at the bar with a reserved sign in front of them. I assumed that's where we were headed, and I wasn't wrong. As soon as we sat down, the bartender pulled out an old-fashioned looking lamp from below the counter and put it between us. Then, without asking, got us each a drink, a rye and ginger for me and a beer for Nate.

At first, I was a little miffed that he'd not asked me what I wanted, but it dawned on me that Nate might be recreating the first time we met.

I swiveled myself to face him. "Are you going to turn the lights out now?"

A huge grin took over Nate's face. "No. But I'm glad you're catching on to the theme."

"It's not exactly the same. It's changed in here since then."

A waitress appeared from behind and reached between us and set two bowls of ice cream on the bar, one chocolate, one vanilla.

I laughed. "I forgot about the ice cream."

Nate slid the chocolate one towards me. "I've not forgotten a moment of that night. There was something about you…"

"I guess this was where it all started." I took a spoonful of ice cream. It was dark chocolate and delicious. "I think the ice cream is better now."

Nate smiled. "Well that's good because I'm trying to do everything better this time." He got up from his stool and reached into the pocket of his jacket. He pulled out a box that was obviously from a jewelry store. My heart started to beat faster as he sunk down beside me on one knee.

"Miss Maddie Cole. You walked into my life when I was truly in the dark. But I've seen the light. My world is brightest when you're in it. My heart is fullest when I'm near you. I want to spend the rest of my life with you, and I humbly ask if you would be my wife." He opened the box and handed it to me.

I looked inside. It was not a traditional engagement ring but a large ruby set in an intertwined double band inset with diamonds. I stared at the ring, still not quite believing what was happening.

Nate put his hand on mine. "I hope you like it."

"Of course. It's beautiful."

At first, his expression beamed with pride in his gift, but it morphed into an anxious look. "Are you going to give me an answer?"

My mind tumbled through a cyclone of thoughts and emotions, but my heart blurted out the answer. "Yes."

Nate popped up from the floor and kissed me. "You've made me the happiest man alive."

We shared an inappropriately long kiss, given our surroundings. There was a hoot from a table nearby and several people clapped. I could feel my cheeks warming. A wide grin spread across Nate's face, and he was beaming with delight.

"What are we getting ourselves into?" My mind was finally starting to settle into some logical thoughts.

Nate sat down on his stool. "Are you going to try it on?" He reached for the ring box, pulled the ring out, and reached for my hand.

I extended my ring finger, and he slipped it on.

"Fits. Just like us." He let go of my hand and put the ring box into his pocket.

"It does. And you're right. We do. But…"

"No buts."

I held my hand up and looked at the ring. "I suppose getting engaged for my birthday is a pretty good gift."

Nate's eyes flashed with mischief. "This isn't your birthday gift. That's still coming." He was full of nervous energy and had a youthful, boyish charm.

I couldn't help but find him absolutely adorable. "I think you're even more excited about it than I am."

"That's because I know what's coming. Now eat your ice cream."

"Are we in a hurry?"

Nate grinned and took a leisurely sip of his beer. "If the idea of birthday surprises doesn't excite you, we can take our time."

"Oh, but it does."

We didn't rush, but we didn't dawdle, and Nate didn't offer a second drink. He settled our bar tab, and we headed back to the hotel lobby.

He handed me a slip of paper with a number on it. "Perhaps you'd like to give this to the valet?"

"You want me to get your car?"

"You've always been a thoroughly modern woman. Why wouldn't you get the car?" He was struggling to keep a straight face. He was definitely up to something, but he had a point. I was accustomed to doing things for myself. I went out through the revolving door and handed the ticket to the valet.

"Yes Ma'am. It'll be right up." He picked up the small radio and read the number, presumably to someone in the parking garage.

I looked around for Nate. He made no motion to come forward to stand beside me. He stood back by the stone wall beside the door, rocking back and forth on his heels, his hands behind his back and grinning.

I turned around with my back to the driveway. "Are you going to make me drive, too?"

"I think you're going to want to." Nate nodded to the car that was rumbling up behind me.

It wasn't Nate's car. It was a 1955 Ford Crown Victoria Skyliner, baby blue and snowshoe white. The driver was in a hotel valet uniform, and he got out and handed me the keys.

I turned to Nate. "It's just like my first car."

"It isn't just like your first car. It is your first car."

This car couldn't be mine. Mine had been dragged out of my garage when I'd sold it for parts to make room for Anne's art studio.

"This car is in much better shape."

"She's had some work done. But it's yours. Then and now." Nate walked around the car to the driver's side and opened the door. "Are you just going to stand there, or are you going to drive it home?"

I had that slightly dizzy feeling of déjà vu again as I slid behind the wheel. My eyes were drawn to the chrome centerpiece. There was a familiar nick on the edge of the logo. It really was my car.

Nate slid in on the bench beside me and tugged at something under me. "It's got seatbelts now. But I'm told everything else is factory original parts."

I put on my seat belt and started the car. The familiar rumble of the V8 instantly brought back the feeling of freedom and anticipation of adventure that this car had inspired almost fifty years before. "This is unbelievable."

"Believe it baby." Nate pointed to the street. "Let's cruise."

For the first few blocks, I felt like I was wrestling with the car, and I was nervous navigating through the city traffic using the tiny mirrors that didn't do much to help me see. But by the time we accelerated up the ramp to the Gardener Expressway, I felt right at home. And I enjoyed the attention we got. We turned heads the whole drive to my house.

I was so focused on the car and driving that when I pulled into my driveway, I didn't immediately notice there were people in my backyard. The car was quickly surrounded by familiar faces: Claire, Theo, Ann and Brandon and Anne.

Anne opened my door. "Wow. When Nate says he's got a big surprise planned, he's not kidding."

Claire pulled me from the car and gave me a hug. "Bonne Fête Mon Amie."

I got birthday hugs from everyone in turn. Brandon and Theo stayed behind with Nate and were looking over the car while Claire led us ladies towards the house.

My backyard had undergone a transformation in the few hours I'd been away. There was a large gazebo tent to shade us from the hot sun, and under it there was a heavy-looking picnic table covered in brown paper. Two women in white and black uniforms were standing to one side, each holding a tray of drinks. Outside the tent towards the back of my yard was a makeshift outdoor kitchen with tables, a big pot on a large propane burner, and several coolers.

"Were you in on this?" I asked Claire as we were handed drinks.

"Only a little. Just so there was someone here while they were setting up. You should have seen the army of people that arrived right after you left."

"Anne said she was texting her friend. But it was you, wasn't it?"

Claire wasn't listening to me. She grabbed my hand. "This is new."

I looked around for Nate. We hadn't discussed how or when we would tell everyone our news. And with the day being a whirlwind of surprises, I hadn't had a chance to properly process our engagement, so I wasn't even sure what I wanted to say.

Sensing my discomfort, Claire leaned in closer. "Is this what it looks like?" Her voice was an excited whisper.

"It just happened…" I could see Nate approaching.

Claire's Cheshire Cat grin spread across her face as she let go of my hand and positioned herself by my side, waiting for Nate to join us before speaking again. "Anything you'd like to tell us, Nate?"

Nate looked at me. "Do you want to share?"

"I guess they'll find out eventually."

Nate waved his arms and said in a loud voice, "Everyone, grab a drink. I'd like to propose a toast."

"I think he's already done some proposing," Claire whispered in my ear.

We all gathered under the tent and the two ladies handed out the remaining drinks from their trays, so everyone had one.

"Thank you all for coming to help celebrate Maddie's birthday. As if that wasn't enough of a reason to have a fabulous backyard lobster boil…" He turned to me. "That's what's for dinner by the way." He turned back to face the group. "But we have another reason to be here celebrating together. This afternoon Miss Maddie Cole agreed to marry me, and I hope you'll all join me in a toast to my beautiful fiancée."

I wasn't sure how they would react, but their enthusiasm went beyond what I could have imagined. Anne and Ann simultaneously crushed me in a hug. Theo and Brandon cheered and patted Nate on the back and Claire nodded with a smug smile, as if things were falling into place just as she'd expected.

Ann gave me a squeeze before letting go and moving on to hug her father. "I knew you were up to something when you mentioned you'd rented your place in Boston, and would be up here for the summer."

"That's a bold move," said Anne, taking her turn hugging Nate.

Nate looked at me and grinned. "Good thing she said yes. Might have been awkward being around all the time."

"You didn't tell me about that." Despite feeling unsettled by his decision to keep me in the dark, I was delighted that he was going out of his way to be near me.

Nate moved to stand beside me and put his arm around me. "You didn't wonder why I've not been back to Boston since I closed on the condo?"

"I thought you were just taking your time getting it set up the way you wanted."

Nate kissed my cheek. "I have everything the way I want it every moment we're together."

Anne groaned. "Enough of the mushy stuff. It's time to get cracking." She brought our attention to the two women who had served us drinks. They were standing on either side of the big pot in the back of the yard. They lifted the wire basket from inside, letting it drain before dumping the contents into an enormous bowl. They ladled in melted butter and shook the bowl to mix everything. Then they carried it across the yard and dumped the contents onto the paper-covered table. Potatoes, corn, clams and lobsters tumbled out.

Nate gestured to us to be seated. "Grab your picks and hammers, everyone. Dinner is served."

CHAPTER 67

It was easy enough to go from Boston to Toronto. I'd packed up the car with the items I wanted to move to the condo in Toronto along with my summer wardrobe and ten hours later, I was pulling into the underground garage. But I didn't want to be limited to the 180 days I was legally allowed to stay as a visitor, so I'd retained Ms. Raindew, an immigration and family law attorney, to advise me.

I was thrilled when she told me there was a pilot program I could apply for. It was a type of super visa that would allow me to stay for up to two years because I had Canadian grandchildren. There were a few things I needed to arrange, like health insurance and proof that I had financial support, but within a few weeks, she'd secured the visa for me.

When Maddie accepted my marriage proposal, I made an appointment the next day to find out what I needed to do to get married in Canada as a US citizen.

She'd been reassuring. "Don't worry, Mr. Jacobs. It will take a little time to get the apostilles, for your documents but, other than that, the process for getting a marriage licence is straightforward."

Although I had my passport with me, I had to go back to Boston to my safe deposit box to get original copies of my birth certificate and divorce decree. I needed to send them to the Secretary of State of the states that issued them to get the apostille from them. Although Ms. Raindew said she could do it for me, I didn't see the need because it was a simple matter of filling out the applications, paying a fee and providing the self-addressed stamped envelopes for the documents' return.

Everything was falling into place, and I couldn't have been happier. The only thing left for us to do was to plan a wedding. I wanted it to be the perfect wedding for my perfect bride and, of course, I wanted to marry her as soon as possible.

CHAPTER 68

"Nate, your phone's ringing," I called to him from the balcony where we'd been sitting enjoying the unusually warm late October evening.

"Answer it. I'll be right there."

I picked up his mobile phone from the side table where he'd left it to go get the champagne bottle from the kitchen. The caller ID showed it was Ann calling from her mobile.

I answered and put her on speaker so Nate could overhear. "Hi Ann. It's Maddie. Nate's coming."

"That's ok. I'm glad you're there. I was just calling to let you know I've got the proofs of your wedding pictures."

"You do?"

"Ya. I was at Mina's meeting about the Oakville Christmas Art Gala, and she asked if I wanted to pick them up for you."

"That was quick. Thanks for getting them." I'd initially resisted the idea of hiring an expensive photographer for our wedding, thinking I'd ask a friend from my photography club who would do it for the experience and a small fee. But both Anne and Ann insisted we properly document the day. Ann had talked her friend Mina, a highly regarded photographer, whose studio was just a few doors down from Ann's gallery, into being our photographer. One would normally have to book her at least a year in advance, but since we had decided to get married on a Thursday, she was available. Nate leaned over me to get closer to the phone to talk. "We could drive out and get them tomorrow."

"I could bring them to you tonight if you'd like."

Nate shook his head.

I answered, "You don't have to do that, honey."

"It's no problem. Brandon and the boys are out tonight. Where are you now?"

"The condo," we said in unison.

Ann must have already been in the car when she called because about 20 minutes later she was buzzing to come up. I brought our glasses in from the balcony while Nate went to open the door for her.

She wasn't interested in a drink or anything to eat, even though Nate had offered her both.

It was a toss-up which of us was more excited to see the pictures. She tapped on the box she'd placed on the counter. "Are you going to open it?"

I slid the lid off the sturdy cardboard box and pulled out the thick binder inside labelled Cole-Jacobs Wedding Proofs. It was filled with plastic sleeves, each holding eight pictures, four on each side. Ann and I took seats on the stools with the binder in front of us, and Nate stood behind me, looking over my shoulder.

The photos were all in chronological order, and flipping through them gave me a strange sensation. My memories superimposed on a voyeur's perspective was the emotional equivalent of putting on 3D glasses, adding another dimension to the pictures.

Our wedding day started with Anne knocking on the door of our hotel room to go down for breakfast. Nate had wanted to book us separate rooms for the night before our wedding in order to stave off any bad luck, but I convinced him that only applied to first weddings. He'd already gotten up, gone out, and come back with coffee for me, so I was in no rush to go down. I was enjoying the view of the hotel garden and the falling leaves while sipping my coffee. Despite our wedding being a small, private affair, I was content to have a leisurely morning because I knew I would be on my feet a lot.

The previous day, Anne and I had been exploring Niagara-on-the-Lake. Nate had shooed us away from the hotel because he said he had things to do, so we'd ventured out for a mother-daughter day. We'd started by weaving our way along the main street, hitting the artisan shops, and then decided on an ambitious plan to walk along the Niagara Riverfront Trail as far as we could. However, we'd gotten sidetracked when we discovered there were several small wineries we could visit within a couple kilometres of our hotel. After stopping at three wineries, we'd called Nate to come pick us up.

The first pages of the album were photos of me and Anne in our jeans, in full makeup and hairdos, having come back from the spa appointments Nate had surprised us with. The picture of the two of us standing on the veranda of the hotel with the backdrop of the garden caught my eye.

"I bet Anne would like this one."

Nate noted the number on a pad of paper he'd set on the counter beside me.

There were photos of Anne and me while I was getting ready, as well as a series that included Ann and Claire. The three of them had worked together to come up with the traditional things a bride carries for luck. Something old and borrowed came from Claire, a vintage beaded evening bag that had been her mother's prized possession as it had come from France. The something new was from Ann, a pearl bracelet that matched the classic double string of pearls I'd chosen to wear that had been my mother's. Lastly, Anne handed me a package. It was wrapped in blue paper, and she'd used a blue and white garter in place of a ribbon and bow.

She grinned mischievously as I slipped off the garter. "I got you two blue, because that one's kinda for Nate."

"This is too." I picked at the cellophane wrap sealing the box containing the deep blue round bottle of Je Reviens perfume.

"The scent makes me think of you and special occasions. And I noticed you had an empty bottle on your dresser."

"And the name is *à propos*. I'll be back," said Claire. "And you have found your way back."

There was a photograph of the four of us laughing, and I'm pretty sure it was taken right after Ann repeated, "I'll be back" several times trying to get her imitation of Arnold Schwarzenegger just right.

"Looks like I missed out on some fun," said Nate.

The next series of photographs was of Nate in his tuxedo in the hotel's foyer. The photos captured him greeting our wedding guests. Our wedding guest list was small but included immediate family and old friends that had joyfully accepted our engagement.

In the intervening months between our engagement and wedding, Nate had reconnected with some of our shared colleagues and had happily integrated himself into my social circle as well. Claire and I had resurrected our supper club, and Franklin and Diana and Farly and Agnes had become regular members. Nate had even joined the curling club under my membership, and we'd formed a new mixed rink with Claire and Theo for the upcoming season.

What had come as a surprise was the enthusiasm to attend our wedding event. Along with the room for our long weekend honeymoon, Nate had also booked the entire hotel for the night of the wedding so that we could have the beautiful mansion hotel to ourselves. I didn't think that we would fill all twelve rooms, but everyone that we'd invited accepted.

"It was a magical evening," said Ann, as we got to the pages with photos of the ceremony.

"Everything was perfect, thanks to my awesome wedding planner." I leaned back and gave Nate a nudge.

Nate leaned in and nuzzled my neck. "Yes. He was exceptional."

Ann groaned. "I'd say he was a bit of a groomzilla. He just had to have everything perfect."

"And it was. I wouldn't have changed a thing." I reached behind me and stroked Nate's leg. My words weren't empty platitudes. From the fire tables he'd rented for the veranda that cast a warm glow on our ceremony to the rose petal heart on our bed, no detail was overlooked.

"You two look so connected in this one." Ann pulled the photo from the sleeve to get a better look. It was a photo of us facing each other as we repeated our vows. The words came flooding back.

Nate, life has given us a second chance.
Though our bond is rooted in friendship,
our hearts have always whispered we are soulmates.
With you, I laugh, I smile, I dare to dream.
On this day, I give you my love,
and eagerly await the adventures life has in store for us.
I promise to be the shoulder you can lean on, the rock on which you rest,
and your companion for life.
I vow to be faithfully by your side for as long as we both shall live.

Nate pointed to a picture of us with our daughters, who had stood up for us. "Look at me with my lovely girls. You are all so beautiful."

"Your dress was stunning," said Ann. "Unconventional, yet elegant. Just like you."

I nodded agreement but couldn't take credit. "Thanks to Claire."

She'd gone with me to search for my wedding outfit and had helped me put it all together. It was three separate pieces. A white bustier in silk taffeta with an intricate short sleeved lace top over it and a full length flowing deep ruby red taffeta skirt.

There were pictures that captured all the wedding guests and the champagne toast that took place once we were pronounced husband and wife. I remembered how the photographer's assistant had set up a step stool so she could climb up high behind us to take in all the guests. The final few pages of the album had the formal portraits of the two of us and those with our families. Nate and me with Anne and then with Ann, Brandon and the boys.

"Your boys were so good," I said.

"They were thrilled to stay in the Safari suite. They were more than happy to go up and play video games in the room after dinner and let the adults have their fun downstairs."

"It was a lucky co-incidence that room had a big screen tv where they could hook up their game thing," said Nate.

I closed the binder. "It was a very lucky day all around, mainly because you didn't leave anything to chance."

Ann checked the time on her phone and stood. "I better run. The boys will be home soon."

Nate put his arm around her and gave her a sidelong hug. "Thanks for bringing the proofs."

"Mina said you can email her a list of the prints you want, but if you want to pick out frames or an album to drop in at the store."

"Thank you." I gave her a hug as well.

"It was great to be here to see the pictures with you. I got the feeling you were reliving the day as we went through them."

Nate answered before I did. "You're spot on."

It sent a warm feeling through me, knowing the photos had swept us both back to our wedding day.

Ann left and Nate fetched the bottle of champagne we'd been drinking from the fridge and poured the last of it into our glasses.

He handed me mine. "Shall we continue our celebration?"

"Blissfully married for two whole weeks. That's something to celebrate."

He came around the kitchen island and pulled me into his arms. "Two weeks, two years, two decades, two centuries… no matter how much time we have together, it won't be enough for me to stop wanting more time with you."

"I think the centuries might be overly optimistic. Unless we find the fountain of youth or something."

"Well, just to prove I don't need no fountain…" Nate set his glass down and went to get something from his study.

He set a small portable speaker and connected an iPod. "Show you how hip I am." He pushed buttons and the song we danced to for our first dance started to play.

I put my glass down and Nate took me in his arms and we danced to Elvis's *Can't Help Falling in Love*. Nate sang softly in my ear as he danced me around the kitchen. As it came to an end, we kissed as we had on our wedding day, but we lingered longer and kissed deeper than we had with our friends and family all around us.

The iPod continued to play, and I realized that it was another song from our wedding playlist. "Did Anne give you the wedding playlist?" Anne was our family's self-appointed mixtape queen, having made tapes for our road trips and parties for years. It was only natural she was in charge of the music for our wedding and it had been a hit with everyone dancing and singing along with the songs she'd selected.

"She gave me this little set up so we could relive our wedding night any time we wanted to."

"Right now, there's another part of our wedding night I'd like to relive." I nodded towards the bedroom.

Nate grinned and leaned over and tried to pick me up as if he was going to carry me over the threshold.

"Don't you dare. No hurting yourself while we're still newlyweds."

Nate abandoned his effort. "Just one more reason I need to marry you sooner, when I'm young enough and strong enough to do it all with you."

"We can still do it all. Just a little slower and with a lot more experience." I led the way to the bedroom.

EPILOGUE

Brandon greeted us at the entrance of the funeral parlor. "Thank you for coming."

Maddie gave him a big hug. "How's Ann holding up?"

"She's powering through. Not sure it's sunk in yet."

I saw my two grandsons, dressed in matching dark gray suits, come out into the hall and trotting away in opposite direction from us. "The boys are in a hurry."

Brandon looked over his shoulder at them. "There's a salon for the family. They're probably going for more sandwiches or donuts. Teenage boys are apparently hollow and must be refilled frequently." He gestured to the door the boys had exited. "If you want to go in, it's not busy right now."

The room was filled with a cascade of floral arrangements, their vibrant colors in stark contrast with the black suits worn by everyone. My daughter was standing between Betsy's husband Charles and her brother Beau. I recognized some of Beau's family, but not all the people standing in the receiving line leading to Betsy's casket.

I was grateful it wasn't an open casket. They had instead placed a life-sized portrait of Betsy on a stand adjacent to it. I could tell the picture was recent because she looked just like she did in the holiday photos Ann had shared.

Ann noticed us and came right over. "It's really sweet of you to come all this way." She knew that we'd been in Italy when she'd called me to let me know that Betsy had passed.

I opened my arms, and she folded in for a long hug. Given the complicated relationship she had with her mother, I was certain she was engulfed by conflicting feelings.

She hugged Maddie next. "Thank you for being here."

"Losing a parent is never easy. We're here for you. Do you need anything?" Maddie's voice shook a little, and I was touched by her deep connection to my daughter.

"No. I wish I had more to keep me busy."

Maddie nodded to the receiving line. "We should pay our respects."

Ann's smile was thin but genuine. "Yes. Do. I'm going to go check on the boys."

I introduced Maddie to Betsy's brother Beau, who took over and introduced her to his wife and family and to Charles.

Once we'd given our condolences, there was no compelling reason for us to stay for the entire visitation period. Ann had returned from checking on the boys and was busy meeting and speaking with her mother's friends, who had come to pay their respects.

We stopped to let Ann know we were going.

"You're joining us for dinner, right? We're here until seven, then we're heading to the club directly."

"We don't want to intrude," said Maddie.

Ann shook her head. "Nonsense. I want you there. Get the address from Brandon." She motioned to him to give us a copy of the directions he'd prepared.

I took the page from Brandon, but I wasn't going to need directions. It had changed names, but I knew the location well. It had been Betsy's father's country club.

We had a few hours before we had to meet them for dinner, so I started driving towards the historic downtown rather than back to our hotel.

Maddie read my mind. "Are you taking me to the place we first met?"

"I doubt there's an empty lot on Central Avenue these days… but I thought we'd try."

I'd not been in St. Petersburg since Betsy and I had separated. When Betsy's father passed, Ann told me she'd suggested my attendance was unnecessary, a subtle yet clear message I wasn't welcome.

Things had changed a lot in the intervening years. There were larger and taller apartment buildings and the stores and restaurants had changed. But the artistic vibe that had started in the sixties had thrived.

I found a parking spot, and we got out and walked. More accurately, we wandered, looking in the windows, going into galleries that looked interesting and weaving our way around dog walkers, strollers and scooters. We'd been doing a lot of this kind of exploring as husband and wife, traveling to places that had touched our lives and making a point of sharing them with each other. London, Paris, Venice, Tokyo… great cities on multiple continents.

I caught our reflection in one of the windows. Maddie had stopped to admire the glass art pieces inside and we were standing side by side looking in. Our faces were softened by the late afternoon light, and I could see our younger selves looking back at us.

"Aren't they beautiful?" said Maddie.

I knew she was referring to the intricate colored glass, but I wasn't looking at it. "You are."

She smiled, and I saw her eyes focus on my reflection beside hers. "We look good in this light."

"I should have chased you down this street and never let you go."

"That might have been creepy."

"But we'd have had a lifetime together. I'm sure of it."

She turned and gave me a sweet peck on the cheek. "Lucky for us we're having our time now." We were lucky. We'd found and lost each other multiple times, but we'd eventually gotten it right.

I took her hand and turned her to face me. "If I could do it all over, I'd make our whole lives our time."

ACKNOWLEDGMENTS

My husband, Mike, deserves the utmost recognition for his unwavering belief that I could write a novel worth reading. His perpetual words of encouragement and ever-present support have fueled my progress in this writing journey. He enthusiastically brainstormed when I got stuck, read every word I wrote, and critiqued, edited, and proofed multiple drafts. He's made Maddie and Nate's story better at every step in the process.

My inspiration for this novel, and the others in this series, is a theory that's always intrigued me. In the mind-bending concept of the multiverse (or many worlds), every quantum event leads to the birth of a new universe, forming an immense tapestry of parallel realities where all possible outcomes exist. If all possibilities exist in parallel universes, what would we experience if we looked in on a different life from the one we are currently observing? This book is the second in the series exploring this concept through multiple versions of Maddie and Nate's lives. I hope you're looking forward to the next book in the series, Our Time, that observes a version of their love story when they meet even sooner in their life timeline.

I am grateful for the support of my friends and family who have participated in this creative journey with me. A special thank you to Norm Stewart for sharing his experience in the corporate legal profession, Maurizio Bagnasco for being my Torinese culinary expert, Glenn Reynolds for educating me about the evolution of the environmental industry, Kim Maron for sharing her love and knowledge of ringette, and to all the many others who I asked random questions about recipes, history and culture in the sixties and seventies because I am too young to have experienced those years as an adult.

A giant thank you to my beta readers Marie Jakubowski, Stephanie Murray-Watson, Rhona Shanker and Corine Telawski. You pointed out the errors and flaws but also provided great feedback and encouragement to help me re-write with confidence.

And last, but certainly not least, thank you to my design team, that helped me put the final package together. Thank you to Cathy DardenLentz for applying her creative vision and artistry to designing a beautiful cover and to Garry Tosti for making every page look good!